THE BUDDHA OF BREWER STREET

Michael Dobbs

CHIVERS PRESS
BATH

First published 1998
by
HarperCollins *Publishers*
This Large Print edition published by
Chivers Press
by arrangement with
HarperCollins Publishers Ltd
1999

ISBN 0 7540 2142 4

054-021-424-2949

British Library Cataloguing in Publication Data available

Printed and bound in Great Britain by
REDWOOD BOOKS, Trowbridge, Wiltshire

To Naljorma ö-Sel Nyima Chèrdröl Khandro.
May we never forget how to laugh and to love

PROLOGUE

Tibet, 1959

Death arrived in the hour before dawn, but if it counted on an element of surprise it had reckoned without Kunga Tashi. And the geese.

Kunga Tashi was attending to the first daily duty of many young monks. He was helping prepare a churn of butter tea for his elders. It wasn't yet sunrise and spring had still to find its way through the thick monastery walls, yet Kunga was happy. The kitchen was welcoming and warm, heated by the constant fires and filled with encouraging aromas. Far better than being told to fetch the water, which was usually hiding beneath a thick layer of ice at the bottom of the well, or being sent directly to the draughty memorizing class where he would have to squat for endless hours reciting scripture and fighting the temptation to fall back to sleep. Anyway, kitchen duties meant he got his tea first.

He dropped into the steaming churn another scoop of the pungent butter that gave the tea its characteristic kick, enough to spark the enthusiasm of the drowsiest of monks, and threw a pat of yak dung on the fire. These moments were special for Kunga. Barely fourteen and with a sense of mischief as unbalanced as that of any boy of his age, nevertheless he had an anticipation of life that stretched considerably beyond his years and dawn was the most precious moment of his day. As the early light began to burn across the mountain peaks

1

he ran to the unglazed window from where he could look down upon the Lake of Four Winds. The lake was the colour of deepest lapis, its water still and brooding. Mystical spirits were supposed to live in its depths, although Kunga had never seen them. He never lost hope that some day he might catch one by surprise, hiding in the mists or creeping back through the shadows of early morning. But all he could see was a scattered flock of sheep grazing stubbornly on its banks and the reflection of the mighty Himalayas, covered in perpetual snow that steamed and caught fire in the early sun.

It was because he had his head stuck out of the window that Kunga was the first to hear the approach of Death and its workmen. Sound carries great distances in the emaciated air of Tibet and they were still three miles down the valley, just entering the village. The startled cries of old Wangmo's geese gave the alarm. At first Kunga could see only dust, a cloud that rose above the low rooftops, but it was drawing closer. Shouts echoed through the bazaar. Followed by a single shot. Then silence, except for dogs and geese. And the tramp of boots. Not Tibetans, these. Not in metal-tipped boots.

Chinese.

They had come the previous week. A bomb had gone off in the provincial capital, Nagormo, and they suspected the monks. They always suspected the monks. If the sun didn't shine, if the barley ran short, if the roads turned to mud, it was always the fault of the monks. Superstitious lot, these Communists. And sickly, too. They couldn't take the altitude; many of them got sick, frothed pink at

2

the mouth and fell over. Some died. Those that didn't blamed the monks. For everything, particularly the bombs.

A week ago they had gathered all the monks in the monastery's main courtyard and issued a warning. Any more trouble 'from splittists and insurrectionists', as they called them, and retribution would be swift. While the officer threatened, the troops had trashed the living quarters and dormitories. But, strangely enough, not the temple or the burial *chortens.* Yes, superstitious lot, these Communists. Kunga had made up a song about them, about how all Chinese soldiers fell over, defeated by the effects of heavy Tibetan alcohol and thin Tibetan air. The other boy monks had laughed. Now, as he saw the column approaching, he wished it were true.

More shots. Kunga jumped in alarm and ran through the corridors shouting at the top of his voice. Soon others were joining in and their cries cascaded down the long stone passages, the noise dragging the abbot from his bed. The head of the monastery was elderly, rheumy-eyed and still dishevelled with sleep, his wits dulled by declining years, and he danced in anxiety as he sought to discover the reason for the disturbance. When he was told, he danced some more while he tried to decide what he should do about it. All around him monks were gesticulating and offering him every sort of advice. This served only to confuse him further, and it was several minutes before he was able to come to a decision. He gave one hop, then another, like a crane balancing on one foot, then ordered the gates to be shut.

The only entrance to the monastery was by way

3

of a narrow bridge across a precipitous ravine. Security, of sorts. Particularly with the gates locked. But although he had given his orders, the abbot continued his inelegant dance, wary of the Chinese and fearful of the consequences of defying them. They could be so short of temper. A fresh hop. A wail of indecision. A line of mantra seeking protection. Then he turned a full circle, his monk's shawl streaming out behind him, and changed his mind. The gates should be left open after all.

More confusion. Raised voices. Even the ancient hinges joined in with screeches of complaint. It took the combined efforts of several senior monks to turn the abbot yet again, by which time the Chinese had drawn much closer, but at last he was persuaded. The heavy wooden gates were barred tight.

While his elders argued, Kunga climbed the outer wall of the monastery. From here he could see the Chinese troops clearly, ragged in dress but tight in formation, their faces and uniforms smeared in the eternal dust blown up from the dry Tibetan plains. The officer rode a mule, the rest were on foot. No vehicles, none of the great grinding tanks Kunga had heard about. And no way through the gates. The monastery was safe, for a while. The monks had food for weeks, and they had the well. A few old rifles, too. Kunga desperately hoped the weapons would be used. To a Buddhist all life is sacrosanct—flies, worms, even Chinese— but there is a bit of cowboy in every fourteen-year-old. It would be like hitting a mad dog. Why, it was almost a public duty, he told himself.

Boys are creatures of wild imagination, and suddenly Kunga wondered if the troops had come

4

to look for him, to punish him for his ribald song. He felt sure that somehow they had found out. He grew afraid, and the butter tea turned to stone in his stomach. Cautiously he peered over the parapet of the monastery wall as the Chinese assembled on the other side of the bridge. There were more than two hundred, he reckoned, many more than had come last week. He wasn't to know that another bomb had gone off, inside the town hall at Nagormo, killing the Chinese administrator who had recently taken up residence. After that there weren't going to be any more warnings.

The officer sat on his mule on the far side of the bridge and through an interpreter demanded to speak to the abbot. In the name of the Central Committee of the Communist Party of the Tibetan Autonomous Region, open the gates! Hesitantly, the abbot raised his head above the parapet. Who was this Central Committee of the Communist Party of whatever it was? he responded. He'd never heard of such a thing. The officer shouted back that the abbot was speaking like an agent of imperialism. Even through an interpreter there was no hiding the anger. I owe allegiance to no one other than His Holiness the Dalai Lama, the abbot answered, growing emboldened, his head held higher—he always enjoyed a good debate. Your Lama, the monk-king, is gone, the Chinese replied. Impossible! His Holiness's position is guaranteed under the Seventeen Point Agreement between Tibet and China along with many other . . . You're wasting your breath, old monk. He's gone. Deserted you. Crawled away to India. Exile. So open your stinking gates.

Kunga had never seen a weapon bigger than a

rifle, and most of those he'd seen were ancient, single-shot affairs left behind by Younghusband and the British. Nothing like that could break down the great gates to the monastery, and there was no chance the officer's scraggy mule could kick them down. It seemed simple, the Chinese could sit outside and stew until the next Losar holiday. So the argument continued with the abbot disputing the point, much as he was accustomed to do in the formalized debates that were held within the courtyard. But the officer appeared to be taking little further interest. Perhaps, thought Kunga, he had accepted that he'd lost the argument and was looking for a means of withdrawing from his position. The officer was gesticulating, but not in the proper manner of courtyard debates. The Chinaman didn't seem to know the rules, Kunga thought contemptuously.

But in Tibet, the Chinese made up their own rules.

As the boy watched, a soldier knelt on the far side of the bridge and put something to his shoulder that was considerably larger than any rifle. He raised it, seemed to take aim. Then, with a single grenade, the soldier reduced the abbot's arguments and the great monastery gates to matchwood.

With a ferocious cry the troops threw themselves across the narrow bridge, their boots pounding upon the wooden boards like the clatter of machine guns. They swarmed into the central courtyard, forcing the monks back with rifle butts and impatient boots. But there was no resistance.

High on the monastery wall, Kunga Tashi discovered that his youthful bravado had been left

6

in pieces along with the gates. He found he couldn't move. His senses had been dragged away in terror while his body was left frozen and far behind. Below him in the courtyard, events were unfolding in what appeared to be a new and altogether different world. It was a world unknown to Kunga, of disharmonies and great dangers, but it was a world through which he would have to pass. He had risen that morning a mere boy, not fully formed, inexperienced. Come the night he would have changed, grown. If he still lived. The great Wheel of Life was turning.

Once the courtyard had been secured the officer, now dismounted, strode into its middle. Behind him was dragged the abbot—quite literally dragged, his arms tied in traditional Chinese style, diagonally behind his back, which made standing very difficult. It required only the lightest prod of the officer's riding crop to force him to his knees upon the time-sanded stone. A growl of objection rose from the monks, quickly extinguished by a few well-directed rifle butts. The abbot began to recite a mantra, trying to focus his mind elsewhere, but before he could utter more than a few syllables the leather riding crop was under his chin, forcing his head back and exposing his throat like a whipped dog. The officer said not a word, simply allowing the abbot time to contemplate his own extreme vulnerability. For many painful moments the abbot was held there, neck stretched, shuddering, until the whip was removed and his head fell forward in submission.

A rough-hewn wooden bowl was produced, one of the bowls from which the monks normally ate their staple diet of ground barley *tsampa*, and was

7

placed on the flagstones directly in front of the kneeling abbot. Then, with almost comic arrogance considering his short stature and the action he was taking, the officer unbuttoned his trousers and proceeded to piss into it, allowing the stream of water to rise and fall but never to miss its target, until the bowl bubbled and steamed in the ice air and eventually overflowed.

Two soldiers picked up the bowl and put it to the abbot's lips.

Kunga wanted to shout at the top of his lungs, to scream his outrage at the wickedness of the Chinese invaders, and he took a deep breath, so sudden that the back of his throat burned. But no sound came. He noticed he was trembling, and not from the cold.

The abbot shook his head in disgust, trying to spill the bowl and its contents, but both the bowl and its contents came back. A second time he wriggled, trying to thrust the foulness away from him, but once more it was brought back to his lips and this time the crop was beneath his chin, forcing his head back again, stretching the vulnerable neck, until his eyes stared directly to the heavens with his lips prised apart.

And they poured until the liquid spilled down his chin and stained his robes.

Still the officer said nothing. He was bored with debate, with words. He didn't need words to put a Tibetan in his place, only a mule crop and a bowlful of Chinese piss.

The abbot slumped forward, retching. The officer strode around behind him. He had not been long in this uncomfortable world of Tibet and he didn't care for it, this frozen, relentless land, full of

8

strange disease. And a very long way from his family in Chungking. He had no particular dislike for the ordinary Tibetans, even though they were stubborn, with their strange superstitions and miserable food. But their monks were worthless. They contributed nothing, parasites who lived off the labour of others, And now far, far worse. They had started killing Chinese. They had left the administrator in Nagormo in so many pieces that his wife wouldn't be able to bury anything other than scraps. So it must be brought to an end, all this bloodshed, before it spread like rats through a harvest. Otherwise he and his troops would never get back to Chungking.

As the sun rose above the monastery walls, the officer's shadow scythed across the bowed figure of the abbot. The Tibetan was an old man, shaven headed with skin like the husk of a walnut. Harmless, in his own way, the soldier thought, and perhaps even innocent. But what did innocence matter? It was his very existence that posed the threat. No, all this had to stop, right here.

The officer cleared his throat. It was the only sound he had made since entering the monastery. His mind was made up. For the peace of the community, the good of the many. The Chinaman raised his arm, which he stretched out stiff before him, pointing. Then he put a bullet through the back of the abbot's head.

The two worlds between which Kunga had floated, the one inside him and the one that was laid out before him in the courtyard, suddenly collided and broke into a million fragments. All around him there were screams, cries of pain and fear, the sounds of destruction. And shots. The narrow stone alleyways of the monastery filled with the frantic slipping and scraping of the monks' soft leather sandals as they tried to flee, pursued by the pounding of steel-tipped boots. Wherever there was resistance, and particularly the pernicious resistance of prayer, a single monk was set upon by three, four, sometimes six soldiers, breaking him with boots and blows from their rifles. Then they moved on to the next.

Nothing was to remain. Brocade-mounted *thanka* paintings were ripped from walls they had adorned for generations, precious buddha images were broken, every one of the monastery's effigies of compassion was crushed underfoot. This was not simply punishment, it was to be persecution.

Behind one door the soldiers discovered a hall filled with endless shelves laden with leather-bound books and parchment scrolls and ancient wooden printing blocks. The library. It contained nearly a thousand years of learning and memories. It was destroyed in as many seconds.

As the library was put to the torch a spiral of glowing ashes and smoke rose from the flames and spread across the sun. Beneath its wrathful shadow the soldiers began herding the monks who could still walk across the narrow bridge. An ancient librarian-monk, a rifle butt at his back, cried in anguish and fell to his knees, his toothless mouth praying for strength. The guards swore at him. They were about to set upon him when he rose unsteadily to his feet and with stubborn care began brushing the dust from his robes. They shouted at him to move on, but he shook his head. 'Everything is impermanence,' he said, uttering the last words of the Great Buddha himself. For one lingering moment he looked back to the monastery that had been his world for a lifetime, perhaps several lifetimes. His old eyes brimmed with gratitude. Then he walked to the side of the bridge and stepped off into eternity.

He fell for what seemed like forever, and as he plunged, the buttercup and claret of the monk's robes opened and fluttered like the wings of a gentle butterfly. Until, in the darkness that clung to the very bottom of the ravine, the wings broke and lay still.

The soldiers shouted in anger, sensing they had been cheated. Older monks chanted in sorrow, while the younger ones hustled forward with a renewed sense of urgency.

Kunga watched all this from his vantage point. He was too insignificant to be a prime target for the soldiers, too frozen with fear to move. And high on that wall, surrounded by death and the destruction of so much that he loved, Kunga passed into manhood. He began to hate. He knew it was a passion he should not feel, but there it was, undeniable, embracing, and empowering.

Hate!

He'd have to deal with its karmic consequences later, but later could take care of itself. For now it warmed his blood, unfroze him, drove him on, running. Amidst the ruination that was spreading around him, he knew there was one thing he must save, one treasure that must be kept from the hateful Chinese even at the risk of his life.

His route to the great prayer hall was blocked by many soldiers, but he was small and too deft for them, ducking beneath their outstretched arms and rifles. Up close they looked so much less fearsome, their uniforms ragged and patched, their faces all but obliterated by crustings of dirt that gave them the appearance of lizards. Many seemed only a few years older than Kunga. Some seemed almost as scared. At the head of the broad stone steps that led to the prayer hall a group of monks had gathered to try to block the way of the troops, but they had nothing with which to resist other than their own bodies. Resistance became sacrifice as the Army of Liberation fell greedily upon its prey. Mao was right. The power of the human spirit was no match for the butt end of a gun. In every corner claret robes flapped and fell. More broken butterfly wings.

Kunga was quick, but not quick enough. As he rushed through the midst of the clubbing and systematic dislocation of bones, a single blow struck him on the shoulder. It sent him sprawling through the entrance to the prayer hall, where he lay stunned on the floor, defenceless. But the soldiers were like foxes in the chicken pen, distracted by too much choice. The boy could wait, until later.

The great hall at first seemed dark. Most of the butter lamps had not been lit that morning. But from all around came the sounds of the Chinese troops at their work, tearing at the magnificent hangings of satin and silk; smashing every piece of glass. Delicate wood carvings were reduced to splinters, tall stucco statues as old as the monastery itself were toppled and turned to dust beneath their boots. Along one wall ran shelves on which were set out sacred images of the Buddha, fashioned by monks from wood and bronze and plaster and even pressed butter. These were works of devotion and skill. Of many different sizes. Numbering in all more than a thousand. The work of countless lifetimes. A laughing soldier ran along the shelves with the barrel of his rifle and swept away every trace.

Spreadeagled on the cold stone floor, Kunga slowly revived, his wits restored by the heavy aroma of incense which stung his nostrils and irritated his deadened senses. He could smell something else, too, something new. His own fear. He crawled forward. He could see more clearly now, for they had started a fire at the foot of one of the great carved wooden columns that soared towards the timber roof, and onto the flames they were piling anything that might burn. The flickering light fell upon the statue of Padmasambhava, the ancient who had first brought Buddhist teachings to Tibet from the sweltering plains of India, a figure almost fifteen feet tall that filled the far end of the prayer hall. Padmasambhava appeared awesome, red eyed, his gilded skin afire, the dancing shadows lending him an expression of the most intense wrath. He held a trident in his hand, decorated with a skull and other fearsome symbols that Kunga didn't yet fully understand, and for a moment Kunga prayed that the great Buddha himself might materialize to overwhelm the enemy and add a few more skulls to his tally.

But it was only a statue. Two soldiers began attacking it with bayonets, hacking away at the riches of precious stones and inlays that decorated its base. They were too busy with their ransacking to notice Kunga as he stole past in the shadows.

At last he was there, before a glazed shrine cabinet on the wall behind the statue. A single butter lamp flickered at the foot of a small clay

13

Buddha, a cracked and age-brushed figure that had been made by Lama Chogyal Lumpo himself, the teacher who had founded this monastery more than a thousand years before. Kunga had always felt a special tie to Lama Chogyal. Perhaps in a previous life Kunga had been a close friend or assistant, maybe even the Lama himself. And perhaps one day Kunga would be recognized as the Lama's reincarnation. He didn't fully comprehend these things, but of one thing he had no doubt—he, Kunga Tashi, had a special role to play in protecting the memory of the Lama, and in particular in protecting this clay figure, the only relic of the master to survive all the accidents and indignities of time and to have passed unscathed through the ages.

It was as he stretched to his full height to open the glass-fronted cabinet that the rifle butt smashed through it. He had been caught unawares. One of the soldiers was upon him. Shards of flying glass cut across Kunga's face and hands. Blood flowed into one eye. But hope! The figure was still intact. It wasn't too late.

Desperately Kunga snatched it from its place, even as the soldier pushed him aside. He fell heavily, cracking an elbow, but still he clutched the statue. As he looked up, the soldier was standing above him, rifle raised. Kunga knew he was going to die. But if his death could help preserve the memory of the Lama, it would be a sacrifice willingly given . . .

The rifle butt smashed down. Not on his head, but on the clay statue. He could feel it break, yet still he refused to release it. His crippled fingers struggled to cover the fragments on the stone floor.

14

Again and again the rifle came down, shattering both bone and clay until there was nothing of any form left. Only pain. Savage pain. Excruciating pain. Unlike anything Kunga had ever known. Once more he felt his consciousness leave his body, drifting away as he watched the soldier bring down the rifle butt time after time. Still Kunga would not let go of the statue. He would not, until both his consciousness and the pain had drifted away into darkness.

CHAPTER ONE

Westminster, some forty years later

Perhaps it had something to do with the ley lines, Goodfellowe wondered. Two main sets of them were supposed to converge at Westminster, directly beneath the altar of the Abbey, in fact, where once had stood a Druid temple. The Michael Ley and the Mary Ley, male and female, all options covered and chaos guaranteed. Avenues of prehistoric energy that gave this place its unusual intensity— and that edge of insanity.

He was standing barely a hundred yards from the supposed confluence of the ley lines, in the Cholmondeley Room (pronounced Chumley, sometimes through the nose), which stood at the back of the House of Lords. He'd never had much liking for diplomatic receptions even though they were an inescapable part of the duties required of Her Britannic Majesty's Minister for Foreign and Commonwealth Affairs. Sod the lot of 'em. Sod 'em all! Being nice to foreigners didn't figure prominently on his Christmas shopping list but perhaps that's why the Prime Minister regarded him so highly. At least until tomorrow afternoon. (He'd have arranged the announcement for the morning, except the *Evening Standard* had recently done him a disservice and he didn't fancy giving them an exclusive. A tiny spite, not much of a revenge, but the best he could run to at a time like this.) The letter was already signed and sealed, waiting only to be taken by messenger the few yards

17

that separated the Foreign and Commonwealth Office from the source of power at 10 Downing Street. It would take the messenger less than three minutes in the morning. And that would be that. Close of innings. The end. Like some desperate Indian academic qualification. Thomas Goodfellowe. MP, BA University of Marshwood (Failed).

His feelings of distaste, at first generalized and unfocused, now took on physical form. Lucretia—he didn't know her real name and didn't care to know, but the name fitted like a corset—Lucretia had managed to get her elbow into his stomach and was using it like a jemmy to force herself between him and his companion, a fine-featured man in his early forties who possessed the glossiest of ebony faces. Lucretia was of a similar age but the gloss was evidently applied.

'I am delighted to meet you,' she offered in a narrow voice that matched her artificially pinched waist, addressing the black man. *Dig.* She slid in the jemmy a few more inches. 'I do so enjoy such occasions. The opportunity to meet interesting new people?'

She now had her back fully towards Goodfellowe. He wasn't used to being ignored, usually he was a centre of attention, but maybe his reclusive body language betrayed him tonight. Anyway, he'd better get used to it. *Dig.* Her buttock was now brushing against him, forcing him back; he could almost feel what was left of her ovaries rattling. Yes, definitely the ley lines, he concluded.

Her hand was clamped firmly onto the black man's sleeve in a manner that implied—no, screamed—it would take either a court injunction

18

or unrestrained coitus to effect his release. There was no doubting Lucretia's preference. 'And tell me, is it hot back home?'

'Mild. For the time of year,' he replied, attempting a noncommittal smile. His words bore only the slightest trace of an accent. Probably an educated African, she decided.

'I have such a fascination for the Third World.' *Dig. Dig.* The parting of the ways between Goodfellowe and his companion was clearly intended to be permanent. 'And of course for its people. Such fascinating cultures, such tremendous challenges. Tell me, Your Excellency, is there much poverty in your country?'

His eyes widened. They caught Goodfellowe's only briefly before returning to Lucretia. 'A crushing issue, where I come from,' he admitted. His tone implied it was all but a matter of mass starvation. Her fingers made their way from the sleeve to his hand in sympathy. They were very large hands, she noticed, powerful, but soft for a man of his age. Educated hands, she hoped, with just the necessary touch of native roughness.

'And tell me, where is it that you come from? No, let me guess, do,' she insisted. 'But you must give me a clue. Does your country play cricket?'

'Candidly, not as well as it might. The world does not truly regard us as a great cricketing nation,' he acknowledged with remorse, as though she was ripping his conscience bare. 'Although personally I have always taken the sport very seriously.'

'Then it is definitely not Caribbean,' she declared in triumph. Her first instincts were right. African. And she was a woman of exceedingly strong instincts. 'So tell me, you are the High

19

Commissioner for which country? Nigeria? Ghana?'

'No, Cricklewood.'

'Where?'

'I come from Cricklewood, madam. In North London.'

'But Cricklewood doesn't have a . . . You're not a High Commissioner?'

'No.'

'Then you are . . . ?' She was unable to find the social courage to finish the sentence.

'Matthew O'Reilly, madam. A government driver. I drive Mr Goodfellowe here. Have done for years.' Matthew beamed and Lucretia, on the brink of devastation, turned.

'Mr . . . Goodfellowe?' At last, he existed. She withdrew her hand rapidly from Matthew's and considered offering it to Goodfellowe, but could find no appropriate words and instead waved it in the general direction of the throng. 'Such interesting people,' she declaimed, and without a further word launched herself into their midst.

'I do hope the bloody cricket improves.' Matthew smiled in her wake.

'You could have kept up the pretence. She is obviously a serious collector of . . .'

'Colonial conquests?'

'High Commissioners. Men of elevated position.'

'Then both of us are safe.' Matthew chuckled. He examined Goodfellowe more critically. 'You ought to go mix.'

'Do I look as if I want to mix?'

Matthew shook his head.

'Then you'll have to do, O'Reilly.'

'Sure thing, bwana,' Matthew joked, but it fell on

stone. 'So, how is it on the western front?' he enquired, picking up the threads of their conversation.

Goodfellowe considered the point. 'Splendid,' he suggested, but the eyes remained cold and untouched.

'Bad as that, eh?'

The drowning of Goodfellowe's teenage son Stevie in a holiday accident seven months earlier had been the cause of genuine sympathy in Westminster. Colleagues could see the loneliness in Goodfellowe's features; those who knew him better could also detect the flecks of guilt. And it had got no better.

'How's the family?' Matthew enquired quietly.

Matthew had driven Goodfellowe and his wife, Elinor, and their daughter Sam to the church, not just as a close work colleague but also as a friend. He had seen the bewilderment in young Sam's eyes and noted with concern the vacant, almost detached look in Elinor's, as though the funeral was merely another tedious official obligation that got in the way of all the private joys she would once again share with Stevie as soon as she returned home. When her longest day was over and at last she had walked back through her front door, past his new jacket that still hung on the rack and the polished boots that still waited for the new school term, she had taken herself to bed and hadn't appeared for a week. Waiting.

'I thought Elinor was getting a little better, but ...' Goodfellowe shrugged his shoulders. That's what men do. Shrug. Never admit to pain. 'And it's tough on Samantha.'

'It would be on any twelve-year-old. I'm very

sorry, Tom.'

'Thanks. But we'll survive.' Sure they would. At least, that's what he'd thought. Though now he wasn't quite so confident. Nor were Elinor's doctors. There was talk of a nursing home.

Matthew could sense the loneliness. 'You fancy coming round for a curry one evening? Flo-Jo would love to see you.' Matthew and Goodfellowe had shared many snatched meals during their time on the Ministerial tour together and Goodfellowe had taken a particular fancy to the food that Matthew's wife always seemed able to produce at a moment's notice. Green chicken curry was his favourite. With extra chilli and plenty of plump, sweet sultanas. Mind-blowing. Flo-Jo wasn't her real name, but a pet name insisted on by Matthew. 'From the first night I met her she's never hung around,' he once explained; 'the fastest woman I've ever known.' And Goodfellowe assumed he wasn't referring simply to her cooking.

'Be great. Love to.' And meant it. But not tonight. He wasn't in the mood to do justice to either the cooking or the company. Lucretia, bloody Lucretia, had offended his manhood, ignored him, and after painful months being denied proper female companionship such insults were especially wounding. He had to leave, before he began to find Lucretia—or someone like her— almost desirable and made a fool of himself. He glanced at his watch. 'Got places to go.'

Matthew knew this was a lie. He had his own copy of the Ministerial diary. 'Then I'll take you.'

'No, old friend. I need some time on my own.'

'Then as an old friend I've got to tell you that's the last thing you need.'

22

'It's a big day tomorrow. I'll see you then.' And with that Goodfellowe left one of the few reliable friends he had ever found in politics.

Goodfellowe decided to slip out quietly. He hadn't met the guest of honour, and to leave without exchanging some form of greeting would unquestionably be regarded as rude. But the guest was besieged by admirers and Goodfellowe had had enough of crowds and impatient elbows for one evening. Anyway, an audience was included in Goodfellowe's diary of official duties towards the end of the week—although by that time it would scarcely matter. Nothing seemed to matter very much any more.

He edged his way around the mass of people to the point where he was passing directly beneath the Second Earl of Cholmondeley (or at least his portrait) when his way was abruptly barred by a man clad in a wine-red shawl, right arm bare to the shoulder and holding his hands together and upright in the traditional Buddhist form of greeting.

It was the Dalai Lama.

Suddenly the room no longer seemed so crowded, so claustrophobic. Others had drawn back a pace, leaving Goodfellowe to effect his own introduction. 'Thomas Goodfellowe,' the politician offered.

The Lama laughed, a resonant noise like drums being beaten deep within his breast, and behind his glasses the eyes puckered in humour. 'Of course you are. Goodfellowe. Goodfellowe!' The name seemed to cause him considerable mirth and he swiped at the name like a benevolent cat might play with a mouse. The Dalai Lama, exiled leader of the

23

distant Buddhist kingdom of Tibet, advanced and took both of the Minister's hands eagerly in his own, as if he were greeting a long-lost friend. He continued to chuckle and smile, nodding a head that was scraped almost hairless in monastic style. 'I am very pleased to meet you, Thomas Goodfellowe.' The mouth and ears were small, the brown skin weathered by exposure to elements and adversity, the glasses prominent; all the features led Goodfellowe's attention to the Lama's eyes, which sparkled and danced, like small crescents of the moon. Some aspect of those eyes, some attribute hidden deep away, seemed somehow familiar, like an elusive memory.

'I am a considerable admirer of your country,' Goodfellowe offered, since the Lama showed no indication of wanting to lead the conversation. 'At home I have a beautiful bronze Buddha's head.' He'd picked it up on impulse one Saturday morning a few years ago, from Ormonde's in the Portobello Road, a piece whose serenity had captivated him. 'Sadly, I suspect, torn from one of your temples.'

'Everything of value has been torn from our temples, Thomas Goodfellowe.'

'I am sorry,' Goodfellowe offered, taking the Lama's comment as a rebuke.

But the deep bass drums within the Lama's chest began to resound with laughter once again. 'Better you have it and appreciate it, than it lie unnoticed beneath the boots of the Chinese Army. Indeed, perhaps that is the true task of the People's Liberation Army. To make sure that the message and beauty of Tibetan Buddhism will be spread throughout the world.' His arm waved expansively.

'Like bees spreading pollen.'

'I suppose so,' Goodfellowe responded cautiously, finding the analogy uncomfortable.

The Lama laid a hand upon Goodfellowe's shoulder. The gesture brought them still closer together but Goodfellowe felt none of the typical English diffidence at the unexpected intimacy; somehow it felt entirely natural. 'At last our paths cross. In this life,' the Lama offered.

At least, that's what Goodfellowe thought he heard him say. Our paths cross. In this life. With the punctuation between the two thoughts definitive and deliberate. As though their paths might have crossed before.

' "In this life"?' Goodfellowe enquired.

'We Buddhists believe in many lives.' The voice was remarkably resonant; it seemed to spend an exceptionally long time travelling through the passages of the skull, giving it an unusual and deep timbre.

'And you believe ... we may have met before?' Goodfellowe asked incredulously. 'In a previous life?'

'Who is to know?' the Lama responded. 'But the past is no more than a signpost on our way. It is the future that must concern us, Thomas Goodfellowe. You will be important to our future, I think.'

'Me?'

Someone was at the Lama's elbow now, trying to guide him on.

'I wish you well tomorrow, Thomas Goodfellowe.'

'Tomorrow?' Goodfellowe was perplexed. How could the Lama know? But surely it was just another ambiguous turn of phrase. Like a fairground fortune teller.

'And for all your days thereafter. We shall meet again.'

He was turning to leave but Goodfellowe placed a restraining hand on his arm, puzzled by the ambiguities, angered by the almost casual manner in which the Lama pretended to know more, much more, than he obviously could. Or should.

'When? When shall we meet?'

The Lama took both of his hands once more and stared directly into his eyes. The wrinkles of amusement were gone.

'Perhaps only after many troubles, Thomas Goodfellowe, my friend. But I want you to remember two things. That whatever it is you do, it is your motivation that matters above all else. Many may misunderstand you, but it matters not, so long as you understand yourself.'

The words struck him like a slap across the face. Understand himself? How could he? Goodfellowe was lost on the great ocean of life. His son drowned. Sails torn. His compass gone. The only thing he understood was that he couldn't take much more of it. He felt angry again, as though the Lama had penetrated his soul and ransacked his emotions. The guest of honour was turning to leave.

'What is the second thing?' Goodfellowe shouted after him.

The Lama half turned. 'That the future has a Chinese face.' Then in a sweep of colourful robe he was gone.

Suddenly Goodfellowe felt flushed, bemused. What on earth did this strange-sounding Lama mean? What future? And why a Chinese face? It sounded surprisingly defeatist, coming from a man who had spent a lifetime trying to ensure that the only part of the Chinese anatomy his countrymen saw was the back. Above him George, the second Earl of Cholmondeley, stared down. Three hundred years earlier the good earl had been a groom to the bedchamber, Member of Parliament, lord-lieutenant of half a dozen counties and an excellent marshal who had rallied troops to the cause of four monarchs. That's what the Dalai Lama was doing, Goodfellowe decided: trying to recruit him for the cause. He'd probably get a letter in a couple of days asking for a donation, or perhaps a subscription to some Himalayan hill-walking society. Well, tough. Money was tight and charity ran out at the door of Elinor's nursing home.

As he was leaving, for the first time he noticed that he was holding a string of prayer beads, small circular pieces of old sandalwood threaded on silk. The Lama had left them with him; he hadn't noticed.

That night, Goodfellowe dreamed, more vividly than he had ever dreamed before. He was sitting on a rock at the mouth of a cave. Alone. In the distance he could see mountains more vast than any he had ever known, great slabs of grey-green rock and shadows of deepest purple, leaping up from the land and stretching from the sky. A sky the colour of polished lapis. Before the mountains lay a great plain, filled with snow so intensely white that it must have been many feet thick and perhaps many centuries old. From somewhere nearby, but unseen, came the rushing of meltwater. Then the meltwater came into view, spreading like a stain

27

across the snow. A deep red stain. Like the flowing of a lama's robe.

The colour of flowing blood.

Goodfellowe woke with sweat trickling down his chest. No matter how hard he tried, he couldn't get back to sleep that night. And, after he had put in his letter of resignation to the Prime Minister, not for many nights to come.

*   *   *

'Madame Lin!' Goodfellowe exclaimed, almost as if in surprise. 'What a pleasure. Please—come in.'

The expression on the face of the veteran Chinese diplomat made it evident that this was not one of those pleasures to be shared. Hers was an elegant face, not round and androgynous in the manner of many ageing Chinese but with high cheekbones and full lips that, when they smiled, were still very feminine. This morning, however, they were not smiling. The bun that held back the fine silver sixty-something hair seemed to have been tightened an extra turn and the dark-spice eyes, which so often glowed with humour, were narrowed and deliberately inscrutable. Her hand barely brushed the Minister's palm in greeting.

The Ambassador was followed into Goodfellowe's Ministerial office by her interpreter. Madame Lin spoke excellent English—with an American undertow picked up at Harvard—but there were rules of engagement to be followed this morning. Diplomatic violence was always to be undertaken in the mother tongue. For a moment Goodfellowe wondered whether he should have greeted her in the Ambassadors' Waiting Room, a gesture of cordiality, a symbolic willingness to meet her half-way that might help soften the blow. But it could also have been taken as a sign of weakness, and such gestures had the propensity for being horribly misconstrued. There were tales filed away in the private office, and brought out only late at night, of an incident in the waiting room between one of Goodfellowe's female predecessors and the diminutive Ambassador from the Dominican Republic, although who first laid a hand on whom varied according to the teller and the amount of water in the whisky. The Minister concerned had since gone off to become a cable TV agony aunt at three times her Ministerial salary, leaving a deep sense of loss around the masculine fringes of the Court of St James's.

Would he be missed? Goodfellowe wondered. The Prime Minister had suggested as much when he had handed in his resignation two days before, and indeed had spent a few minutes trying to argue him out of it. But he'd soon given up. Goodfellowe was adamant, his family truly needed more of his time. Anyway, perhaps Goodfellowe's talents were just a little too apparent for his leader's comfort; they all but demanded his inclusion in the Cabinet at the next reshuffle. Prime Ministers like to feel they have a measure of choice in the disposition of favours, which is why they are constantly in search of abilities less evident than their own.

'You'll be back,' the Prime Minister had said, not meaning it.

'Sure,' Goodfellowe had replied, not believing it.

But at the Prime Minister's request Goodfellowe had agreed to stay on until the weekend to allow a decision on his replacement to be taken with deliberation, so for now Goodfellowe was going through the motions. A diplomatic game of charades. One word. Nonentity. And after the news had leaked the whole world knew it. What was still more relevant at this moment, Madame Lin knew it, too.

She refused to make herself comfortable on the sofa, insisting on perching on its edge as though ready to walk out at a moment's notice. He sat in the easy chair beside her.

'I have been instructed by the Government of the People's Republic of China to protest in the strongest possible terms,' she intoned, reading from a formal statement. The voice was husky from tobacco.

Tonelessly the interpreter translated while Goodfellowe's private secretary scribbled hurried notes. So what else was new? Complaints from Beijing nowadays fell like apples in autumn and were normally left to rot on the ground. Particularly after Hong Kong. In Goodfellowe's view, handing over the colony had been a great mistake, but for the Chinese it had proved to be a time of great deception, the euphoria soon draining away into what Goodfellowe described as China's 'duckpond of despairs'. The great tiger economy had developed ingrowing toenails. Corruption. Food riots. Then had come the failure of the absurd military adventure to retake a small outlying island off Taiwan. As the world had watched through CNN, America had coughed and the Chinese had caught a very public cold. It was all unravelling in Beijing. So they complained, endlessly and usually without merit.

'The Dalai Lama is a splittist and a renegade and

a tool of imperialism,' Madame Lin continued, her brow furrowed. Frowning didn't suit her, thought Goodfellowe; she had remarkably smooth skin for her age, and in her earlier years must have been something of a beauty. Is that how she had prospered? It was an ungallant thought, but Maoism was a peculiarly ungallant creed.

'The People's Republic of China has objected most strenuously to his presence in this country,' she continued, 'but we were assured that this was an informal visit, with no political overtones. Yet Ministers of the British Government have already met with the Dalai Lama and tonight he is to be a guest at the Foreign Secretary's official residence in Carlton Gardens.'

A rather frumpy residence, in Goodfellowe's view, but with some fine Ming blue-and-white expropriated by British troops for safekeeping while they and the French were ransacking the Summer Palace. Not the British Empire's most laudable episode, just another in a long line of imperial punishments handed out during the last century, which was perhaps why no one had ever bothered to tell the Chinese of the porcelain's ancestry. Although inevitably, in this brave new and abominably correct world, suggestions had been floated that the porcelain might be handed back, as a gesture of goodwill, an opportunity to creep a little closer to a market of more than a billion wallets. Goodfellowe had dug in his heels so deep he thought there was a chance he might emerge in the Yellow River. He was fed up with apologizing for the past, and with giving things back. So long as he had any say in the matter, they weren't getting the bloody vases. As he had scrawled on the relevant memo, *'No. They'll just have to make do with Hong Kong.'*

On the sofa, Madame Lin took a deep breath, trying to draw up her diminutive figure to its full height. The cliches of diplomatic protest were laid before him. 'Gross interference in China's internal affairs ... my Government's serious concerns ... Britain has turned a deaf ear ... Dalai's lies and slanders ... in complete disregard of the major progress on human rights made in Tibet.'

One day, just one day, Goodfellowe promised himself, he'd get to ask a Chinese why, since they claimed to have delivered Tibet from serfdom, so many of these newly liberated serfs still risked their lives trying to escape from this Maoist paradise. They walked for weeks through the Himalayas, across the highest mountains in the world, equipped with nothing more than hope and prayer. Some made it, some didn't. Many froze. Others starved. Vulture pickings. But still they came, thousands every year. Fleeing from paradise. Yes, one day he'd ask why. But not today.

He raised his eyes. The bookcase behind Madame Lin was laden with the doodles of diplomacy—the boxes of inscribed mementoes, the paperweights and pen sets and other assorted knick-knacks that Foreign Ministers seemed compelled to exchange with each other. Most of it was engraved, over-embellished, and crap. Before every meeting one of his private secretaries would scour the room, ensuring that the gift from the visitor's country was on prominent display. Rather like pulling the photograph of mother-in-law out of the drawer. In their own turn the Chinese were rather more subtle. Visitors to Beijing were invited

32

to the Pearl Room where a table would be laden with strings of raw pearls, all carefully sized. They were for purchase, but at very generous prices. Yet inevitably in the diplomatic marketplace there was a careful order of things. Goodfellowe had been shown which sizes of pearl had been selected by his French counterpart, and then he had been shown those chosen by his Whitehall superior, and with great Oriental deftness had been encouraged to go a little bit better than the first while not daring to go as far as the second.

Characteristically, Goodfellowe had screwed up the system and bought nothing. Couldn't afford it, not at any price, not nowadays. Anyway, Elinor no longer had an appreciation of such things. Of anything, come to that, in those weeks when she climbed into her pit of depression and pulled the roof in on herself. It affected Goodfellowe, too. Despair would snap at his heels like a Black Dog, determined to pursue him. He called them Black Dog days—Churchill's expression, and so apt; the initial effect was like hearing a dog growl, from very close behind on a stormy night. And recently there had been more of them. That's why he'd had to get out. Before he was pulled down in the same way as Elinor.

He dragged his attention back into the room. Madame Lin was nearing the end of her homily. Something about her Government's desire to ensure that the contents of this protest be communicated directly to the highest levels of the British Government. A matter of the most considerable significance. Her sadness that the Secretary of State himself was abroad, unavailable. The strong implication that she was deeply

33

dissatisfied at being able to see only Goodfellowe. A mere Minister. Here today, a has-been tomorrow. She didn't use those words, but the sense hung heavily in her tone.

That hurt. Of course the snub of offering up only him to hear the complaint was deliberate, the British Government getting its retaliation in first, but it served to emphasize that already he was a man of overwhelming unimportance. Thomas Goodfellowe. A sensation when at the Home Office. The rising star of the FCO. A man who with fortune might eventually have gone all the way. But not any more. Politicians never came back. There were too many colleagues to trample on the fallen. It was over. He was nothing. She knew it and was making it part of her official complaint. And he had to sit there and take it.

Then it was over and he was handed a formal copy of the complaint, like an irresponsible driver receiving a speeding ticket. A pity, he thought. She was new in her post and, on the couple of occasions they had met, Goodfellowe had warmed to Madame Lin. Sad to end on such a sour note.

He didn't waste much time with his official response; they both knew the script by heart; indeed the details had been discussed beforehand by their underlings and advisers. The Dalai Lama was visiting Britain privately, not in any official capacity. Any contact he had with Ministers was in his role as a religious leader and Nobel Peace Prize winner, not as a political figure. And platitudes about there being no intention of Her Majesty's Government to interfere in China's internal affairs. After all, thought Goodfellowe, they were making enough of a mess of it on their own; they scarcely needed Britain's help to add to the chaos.

And then it was over. Madame Lin rose, bowed and made for the door. His last formal visitor as Minister of State was leaving. He thought the occasion should have been marked in some way. A little ceremony, a short speech, a small dedication, even a bottle or two. But already his private office was preparing for a new master. The contents of his red boxes for the last two days had dwindled to nothing but personal matters, letters from colleagues, an invoice from the office for expenses that couldn't be claimed. He'd get that drink eventually, but on his own. He was drinking too much on his own.

It was as Goodfellowe's private secretary was showing out the visitors that she turned. Both the private secretary and the interpreter hesitated, wanting to stay, but Madame Lin ushered them onward. The private secretary stood his ground, reluctant to leave his Minister alone with the diplomat, fearful of the damage that might result from an unguided discussion. Yet Goodfellowe didn't care for his private secretary, Maurice, nor the bureaucratic games he played. Like handing him speaking notes so late that Goodfellowe had no chance of considering them, let alone altering them. Or hiding all the important papers that Maurice didn't want the Minister to study too carefully in the middle of the pile. And stuffing Goodfellowe's diary so full he didn't even have time to break wind. Should have got rid of this wretched man months ago. Now was his very last chance.

'Don't you have some papers to shuffle? Or spies to catch, Maurice?'

Maurice smiled, lips parting like the drawer of a well-oiled filing cabinet. 'Did all that last week, Minister.'

'Do it again, will you? Can't be too careful. Not about paper.'

Maurice hesitated. 'Yes. I'm sure we have a few last items of yours to clear, Minister. Wouldn't want to miss any.'

The door was closed as though on a lepers' ward. They were alone.

'Thank you, Mr Goodfellowe.' Madame Lin was smiling, the dark eyes open and amused. 'Now the formalities are over, I wondered: the opportunity for a private word, perhaps?'

'So long as you have finished chastising me.'

'It was never my intention to be unkind to you. Nor about you. I wanted to make that clear. I am deeply saddened by your loss of office; it was not my wish to refer to it in the official remarks. But my masters in Beijing insisted.'

'As we thought they would.'

'Which, of course, is why you did it.' She laughed, a throaty, surprisingly masculine sound.

'It's kind of you to wish me well,' he responded, trying to divert the conversation. She was unusually direct for a diplomat, astonishingly so for a Chinese.

'I have enjoyed our meetings, no matter how brief. We could have done business together. Perhaps we shall in the future.'

'A pleasant thought. But, as we both know, not very realistic.'

She crossed slowly to the old globe that stood in the corner of his office, by the window that overlooked the great Horse Guards Parade. The globe was an artefact of considerable value, if not of the greatest age. 1910. And about forty grand at auction. Her finger tracked slowly through the continents of Europe and Asia.

'Life often comes full circle, Mr Goodfellowe. It changes. Then it changes again. Look at this globe. No Soviet Union, just a collection of nation states. As it was then, and as it is once more. Don't give up hope. Life is a turning wheel.'

'Funny. The Tibetans agree with you about that. The Wheel of Life turns. Uplifting. Turns again. Crushing. Your point of view depends on whether you are pushing the wheel or strapped beneath it, I suppose.'

'I did not stay to continue the argument about Tibet.' The eyes clouded in warning, then relaxed. 'Merely to express my sincere condolences. To sacrifice office for your family is an act of honour. And of courage.'

'You are very kind.'

'I know the power of family, Mr Goodfellowe. I have but one daughter, no sons. Rather like you. And of all the many hopes I have for myself, my greatest ambition is to be a grandmother. I would like many grandchildren.'

Strange, Goodfellowe thought. The Chinese pursued the most ruthless birth-control policies of any power on earth. Compulsory abortions. Enforced sterilization. Infants, particularly daughters, left to die. Literally discarded, thrown away. In China, population control was nothing more than a crude numbers game. Yet undoubtedly she meant what she said.

'Ah, I read your brow. You are wondering how I as a representative of the Beijing Government can

37

favour large families?'

Extraordinary, thought Goodfellowe. Diplomat. Grandmother. And psychic. 'May I speak personally?'

She nodded.

'They're barbaric, your Government's policies on birth control. I understand the practice is often to inject the unborn foetus directly in the head to induce a miscarriage. Nothing short of barbaric. If I may speak personally.'

He had expected an animated response, but she remained collected. 'I do not have to agree with all the acrobatics of my Government's policies. Not here in my heart. Any more than you do, Mr Goodfellowe. But I hold my office with pride, and office brings with it responsibilities. But also certain ... what is the word? Privileges. If one of those privileges is the opportunity to ensure I can have many grandchildren, don't expect me to apologize or feel shame. Above all, my family comes first. Which is why I understand the sacrifice you have made.' She turned the globe slowly. 'I think we are much alike.'

'Except there is a difference between us, or at least between our systems. We both wish to protect our families. In your system, that means you must retain your office. Yet in my system, it seems, I have to give up my office. A curious contrast.'

Her fingers began to drum in agitation, the sign of a chain-smoker denied her support. 'I must go. My staff will be getting inquisitive. It does not do in these testing times to be out of step with one's Government, or out of earshot of others. They become suspicious.'

'I appreciate your staying on.'

She held out her hand. This time her grip was firm. 'I hope we shall meet again.'

'Me too.'

And with that she was gone.

*   *   *

Rain. Brutal. Belligerent. Yet the Dalai Lama left the car window open. He wanted the wind on his face, the same monsoon wind that, once it had poured its heart out on this side of the Himalayas, would climb into Tibet and quarrel its way around the dusty plains. For that reason he envied the wind. And blessed it. The wind spoke to him while he in turn whispered prayers that would be wrapped within its folds and carried all the way to his homeland, slipping clean through the outstretched fingers of the People's Propaganda Unit.

The rain smothered the landscape in a relentless khaki shroud, turning the world to mud. Crops bent and were borne away, man and his beast stood miserable under dripping trees. The highway that had guided them away from the airport at Delhi was, ten hours later, little more than a track, and in some places not even that. Water rushed down the mountainside in great brown cork-screws, gouging and chafing at everything in its path. It was said in the state capital that at least a quarter of the road leading up into the hills from Kangra was waiting for repair; it was also said that the rest waited only for God.

The car wheels spun before finding their grip and climbing out of yet another pothole, and the Lama sighed wearily, comforting himself that after his long trip to Europe he would soon be home—or at least what passed for home in a life of exile. As the small convoy of cars with its Indian police escort began the last stretch of the journey, the drivers were tired, the road grew more tortuous and the cascade of floodwater swept ever more implacably across their path.

Trouble was inevitable, so they said. Afterwards. Inevitable.

The Indian Army captain who conducted preliminary forensics at the scene was meticulous, and reported indications that some sort of explosion might have caused the landslide that carried away two of the cars.

His colonel, who was in charge of the investigation and up for promotion, emphasized in his own report that these traces of explosion were indistinct and inevitably ambiguous.

Meanwhile, the general in receipt of the colonel's report weighed up the carefully worded ambiguities and found them wanting. He took advice on the matter, and as a consequence omitted all mention of explosives in the summary that was laid before the Cabinet.

The advice not to mention any explosion came from the Minister of Defence. His logic was clear. There was only one enemy of the Dalai Lama. China. But China was India's powerful neighbour and not its enemy, not for the moment at least. And to rush into confrontation with China through uttering accusations they couldn't support would be distinctly prejudicial, quite possibly to national security, most certainly to the accusers, be they military or Ministerial. Best say nothing, he had suggested. Not even a hint. Not until they were

40

certain. Which, on the rain-soaked road leading up from Iangra, they never could be.

So, for want of an explanation, they simply termed the accident 'inevitable'. An act of God. And in India they had gods galore on whom to lay the blame.

However, this explanation did not satisfy the Dalai Lama himself, who had an enquiring and almost scientific mind, and who in any event as an atheist did not believe in God.

It was common ground that there had been a landslide. It was also common ground that the landslide had tossed the car carrying his private secretary and interpreter sideways into a ravine two thousand feet deep. There was still more common ground that such a landslide could have been caused by the incessant rain, as the official report suggested.

But rain, no matter how heavy, couldn't explain why the Lama's own car was thrown not sideways, but backwards. Neither could rain explain the sharp stench of burning that filled his nostrils for days afterwards, nor the rock that was thrown with great force through the windscreen, striking him high on the right-hand side of his face. And rain would never explain the extraordinary blue-white light that filled his head as a result, blazing with an intensity of a kind he had never experienced before.

And, when the light had finally flickered and died, would never experience again.

The rock had damaged the optic nerve. He was blind.

But what is blindness to a man who had spent a lifetime, indeed a whole succession of lifetimes,

41

seeing beyond this world? At least, that is what the Dalai Lama told those who tried to commiserate with him. He could accept his blindness.

But what he could never accept was that he had now become a target, and as a result of being a target he had become a threat to the lives of all those around him. His own death was something his religion required him to contemplate daily and which he had never feared. Death was an achievement, in its own time. But killing, the taking of life, was as repulsive and as abominable as any act he could imagine. And now his very existence threatened to inflict precisely that on those who were closest to him.

The darkness that fell across his life as a result made blindness the lightest of his burdens.

CHAPTER TWO

Defunct Ministers generate surprising attributes. Such as becoming invisible. The female lobbyist who only a few weeks before had pestered him to the point of exhaustion now passed him in the crush of Parliament Street without even a fleeting sign of recognition, let alone remorse. Goodfellowe had also developed what appeared to be a case of infectious incontinence. Although he noticed no change in his own personal habits, he had become aware of the large number of people who in his presence seemed suddenly to find the need to rush away. This was particularly so in the case of the Whip who informed him that, as he was no longer a Minister, he would have to hand over possession of his large office in the House of Commons and move immediately to less salubrious surroundings. At least the Whip had the decency to appear embarrassed before rushing off. Well, perhaps it was his prostate, thought Goodfellowe kindly. But there were no kind thoughts for Maurice who, to the end, to the very end, remained the complete uncivil servant. As a final gesture Maurice had taken great delight in handing him a small plastic bag that contained all the mementoes Goodfellowe would never have wished to see again. The name card from his Ministerial door. An ashtray from some banana republic engraved with the image of its fat-jowelled president-for-life. Even a half-eaten tube of mints wrapped in a packet of tissues that had been found hiding down the back seat of his Ministerial car. Or rather, his ex-Ministerial car.

Yet perhaps the most distressing circumstance was that concerning his House of Commons secretary, Veronica, a single lady in her early forties who had been a model of efficiency, ambition and detachment. In this instance it was the second quality of ambition that led to the third, detachment, for she basked in the reflected glory of her employers and had no time for lingering in shadows. Within a month of his resignation Veronica had followed suit and thrown in her Tippex. But her prime quality of efficiency was never to be doubted; she had already found alternative employment with a Cabinet Minister.

So it had fallen to Goodfellowe to find a replacement secretary, not the easiest of tasks in the middle of a parliamentary session. They told him he would have to look outside the system and indeed he had, interviewing a succession of spinsters and matrons whom he had found to be 'just right for the job'—like Veronica. Yet he was still getting used to the role of the Invisible Man; he was lonely, at times despondent, in need of . . . well, doing something different for a change. Something unexpected. Unpredictable. Then in walked Mickey Ross. Quite literally.

He had been in the Central Lobby one afternoon chatting to Gladstone. Gladstone was a tramp. He slept in the doorway of a gentleman's tailor in the Strand and frequently came to the Central Lobby to exercise his democratic right to comfort and a little companionship. He'd become something of a celebrity fixture. Although he was homeless he managed to dress himself in an orderly fashion and possessed a wit as polished as his shoes were scuffed. No one knew his real name but he held court at the foot of the statue of the great nineteenth-century Prime Minister and night stalker, after whom he was affectionately known. One 'senior backbencher'—the parliamentary term usually reserved for someone who had achieved very little and had stretched it over a great period of time—had once indulged in the folly of seeking Gladstone's removal from his place of comfort. A waspish article in that day's *Evening Standard* had ensured the request was hastily withdrawn and Gladstone informally offered tenure of the end of his leather bench. And Goodfellowe rather enjoyed his company, for the tramp was a great observer of people and life. It was while they were chatting away contrasting the qualities of Bulgarian Riesling and surgical spirit that he felt a hand on his sleeve.

'Excuse me. Do you work here?' It was a young woman, handsome and earnest.

44

'I suppose I do.'

'It's just that I'm looking for a job. Don't know if there's any going, do you?'

He stared hard. She had a raw energy and an almost combative presence that he found immensely appealing. And a touch of East End in her elocution. No nonsense.

'What sort of job?'

'Secretary, I guess. Or personal assistant. I've got GCSEs.'

'Happens I might know someone. Care to talk about it over a drink?'

'Champagne?'

'No, only tea, I'm afraid.'

'Then you're on. My mother told me never to drink champagne with a man until you know his name.'

'Tom Goodfellowe,' he offered.

'I'm sure you are,' she replied, holding out her hand. 'Mickey Ross.'

And he had taken her down to the Terrace of the House of Commons, which overlooks the Thames. There was a gentle breeze and the sun played on the bow waves of the tugs and pleasure cruisers that plied back and forth. It also shone on her hair, auburn, which had been brushed to perfection. She was meticulous about her appearance. Women with large breasts such as hers could sometimes look so untidy, but every part of Mickey Ross looked as though it knew what it was about.

'As it happens, I'm looking for a secretary.'

'Who are you then, Tom?'

'The Member of Parliament for Marshwood.'

'Whoops. Never figured it, not with you talking to that tramp.'

45

'That is not a tramp, that is Gladstone.'

'Gladstone was a randy old sod who spent his days making great moral statements while he spent his evenings wandering around the streets of London picking up women of doubtful virtue. I've always wondered if that's why he didn't manage to get the relief column to Khartoum in time to rescue General Gordon. You know: too many distractions.'

He bowed his head in deference. 'You are remarkably well informed.'

'As I said, I've got my GCSEs.'

He chuckled in admiration. Several Members who passed by took note, staring just a little too long. A Whip frowned and raised an eyebrow, rather like a warning flag on a beach. Treacherous Bathing. Do Not Enter These Waters. He was right, of course. She was far too young, lacking in the long years of experience that would allow her to dominate the job. And she was also far, far too obviously feminine for Goodfellowe's comfort. And Jewish. He had made a mistake.

'This can be rather a dull job at times,' Goodfellowe suggested, deciding he should let her down gently.

'It would be different. I might be willing to give it a go.'

'A lot of dusty procedure.'

'That's no problem. I work extremely hard.' She smiled, two large dimples appearing on her cheeks. 'And I pick things up easily.'

Her eyes held a glint of dark mischief which Goodfellowe decided could so easily turn to mayhem. He concentrated on his tea.

'But why do you want to work in Westminster?'

She paused, considering her reply. 'I could tell you of my fascination with politics, my respect for the great institutions of state. Or do you want the truth?'

'This is the House of Commons. But let's start with the truth.'

'A bet. I did it for a bet.'

'You what?'

'I was bored with my old job in the City. And my boss and I fell out. We had very different ideas about holiday entitlement. He seemed to think he was entitled to take me on his holidays, or at least his weekends away.'

'You disapprove of such goings-on?' Goodfellowe nodded in rather avuncular fashion, then despised himself. He knew he'd like nothing better.

'To Grimsby, sure I do. If he wants the seaside, what's wrong with Venice? Anyway, it was time for a change. I was at a hen night. A girlfriend bet me I couldn't get a job in the Palace. I think she meant Buckingham Palace, but I couldn't work in a place filled with all that museum furniture. And far too many divorced men. So I decided to try the Palace of Westminster.'

'Doesn't sound like high motivation, Miss Ross.' He found himself sounding pompous.

She retaliated. 'I thought of joining the Army. You know, all that foreign travel. But have you seen the footwear?' She studied her hands. 'And what would it do to my manicure?'

'Sorry. I get the message.'

'Seriously, I'm twenty-two. I'm not sure what I want to do. Whatever I do is going to be a leap into the unknown. What matters to me is the people I take that leap with. Whether we're right for each other.'

'A fair point. You ought to know that my personal circumstances aren't easy. I'm not flavour of the month. I've just resigned from the Government. My family life is difficult, intrusive.' He sighed. He really must dissuade her. What the hell, he knew he was trying to dissuade himself. She couldn't possibly work out. 'This isn't the most glamorous post in Parliament.'

'Now I remember. You're *that* Goodfellowe. The one who resigned because of his family. I read about you. I admire what you've done. Is it all right to say that?'

This was impossible, he decided. Ankles and admiration. He was hiding in his tea again; she resolved to lighten the atmosphere.

'Anyway, I'm not certain I want the job yet. I need more information about the perks and conditions. Do I get Jewish holidays and my mother's birthday off? Is there a Face Lift Fund?'

'A what?'

'A Face Lift Fund. Insurance. Like a pension plan. A girl's got to look ahead, Mr Goodfellowe.'

Goodfellowe began wriggling, trying to suppress the laughter, and failed. The Whip turned to stare from his nearby table, the flag hoisted and warning of storms, damn him. It had been such a long time since Goodfellowe had laughed.

He wiped an eye. 'I needed that. Cheering up.'

'Hey, then I'm your girl.'

He took a deep breath, felt a touch of vertigo, then dived in. 'You know, Miss Ross, I think perhaps you are.'

The mouth of the cave was well concealed. Although the boy thought he knew every boulder and crevice on this side of the mountain, he hadn't discovered this cave before, and wouldn't have discovered it now had it not been for the curious old monk. Every day at dawn for almost two weeks Lobsang had watched the monk make his solitary way up the path to the point beyond the shrivelled fir, disappearing behind the great temple-sized slab of granite, from where he didn't return until last light. Lobsang was rather afraid of this monk with the strange, twisted hands and sad face, who seemed to know more about Lobsang's playground than the boy did himself, but he was of an age when in the end curiosity inevitably overcame caution. Today Lobsang had followed.

Behind the temple-boulder he discovered a narrow fissure that formed a path of loose rock and slippery lichens. Step by uncertain step, the pathway led him up to a point overlooking the Kangra Valley, from where he could see out to the endless plains of India, a view of mists and soaring snow eagles. Even for young eyes accustomed to such sights, this was special. Beneath him, nestling in forests of sugar pine and oak, was McLeod Ganj and beyond, on top of a ridge, stood the low roofs of Namgyal Monastery. Lobsang had unsound views about the monastery. It was said that when he finished his next year at school he might join his brother there as a novice monk. A great blessing, his grandmother had said, but to Lobsang it seemed a blessing of a particularly well-hidden kind. It would mean rising at four thirty every

49

morning to sit on the cold floor of the memorizing class in order to drum into his brain the texts and scriptures that bound together a monk's world. And the food, although plentiful, was dull. He had decided—though he hadn't yet told his grandmother—that he'd rather go to Switzerland and become a banker, like his cousin Trijang. There he could earn enough money to support a hundred monks. Or maybe he would go to America and become an astronaut.

Next to the monastery, almost hidden behind a screen of fruit trees and rhododendron bushes, he could see the low, single-storey residence where the Dalai Lama lived. Every year since he had been born, Lobsang had been taken by his parents to the courtyard outside the monastery to line up with the thousands of others who crammed into the tiny space in order to receive the Lama's blessing. As the Lama passed by his parents always cried; Lobsang didn't understand why. But afterwards there would always be a special meal with honey sweets and puppet dancing and stories about life in old Tibet. Lobsang always looked forward to the sweets.

As the boy climbed he could see the monk sitting outside the mouth of the cave, staring into its depths and mouthing silent mantras. Between the crooked fingers of his hands was stretched a string of beads which he manipulated with difficulty, counting off his prayers one by one. Lobsang crept closer. Flat stones had been placed at the entrance to the cave on which flickered butter candles; beside them was an offering of fruit. A holy place, evidently. The air was still, like fresh crystals of ice, and silent. No birds here, no rustling of breeze and

50

leaves. It was as though Nature itself was waiting. But waiting for what?

Lobsang drew closer still, anxious. intruding. He could see something in the dark recesses, but what type of thing he couldn't quite make out—some figure, some form, almost like a . . . As he stretched to see his foot found loose scree and he slipped, sending a cascade of stones quarrelling down the mountainside. The monk turned.

His face was almost completely round, wrinkled and carved with time like a bodhi seed. The skull was scraped to the point of being hairless. Lobsang's first impression was that the monk was as old as Life itself, yet the ears were large and pointed, giving him the appearance of a mischievous sprite. And the eyes brimmed with curiosity. Perhaps he wasn't as ancient as Lobsang had first thought; the body, like the hands, seemed bowed by adversity as much as by age. The hands were now clasped uneasily together for support and were beckoning.

'Come, my little friend. Share some fruit. I'm sure the spirits can spare a few mouthfuls.'

Kunga Tashi held out a pomegranate from the offering bowl and Lobsang, more than a little nervous, stepped forward.

'So you have found my secret place,' the old monk offered in congratulation, and Lobsang nodded, biting greedily into the sweet-sour flesh of the fruit. The juice dribbled down his chin which he wiped with the back of his hand. Then he froze. He could see it now, in the shadow at the back of the cave. A man, bare-chested, sitting in the lotus position in the manner of a meditating monk. The eyes were closed. Not the smallest sign of

51

movement, not the flicker of an eyelid, not even the shallowest of breaths. It was as though the figure had become part of the rock itself.

'It is His Holiness,' Kunga said. 'The Dalai Lama.'

'He's lost his glasses.'

Kunga smiled sadly. 'He doesn't need them any more.'

'Is he meditating?' Lobsang whispered.

'No. He is preparing to die.'

Everything was impermanence, of course. Particularly here, in this place, McLeod Ganj, in the mountains just above Dharamsala. The last time Kunga had been here was more than twenty years ago, when it had been little more than a tiny frontier post, a remnant of the British Raj squeezed into that mountainous part of northern India that lay between Kashmir and Tibet. In those days it had been almost unwanted, a sleepy collection of tin huts and a few crumbling masonry buildings that had somehow survived the great earthquake; now it seemed to him that the old village had disappeared beneath a flood of refugees that had turned every piece of pavement into a private emporium. The narrow, muddy streets bustled and sang. Here it seemed you could buy or sell almost anything.

Its crowded central square was awash with the colours of Pathan, of Tibetan, Hindu, holy men and hippie, Kashmiri and Sikh. And, of course, the claret-robed Buddhist monks. A confusion of cultures—which made it an excellent place for him to hide. For when they had summoned him they had told Kunga that he must hide. There was danger here, great danger, and not just for the monk.

52

They had brought him from his monastery in Tibet in the greatest secrecy. In normal circumstances such trips out of Tibet were difficult and frequently dangerous, the Chinese authorities suspicious of the activities of all monks and particularly those who held senior positions, as Kunga once had. But there was an advantage in being crippled, an anonymity that blinded officialdom and had eased his way through checkpoints and border crossings. He had only to stretch out his withered hands, like the claws of the Devil, and they would retreat in revulsion and confusion, never meeting his eyes. So he had arrived in McLeod Ganj, as he had been instructed, unseen and unannounced.

And he had waited.

They had set aside for him a small hut on the outskirts of the town normally used by monks on solitary retreat. Some of the monks stayed for three years—and what did three years matter in a whole succession of lifetimes? Kunga had waited only three days when, towards dusk, two guides had appeared and taken him onward, down the mountain a little. They hurried past groups of men haggling outside the taxi rank and tea shops. There were bright cafés full of tourists, and video huts where bootleg films were shown. The films were sent up from Delhi, some copied with hand-held cameras from the back of the cinema. You could see the picture shake, even see the audience leaving over the credits. This was McLeod Ganj as Kunga had never known it. He recognised little until they came to the holy way, where aged women walked at last light, wrapped in faded blankets, spinning their prayer wheels as they chanted mantras whose

53

words hadn't changed in a hundred lifetimes. But the guides lowered their eyes and scurried by. They were nervous and Kunga found their anxiety infectious. What did they have to fear? From old women at prayer?

It was now dark. A rock-strewn track led through the woods, the silence of night broken only by the cracking of pine twigs underfoot and the cry of a startled owl. A difficult passage by moonlight. He stumbled, fell badly, grazed his shin, but found willing hands to help him to his feet. Then at last they came upon a high stone wall, inset with a heavy wooden gate. Not the front way, with its guards and prying eyes, but a rear entrance that Kunga hadn't known existed, even though once he had known this place well, almost as well as his own home.

And as the gate creaked and swung open, Kunga couldn't restrain a soft cry of joy. For he was there. Waiting for him. The Dalai Lama. *His* Dalai Lama. Whom he hadn't seen in more than twenty years.

Kunga began to prostrate himself on the rocky ground but the Lama reached out for him, ordered him to rise, and with unrestrained emotion they fell into each other's arms. The Dalai Lama's hands brushed over Kunga's head and they touched foreheads, a greeting which did great honour to the monk. His senses were ablaze, Kunga felt as if he had been touched by the sun.

Only when the Lama's fingers continued to brush around Kunga's head, as though inspecting it for damage, did the truth dawn upon Kunga.

'You . . . are blind?'

'And you, my old friend, are bald!' The Lama chuckled, although the customary humour sounded strangely forced. His hands fell to the monk's lean frame. 'Tell me, don't they feed you in that monastery of yours?'

'Enough. And more than many.' A note of sorrow chilled their spirits.

'How is my homeland, Kunga?'

'Suffering.'

'That will not last.'

'Nothing lasts for ever.'

'No, not for ever. Which is why I have summoned you. And the others—Gompo, and Yeshe. The three I trust most in this world.' Gompo was the Dalai Lama's representative in Geneva, and Yeshe his former private secretary who had only recently completed a lengthy solitary retreat at a monastery in the south.

'These are times of many lies, Kunga. And many enemies,' the Dalai Lama continued. 'I am blind and can no longer see into men's eyes, or tell what is in their hearts. I must be certain of those around me if we are to succeed in the task ahead.'

'And what task is that?' Kunga had asked.

'To help me die . . .'

Outside the cave, Lobsang grew frightened. 'Are you sure? That he's dying?'

'Oh, yes.'

Lobsang let forth an involuntary sob.

'Don't despair, little friend. It was his will. He told me himself. He decided the time had come.'

'You . . . knew him?' Lobsang enquired, embarrassed to use the past tense.

'Long before you were born. For many years I was his translator and adviser. And also his friend.'

'But he looks so . . . alive,' Lobsang exclaimed. He knew that death was corruption, rotten flesh, decay. Yet the Dalai Lama looked as if he were simply asleep.

'Great Lamas don't die like the rest. They pass on. Their spirit leaves their body so gently that the body barely notices. So it doesn't decay, not for a long time.'

Lobsang was gripping the monk's hand for comfort, too distressed to notice that it was little more than a formless mass of bone and skin.

'Remember that in death there is always new life. And new hope. The spirit is reborn in a new body,' Kunga encouraged—just as the Dalai Lama had encouraged them, the three he had gathered together. He had explained his purpose the following day as they sat in his garden, a garden that he himself had planned and planted, a place where they could be overheard only by the birds and the Lama's favourite cats.

'My task is simple, my friends. To die. There is nothing simpler. But your task will be far more hazardous. Your task is to live. If you can. To ensure that my rebirth is safeguarded, to seek out and protect my incarnation.' His voice tightened in sadness, as though a screw were being turned within. 'In that search you will encounter many dangers. And great pain. You may come to envy the peace with which I shall pass from this life.'

The Searchers had argued with him, passionately, and with more than a little fear.

'We want to serve you alive, not dead.'

'Without you—we're lost.'

'And without you Tibet is lost!'

'More than ever we need you . . .'

Until at last he had grown exasperated. 'No more! Enough!' The Lama raised his voice, a rare

56

event, his passion more than a match for theirs. The cats scattered in alarm.

'Listen to me. For a thousand years in Tibet we hid behind the great walls of the Himalayas. Untouched—but also untouching. We guarded our truths selfishly, reluctant to share them. Yet look around. Our world has more wickedness than it has ever known. The people suffer. They need us.'

'So does Tibet,' Gompo responded defiantly.

The Lama raised his hand and pointed beyond the mountains, his voice burning with emotion. 'Our Tibet, that ancient homeland we loved, is no more. It is gone. Perhaps for all time.'

He challenged them to deny it, but no one spoke. What was the point? Hope might spring eternal yet it had no more strength than a summer breeze. And the People's Liberation Army wasn't going to be blown away by a puff of wind.

'We can't go back, not to the way things were. But Tibet is more than just mountains and monasteries. It is a faith, a way of life.'

'And of death?'

'Think of our exile as an opportunity. A chance to send down new roots, to find new strength. And think of my death as a new beginning, not just for me but for all our people.'

'A new beginning? For that we need an army!'

'Perhaps there is another way. A way in which Chinese and Tibetan can be brought together, not in confrontation, but in reconciliation.'

'Reconciliation? How?' demanded Gompo, as ever sceptical.

'Reconciliation . . . through reincarnation!'

The Lama had laughed, a deep booming drum of hope. And cautiously the cats had begun to creep back . . .

Now, as Kunga stared into the shadows of the cave, where the Dalai Lama had taken himself to meditate and to die, he struggled hard to recapture the Lama's optimism. Beside him Lobsang began to shiver.

'Don't be afraid,' Kunga encouraged, placing an arm around the boy's shoulders.

'It is the end.' Lobsang's voice was mournful.

'It is also a beginning. The body is like a set of clothes. When it gets old, you discard it for a fresh one. That's all he has done, decided to discard his body. But not the spirit. That lives on. And will find a new body.'

'When?'

'Soon.'

'Where?'

Kunga gave a low sigh. 'Ah, now that is the mystery.'

The light was fading fast, Kunga trimmed the butter lamps. The last of the gentle breeze had vanished with the light, the flames did not flicker. Everything was still.

'It is almost over, I sense it. Time for you to go, little friend.'

'I'd like to stay. Please? To help you.' A quieter voice. 'To help him.'

And so they had settled for the night, Kunga sitting before the cave, and Lobsang close before him, wrapped in the monk's thick robe, waiting for the Dalai Lama to die.

* * *

Kunga had been determined to stay awake and

vigilant, but he couldn't help himself. He fell into a deep and dreamless sleep. It was Lobsang who woke first.

'He's moved,' the boy whispered, tugging at the monk's robe.

Kunga brushed the night from his eyes and stared. The sun was beginning to light the sky, deepening the shade within the cave, and for a moment his tired eyes struggled to adjust.

'He has moved,' Lobsang insisted. 'That must mean he's still alive, mustn't it?'

It is given to few in the world of Buddhist mysteries to know when the spirit has finally departed; Kunga was one of the few. He shook his head. 'No. It is over. He is gone.'

The Dalai Lama was dead.

But the boy was right, the body had moved. In death the face had turned as though looking out across the world below. Towards the west. It was a sign.

And Kunga felt a strange sensation in his hand. When his hands had been pulverized by the rifle butt of the Chinese soldier, a large fragment of the clay statue had buried itself deep into the flesh of his palm, leaving a vivid scar that had never fully healed. On the day the Lama had taken himself to his cave, the scar had begun to burn, the first sensation other than constant pain he had felt in forty years, a sensation that had grown more fierce with every passing day. Now it felt as though it was on fire. He rubbed the palm against his chest, but it burned still more fiercely. The outline of the scar had grown red, like a map drawn on the parchment of his skin, A map of what, he had no idea. But he knew it was another sign.

59

The book and the black eye arrived in his office together, both being carried by Mickey.

'What the hell have you been up to?' Goodfellowe growled, seeing the mark that not even a copious sponging of Clinique concealer had been able to hide. Then, remembering his manners: 'You all right?'

'Just a little accident.'

'Accident? What accident?'

'The truth?'

'Of course the bloody truth.'

'Stage diving.'

His silence betokened utter ignorance.

'Stage diving,' she repeated. 'You know, when you try to get up on stage?'

'You've been auditioning for *Pygmalion,*' he announced triumphantly. 'And you fell off the casting couch?'

She looked at him waspishly, the slight bump above her left eye giving her an uncharacteristic scowl. 'Bugger off.'

'Whoops, sorry,' he said, not meaning it.

'Stage diving,' she repeated, trying again. 'The stage in question was at the LSE. A university bash. Def Leppard were playing.'

'Deaf who . . . ?'

She rolled her eyes in despair. 'They're a band. Heavy metal. The sort of music with megatons of bass that makes your skull vibrate. The sort that needs tight leather pants just to keep you in.'

'I wonder why I haven't heard of them,' he muttered, all sarcasm.

60

'So the idea is that you work up a rush of blood, jump up onto the stage and try to grab a piece of them.'

'What on earth is the point?'

'Not much. They're ancient, about your age. Most stage divers wouldn't have a clue what to do if we actually caught them. But we don't. The purpose of the exercise is for the roadies—their road crew—to grab hold of you and throw you back into the crowd. Or rather, onto the crowd, since everyone's packed so tight in front of the stage that all they can do is pass you back over their heads. Which means hundreds and hundreds of deliciously sweaty hands tossing you around and passing all over your body.'

'But why would people want to do that?'

She groaned. 'Take a wild guess, Goodfellowe.'

The impression began to form, and he had the grace to look momentarily stunned.

'But last night they must've been down on numbers.' She shrugged. 'They dropped me.'

He studied her, studied her body, very closely, imagining the hands. His hands. He gathered his flustered thoughts. 'Two suggestions. First, don't spread that around this place. Wouldn't do you any good. Or me, for that matter. Say you ran into a filing cabinet; that's the standard parliamentary excuse for a black eye.'

'And second?'

'When I say I want the truth . . .' He winced. 'I'm not sure I always mean it.'

She smiled sweetly. 'I guess you were young once.'

'Don't bet on it. Anyway, enough of your off-duty diversions. What work have we got?'

She handed him a book that was floating on top of the usual pile of daily letters. 'Came this morning. From the Dalai Lama.'

'You're not the only one full of surprises,' he offered as he inspected the book. It was an elderly edition of the writings of Sun Tzu, the Chinese military strategist who had written about the art of warfare more than two thousand years before (although he lived so long ago that scholars debated endlessly about whether he truly wrote the works, or if he even existed). The thick paper was brittle and discoloured with age, the cover of cheap card and scuffed. With great care Goodfellowe opened the book, at random, concerned lest the pages should fall apart in his hands.

'*If you rely on Government to put out the fire, by the time the bucket arrives there is nothing left but ashes,*' he read.

He smiled wryly. 'Two thousand years and nothing's changed.'

'At least in those days the Government could afford a bucket.'

'But I don't understand. Why is a Tibetan man of peace passing on the musings of a Chinese warlord?'

'There's a letter in the back.'

It was written in a bold hand.

'*My dear Thomas Goodfellowe, I have been interested in military strategy since I played with lead soldiers in the Potala Palace as a child. In those days I always won! We Tibetans were once a warrior race, but now we must fight our battles by other means. Sun Tzu often shows how. I thought he might interest you. Especially since the future has a Chinese face.*'

That phrase again. It was dated and signed in

62

Tibetan script that meandered like an ancient river in flood across the page.

'Bit like the bloody *Times* crossword, isn't it?' Mickey interjected. '"The future has a Chinese face." Does that mean he's given up?'

Goodfellowe stared at the letter. 'No, of course he hasn't given up. Can't have given up. This is all about continuing to fight the battle, but by other means.'

'What other means?'

He shook his head. 'Dunno.' He placed the book in a desk drawer and turned to the pile of correspondence. 'And since he's not a constituent I don't suppose we're ever going to have the time to find out. His battles aren't our battles. They weren't when I was a Minister, and can't be now I've no more influence than yesterday's weather forecast.'

Goodfellowe was wrong, of course. He would come to realize that, as soon as he discovered the letter was probably the very last thing the Dalai Lama had written in this life.

*   *   *

Mo could scarcely contain his frustration. He had rushed into the Ambassador's office, perhaps a trifle enthusiastically but only in order to pass on the good news. Yet he had been forced to stand, humiliated, before her desk while the ancient warrior prattled on about courtesy and youth. It wasn't as if she had been busy with anything of importance, merely rearranging the clutter of family photographs that dominated her desk.

'A private secretary should know when privacy is meant to be respected. If they want to remain a private secretary, that is.'

She was constantly changing around those photographs, a daily ritual, like some old woman throwing fortune sticks in the temple. Faded sepia prints of her mother and father, revolutionaries who had met on the Long March, six thousand miles through central China to the caves of Shaanxi. Also one grandmother. Two aunts who had died on that march. Sisters. And of course her only daughter. A sickness her family had, only producing girls. The shame of the Lins.

'Doors are meant for knocking on, not kicking down,' Madame Lin lectured.

Mo hung his head, less in respect than in an attempt to hide the flush on his cheek. Listen to her! Kicking down doors? But that's what the new China was about. The Ambassador was an old woman in an outdated world who had been left behind by the changes that were gripping their country. Sure there was corruption. And chaos. Hadn't there always been? But now there was also something new. Opportunity. Open doors. Even if occasionally those doors needed a little forcing.

He took a deep breath. 'Ambassador, I apologize.'

She waved her hand impatiently, leaving Mo unclear as to whether she was waving away his presence or his offence. He seized the moment.

'But there is wonderful news that I wished you to have.' His tone grew more eager. 'The renegade Lama is dead.'

She became thoughtful, then grew unsettled, almost concerned. He had expected her to respond to the news, but not in this manner.

'I thought you would wish to celebrate,' he

64

added, suddenly uncertain.

'Then your presence is even less appropriate than I thought, Private Secretary.' She always used his formal title when slapping him down. The deep frown was back, creasing her forehead.

'I don't understand, Ambassador.'

'The first perceptive thing you've said all day.'

She was unusually brittle this morning. More bowel trouble, perhaps. Best to pacify. He bowed. 'It would be an honour if you would explain.'

How he hated this vast office at the heart of the Embassy. They might just as well have been back in old Beijing rather than at the centre of a thriving Western capital. When the new Ambassador had arrived it had been an opportunity to bring the place to life with some of the new colour and fashions that were coming out of Shanghai and Hong Kong, but the old woman had turned it into something fit only for the scrapbook of a dowager empress—heavy rosewood chairs complete with antimacassars, dark lacquer screens, heavy rugs, oppressive potted plants. No imagination. All imported from home, even the musty smell, which seemed to have been borrowed from some dank winter's day in central Beijing.

Madame Lin walked across the room to stand silhouetted against the window, where she lit a cigarette and took the smoke down to the bottom of her lungs.

'So the Lama is dead,' she repeated.

'Gone. Wiped away,' Mo enthused.

'No, that's where you are wrong. Simply because he was an enemy you underestimate him.'

'But there is nothing left to underestimate.' He struggled to hide his exasperation, and was not altogether successful.

'In life he was significant. Yet in death he is a still greater uncertainty. And we have enough uncertainty in China today to satisfy even the keenest sceptic. Which is why young men like you are in such a hurry, Mo.'

Her tone was chiding and he wasn't entirely sure what she was getting at. Time to get back to the matter in hand. 'You are suggesting he is more of a threat to us dead?'

'While he lived we knew where he was, what he was up to. Our eyes were always upon him. But how can we follow him now?'

'You can't believe in the absurdity of rebirth?' Mo was aghast. His training at the Foreign Affairs Institute in Beijing had been most specific on the point.

'It doesn't matter what I think. What matters is what millions of Tibetans think, and they believe he will come back to lead them. A new Lama. Like a Messiah. While they are waiting they will make trouble. And when he returns, whoever he may be, they'll make even more trouble. The wind blows cold from those mountains.'

'Then we must remain alert, Ambassador.'

She turned on him. 'The question, Mo, is whether you will remain at all.'

'Ambassador?'

'You take me for a fool. That I cannot tolerate.'

He began to protest. She cut him short.

'You steal antiques and artefacts from the Embassy, Mo. My Embassy.'

Thick cigarette smoke hung in the air, creating an atmosphere that was suddenly clinging and intensely claustrophobic. 'Ambassador, I can assure you . . .'

'You can assure me of nothing. I know, Mo. About how you've been moving antiques around the Embassy. To hide them. Sending them off to your cousin in Amsterdam and having them copied. Then selling the original, and returning the fake to the Embassy.'

She was by the fireplace now, with Mo still protesting.

'Not true. Not true . . .'

As though to prove her point she picked up an earthenware cocoon vase from the mantelpiece, covered in devils' eyes and subtle whorls and the encrustations of age. She held it shoulder-high for his inspection. 'How old would you say, Mo? One thousand? Two thousand? Han dynasty, I think. Yes, two thousand years old.'

Then with remarkable dexterity for a woman of her age she lobbed it across the room in his direction. In alarm Mo reached out and snatched it from the air, juggling desperately with it for a few tangled moments. But he couldn't hold it. It fell. And smashed to fragments.

'Not even two thousand days, Mo. But a very effective copy, nonetheless. Your cousin is to be congratulated.'

Across the vast space which seemed to separate them their eyes met and locked, and a change came over Mo. The cringing of previous moments was replaced by something altogether more substantial. If the game was up, he decided, there was little point in continuing to be horsewhipped by a woman. 'Ambassador, I believe that is the first compliment you have ever paid me or my family.'

She ignored his impudence. 'Why, Mo? Why all

67

this dishonesty?'

He shrugged. 'Only three pieces have gone. The first went to pay your predecessor's gambling debts.' His tone had an edge of disdain.

'You never told me he gambled,' she accused.

'As you would not expect me to gossip to your successor about you.'

'And the second piece? What became of that?'

'It went to pay the outstanding bills on the refurbishment of your Residence.'

'But why? The budget has been exceeded?'

'No, simply not paid by the Foreign Ministry. Our budgets are months behind. I thought it wise to pay the bills and fix your leaking roof. And equally prudent not to tell you about it.'

She nodded. The Chinese economy was in chaos and Embassy expenses were beginning to fall ever farther down the list of Foreign Ministry priorities. The Residence was tired, unkempt, in need of refurbishment. What Mo said made sense. Her tone grew more emollient.

'And the third, Mo? The third piece went for what purpose, please?'

He knew she would come to that. He had carefully dragged his Ambassadors into his little game, paying some of their debts and soiling them by association. But he knew it wouldn't hide his own activities. Mo was one of the brightest and best-qualified young diplomats of his generation. Fudan University before the Foreign Affairs Institute. Every step of his career accompanied by commendations and acclaim. That's why many years earlier than he might have expected he'd ended up in London, one of the most prized of foreign postings. But he and the other staff might just as well have been posted to a warehouse in Ulan Bator. Of London itself they knew and saw practically nothing. They weren't allowed to touch. They lived almost entirely within the Embassy walls. They ate in the Embassy's canteen, worked beneath the Embassy's harsh lights and slept in the Embassy's unwelcoming and lonely beds. The cockroaches here were almost as big as in their old university dorms. And their greatest excitement— oh revolutionary joy!—proved to be a communal bus trip to Brighton. Windy, rain-splattered Brighton. Next year they had been promised Bognor.

Even as the secretaries fluttered at the prospect of Bognor, Mo felt sick with frustration. And his sickness grew. One day he had been permitted (after first reporting to Security) to walk to the Chinese pharmacy in Shaftesbury Avenue so that he might pick up some herbs for the Ambassador. Just down from the pharmacy he had found a young man and his dog, wrapped in a blanket in a doorway. A beggar in the midst of plenty. Proof before his eyes of the Western disease. Except that in his bowl the young man and his dog had made more money in a morning than Mo could spare in a week. A Chinese diplomat, yet he couldn't even look an English beggar in the eye.

It could have been worse, of course. Mo was already on the ladder of privilege which, as he climbed, would eventually bring him advantage and reward. Yes, eventually. He'd just decided it would make sense to short-circuit the system a little. To grab some of the benefits before he was too old to enjoy them. Certainly before he was as old as Madame Lin. But he wasn't about to tell her that.

So he said nothing, simply returning her stare defiantly. Why should he incriminate himself? But in spite of his silence, she knew.

'I see. You had touched forbidden fruit and decided to taste it for yourself.'

'What do you propose to do?'

'The rules say I should send you back to Beijing.'

He flinched. 'Where the People's Republic will show its gratitude by taking me to a football stadium, placing me on my knees in front of the crowd and blowing my brains out through my ears.'

'You have broken the rules.'

'As did your predecessor,' he protested with vehemence. 'But I doubt that he will be kneeling beside me. There are privileges that accompany rank, even in the People's Republic.'

'Perhaps particularly in the People's Republic.'

Mo started. The prospect of being done to death permitted a measure of cynicism. But he hadn't expected Madame Lin to reciprocate.

'Simply because I am an Ambassador does not make me blind, Mo. And simply because I am old does not make me forget.'

'Forget what?'

'That I too was once young. A Red Guard. We shot people too, during the terror of the Cultural Revolution. We shot people who had done much less than you. Some who had done nothing at all. We made mistakes far worse than yours.' She paused. 'There has been too much shooting.'

His heart stuttered in hope and disbelief. An old woman, an old revolutionary, come to repentance? 'What do you intend to do with me?'

'Mo, you are no older than my own daughter. You are a fool in some matters, like politics. But

70

you are adventurous. And adaptable. Such qualities will be necessary in the difficult times ahead.'

'So . . . what do you intend?' he repeated.

She left him hanging for a few pain-filled moments, like a fish impaled on a hook. 'I intend that you should notice the gap on my mantelpiece, Mo. Where there should be something very old.' She reeled him in. 'Perhaps your cousin can fill it for me.'

*   *   *

They came together to remember him in many corners of the globe. Particularly in Tibet, before the baton charges and electric prods of the People's Armed Police forced them to flee. Around the world they gathered in small groups, and in vast crowds, the high and the humble, monarchs and those who were merely mortal, to give thanks for the life of Tenzin Gyatso, the fourteenth Dalai Lama.

On the mountainside in McLeod Ganj, in front of the steps that led to the temple of the Namgyal Monastery, they built a great brass *chorten,* a tomb which they covered in gold leaf and decorated with many precious stones. And above it they built a canopy of blue, yellow, white, red and green, the symbolic colours of the sky, the earth, water, fire and air. And the body of the Dalai Lama was taken from its cave and prepared by embalmers in the ancient tradition, washing the eviscerated body in milk and rubbing it with salt. The face and hands were also covered in gold leaf and the body, wrapped in brocade robes, was placed in its position of meditation within the *chorten.*

71

A small window was left in the side of the *chorten* so that the body might never leave his followers' sight.

The monks, led by the abbot of Namgyal, began to chant the protector rights, praying that his teachings might be preserved and the body might be safeguarded, and also that the reincarnation would be swift. The national flag of Tibet that in normal times flew above the monastery was hauled down and would not be raised again until many weeks of mourning were complete.

And when gifts had been bestowed upon those monks and craftsmen who had laboured to build the *chorten,* the ordinary people came to offer their own prayers and tears, and to make prostrations, giving thanks for his life and many works. And across his empty throne they placed a mountain of white prayer scarves.

Then they waited for his return.

CHAPTER THREE

More than three years had passed since the death of the Lama. Years of emptiness and anticipation for those who were waiting in the hope, or in the fear, that he would come again.

It was spring. Violent. Unpredictable. The ageing sash windows were locked against the dampness but as always they leaked and rattled. All winter long she had nagged her husband to fix them, concerned that the chill winds would get into the child's chest. To no avail; he was always so busy. By the time the task had grabbed his attention it would be high summer. 'There, I told you not to bother,' he would say, looking up from his tea and laughing at her. 'I was born in a mud hut up a mountain and you go on about a few draughts. The child needs a bit of fresh air. You worry too much.' In less defensive moments he had promised that one day they would move into a larger place where she could have room not only for herself but maybe even for another baby, somewhere away from the noise and the traffic. One day, he promised, but for the moment she must be content. The laundry business on the ground floor was still no better than struggling, not a time yet for taking great leaps. She was impatient, at times angry. This was not a part of town to set up a family, and in her opinion it was scarcely a part of town to set up a cleaning business either, not with the condition of some of the clothes and bed linen that were brought in. Only this morning she had repaired one of Sophie's costumes. It had clearly been slashed with a razor. Yet Sophie had merely given her that bold, brash, sad smile of hers and made some excuse about another day, another downer. Do your best, Sophie had asked, and she had done, but the best in this place, like the windows, was never good enough.

She should have fixed the windows herself. Never too late. It only needed a few twists of paper to be forced into the gaps. So she found a roll of brown wrapping paper in the back of the cupboard and began cutting it into pieces. 'Paper. Paper,' she said to the child, encouraging him to repeat the sound, but as yet he had shown no inclination to talk, even at two years of age. He preferred to sit and watch her, as he was doing now, his eyes bright and aware, and exceptionally dark, even for an

73

Oriental. 'Paper, paper,' she repeated, but he merely chuckled and tried to bite the head off his Teletubby.

'You're stubborn. You get that from your father,' she chided, opening the window. From the narrow street below came the clatter of the open-air market. Customers complaining. Car horns blaring. Traders tossing argument and optimism back and forth to get themselves through their long days.

It took her back to her own childhood, when some of her first recollections were of wandering with her own mother through the local market in search of fresh meat and vegetables, and sorting out a little of the freshest gossip while they were about it. That was thirty years ago. Now, down below her, the cries of the market had reached such a pitch that a stranger might think a full-blown quarrel was about to erupt, yet it was nothing more than the hard-handed humour of the street. Just like her childhood.

Except the market of her childhood was now many thousands of miles away. It didn't have hookers like Sophie. And it hadn't sold King Edwards by the pound.

*　　　*　　　*

Beds, beds, and still more beds.

Once he'd had guest beds, granny's bed, bunk beds, beds to bounce on and crawl under and pretend were Wild West forts or Spanish galleons. He'd even once had a water bed, but Elinor had thought that pretentious. He'd had more than enough of every kind of bed, when he'd lived in Holland Park. Whole tribes of children would

74

arrive and promptly disappear into the wonderland of the attic or the wilderness of the basement, far enough away to let their mothers chat in peace and let Goodfellowe get on with his paperwork. Good days. But now he had nothing but his own bed and all he could stretch to for guests, even for Sam, was that cantankerous pull-out thing which called itself a sofa.

And still she couldn't be bothered to clear up after herself, the miserable little madam. But what could he expect of a seventeen-year-old daughter?

The path from relative comfort to adversity had been nothing if not swift, forced out of Holland Park by the effects of AFD Syndrome—Acute Financial Dysfunction Syndrome. (He'd actually heard the phrase used, some psycho-babble given as evidence before the Social Services Select Committee; what bollocks.) That hadn't been his only problem, of course. He'd also failed a breathalyser test which had reduced him to finding living quarters (he couldn't call it home) within a reasonable bicycle ride of Westminster. He'd chosen Gerrard Street. Or, more accurately, Gerrard Street had chosen him. The rent and other expenses came to a thousand a year less than his parliamentary housing allowance, but the Chinese landlord hadn't batted an eyelid when he asked for a receipt for the full amount. The additional thousand meant he could keep Elinor in her nursing home. Parliamentary allowances didn't run to full-time psychiatric care for wives nor, come to that, did they run to a boarding school education for a seventeen-year-old. But what choice did he have? At least without a car he couldn't fiddle his mileage allowance, unlike others.

Sam hadn't found it easy. A small garret studio with a platform for the bed stuck up in the open eaves could never pass as a family home and wasn't particularly comfortable, but at least she found it convenient for the clubs and galleries when she came to London, She'd been coming up more frequently in recent weeks, often with her friend Edwina, and he was always glad to see her. Even if she didn't clear up after herself.

Goodfellowe started throwing the bedclothes into a slightly less rumpled pile and wrestling with the mattress mechanism. A year ago he and Sam had scarcely been able to talk, their conversations sheathed in the mutual embarrassment and misunderstanding which filled the gap between puberty and parenthood. Nowadays the embarrassment was all his. She was growing fast, almost too fast for Goodfellowe, with a lack of self-consciousness that had him averting his eyes and left her underwear strewn over his floor. As he gathered up the sheets and threw them onto the laundry pile, he found himself hoping that her lack of self-consciousness didn't also mean a lack of self-restraint. He knew he should offer her paternal advice, even more so as she lacked a mother's influence, but somehow whenever he ventured onto this particular field his words deserted him and the good intentions froze. His attempts were never less than clumsy and ultimately always proved unsuccessful. 'Don't worry, Dad,' she had once consoled him; 'fathers are always the last to know.'

Yesterday she had arrived unexpectedly with a bundle of brochures and magazines under her arm. 'Got to choose my university for next year,' she had declared. Heavens, was it that time already?

76

Growing up too fast! He wasn't ready for this. But at least she had wanted his advice—or, if he were honest, his approval of her choice. University of London, by preference. Best history-of-art courses in the country.

'And it will be near you,' she had smiled, turning him as soft and as malleable as wax. 'And Bryan.'

'Who the hell's Bryan?' he had demanded.

'Oh, just a boy I like. Nothing too serious yet. If it gets serious I'll introduce you.'

'What's "serious"?' he had enquired.

'Backpacking in Umbria, maybe. Or at least driving lessons. He's suggested it. Got a BMW 3-series. Black. Convertible. With a six-stack Kenwood CD.'

He wasn't sure whether he was being teased. 'You can't take driving lessons in a car like that.'

'Got any better suggestions?'

He had not. He still had several months to go on his ban and had long ago sold his own car. He lapsed into silence, speculating on what other lessons teenagers learnt in a black, 3-series BMW with endless stereo, and whether it made a difference if the soft top was up or down.

She was on the verge of independence and he had no choice but to accept it. University. Separate holidays. Separate lives, for the most part. He could only be grateful that she shared some of her time and came to stay with him, a friend as well as a daughter—even if it did mean him scrabbling around dealing with dirty linen instead of matters of state. Although on reflection perhaps there wasn't all that much difference.

He threw a bundle of university brochures to one side and tried to fold the bed back into the sofa.

But it was stuck, complaining, something in the way. A magazine had become wedged in a spring. It turned out to be a copy of *Metropolitan,* a publication that, in the language of the shout line, 'Makes Young Women Turn On and Turn Over'. It made him feel uncomfortable. He'd never read one before, hadn't realized it carried items like . . . He sat down—no, sank would be a better description—onto the bed. This was clearly going to be one of those growing-up sessions that fathers had to endure when they discovered what truly took their daughters' interests. Like 'Male Lust—Inside the Mind of the Man Inside You'. And 'Bonking Your Way to Greater Brain Power'. The illustrations for 'Nifty Ways to Naughty Nights' were particularly vivid.

He leafed through the pages, becoming involved in it rather more than he had intended. The photographs of the models were about as close as he got to female flesh nowadays, and he found himself making the most of it. Then, to his intense embarrassment, it dawned on him that any one of these full-figured and flawless young women could have been Sam. In pursuit of her interest in art she had posed for life classes, taken her clothes off for strangers, still did for all he knew, and although he had tried to be as dispassionate and as analytical about it as she was, he had failed. He knew what he felt about these young women, their bodies barely covered, their all too evident sexual attractions, and it served only to remind him what other men felt about Sam.

He hurried on. Through the advice of the agony aunt ('His Wife Doesn't Understand Me'), past the breast-enlargement advertisements ('the implant with impact . . .'), skipping over the tarot readings and astrology charts until finally he was done. Nothing left but the classified ads. He was about to toss the magazine to one side when he noticed she had marked one of the ads. Ringed it in ink.

The Unplanned Pregnancy Advice Clinic.

It took a little time for the thought to take hold. It was almost as if he were standing on the deck of a great liner which at first trembled then, very slowly, started to sink. The deck began to tilt and the familiar furniture to shift. He found himself scrabbling for his footing, his uncertainty turning by stages to confusion and then to fear. Little Sam. Pregnant? Suddenly he saw a life with so much promise, overflowing with such potential, now on the brink of—what?

Ruin. His daughter. Just another social statistic. Of course! That's why she'd been coming to London so frequently. Not to see him but to attend a bloody . . . a bloody bun club! He'd been a fool, felt deceived. But he also felt responsible. All those parental conversations he had tried to launch before retreating in embarrassment. That had been his part of the deal and he had failed. He had owed her more than that. Now she was paying the price, not only for her own weakness but for his, too. His fault. More guilt.

And after the guilt came panic. What to do? He didn't know, had no idea. He'd never been a grandfather before.

And who was the father? Bryan? Bryan! He'd kill bloody Bryan-the-little-bastard. Or whoever. Perhaps it wasn't Bryan. Still more panic. No, he wanted it to be Bryan, he didn't want a whole list of suspects.

Little Sam!

He swore, most vividly, but it didn't help. And outside he thought he could hear a Black Dog braying, waiting for him. So, lacking any other inspiration and ignoring the fact that it was still only eleven o'clock, Goodfellowe rose unsteadily from the bed and fixed himself a drink.

*   *   *

A different bed, still more makeshift than the first. Little more than a mass of complaining springs, no mattress, supported by four short and rusting iron legs. It was to the legs that they had tied her.

Sherab should never have returned to Tibet. Such trips always involved risk. She was only a functionary, not a mighty maker of decisions, no more than a manager of Potala Travel in McLeod Ganj. But she handled all the travel arrangements for the Dalai Lama's office and anyone with those sort of connections became a subject of interest to the Chinese. A target. Yet her mother was gravely ill; it might be a final chance for Sherab to see her. She had no choice.

Luck had not travelled with her. Sherab was riding in the back of a vegetable lorry along an ancient Khampa trade route, avoiding the main roads which were heavily patrolled, but every mile took her further east, to where the Chinese presence was most evident and oppressive, drawing her deeper into danger. Her head was covered to protect her from the swirling dust of the high plateau and the stench of burnt diesel, so she did not see the Chinese patrol at the side of the road. They weren't looking for her and had little interest other than in liberating a few vegetables to accompany the yak broth they were brewing, but they became suspicious when they found Sherab hiding in the back, covered, and grew still more interested when they found the money belt packed tight with the savings she had intended for her mother. This was no ordinary peasant, concealed behind sacks, and with such soft hands. They could read fear in her eyes, and fear spelled guilt. Anyway, if she wasn't guilty of something they would have to hand back the money pouch. So she had been apprehended, and Sherab's life was squandered for an armful of vegetables.

She had been taken to Gutsa Gaol to the east of Lhasa, not in the main section but in a wing reserved for the politicals. It was there they unravelled her true identity by matching sex, age, accent and eventually her face to their files. 'Sherab Chendrol,' they had said, 'we believe you wish to be a good citizen. Please co-operate.' And to encourage her they had put her in a 'co-operation' cell fourteen metres square with one overspilling bucket and twenty hideous women, every one of whom was disfigured by some malevolent skin disease that she presumed to be highly contagious. There was no room to hide, no place to wash, and several of the hags had made a point of brushing up against her. When in the morning she had begged to be put in another cell, she was brought down many musty flights of concrete stairs to this new place. It was below ground, dank, with only a single bare light bulb hanging awkwardly from the ceiling and condensation seeping down the walls. But she felt, at first, relief; at least it had a bed. And she was alone, except for the guards, three male and one female, who accompanied her. There seemed to be very little noise down here; it was a long way from any other part of the prison. She wondered why there was no latrine bucket; perhaps that meant she would not be staying here long. It was only then she realized this could be no ordinary cell.

'I am nothing but a travel agent,' she insisted, anxiously. 'I have done nothing wrong.'

'You work for splittists and imperialists who want to destroy China,' one of the guards, evidently the most senior, answered roughly. Then he almost smiled, his tone softening. 'We want nothing more than your co-operation.'

'I only make travel arrangements. Travel arrangements,' she repeated, like a mantra she hoped might keep her from harm.

'For the Dalai Lama clique.'

'I do what I am told.'

'Good. That will keep you out of trouble,' the officer applauded. 'We intend you no harm. All we want is for you to do as you are told. Nothing more.'

She had heard in McLeod Ganj from the thousands of refugees who flooded across the Himalayas of the many outrages that took place in Chinese prisons. But she had done nothing wrong, was of so little importance. If she returned their smiles, maybe they wouldn't . . . She tried to push aside her darkest fears and concentrate on images of her baby daughter, not eighteen months old, with her first teeth, and of her son who was already growing up to look like his father.

'Please, take off your clothes,' the female guard instructed.

Sherab knew there was no point in resistance.

82

She sat on the edge of the bed. She thought of summer, of a picnic by the waterfall at Machchrial. Slowly she began to slip out of her clothes, as though preparing for a swim, and conjured up the sound of children's laughter.

'All of them,' the female guard insisted.

'It is not a problem,' Sherab told herself. 'So long as there is another woman present, it is not a problem. Not a problem. Not a problem.' Another mantra.

As the last item of clothing fell to the floor, the female guard swept up her clothes and without a backward glance disappeared through the door. As it closed, the men drew nearer.

Sherab began to sweat, in spite of the cold. As she sat on the edge of the bed she could feel the raw and rusted metal biting into her flesh.

'You have nothing to fear,' the officer said. He was an inelegant man, balding, with a belly too large for his belt, a figure of contentment that could only result from a privileged position and an attentive wife. His smile, when he used it, was that of an indulgent father.

'Please. Please don't rape me,' Sherab whispered.

The officer shook his head in surprise. 'We don't rape Tibetans,' he protested.

'Better yaks,' one of the other guards sneered. 'Better yaks than Tibetan cows.' And meant it.

Sherab leant forward, trying to cover her nakedness, unable to meet their eyes. A razor's edge of sweat carved its way down her back.

'Nothing to fear,' the officer continued, 'so long as you cooperate. Take yourself back three years. To a moment shortly before the last Dalai died.'

83

The last Dalai. He lingered over the phrase. If only it were true. He began pacing around the bed, which was located in the middle of the cell, until he was unseen and behind her back. 'The Dalai called together some of his most important advisers. From distant parts. In the greatest secrecy. You must remember the occasion because it was the final meeting he ever held in this world. I would like to know what was discussed.'

'But I wasn't present at the meeting,' she protested, her voice hoarse. 'I can tell you nothing.'

'Good. Very good,' the officer commended.

'No, no! You've got it wrong,' she insisted. Despite her circumstances her heart began to lift, for this was clearly a stupid mistake which could be easily resolved. And the officer seemed kindly. 'I wasn't at the meeting.'

'Yet you were often in the Dalai Lama's residence. You even live nearby. With your family. Your young son. And a little baby daughter, I am told.' He knew all about her. And her family. And he wanted her to know that he knew. 'It is perfectly possible that you visited the Residence at the time of the meeting.'

Now she could see his mistake. He didn't understand! But she could soon explain. 'The meeting was a secret. No visitors were allowed that day to His Holiness's quarters. Even the staff were sent away.'

'And you?'

'I wasn't there!'

'But there were many people present at the meeting.'

'No, only three.'

'Three. Only three. You see how easy it is to co-

84

operate with us?'

She had fallen into his trap.

'So what did they discuss?' The question was put again, most gently.

She shook her head in exasperation. How could he not realize? 'I was not there. How could I know what they discussed? I only made the travel arrangements.'

'Precisely. You made the travel arrangements. So you should have no trouble in telling me who the three were.'

Suddenly everything had grown dark and confused in her mind; she could no longer trust her faded wits. The officer leant forward, to whisper. She could feel his breath prickle upon her damp shoulder.

'All we need to know from you, Sherab, before we let you go back to your children, is the names of the three. Just their names. Nothing more. And then you may return.'

She bit her lip to enforce her own silence. It was a mistake. She should have denied knowing who they were, perhaps she might have been believed. But silence implied secrets.

'It seems a fair exchange. Your family for three names.'

She shook her head, trying to clear it of confusion and temptation. Above her head the light bulb was swinging, casting leering shadows on the floor where her eyes were fixed.

'I am a reasonable man,' the voice behind her continued. 'But, if I have a fault, it is impatience. Yes, sadly, I am an impatient man.'

A long silence.

There were to be no further chances. She was

85

grabbed from behind. Jerked backwards. Stretched out on the iron bed. Her senses screaming but too terrified to cry out. Her wrists tied to the metal legs. And her ankles. With wire. Thin, spiteful wire. She was spreadeagled, her woman's parts completely exposed. Vulnerable. Only then did she see why the light bulb had hung so awkwardly, for the fitting allowed for another attachment which was now in place. A long cable trailed from the light bulb to an instrument, like a thick chisel, which was held in the officer's hand. The hand was protected by a thick rubber glove.

She had heard so much about it. In hushed tones, when the refugees had reached the safety of McLeod Ganj. The Devil's Chisel, she had once heard it called. He brushed it almost casually across the damp, perspiring skin of her middle thigh. Less than a second. But time enough for her entire body to arch upwards as though trying to break free and fly through the ceiling. Except, of course, she was manacled, with wire, which was already slicing through the flesh to the bone.

'Impatience is a fault, I know. Please don't encourage it,' her tormentor requested.

She could manage no more than a whimper. Her body sagged back, the rusting springs complained as they lacerated her back. She thought she might have fouled herself but could not tell through the noise of battle that was still being waged throughout her body.

The chisel fell again. This time she managed to scream.

'I don't wish to hurt you,' the officer encouraged, touching the chisel to her nipple. 'All I want is three names.' Now the other nipple, as though it were

86

being scorched in a flame. She began to mumble, her words faint and incoherent, and he bent low over her. He could see terror in the pulp of her eyes, yet he could hear only defiance as her lips tried to form the words of a prayer. He shook his head, now visibly angry. 'When will you Tibetans learn that your religion is nothing more than superstition? Sorcery! A spell cast upon you by that serpent Lama. He can't help you now, can he?'

She continued to form the words of the prayer, with difficulty but with unmistakable deliberation. His response was to stick the chisel inside her mouth.

She tried to focus on her most powerful images. On the children. On the running waters at Machchrial. On butterflies, whose colourful wings beat in front of her mind with such force that they grew blurred like a spinning top. Before she passed into unconsciousness she could smell the burning of her own tongue.

She had no idea how long she remained in darkness. But when she awoke, the guards were still beside her. And the pain was worse.

'Have I managed to change your mind?' the officer asked.

It was all she could do to turn her head stiffly from side to side.

'Please let me explain, Sherab. I ask only for three simple names. But if I cannot persuade you to co-operate, I shall have to hand you over to my colleagues. That would bring me sorrow, loss of face. Compared with them I am a man of unlimited serenity. No more gentle encouragement. They will simply cut off your tits.'

As she turned to look at the other two, she could

see one was gripping a pair of shears, not rusted like the bed but gleaming in the lamplight like rats' teeth. He moved closer. Her breasts were not large and they were covered in perspiration; he had some difficulty in gaining a firm purchase, but then he brought the mouth of the shears up to just below the dark nipple until she could feel the challenge of the steel.

She had fought hard, with all the courage she could summon, but this . . . this was impossible. Death, yes, that she could contemplate, but to live with the pain and the mutilation of her womanhood was simply beyond her.

She mumbled her assent.

Yet still the soldier cut.

She arched her back and then her head in disbelief, too numbed as yet to feel the physical pain.

The guard fumbled at her other nipple. With every fibre of power that was within her, Sherab screamed the three names, over and over and over again, until the guard let her remaining breast fall from his fingers.

'My congratulations, Sherab,' the officer said. The other two laughed coarsely.

Sherab began to sob, with guilt, with excruciating pain, with relief. At least it was over.

Then he pushed the chisel between her thighs, deep, and the light bulb began to waver and flicker as it fought for its share of the current.

Her body continued to twitch long after she had lost consciousness, and possibly for a while even after her death as the electricity continued its assault upon the nerves. Only when the last of them had been burnt away and Sherab lay motionless upon the bed did the soldiers switch off the light and go for tea.

*   *   *

Another bed. But not really a bed at all. Nothing more than the back seat of an open-top tour bus cruising down Unter den Linden. But it would do, he thought. In the circumstances it would do really rather well.

Patrick Baader's day had to this point been filled with the inescapable tedium of duty. Perusing official papers. Pursuing the official 'Line to Take'. Being nice to foreigners. Even over breakfast he'd had to listen patiently to the exhortations of the Ambassador when all he truly wanted to think about was shagging the man's wife. Baader was easily distracted like that. He was Tom Goodfellowe's successor as Minister of State at the Foreign and Commonwealth Office, and in the early days he'd found the job had attractions in abundance. It was, after all, one of the most glittering waiting rooms at the fringes of the Cabinet. Sadly for Baader, however, he'd been waiting too long. Nearly four years. Stuck. Too new in his job to be moved before the last election, yet afterwards too long in the job to be a fresh face. Baader was marooned, stuck on the shelf. Not his fault. Nothing wrong with his talent, only his timing. By day he was adroit enough to be philosophical about his fate, but sometimes by night he prayed that they might all rot in hell.

The combination of power and disappointment had made him incautious. Generally he bore his disappointment with good grace yet increasingly he

89

had come to realize that, no matter how lustrous his job at the Foreign Office might seem to others, this was all he was going to get. At the tender age of fifty-four he was left under full brake in the great parking lot of Westminster, waiting for the time when the Prime Minister required his space for another, more recent model. But that was the game. No point in getting bitter. Others in his position might begin to plot and connive, to play Cassius to the great Caesar in the hope of a better ending than that crafted by Shakespeare, but Baader didn't overestimate his talents as either scriptwriter or assassin.

His talents lay in other areas. Sharp-witted, a former university lecturer—economics and an established red brick, not one of these new concrete academic abattoirs—he was well suited to the role of talking up his country and selling it to foreign investors. The hair may have lost its original colour but it had settled to a fine silver sheen, there was humour in his smile and just a hint of the razor up his sleeve. Men respected that. Yet there was more. Within Baader the pageantry of the diplomatic world was interwoven with the lustre of late nights and just a hint of licence in his pale eyes. Many women found that irresistible. There was never any suggestion of deceit, no idle talk of a misunderstanding wife and certainly no insinuation of loneliness, just the discreet offer of a meander beneath Aphrodite's arch with no threat of complications and without the husband ever knowing. For many Westminster wives it proved a potent and irresistible combination.

But he wasn't in Westminster. His private secretary had prevailed and he was in Berlin.

'You've turned down the invitation for the last three years, Minister; it's really time to put in an appearance.' So for the last two days Baader had been an official UK representative at a European seminar of parliamentarians and assorted advisers, researchers and assistants, shackled within a conference room where he was forced to listen to overstuffed Germans lecturing him, an Englishman, about the mechanics of democracy in Europe. Typical bloody Germans, always thinking they had the solution to 'the problem in the East' and the inherited right to implement it. He'd felt obliged to mention Winston Churchill three times during his own remarks simply to keep himself awake.

The official dinners had been gruesome. Bavarian wine as thin as their sauces were thick. A collective sense of humour as subtle as a trench shovel. And this evening an impromptu lecture from his neighbour at the dining table about the technical standards proposed by the European Commission to curb the explosion of telephonic sex chat services. What was particularly exhausting was that the bloody man was so patently sincere. Wearied, Baader called for an Armagnac and quietly resolved to find himself a new private secretary.

The telephonics expert had paused in order for others to express their moral approval when a voice intervened from further down the table. 'I'm not so sure,' it said brightly. 'This could ruin my relationship with Martin.'

'Martin?' Baader enquired, attracted to any source of dissent.

'My bank manager.'

'I don't understand. He talks dirty down the phone to you?'

'Not poor Martin! He's a telephone banker, the one who has to approve my overdraft. So I have to make sure he understands precisely what I need the overdraft for. Like why I need a new dress. And how it fits. Or where it fits, at least.'

'Martin is a progressive bank manager, then?'

'Good grief, no. He hasn't any idea how a girl has to get through life. So I have to educate him. On the phone. And that's where I might fall foul of the Government's guidelines.'

Mickey Ross had brushed across his life, and Baader's world suddenly began to brighten. Up to that point the entire weekend had been as exhilarating as a correspondence course in bookbinding. Boredom stirred him to excess—which was why he had grown overly interested in the Ambassador's wife and had been fantasizing about a late-night liaison with her in the Embassy lift. Boredom also bred mischief. And impatience. He had now spent two days in this place, two days of the rest of his life. Beyond the age of fifty, these things had begun to matter to him. Time was running out. And the more they crammed his official diary with duty the more he began to think about the things he was missing. Those things that had not yet been done, by him at least. In Baader's judgement the errors of commission were far more excusable than the sins of omission. You learnt more. And had more fun. And after two days of bookbinding Baader was in a mind to commit. He didn't feel like going to bed yet.

The dinner had drawn to its lifeless close and they were huddled together waiting to collect their coats. His official car would be loitering outside, waiting to take him back to the Embassy. To the Ambassador. To his small talk. And to his lissom wife. It was as his mind roved over the appalling trouble he might just get into if he went back to the Embassy in this mood that Baader found himself next to the young woman with the overdraft. He came to an instant decision.

'Fancy a bus ride?'

The bus in question turned out to be of the sightseeing variety, double decked, open topped, touring the sights of Berlin. It was dark, one of the last tours of the evening, and they sat alone on the top deck, the warm wind in their faces and their spirits like birds released from their cage.

He kissed her just as the bus passed the Opera House. A lingering, thirsty kiss. Forceful, almost aggressive.

'You don't object?' he enquired.

'You hear me shouting for help?'

He was about to reach for her again when she interrupted, almost teasing. 'Actually I prefer a Porsche to a bus.'

'Why a Porsche?'

'Has very special vibrational harmonies, totally in tune with my own. Turns me on something rotten. The top of a Number 53 from Clapham has much the same effect, but the other passengers do have a habit of staring so.'

'No passengers tonight.'

'Funny you should notice that.'

By the time the bus had passed the Brandenburg Gate their fingers were exploring, and as they passed into the darkness of the Tiergarten their mutual lack of inhibition had become clear. Zips,

93

buttons, clasps, gasps. Clumsily he helped her remove her tights, which were grabbed by the breeze and flew away into the night, accompanied by their laughter.

Of course it was ridiculous. As a Minister of the Crown what he was doing was extraordinarily dangerous. But as a man—and bugger the Crown—this was nothing less than magnificent. Utterly Bloody Magnificent. And mastering the geometry of the back seat of a swaying sightseeing bus proved to be an inspiring new challenge. He enjoyed new challenges.

Her nipples appeared exaggeratedly dark under the light of the passing street lamps. Everything flickered in the harsh shadows, a little like one of those three-dimensional penny peep shows on Brighton pier he remembered from his childhood. The first time he'd been on a church outing with the choir and had received a good slap when the vicar had caught him. Not now, though, although there were other perils. As she nestled across his lap, both of them contorting to master the awkward shape of the seat, Baader gasped. His back was in knots. He'd have to spend all week on the chiropractor's table. But somehow he didn't give a damn.

'Do you think this could be a big mistake?' she whispered.

'Oh I do hope so,' he replied. 'I do hope so.'

*　　　*　　　*

The final bed was little more than a stone shelf built out from the wall. Uneven, cold, and covered with nothing more than a blanket. It was the middle of the night and the temperature in Kunga Tashi's room had fallen below freezing, but a lifetime of meditation had enabled him to sleep in such conditions without discomfort. For a Tibetan Buddhist, the body can be turned into something that is detached, almost disposable. Kunga often taught such meditation techniques to the younger monks, encouraging them to lift their consciousness to a higher plane of spirituality and disembodiment. And if it helped them to sleep through the icy blasts of a Himalayan winter, so much the better.

It had been a winding road that had led Kunga to the monastery at Rapang. There had been other monasteries in the last ten years, each one offering no more than a brief interlude in his flight from persecution. Or what might alternatively be described as stopping places along the road to enlightenment—it all depended on your outlook. To a Tibetan Buddhist the body is a vehicle for the soul; to those like the Han, the soul is nothing more than deceit, an excuse for the body to sit around a monastery living like a pickpocket off the rest of the community. So the Chinese arrived at each monastery with their political commissars who dismissed the abbot and installed one of their own choice. The monks would then be forced to sign a 'confession' giving up all allegiance to the Dalai Lama, and all pictures of their leader would be smashed. Some monks signed the confession, then hid pictures of the Lama in private places. Others resisted, and in those cases the normal Beijing response was to send in bulldozers and raze the monastery to the ground. Many, like Kunga, fled to other monasteries. But always the Chinese and their commissars followed.

So, many years ago, Kunga had written to the Dalai Lama for his advice. To stay and sign? To lie and deceive? To fight? Or to fly? The monk's dilemma. The Lama's response had been characteristically blunt.

'To Rapang!' his reply had instructed, naming a monastery in the remotest part of north-western Tibet. 'Where there is no electricity. No vegetables. There you will find safety. For where there is no electricity and no vegetables, there you will find no Chinese!'

As Kunga had read the advice he could almost hear the Lama laughing. And how right he had been. The Chinese had no liking for the rigours of Tibetan life and everywhere tried to recreate a miniature version of the Han homeland. Han food. Han fashions. Han laws, of course. Even the language—only Chinese was permitted to be used in the schools. The Han claimed they were a civilizing influence in this feudal land. But they also opened bars and brothels. And gaols. And lost interest in their civilizing role with each mile that led them away from the nearest power station.

Rapang was a very long way from any power station, or serviceable road, or supply of beer. And it was here that Kunga had come several years before to be the chant master and to give himself time for meditation. If that in Chinese eyes made him a parasite, it was a remarkably ill-chosen spot. Not a place to grow fat. But a place of peace, a place where, in normal circumstances, he was able to sleep. Although tonight was different. Kunga lay restless in his cell, unable to push away his thoughts, listening to the complaints of the

96

mountain wind through the shutters and distracted by the scampering of mice as they sought out the offering of rice he had placed before his small shrine.

There was no light. What moon there was lay obscured behind the shutters, closed against the howling wind. The darkness embraced him and once more he tried to open his mind to his dreams, to practise the dream yoga that enabled him to search into the corners of his consciousness. Perhaps that would help him understand why he was so unsettled tonight, why indeed he had been growing increasingly restless for several days. Dreams might help, but only if he could sleep.

He tried to relax his limbs, to drag himself through to sleep, but to no avail. It was as though spirits from another world were prodding his mind with a stick. And gradually that world became clearer. It was a world much like his own. Of mountains and bottomless lakes and air filled with the tang of wood fires and dew on meadows. Of colours as clear as if they had been freshly painted in enamel. And the sun beating down, warming his bones. Suddenly across the fields he could see a man approaching, carrying a small bundle. A man without a face. And as he approached, Kunga could see that the bundle the man was holding was the size and shape of a small child, wrapped in swaddling clothes. But as they drew nearer Kunga could see he had made a mistake. They were not swaddling clothes. They were funeral robes. A voice whispered in his ear that the child had been brought home; one last look, before they buried him. And with a sense of overwhelming terror that all but choked him, Kunga realized that this child,

97

this bundle of rags, was the incarnation. The Lama. Dead. His world destroyed. And the bundle was being brought closer to him, mocking, accusing him, for Kunga had failed. Closer and closer they came until Kunga couldn't breathe and knew that he, too, was going to die. And a shadow fell across the scene that turned the sweat on his body to ice. Now the man was upon him, reaching out to show Kunga the child, announcing the end of all hope. And the man looked up. Kunga at last could see his face, It was smiling. Taunting. It was Chinese.

Kunga uttered a cry and with both hands pushed the vision away from him. He sat on the edge of his bed, gasping for breath, feeling the sweat trickle down his face like tears.

He knew what it meant. The Lama had arrived, had been reborn but already was in mortal danger. As Kunga himself was in danger. A feeling of compelling dread gripped him. The time had come and already he might be too late.

An hour after dawn, and only five after Kunga had fled, a Chinese officer arrived at the monastery in his jeep. He was followed by three truckloads of troops. But to no avail. It would make no difference how many troops he brought with him. For already Kunga had gone, fled, leaving his life behind him.

CHAPTER FOUR

Reg Limping was the topic of the day. And probably would be next Monday too, since the Sunday tabloid had promised to publish 'more exotic antics and stunning images of the

Honourable and Upright Member for Coalbridge'. Bloody photographs! They'd been taken just for fun. A bit of a turn-on. Nothing more than a few Polaroids to perk him up, And on his mother's grave he'd have sworn that only a mental patient would allow them to be published. He had reckoned without the publicity-seeking out-of-work actress who also featured in them. Limping braced his shoulders and continued his uneasy progress around the Central Lobby of the House of Commons, lips set in what he hoped was defiant form as his eyes searched for colleagues who might engage him in conversation for longer than ten seconds. Hell, he was sure they would understand. Why, could've happened to anyone.

Not quite anyone, Goodfellowe thought. To have conducted an affair with a snap-happy actress born three years after your own wedding was careless. To have put the young woman on public display at one of the Prime Minister's receptions at Chequers was crass. Getting caught by a police patrol car consummating the affair in his Range Rover in a Buckinghamshire lay-by on the way home was little short of cretinous. And attempting to drive away from the scene so hurriedly that his trousers flew out of the window ensured that, whatever else happened in Limping's undistinguished career, he would never be forgotten. He had not only ensured an eventual obituary in *The Times,* but had already tied up its content. *'An unremarkable career made notable, indeed notorious, by an incident in a lay-by when . . .'*

Yet, in his guts, Goodfellowe was eaten with envy. His own social life was little more than a shroud, his sex life the dust within its folds. On days

99

like this he'd have given his left nut to have been in—or out—of Limping's trousers. It was one of those days when he had visited Elinor.

His wife's condition had grown steadily worse. The processes of the mind and the spirit subjected to unimaginable pain are still broadly a mystery to the medical profession, which, in many instances, can offer little more than condolence and bromides. Within Elinor something had snapped, that internal pathway which connects hope with resistance, and not all their efforts had been able to sew the connection back together again. So she had been sectioned, locked away as a danger to herself, where she spent her time slipping deeper and deeper inside herself. That morning Goodfellowe had visited and she hadn't stirred. She had responded neither to his presence nor to his voice; not to the massage of her arms that he had given nor even, in a final act of tearful desperation, to the violent shaking of her shoulders. He thought that she was going to break in two. She had shrunk, grown so frail, her skin like parchment gathered from the floor of an Egyptian sarcophagus. But it was her eyes that affected him most. They were opened wide, but led nowhere. There was nothing within. Nothing stirred.

Yet he needed her more than ever. He had sat at the end of her bed and talked about Sam and pregnancy and his own inadequacies in dealing with the situation, begging Elinor for help. She had not stirred. Hadn't been there, wouldn't be there, for him or for Sam.

He blamed Elinor. He blamed Sam. He even— God forgive him—at times even blamed little Stevie for getting drowned and destroying all their lives. Hell, he could throw blame around like children throw fireworks on Guy Fawkes Night. Above all, he blamed himself. It was going to be another of those days when he would end up at home, drunk, on his own, bathing in self-pity and listening to the slavering of the Black Dog.

Yet as he watched Limping's pathetic journey around his colleagues, something changed inside Goodfellowe. He suspected it wouldn't be long before he was making the same journey, for he knew that after a single glass he would give anything to be in a lay-by getting worked over by some young nymphet, and after three he wouldn't be giving a damn if the entire population of Buckinghamshire was at the window looking on. And, night after night in recent weeks, there had been many more than three glasses. Yes, Limping's trousers would undoubtedly fit him rather well.

So what? Elinor wouldn't mind, wouldn't even know. And he didn't give much of a damn about anyone else's opinion. Except for Sam. Ah, but there it was. Whoever else he owed, he owed Sam more, and considerably more than he was able to give on his own, particularly with this nightmare of her pregnancy. Which meant he needed someone else. A woman, of course. *Woman!* Which meant a really good shagger . . . No, no, forget the shagging, don't get distracted! He needed a friend, a source of feminine advice, that's how he'd meant to explain it. Someone who could help him with Sam. Maybe using Sam as an excuse was pathetic but, as he watched colleagues turning their backs on Limping after offering nothing but mouthfuls of banalities and disingenuous smirks, he knew what he wanted. A woman who could not only shag his brains out so that he wouldn't remember his guilt but who could also be his guide with Sam, and bury some of that guilt too.

His thoughts turned to Elizabeth.

Elizabeth de Vries. Late thirties. Divorced. Marmalade eyes and lips which, when they smiled, seemed to put an earthquake through his sorrows. Not that they had smiled much in his presence recently. They had been about to become lovers the previous year until circumstance had intervened in the form of a press insinuation that he was having an affair with an eighteen-year-old Chinese girl. A misunderstanding, of course. Practically bloody libellous. But the damage had been done. Their silences were no longer filled with unspoken understanding but simply voids where their minds refused to meet and meld. So he had stopped visiting The Kremlin, the fine Russian restaurant she owned, and had begun drinking at home. Alone.

But he needed her. Sam needed her, too, or someone like her.

As Goodfellowe watched, an agent of parliamentary retribution, a Whip, had come up to Limping's elbow. Brief words were exchanged. A restraining hand placed on Limping's arm. As though he were under arrest. They left together in the direction of the Chief Whip's office, Limping's smile even less convincing.

No, that wasn't the way, not for Goodfellowe. There was still a faint smear of pride upon his soul. And so it was resolved. He needed help. He needed the help of a woman. He would give Elizabeth a call.

Kunga had only a few hours' start and was on foot, but that was enough. He knew the tracks and rock-strewn trails in this area, while the Chinese would be confined to the one, useless road that had brought them bouncing and bruised to the monastery.

The Chinese would be consumed with anger when they discovered he was gone. The monastery would suffer. The abbot had known that. Which is why he had asked Kunga to take Dawa with him. Dawa was a fourteen-year-old *tulku,* or incarnation of a great teacher, one of the monastery's most precious assets; he must be kept from the Han. And in addition they took Tenzin, a strong young man and one of Kunga's favourite pupil monks, for they would need much help and strength to get them through the mountains. There had been no time for preparations, no special clothing, not even boots, only a little money and the food that could be wrapped hurriedly in a blanket. And sunglasses. The abbot found them each a pair of sunglasses. Cheap, and Chinese. But, when the snowfields were stirred by the sun to the intensity of a laser, their eyes and their lives might depend upon them.

They followed the river for many kilometres as it tumbled and frothed downstream in the direction of the distant highway, their calf muscles aching with strain, then hitched rides and took buses in the direction of the southern border town of Dram. Dawa slept most of the way. Kunga couldn't resist many fleeting moments of envy. Axles on Tibetan roads spend a life in constant torment, and they put Kunga in touch with every part of his body in a manner he rapidly came to regret. But apart from the discomfort, for two days they encountered few problems. Tibetans are naturally nomadic and help is freely given to travellers. At a small monastery they exchanged their monks' robes for sheepskin *chubas* and in the local marketplace bought some *tsampa* barley and honey to augment their meagre supplies. They had no travel permits, of course, but that was not unusual. At every checkpoint they 'broke a few ribs'—paid bribes to the People's Armed Police, which was also not unusual. On the third day, however, the atmosphere changed. At the checkpoint fifty kilometres north of Dram, at the entrance to the border zone, the procedures grew slower, distinctly more methodical. The police were looking for something. Or someone. But not a family group, they gambled. So an obliging young Tibetan woman pretended to be Tenzin's wife while Kunga put on the appearance of a demented patriarch possessed by demons. The superstitious Chinese recoiled from this by-now filthy and overripe old man with hideous waving hands and let them through. But they knew they might not be as lucky next time. When at last they entered Dram they shied away from the main thoroughfares, losing themselves in the dusty alleyways and crowded markets of the back streets. It was on one of these back streets, in a grimy mud-walled tea shop, that they made contact with their guide. He had only one eye and the fingers of his left hand were stunted with frostbite. And he appeared reluctant. If they wanted over the mountain, he would lead them, but only for twice the normal price. The border patrols had doubled, he said, and so had the risks. The guide studied them closely—

104

one strong, one young, one old, all appallingly equipped—and shook his head. They wouldn't all survive.

They set out the following night, doubling back a little to escape the more obvious patrols. As dawn broke they stepped off the mountain road at a point below a ruined monastery, its empty windows and gateway standing like a bleached skull against the dark mountainside. Kunga noticed a solitary white vulture wheeling in the skies above the ruin. An omen.

The guide led them, inexorably upwards, deeper into the mountains, along trails that were invisible to the others. There is great beauty in such places. This is the land of snow eagle and snow leopard, of lammergeier, red bear and lynx. The air has a purity that enables sight and sound to travel immense distances, giving the world great clarity and a sense of oneness. In a landscape touched only by sunlight upon virgin snow, there is peace. And amidst this beauty there is also great danger.

The mountains give no second chance. A wrenched ankle is a death warrant, and all they had as protection was counterfeit Adidas tennis shoes picked up in the local market. Tennis shoes, to walk across the roof of the world. And the abbot's sunglasses to ward off snow blindness. But against the snow itself they had no real protection. Every year thousands of Tibetans walk into exile across the Himalayas, even in tennis shoes, and the favoured time is winter, when it is dry and the snow is crisp and firm, and the patrols are fewer. But Kunga had no choice. He couldn't wait for winter. And on the fourth day of their trek the air lost its quality of crystal and the storm arrived, ripping the veil of peace from the mountains. It was as though all the furies of the universe had been thrown against this one spot. The wind screamed in pain, daylight was turned to blue-grey darkness and the snow attacked their faces like an endless volley of arrows. Their eyes could not see, their lungs turned to ice. They could not go on. Yet there was nowhere to hide. They managed to build a small windbreak of rocks and huddled behind it, sharing their body heat, but the yak's dung they had gathered for fuel refused to burn, and they couldn't make tea. They chewed on a little dried meat and cubes of cheese, using up precious supplies of both food and faith. For almost two days they sat and waited for death.

Then it was over. The storm broke and skies of cobalt blue returned. Sun. Hope. At last they could light a fire, melt the evil snow and make butter tea and *tsampa* dough. But the danger had not gone, only changed its cunning, for when they resumed their trek they found the snow soft, like walking through a deep marsh. At many points it was as high as Dawa's chest. Their progress was slow, painful. The snow sneaked inside their clothes, down into their shoes, and the needle pricks of frostbite began to attack their fingers and toes. By nightfall no one but the guide, who was better equipped, could feel their feet. They lit a small fire and slowly the feeling began to return, but it was as though their feet were being slashed by burning razors. Their only consolation was that while they could still feel the pain, they had a chance to stay alive.

In the morning a helicopter with the markings of the People's Armed Police flew down the valley, but they were covered with snow and it did not see them. After it had disappeared and they prepared to move on, Dawa discovered he had no feeling in his feet and could not walk. So, for a while, Tenzin carried him on his back through the drifts of fresh snow. Then as evening approached, the storm returned. This time there was no room for doubt. Every one of them knew they were going to die.

*   *   *

The mother had planned to take her son out to the park for the morning, but it turned blustery, a typical English spring day. They stayed inside instead. The windows were still rattling, so she closed them, worrying a little whether the fumes from the dry-cleaning plant downstairs would make him cough. But the two-year-old seemed contented enough.

During the last few weeks the child had begun to make new sounds, stretching his lips to mimic the noises his mother made in play. Sounds like a train. The motorcycles of the despatch riders who roared down the street. Even a washing machine on spin cycle. But still nothing identifiable as a word. Yet any day now, she hoped. Perhaps even today. She called to him and he tumbled across the room, arms outstretched.

'Come to Mother—Ama. Ama. Ama,' she encouraged in her native tongue.

Suddenly he stopped in front of her, head to one side, listening attentively.

'Ama. Ama,' she repeated.

His lips began to change their shape. He was trying.

'Ama! Ama! Ama!' she cried.

The child's eyes began to twinkle with mischief. His lips trembled, trying to take the necessary shape.

Then it happened. His first words.

'Lama! Lama! Lama!' he chortled.

*   *   *

Ironically it was the cold that came to their rescue. For a while, at least. The storm broke once more and the soft snow it had thrown upon the mountains rapidly turned to crunching ice. You can walk on ice. It may be only a thin crust, you may never know whether your next step will take you tumbling through the crust and into a bottomless chasm or carry you off in an avalanche, but standing still on a mountain is not an option. You freeze. Or starve to death.

They walked on across the fields of snow, vast arenas of glaring light that attacked the eyes, where they felt lost in the emptiness. Even the guide had difficulty in marking their way since the snow had covered many familiar landmarks, but all the while he kept the holy mountain of Everest in his sights, to their left, and they came ever closer. By day they warmed in the sunlight reflected from the snow, while during the coldest part of the night they snatched three or four hours' sleep, before carrying on by moonlight. They had to keep moving. Already the nails on Tenzin's hand were turning black, fossilized, like coal. Dead. Those nails would eventually drop off. And unless they made more rapid progress, so would the tips of the fingers, to the knuckle. It was the same with Dawa's toes. But all the time they were drawing nearer Nangpa-la, the pass that would take them over the roof of the world and to safety.

They were almost there, at nineteen thousand feet, the highest part of their journey, more than three times the altitude of most ski resorts. Standing in tennis shoes. From here they felt they could almost touch the sky. White clouds snagged on the summit of Everest like prayer flags waving in welcome. They could still hear and occasionally see the helicopters that searched for them, but the guide had taken them high in search of firmer footing, and when the helicopters came into view they were usually far below them, scouring the valleys. It had been days since they had seen any other sign of life, even vultures, and up here they felt as though they were riding sky boats into the next world, Soon they would start to descend, towards Nepal, there would be warmth again, and life. Their hopes rose.

But first. they had to traverse the ravine, a great hole in the granite that cut through the mountains and seemed to fall away into the bowels of the earth. Mists clung to the bottom, which never saw sunlight, perhaps had never seen the sunlight in a hundred thousand years. The ice here was thick, their path treacherous, but there was no other way. Nangpa-la beckoned in the distance. The ravine was of no great length, no more than twenty miles, but every step had to be measured, tennis shoes on sheer ice, and by nightfall on the second day of their passage they had still not reached its end. They were impatient; tomorrow would see the finish of it. And when dawn broke they could at last see where the sun met the mountain once more.

109

They prepared a brief meal of warm tea and *tsampa* mixed with cheese, then divided their load. The guide would take no more than his own supplies and Dawa's feet were so bad he could take nothing, so Kunga took the bag with the last of the yak dung on his back while Tenzin tied the heavy bundle of food across his own. He was the strongest; they would travel more quickly this way.

It happened just as they hit the section that was being warmed by the morning sun. Here the snow path had begun to melt. It wasn't melting much because the air temperature was almost twenty below, but enough to leave a film of perspiration on the ice.

The guide led with Dawa following, while Kunga and Tenzin, weighed down by their loads, lagged behind. Then Tenzin paid the price of his cheap shoes. He slipped. His feet went from under him and he hit the ground clumsily. Then rolled. And rolled once more. Until he disappeared over the side of the ravine.

Kunga rushed to the edge, expecting disaster, but found Tenzin hanging on to a rock a few feet below. Their eyes met in despair. Kunga began to reach down, but his bag was dragging him over the precipice, too. He wrenched it off then reached down once more, grasping for Tenzin's outstretched hand, but his crippled fingers could gain no grip, he was only scratching at the other man's thin gloves. And Tenzin's own heavy load prevented him from climbing.

'Drop the bundle!' Kunga gasped.

Tenzin shook his head.

'Drop it!'

'It has all our food inside.'

110

'If you don't you will die.'

'If I do, we shall all die,' Tenzin replied stubbornly.

'But I cannot pull you up.'

The guide was still trying to make his way back to them, step by deadly step across the sweating ice. He wouldn't make it in time. Tenzin's hold on the rock was beginning to slip.

Tenzin wriggled. He was trying to shrug the load from his back. He'd already succeeded in unfastening one of the restraining ropes. The bundle was now swinging from just one arm.

'Come closer,' he beckoned to Kunga. 'Let me throw the food up. Hook your arm through the rope.'

Kunga reached down as far as he dared, every additional inch threatening to topple him forward. Tenzin heaved. Heaved once more. The rope looped over Kunga's arm.

The food! Their food was saved! And Tenzin might be, too.

But the effort of saving the food had made him slip way beyond Kunga's reach. And with every moment he was slipping further still.

Kunga flayed the air with his free arm, reaching down, but they both knew it was hopeless. Tenzin was clinging with all his strength to the rock, but he was slipping, almost gone.

He held on long enough for his dark eyes to give thanks. For life. For enlightenment. And to pray for the next life.

Then, with great care, he took one of his hands away from the rock and reached towards Kunga, not in vain hope of salvation but in a wave of gratitude. Their eyes held for a moment. There was

111

no fear; Tenzin was smiling.

'I shall try to enjoy the view on the way down, master.'

Then he was gone, into the mists, and below him Kunga could see nothing but eternity.

*   *   *

'Hello? Elizabeth?'

'Speaking.'

'It's Tom.'

'Tom who?'

'Try Goodfellowe.'

She knew exactly who it was, but there was scar tissue to fight through. Keep him pedalling backwards. 'Been a long time, Goodfellowe.'

'Precisely. Too long, I was thinking.'

'You'd like to make a reservation?'

'Not exactly. More a date. I'd like to see you again.'

'Wow.' A pause. 'I'm not sure that's wise. Once bitten.'

'You've never struck me as being the shy type.'

'Nor a masochist, either.'

'Look, I've no idea whether seeing each other again would be fun or complete folly.' A brief pause. 'But I'd like to find out.'

'What brought this on?'

'You know me. Decisive as always.'

That brought a peal of laughter down the phone, and he could feel her melting slightly.

'I saw you the other day on the Embankment. On your bike. Nearly ran you down.'

'That was you? That flash Mercedes?'

'What's the point of spending forty grand on a
112

car if it's not flash?'

'I was too busy picking myself up from the gutter to see you. Was the assault deliberate?'

'You know, I'm not sure. I'd probably need to go through years of analysis to find out. Was I trying to get my own back, perhaps? Or maybe just trying to attract your attention?'

'You've never had any trouble doing that.'

'Goodfellowe, this is me, remember. I could shove a distress flare up your arse and still not get your attention.'

Ouch. 'Even so, splattering me all over the highway seems a little extreme.'

'OK, so I owe you.'

'Agreed. So how about Thursday?'

A slight pause. 'Can't. Already busy. Going to the theatre.'

May it be the worst show this side of Sevenoaks, he prayed. He couldn't hide the trace of frustration. Or jealousy. 'The following Tuesday?'

'They'll let you out of that Palace of Intoxication before midnight?'

'Wanting to see you again must by definition make me unsound of mind. They'll have to put me on the sick list.'

Another pause. 'You still living in that little apartment in Gerrard Street?'

'Why?'

'Because most of the Members of Parliament I know are interested only in two things: a free meal and a lot of leg-over. In which case, perhaps I should cook for you. But I'm not parking my flash new Mercedes in the middle of Chinatown. You'd better come over here.'

'To the restaurant?'

'No, the house.'

'For a free meal?'

'Free, yes, but not exactly costless. Don't expect an easy ride.'

'Next Tuesday.'

'Timing is everything with a girl, Goodfellowe.'

'Well, you know me. I'm a very patient man.'

'Bollocks,' she said, then rang off.

A free meal and a lot of leg-over. Guilty as charged, the lot of 'em. But it left Goodfellowe wondering just how many of his fellow MPs her experience was based on.

*   *   *

It was Tenzin's death that, in the end, saved them all.

The storms had slowed their progress, as had the frostbite on Dawa's toes. In spite of the extra ration, the food had run out after seventeen days. For the next three they had nothing but snow and dwindling hope to fill their stomachs. Had Tenzin still been alive they would all have died. Even so, they hadn't long to live.

Then the guide broke into a run, stumbling weakly through the snow. They had been walking downhill for a week, through barren wastelands of rock and ice; now, ahead of them, they could see the tree line marked by a thin forest of stunted and withered pines which, as they looked further down the mountain, began to grow in confidence. They also saw a small stone bridge across a tumbling stream and it was here the guide had stopped, waving his arms.

Behind them stood Tibet. On the other side of

114

the bridge lay the mountain kingdom of Nepal.

Freedom. And exile.

To one side of the bridge rose a handful of rough-hewn sticks. From these fluttered the remnants of prayer flags, wind torn and faded by the sun, but whose messages left by previous trekkers were intended to bring encouragement to those who followed.

And beside the canes, reaching towards them, they saw a hand protruding through the snow.

Kunga and the guide knelt to sweep away the snow. Bodies on this route were not unusual. Of the thousands who began the march into exile every year across the world's highest mountains, many did not complete the journey, particularly the young and the old. Their bodies lay like signposts on the mountainside, marking the route away from oppression. But this was not one such body.

As Kunga brushed the snow away from the face, he flinched and drew back in astonishment. He knew this face, knew it well. It was Osel, a young monk from his own monastery. As they scrabbled to remove the rest of the snow the story of Osel's fate became clear. For he was stripped naked, his body encased in rock-hard ice. Tears of understanding trickled from Kunga's eyes, freezing even as they fell.

'They found me gone. So they decided others should suffer in my place.'

They had brought Osel to this point, stripped him, and poured water over his bare body. He had struggled for a while, running around in the snow, beating his own body with his fists in an attempt to keep warm, while the soldiers laughed. And poured more water. Slowly he had sunk to his knees, his

115

arms wrapped vainly around himself. Then he had fallen to the ground. And still they poured, even as Osel reached out for the power of the prayer flags, until the ice formed a glass coffin around his young corpse.

'This is their warning. They want me dead.'

The guide's single eye glanced around in anxiety, as though expecting the border guards to appear at any moment. 'But how did they know we would use this route? There are a dozen crossing points we might have used.'

'That is the point. They didn't know,' muttered Kunga grimly. 'They only know the crossing points. The same message will have been left at every one.'

In spite of the guide's concern, Kunga and Dawa sat in the snow to recite mantras for Osel and for Tenzin, and for the others unknown whose bodies now littered the many paths to freedom.

When they had finished, Kunga rose, a new energy and sense of urgency written upon his face. 'We must hurry. They will not stop until they have the Lama. And neither must we.'

*   *   *

A man who has had no sex for five months may begin to doubt whether he is still a man. For a man who, like Goodfellowe, hadn't had sex for five years, that doubt begins to turn to riveting certainty. And when that man is in the middle years of his life, he begins to wonder whether he will ever be a complete man again. At the age of fifty he becomes as fifteen, where sex is not just an issue but the *only* issue that matters in his life. Goodfellowe was not yet fifty, but was not far off it,

116

and dinner with Elizabeth had begun to take on proportions that overwhelmed the other parts of his life.

He had started to take stock of himself as a man. The mirror told its own story. Those misleading photographs of himself he hated so much were not so misleading after all. While the man within was still in his early twenties, the man on the outside had begun to show that frosting at the temples which in others he found distinguished yet in himself he viewed with alarm. The deep blue eyes, always turbulent, still sparkled and the spirit was as willing as ever, but the body was not what it once was. He would never play wing forward at Twickenham, not even in his dreams.

But to merry hell with misery. He took himself off to the traditional panelled salon of Trumpers in Curzon Street where Adam, the young hairdresser, set about his hair. That wasn't all. While he was cutting, Adam also gave him an education, initiating him into the distinctions between heavy metal and funk. Goodfellowe probably wouldn't like either, scarcely music at all, but he felt adventurous. Might give it a go. Perhaps Mickey would take him. And as they talked, Adam snipped away most of the frazzle and frosting and trimmed in some style. Goodfellowe was left looking elegant, feeling refreshed. Not young enough for a bash at the LSE with the Deaf Lollipops, perhaps, but at least he was still alive. He also bought a new silk tie. Clothes were not Goodfellowe's strongest point, squeezed as he was between the twin aesthetic disasters of his bicycle and his bank balance, but the new neckpiece was colourful and fun. Suddenly it mattered once more to

Goodfellowe what he looked like. And he took himself off to the House of Commons gym. For the first time in years Goodfellowe was reminded that he was a man of many parts—a spirit, a physique, a wit, an intellect—not just a machine designed for the drudgeries of duty. He enjoyed the gym, sweating away many of the years and the worries he had brought with him. So, the next day, he went back. And the next. By the time Monday arrived, the day before their dinner, the twenty-year-old that lurked deep inside had reasserted himself and he completed a full extra circuit and an additional ten minutes on the rowing machine.

By Tuesday he could barely walk. His muscles had turned to permafrost and each step gave him agonies. As he cycled to Elizabeth's mews house in Notting Hill he could feel every tormented muscle. This search for youth was folly, of course, but so what? Between the stabs of pain his body was pumping in anticipation.

The moment he arrived, the high spirits he carried with him went into spasm. He had expected an intimate evening *à deux,* not a full-scale dinner party with half a dozen strangers who were already well awash. Colleagues of Elizabeth from the restaurant trade. Lots of in-house gossip. Croutons and cretins. He felt like a fifth wheel, being carried just for the ride.

During the quieter corners of the pre-dinner conversation he looked around Elizabeth's small house. It was the first time he'd seen her on home turf. Everything was immaculate, no traditional feminine frills but strong colours and individual pieces, which contradicted and argued but which were stimulating and sensual. Just like Elizabeth.

118

There was a magnificent faceless nude on the wall, painted in exquisite detail. The suggestion of a birthmark high on magnificent legs. He wondered whether it might be Elizabeth herself. He also wondered whether anyone had paintings like that of Sam. The previous year she had taken to modelling in life classes—'not just for the money, Daddy, but for the experience. For an artist it's part of growing up.' He'd had to grow up, too. Overcome all the male hang-ups and parental concerns about his daughter baring her body to anyone with a five-pound arts club subscription and a paintbrush. She was proud of her body, he was proud of her, so it ought to have been easy for him. But it wasn't. No point in arguing with her. She was too strong willed. Anyway, if it resulted in paintings such as this, works of art of considerable beauty, how could he object? He continued to stare at the nude.

This was a beautiful room. In particular the lighting was exquisite, creating atmosphere, bringing people together. But perhaps, he considered, it was all a little too carefully planned, too perfect. Was that Elizabeth also? Immaculate on the outside. But what lay behind the presentation? She was divorced. Had spent time in Eastern Europe. On the back of that had opened a restaurant and called it The Kremlin. With an exuberance that made people laugh and fall in love with her wherever she went, which only made her laugh all the more. Her wit was sharp, occasionally cruel, but Goodfellowe began to wonder whether she used it as a buffer. A barrier, perhaps, behind which she could study others while they were kept at a distance. It dawned on Goodfellowe that he knew very little about her and had succeeded in finding out very little about her. Perhaps he hadn't truly tried. He'd used her selfishly, as a crutch, was still using her as a crutch. He'd been totally one-sided about their relationship. Now he gazed at her, tall, almost statuesque, hair of ripe chestnuts, dressed in silk that shimmered seductively in the candlelight. Is that all he had seen, a body, a place to rest his sorrows and insecurities? Had he touched the person within? Suddenly his great expectation had turned to doubt.

Then the doubt turned to disillusion. He knew it was ridiculous and petty, but when he was honest with himself he recognized that he had long ago stopped educating his emotions and under pressure became woefully stubborn. And inadequate. It was inexcusable to get in a huff about the wine, but for God's sake! She knew he wouldn't drink wine that had been produced with a subsidy from the wretched European Union, it was one of his silly male hallmarks. But it was *his* hallmark, and she knew it. Or had she simply forgotten? After all, it had been so long.

So they sat around the table and he misbehaved. Invariably on such occasions, the politician seems to be put into a metaphorical corner while the whole world lines up to tell him what a bloody awful job his Government—and by implication he himself—is doing. And the restaurateurs, by profession characteristically garrulous and opinionated, responded to his increasingly sour mood by giving him hell. Elizabeth had sat at the end of the table and simply smiled, never once coming to his relief. He was like Mafeking, surrounded, nothing to drink, waiting to be

120

stormed.

And she looked sensational. He didn't want to share her. The New England lobster she served was one of his favourites—had she known?—but he gulped it in impatient mouthfuls and had no interest in tussling with the sweet tendrils.

So he took his revenge. As the rest of the table grew increasingly informal under the influence of a splendid Ribera del Duero drawn from the dustbowl of central Spain and full of blackcurrants and vanilla, he raised the subject of adultery. It had been put to him by one of the dinner guests that the life of a backbencher was pointless, nothing but lobby fodder and lunch. The gibe happened to coincide with a spasm of cramp in his calf. That did it for Goodfellowe. He was irritated, in pain, and flatulent from the fizzy water he'd drunk while the others were erasing their inhibitions in the oak-aged Reserva. The time had come to fight back.

'You're wrong,' he countered firmly. 'I may not run the country, but I can help my constituents. Ordinary people. It's like being a social service. Just last week, for instance, a woman came to me and said she was living in a council house. Her children had left home and her husband was away on business more often than not. She felt dreadfully neglected and lonely. She had found a friend, a man. She wanted to sleep with him, when her husband was away. But she was afraid of two things. That she might lose her council house. And she might lose her self-respect. What did I think?'

'Well, what did you think?' demanded the woman across the table, jabbing her fork in his direction in a manner that in Sloane Square might have got her arrested for threatening behaviour.

121

'I said there was no chance of losing her council house.'

'Sod the council house. What about her self-respect? What did you tell her about her self-respect?' The prongs of the fork waved ferociously, if a little unsteadily.

Goodfellowe put forward his most earnest expression. 'I told her she should try to encourage her husband to come home more.'

The feminine outrage was immediate and overwhelming. On all sides he was assailed by the women who demanded that the husband be castrated in his sleep and that the wife get the fun and romance and mind-blowingly good leg-spreading she deserved. All the women were in excitable agreement—all, that is, except for Elizabeth, who kept her silence. As did the husbands, for a while. These were all men who spent a lot of time away from home. Busy men. Working men. And, yes, probably adulterous men. None of whom cared to think that while they were away their wives were busy with anything other than coffee mornings and aerobics classes or would spend time on their backs with anyone other than their gynaecologists. Battle standards were raised on all sides, the arguments engaged. Goodfellowe, at last content, retired from the field to the spectator stands in the company of a malt whisky.

The couples were still bickering as they departed, overfortified and fractious. Goodfellowe, left alone at last with Elizabeth, smirked wickedly as he helped her carry dishes into the small galley kitchen.

'That was splendid,' he suggested. 'A dinner table should be like a battlefield. There should always be casualties.'

'With you left to bayonet the wounded, I suppose.'

'Merely putting them out of their misery.' He smiled a trifle smugly.

'You really gave the woman that advice? About her husband?'

'Good God, no. It was all nonsense. I made it up.'

She turned from the sink to study him. 'But what would you have said if the woman *had* asked you for advice?'

'Frankly?' He took a swig of whisky and considered. 'No bloody idea. I would have done, once. But not any more.'

'You don't understand women very well, do you?'

'Not up close. Not a lot of practice recently. And understanding women at a distance seems to be a peculiarly pointless type of torment.'

She dried her hands thoroughly. 'One thing I want you to understand is that I deliberately gave you a hard time this evening.'

'You succeeded. But why?'

'To pay you back a little. To say to hell with your unreliability, with your committees and distractions and late-night votes and absurd diary. Always insisting on being the centre of attention, then dashing off for some other performance. In front of someone else. Politicians make lousy lovers.'

'I've hurt you.' Just for a moment he wondered if others had, too. 'I'm sorry.'

'But I also wanted to show you something else. That if you're interested in picking up our relationship, it's not going to be smooth and simple.

Or on your terms. I like you, Tom, in fact I could like you a lot. But if you're not going to be there when I want you, don't expect me to be hanging around waiting for the odd day when you've found a spare slot in your Filofax.'

He felt uncomfortable. He stretched his painful leg, but it didn't seem to help. 'It seems my education has begun.'

'And it's not finished yet.'

'Meaning?'

She was facing him. 'Remember I told you that timing was everything with a woman?'

'Sure.'

Her long, sensuous fingers with their elegant nails reached up to her neck, hesitated, trapped his eyes, then slowly descended and brushed the straps from her shoulders. Her dress fell open to the waist. She sucked in a huge, lung-bursting breath; he could count every rib.

'Goodfellowe, I think it's time . . .'

Suddenly, and for the first time in many years, he stopped feeling sore.

CHAPTER FIVE

They knew who. They'd squeezed that much from Sherab. But they had no idea where. To the Chinese eyes that sought them, the three Searchers had become less than grains of sand in the desert.

They had kept careful watch for Kunga on the roads leading down from the mountains, particularly at Namche Bazar, the first village on the Nepali side, and at the reception centres in

124

Kathmandu. But Kunga knew they would be waiting there, the body of Osel had told him so. He and Dawa walked through Nepal at night, and outwitted them once again.

The other two Searchers were equally elusive at first. Gompo had left his post in Geneva almost two years before, no one knew for where, while the ascetic Yeshe had spent half a lifetime in solitary retreat and seemed to have retreated once more. The Chinese had their informants, particularly in McLeod Ganj—like the official in the Ministry of Information and International Relations whose family in Tibet was under arrest in Gutsa Gaol. Then there was the member of the Kashag, or Parliament-in-Exile, whom the Chinese corrupted with whisky and women, while the lowly secretary in the Dalai Lama's office they had simply bought. Now these informants were both bribed and bullied, even occasionally bruised, but none knew or could do anything other than speculate wildly. Until Yeshe—soft, innocent, unworldly Yeshe— applied for a visa.

The application had arrived at the British High Commission in New Delhi, flagged with an appeal that it should be processed urgently. So the reference was taken up, which marked a trail back to McLeod Ganj—and to one of the many Chinese informers. The paper trail then led to where Yeshe was hiding, in Old Delhi, in the part of the ancient Mogul city that is a vortex of noise and poverty and dust, a community apparently held together by little more than a cat's cradle of illicit power cables that snake across roads and around buildings in an organized conspiracy to defraud the authorities. Old Delhi was a good place to hide, but it was a terrible place to be trapped. For once you were caught, no one would ever find you, or even notice you were missing.

Old Delhi is a city of open palms. There were many hands for hire on the back streets, with no questions asked. It was a city of blind eyes and deaf ears, so no one saw the minor scuffle in the night. It disturbed no one but the alley cats. No one heard the brief strangled shout of dismay announcing that Yeshe was theirs, and no one cared as they dragged him back to a room above an empty warehouse on the Street of Sorrows. There they hung him by his thumbs from a rafter so that his toes barely touched the floor. They left him overnight. By morning both his shoulders were dislocated and he was in agony.

There is little point in recounting the details of the many tortures to which Yeshe was subjected over two days. They wanted what he knew, and in a hurry, but he would not tell them, not even after many of his bones were broken. Only once did they release him from the chair to which they had bound him. The pain had made him foul himself, and even his tormentors were beginning to find the conditions unbearable. So they untied him in order that he could clean himself up in the corner. And with so many fractures, he was scarcely in a position to walk, let alone run.

Yet a Buddhist's training enables him, or her, at higher levels of enlightenment to separate mind from body and to block out many of the physical traumas that distract the spirit. Yeshe was better trained than most, but he knew that even his reserves of detachment were failing. Soon he would have no choice. He would give them everything they wanted. Had they left him alone for a night, he

126

would have willed the consciousness to leave his body and by morning they would have found nothing but a husk. But these people would never leave him alone. And he had little strength left. He must focus it, and his mind.

How a man who can scarcely walk could throw himself through a glass window three storeys up was beyond the understanding of either his captors or their angry superiors. Their only benefit from the entire incident was that when Yeshe's body hit the Street of Sorrows it was immediately run over by an oil truck, so hiding many of the marks of his ordeal. Only the undertaker's assistant noticed that every single one of the knuckles on the victim's fingers had been broken, and both forearms smashed in two places. Unusual injuries for a traffic accident. Practically unique. But nobody was interested in his observations. This was just another body on the Street of Sorrows, one amongst so many.

On reflection, however, this was not the only benefit that accrued to Yeshe's captors. After all, they knew there had been three Searchers. Now there were only two.

And Yeshe had been heading for Britain. So now they knew where to look for the others. And for the Lama.

*　　　*　　　*

Mo resented his new duties, but had learned not to allow his feelings to show. It was irritating that a woman who seemed to have so much difficulty dealing with her own emotions was often notably lacking in sympathy for the feelings of others. He had performed many duties for his Ambassadors— lied, covered up, even stolen for them. Babysitting went beyond the limit.

It had been two years since Madame Lin's only daughter had given birth to a strapping and healthy boy who, in Mo's view, rather resembled a frog. Sadly, the overcrowded Beijing hospital at which the birth took place had failed to notice the pre-eclampsia until it was too late and the new mother, Madame Lin's daughter, had succumbed without ever seeing her child. That sad episode had marked a change in Madame Lin. While she remained the consummate professional, her disillusionment about the state of affairs in the homeland had grown ever more apparent to those like Mo who were close to her. Even for a diplomat stationed in a distant land, there was no escaping the problems that grew like mould on rotten fruit. The Ministry of Foreign Affairs had sunk into chaos. The bills weren't being paid, the instructions were constantly countermanded as Beijing's rulers squabbled. And in the confusion that had become China, daughters died. Unnecessarily. Without cause. Unnoticed and unmourned by any except close family. For what is one life in a country where the lives of hundreds of millions are daily at risk?

Yet it mattered to Madame Lin. Her grandson was her only family and became the prime focus of her life. She had brought him from Beijing to London, away from confusion, so that she might be responsible for his welfare. And every day at lunchtime she had the child brought from the Residence in Hampstead to the Embassy, where they would play while she doted like an old *amah*— except on days such as this when unexpected

128

official duties got in the way and Mo was instructed to take over. How he hated it. Babysitting a mewling two-year-old.

He gave a sigh. Get it in perspective, Mo. There were sacrifices to be made in order to remain at the right hand of one of the most powerful Ambassadors anywhere in the world. In her own way, because she controlled him, she trusted him. His was a position of privilege.

And whichever way he looked at it, this was better than being taken to a football stadium, knelt down in front of a baying mob and having his brains blown out through his ears.

'Come on, Frog-Face,' he instructed, taking the boy by the hand. 'Let's go and kick a few vases. With any luck you'll break a few.' He brightened. 'Then you can take the blame.'

*   *   *

The obscure birthmark of the painting had turned out to be a tattoo. Small but exquisite—in Goodfellowe's eyes, at least. High on the front-inside of her thigh, the smoothest of flesh for a canvas. And colourful. As he came to examine it more closely he saw that it was not the regulation butterfly of air hostesses or entwined cobra of the leather brigade, but a most unexpected delight. He brushed it gently with his thumb to make sure, once, twice. It was a hammer and sickle.

'The inspiration came from my husband. My ex-husband,' she explained. 'We met when we were both in the security services.'

'You? A spy?'

'A dirty job but somebody has to do it. Like

129

washing-up. Or sleeping with politicians.' She adjusted her position to make his weight more comfortable. 'I resigned when we got married, to give our relationship a chance. Should've known. He was totally dedicated to his job. Lived, breathed, ate and slept it. I got drunk in Prague one night and decided he might as well screw it, too.' The faintest touch of acid. 'Took him three months even to notice.'

'I'd have defected, no question,' Goodfellowe ventured.

'Then my husband would have had you shot.'

'Elizabeth, you could've won the Cold War single-handed . . .' her fingernail trickled down through the hair around his navel, bringing forth a low moan of distraction—'or . . . whatever . . . the appropriate anatomical metaphor is.'

'Why, Goodfellowe, you make it sound like a patriotic duty. Which, in the view of the security services, is precisely what it was.'

He was intrigued. He found everything about her tantalizing. The more he knew, the more mysterious and challenging she became. He propped himself up on one elbow. 'Did you? Did you ever? You know, as a patriotic duty?'

'As a politician you should be familiar with the concept of personal sacrifice,' she replied evasively.

'Yeah. But only of others.'

Was she merely teasing? Or hiding something from her past? He didn't find out that night, but by the following morning he reckoned he could recreate every twist and curve of the tattoo. It was only a hammer and sickle, of course, but for Goodfellowe it was one of the major triumphs of his life.

130

Inevitably, in the days that followed, Goodfellowe found himself thinking of little else. Everywhere it seemed there were reminders of that night—references to Prague, foreign correspondents reporting from in front of the Kremlin, even an article in *Time* magazine on tattoos. Everything seemed to conspire to inflame his imagination and to raise unanswered questions. The most disturbing question for Goodfellowe was whether it had ever, even once, been like that with Elinor? Or with any woman? He couldn't recall anything like it and it was difficult to escape the conclusion that this had been the most mind-mincing sex he'd ever had. Yet one night seemed tragically little on which to base such a devastating conclusion. He decided he would reserve judgement, pending further enquiries.

But, amidst the fanfare and newly resprayed colours of his thoughts, other echoes of the past kept intruding. At the back of a drawer he found the prayer beads given to him those years before by the Dalai Lama. On the long nights when once again he was alone, wishing he could be with Elizabeth, he found the small sandalwood beads of great comfort. He took to carrying them with him all the time in his pocket. He also found himself reading the copy of Sun Tzu, which told him how the finest doctors are those whose patients never fall sick and the greatest warriors are those whose armies never need to go to war. True, of course. But also a little naive. Who would have heard of Joshua if it hadn't been for Jericho, or remembered Hannibal without his elephants? The lesson of all history was unmistakable—bring me chaos and bring me fame! Otherwise they would all die old and unmourned. Funny, he had once wanted very much to die famous, as Prime Minister, to leave behind him the great and rehabilitated name of Goodfellowe that his swindling father had destroyed. Now he decided he'd much rather live, a very long life, preferably lost between the legs of Elizabeth and without the attention of the world's media gathered on his doorstep.

He found his sleep, like his life, had taken on more colour, too. The dreams had grown vivid— not taunting dreams as they had been during his worst times, but images of mountains, of great lakes covered in mist and lands he had never known yet which seemed almost like home. The Dalai Lama entered into one dream, sitting in a cave. He said nothing, simply smiled and laughed in that deep, booming manner of his. And beckoned.

Goodfellowe was lost in a daydream, feet up on his House of Commons desk while trying to figure out this strange new world of his, when Mickey walked in bearing the daily mountain of correspondence.

'Mickey, tell me true. Could you fancy me?'

She studied him carefully. 'Do you have an Aston Martin?'

'Not even a tandem.'

'Next question.'

'You're a real morale booster, you know.'

'What do you want? Platitudes? You want encouragement to go out there and make a complete fool of yourself?'

'Very much.'

'I see. So you got your date with Elizabeth.'

'That's right.'

She sat coquettishly on the edge of his desk, the

132

twinkle of interrogation in her dark eyes. 'And did the earth move for you?'

'Mind your own bloody business!' He paused, tried to look fierce, and failed. 'Well, she lives above the underground line. It might just have been the passing of a late-night train.'

'Way to go, Goodfellowe,' she congratulated softly, leaning forward and kissing him warmly on the forehead. 'You deserve it.'

Goodfellowe became distracted. As she leaned forward, his horizon suddenly consisted of nothing but cleavage. Generous, free-spirited and . . . well, there. Right there. In front of his nose. Scarcely a night out of Elizabeth's bed and already he wanted to be a slut. As her breasts loomed ever larger they brushed across the letter on top of the mountain. It became dislodged and fluttered to the floor. Hastily he ducked to retrieve it.

The letter was marked 'Strictly Personal and Confidential'. He allowed Mickey to open all his mail on the basis that with a life like his he never received correspondence that was strictly personal, let alone confidential, except from madmen and the Inland Revenue. With luck and Elizabeth, that might have to change.

The letter, on cheap off-coloured paper and written in a neat but rather archaic hand, was from Lhamo, who introduced himself as the late Dalai Lama's private secretary.

'We did not meet during His Holiness's last trip to Britain but I am, of course, aware of your close personal association with him . . .'

What close association? Goodfellowe wondered. Why were they always trying to treat him as part of the family?

133

'Through the means of this letter I have the honour of introducing to you Representative Gompo Cherdrol Khendro, one of His Holiness's most intimate associates who is currently engaged on a vital mission on behalf of the late Dalai Lama . . .'

And taking one hell of a time to finish the job, Goodfellowe considered. The Lama'd been dead three years.

'I regret to inform you that, sadly, this mission has become one of considerable danger. Another colleague engaged on the same task was recently murdered, we believe by forces opposed to a Free Tibet. I must therefore ask you to treat the contents of this letter as an issue of the gravest consequence, indeed a matter of life and death . . .'

Goodfellowe found himself uttering a highly unimaginative oath.

'Representative Gompo is currently hiding in St Petersburg.'

Russia? Why on earth Russia . . . ?

'We wish to obtain for him a visitor's visa to your country, but believe there may be extreme danger in applying through the orthodox channels. The purpose of this letter is therefore to ask you to use your good offices to secure for him a visa in a manner that is both speedy and completely confidential.'

This was a joke. A hoax. Had to be. 'You still got the envelope?'

'Yes. Pretty stamp. From India.'

So a long-distance joke. But he didn't know anybody in India. Except, of course, for the . . .

He found himself fingering the prayer beads in his pocket, slipping them along their silk cord. It seemed to help him order his thoughts, get them into line, one after the other. Mickey was still

134

leaning over the desk. In his mind her cleavage had been transformed into images of great valleys. Mountains. Fields of snow. Strange lands. And the Dalai Lama's face, laughing at him.

'I need to see Paddy Baader. Today, if he's in town.'

'I think I heard he's in town.'

'Then try to arrange five minutes for me.'

She was very businesslike. 'I might be able to pull a few strings.'

'Pull them, will you? I've got a funny feeling about this one . . .'

Mickey decided not to mention her own funny little feeling.

They found a quiet corner of the Smoking Room early that evening, before the vote. Mind you, every corner of the Smoking Room was quiet nowadays. The influx of women into the House seemed to have drained the place of much of its conspiratorial mood, and the old leather sofas of the Smoking Room no longer creaked beneath the weight of collusion and cabal. It had become an echoing relic of an era when plots were laid most publicly and Ministerial reputations mauled before dinner. Nowadays the plots were hatched underground. In quiet corners. From houses in Gayfere Street and beneath duvets in Dolphin Square, where their intent was all too easily diverted. Progress, of a sort. But it left Ministers with untied hands and encouraged arrogance in office. Life on the backbenches should be like that of a pack of hounds, thought Goodfellowe. Better stirred up, quarrelling, fractious, snapping at the heels of Ministers, than lying supine at their feet. But Parliament had developed into one great powder room. Even the Prime Minister had his own personal compact. As for the Smoking Room, they'd probably convert it into a creche.

They sat in the corner by the window. A storm was sweeping up from the estuary and the great velvet curtains were drawn, obscuring the view across the river and adding to the atmosphere of intimacy. The leaded windows rattled against the wind.

'Drink, Tom?'

'Maybe some tea. I'm trying to cut down on the alcohol. Lose a bit of weight.'

'A sinner come to repentance! But I'll have a whisky, if you don't mind. After a day playing the bloody white man I deserve it. And need it. I'll have the usual three boxes of telegrams and Foreign Office tittle-tattle waiting for me when I get home. Never a dull moment.'

'I think I can remember . . .'—with only a trace of wistfulness.

'You know, Tom, I've always been grateful to you,' Baader began. 'My predecessor. A damn good one. Would've been all too easy for you to double-guess, to offer me "helpful suggestions" from the backbenches that always implied you knew better. You never have. I appreciate that.'

'Don't think I haven't been tempted.'

'Ah, Temptation, whither hast thou fled? When I was a college lecturer I was surrounded by it. So much young, raw, unharnessed talent.' He sighed wistfully.

'And now?'

'You know I can't do anything without the say-so of my bloody private office. Temptation isn't one of the "Lines to Take". And there's no room for it in

136

my diary. Simply no time for it.'

They both started laughing in recognition of flagrant bullshit.

'Anyway, now I've landed up on the side of the angels, what can I do for you, Tom?'

Over Baader's second whisky, Goodfellowe had explained his purpose, about Gompo and St Petersburg and the letter he had received.

'So what is the mission this fellow is supposed to be on?'

'I'm not entirely sure. I know it's all a bit flimsy. But I'll vouch for him, I'd be grateful if you'd have a look at it. See what you can do. As a personal favour.'

'Well, I owe you that much.'

'And these people are decent. Not troublemakers.'

'Tell that to the Chinese. You know, you've got to consider that angle, Tom. If we help the Tibetans we hack off one billion Chinese. We're negotiating huge contracts with Beijing right now. New docks, hotel projects, aero engines. It's the first big breakthrough we've had in that market since we fell out over Hong Kong. Putting that at risk isn't one of our great national priorities.'

'I'm not asking you to declare war, simply look at one individual case.'

'Not that easy, Tom. I'll have a look at it, of course, get the Consular & Visa boys on to it . . .'

'Quietly, please,' Goodfellowe insisted. 'This is very sensitive. Dangerous, perhaps.'

'Which makes it all the more mysterious . . .' He stopped in mid-sentence. The message pager he wore at his belt was vibrating, someone was trying to make contact. 'Forgive me, I've got to go,' he explained, studying the message. 'I'll look into it. Do my best. I promise.'

'Be careful,' Goodfellowe urged.

'You know me, Tom. I'm always careful.'

Which, in matters of diplomacy, was perhaps true. But not in other areas of his life. The message had been from Mickey. Fifteen minutes later Baader was guiding her down to the crypt beneath the Palace of Westminster.

'So we're into sightseeing,' she muttered, perplexed.

'You ever seen the crypt before?'

'Only in horror movies.'

'Not this one.' And he was right. Ancient stone stairs led down from the Great Hall to a low-ceilinged chapel the likes of which Mickey had never seen. A Gothic extravaganza of gilded frescoes and tiling and metalwork which threw everything at the eye in blinding confusion. 'What do you think?' he enquired.

'You can think with all this around you?'

He laughed. 'Actually, I didn't bring you down here to think.'

'Nor to pray for forgiveness, I hope.'

'No. To show you the finest cupboard in the Palace.'

A little way from the vestibule, near the font, he opened the panelled oak door to a large walk-in cupboard. For the cleaners. Where they kept the tools of their trade—mops, brooms, buckets and a large commercial vacuum cleaner.

'You brought me here to show me a vacuum cleaner?'

'Stop being so blindingly impatient. Look around. This is a place of history.' He switched on the light and ran his hand across a commemorative brass plaque on the inside of the door, as though he were back at university giving a tutorial. 'In the good old days, before we men went soft in the head and allowed women into this place, a certain Mrs Emily Wilding Davison decided she was going to make complete idiots of us. She wanted the 1911 census to record that even though she couldn't be a Member of Parliament and didn't have a vote, she spent the night in the House of Commons. So on the night the census was taken'—he closed the door behind them—'she hid in here.'

With the door closed they were suddenly in much closer physical proximity. Yes, as though he were back at university giving a tutorial in that cramped room of his overlooking the river. A room of so many memories. So many tutorials. So much temptation . . .

Baader was never destined to stay in that room for long. Partly because he wanted so much more for himself. And partly because he had never been able to command the full respect of his university colleagues. He was an intellectual cuckoo, with the sort of mind that was capable of arguing any case but incapable of sticking to one. Less of a problem in politics, he had discovered. He had also been too fond of screwing a large proportion of the many young women he found around him. Again, less of a problem in politics. And, surprisingly, in his marriage. His wife didn't share his flexible approach to fidelity but she was too intimidated by his intellectual agility and too comfortable with the established order of their lives to object. She had demanded only discretion, that he 'be careful'. They'd discussed it quite openly. Which in itself created a problem. For his wife's acceptance had made commonplace adultery almost bland, put it within the rules. And Baader's excitement and inspiration came not from fitting in with the rules but in bending, bruising and where necessary breaking them. Most Ministers took cover, Baader took risks. That's what motivated him. Risk. A bit like Emily Wilding Davison. He rather admired her. Would like to have known her. Well.

'So ... was the delightful Mrs Davison on her own in the cupboard?' Mickey asked, as though picking up on his thoughts.

'Sadly, yes.'

'Then she didn't come to a sticky end?'

'Oh, but she did. A couple of years later she threw herself in front of the King's horse at the Derby. Got herself trampled to death.'

'Ouch. Not a nice way to go.' She could feel the heat of his breath.

'Can think of better.'

'Such as?'

And they were in each other's arms. A bucket full of brooms toppled as they fumbled.

'You want it here, Patrick? In the bloody cupboard? In the crypt?'

'I like living dangerously.'

'Is there a lock on the door?'

'No way.'

'You've been here before,' Suddenly Mickey drew back.

'What's the matter?' he asked. 'Jealous?'

'I don't do jealousy.'

'Then what?'

'The visa.'

Exasperated—'What about the bloody visa?'

140

'Have you agreed to give it to Tom?'

'You trying to blackmail me?'

'No, just trying to mix a little business with pleasure. Satisfying mutual desires. So, do we get the visa?'

He ran his fingers up the crease of her back, tickling, tempting. 'You and Tom hunt as a pack?'

'Not on all things.' She grabbed his hands, which had moved to her breasts, and held them away from her. 'Do we get the visa?'

'I have my principles to think of,' he objected.

'So think of your principles. Then think of these . . .'—she placed his hands back on her breasts, cold fingers on warm flesh that sprang to attention at the touch—'and make up your mind.'

He closed his eyes against temptation, considering the options, particularly the hard nipples. No contest. Slowly he nodded.

'Promise?' she demanded.

'I promise. If you will.'

She did, and kept her promise, too.

Afterwards, as they readjusted themselves and picked up the fallen brooms and mops, he turned to her.

'You drive a hard bargain,' he complained. 'But you know something? I was going to let you have it anyway.'

'That's funny,' she smiled in triumph. 'I was going to let you have it too.'

*   *   *

Goodfellowe and Sam spent the weekend at the family home in Marshwood.

Memories.

141

Sam had been born here. And near here Stevie had died. In this house they had once been a family. Now the family was no more. Just he and Sam.

There had been a tension at the breakfast table. Things, difficult things, needed saying.

'I'd like your help this weekend, Sam. To clear a few wardrobes.'

'Mum's things?'

He sipped his tea carefully as though tasting it for the first time. 'The doctors are very clear. Mummy's not coming home, not for a long time. And if she does, she won't be the person we've known.'

'I don't think she's ever coming home,' she said. Sam's voice was matter-of-fact. but her eyes remained fixed on her cereal bowl. Around this table there had once been so much noise and banter, so many plans laid, so many arguments started and settled.

His mind went back almost ten years, when he had been sitting at this same table. Then the conversation had been of horses and dolls, pigtails and party dresses. And rabbits. At least, one rabbit. It had been so wonderfully ludicrous, They had a Jack Russell, and next door had a rabbit. One day, when the neighbours were off for a weekend break, the Jack Russell had come back with the rabbit in its mouth, very dirty and very, very dead. Sam had burst into tears. She was inconsolable, convinced the neighbours would demand that her own pet be destroyed just as he had destroyed theirs. An eye for an eye. But Goodfellowe had been a match for the task. Together they had washed the rabbit in the kitchen sink, carefully dried its fur with Elinor's hair dryer, then like thieves in the night had

142

sneaked into the neighbours' garden to replace the rabbit in its hutch. All seemed well, until the neighbours returned.

'Anything strange been going on this weekend?' they had demanded.

He had squeezed Sam's hand tightly. This was an appalling exercise in deceit for such a young girl, but not a bad lesson in survival.

'Why do you ask?'

'Something damned funny with the rabbit,' the neighbour had complained, troubled. 'It died just before we left, so we buried it. Blow me down, but it's back in its hutch looking like it's about to enter a Beautiful Bunny competition.'

And he and Sam had hugged themselves so tightly he thought he would burst. Happy days. Another world.

Now there was a small but exceedingly painful silence. The words had been used, the thought expressed. Elinor was never coming home.

'That's possible,' he agreed at last, as though pleading guilty in a small voice to the most unspeakable of crimes.

'No point living in the past, Daddy.'

He took a deep breath. 'It means we might have to sell the house. I can't afford the nursing-home fees otherwise. Would you mind?'

'Would she notice?'

'Would who notice?'

'Would Mummy notice if she were in a less expensive home? She seems not to notice anything much nowadays. She wouldn't mind.'

He clenched his fists in frustration. She was right, of course. So down-to-earth. The sort of girl who without complaint worked through her holidays rather than dreaming idly about skiing or surfing trips with her schoolfriends that her father couldn't afford. 'That can come later, Daddy.' Sam deserved better. But Elinor deserved the best, the very best he could possibly afford. How dare Sam be so bloody practical, particularly at seventeen. Couldn't she at least show a little hurt? Or share some of his?

'Mummy might not mind. But I would.'

'Your choice, Daddy.'

So they had set to work on the wardrobes. His approach was to take out each item, and fold it carefully, tenderly, guiltily. But he was not seventeen. She gave each item a cursory examination then threw it in the Oxfam bag.

She was growing, changing. It was particularly noticeable this weekend. She had come home on *exeat* from her boarding school with her hair in tight braids and many of those braids embroidered with brightly coloured beads.

'Your hair. It's . . .'

'Egyptian,' she had offered, filling in the gap.

The effect was magnificent, but it wasn't Sam.

'Cleopatra,' she had explained. 'It's this year's Shakespeare at school. And I've got the leading role. And special permission to leave my hair like this for a month—so I can feel the part.' She giggled as she threw one of Elinor's favourite coats, a birthday gift from him, into the bag. 'The other girls are just dying over it.'

The boys, too, he didn't doubt. And Bryan? He studied her carefully, this young woman, this part-time stranger, the thing he loved most in the world. A year ago she had offered little but problems—introspection, rebellion, premeditated deafness,

144

still suffering from the loss of her brother and mother, and, he had no doubt, from the inevitable absence of her politician father. But through her painting she had succeeded in finding confidence and a form of expression other than outburst or silence. That damned school had been worth every penny he'd been able to scrape together. They'd even given her a small scholarship in recognition of her artistic talent—and also, he suspected, in recognition of his unflagging inability to pay the fees on time. Now, the headmistress had suggested, she might be in line to be head girl next term. Oh, God, if she were still at school next term . . .

As he looked he couldn't help but try to search for any little bulge at the abdomen, any tell-tale sign that would signify the end of the scholarship. Of her hopes for university. Of being a teenager. Yet Elizabeth had been adamant in her advice. Let her come to you. Don't force the issue. Don't let it all end up in a shouting match that may make you say and Sam do something stupid. But it had been three weeks since he had found the pregnancy advertisement. She must be at least—what, eight weeks pregnant, perhaps more? Time was not on his side. Nor on Sam's.

Perhaps if he made the first move, shared something deeply personal with her, it would give her the confidence to do the same. What had he got to lose? In any event the subject of Elizabeth was going to have to come up sometime.

He sat on the edge of the bed. 'Can we talk? You know, man to woman?'

Her eyes teased. 'So you're growing up at last. What do you want to know, Daddy?'

He licked his dry lips. 'Mummy isn't coming

home. May never come home. It's made life very difficult for me . . .'

'I know.' She sat on the duvet beside him, sharing, and held his hand.

'I've been very lonely at times. Particularly now you're away at school.'

'You need some new friends.'

'I've found some. Well, one at least.'

'Who, Daddy? Tell.'

'You've met her before. Elizabeth. The lady at The Kremlin. We've become . . . close.'

'How close?'

'Very.'

'You mean you're sleeping with her?' she asked slowly, very earnest.

He thanked the gods she was so direct and practical, so understanding. He nodded. 'Yes.'

Goodfellowe might understand public finances and the finer details of arms control treaties, but he wasn't close to understanding women. Certainly not teenagers. Sam shot to her feet.

'You're cheating on Mummy? I can't believe I'm hearing this. Mummy's in a hospital bed and you're . . .' She couldn't find the words. She looked around the room despairingly as though she might find the words hiding in the corner, or Elizabeth lurking in the back of the wardrobe. 'Is that why you want me to clear out Mummy's clothes? So you can move another woman in? To her bedroom?'

'No . . .'

'That's why you want to sell the house, isn't it? To buy a new one for another woman.' The complete inconsistency between her two accusations seemed not to bother her. But the anger came bubbling through. The veneer of

146

maturity and almost ruthless practicality was stripped away to reveal the frightened teenager that still lay beneath. 'Are you going to divorce Mummy?' She seemed on the edge of panic.

'No, no, no, darling . . .'

'I can't believe you could do such a thing! It's disgusting!' she screamed, heedless. She fled from the room in tears.

There was no point in chasing her, not yet at least. He had tried to share, to bring them closer together. Instead he had split them still further apart. He wanted to help her. Instead it would have been kinder if he had hit her over the head with a lump of wood. Then used it on himself.

*   *   *

There were two. And after the discovery of Osel on the mountainside and death of Yeshe in the gutters of the Street of Sorrows, each of them knew they were in great peril.

Gompo was a Tibetan of considerable worldly experience. Born in India, he had served the Dalai Lama in New York and Europe. He drank whisky, preferring a single malt, loved Baskin Robbins (anything but Rocky Road) and was an accomplished guitar player and ten-pin bowler. But above all else he was Tibetan. As a child he had been recognized as the incarnation of Lama Thubten Sonam Norbu, an incarnated teacher of great seniority. Lama Thubten had, until his death at a considerable age in 1953, been one of the young Dalai Lama's personal tutors and closest confidants. Gompo had followed in similar footsteps.

147

Gompo was a man of unconventional outlooks and rarely met the expectations of the rest of the world. So, when he grew to appreciate just how much danger he faced in McLeod Ganj, and at a point when most men would have flown as far away from Tibet and the Chinese as their resources would allow, he did precisely the opposite. He travelled to Tibet. Where he would be amongst friends. And the last place on earth the Chinese would think of searching for him.

Yet his homeland could be no more than a brief stopping place. From Lhasa he travelled by bus and lorry to the Chinese city of Lanzhou, amongst the Han themselves, and then by train to Mongolia, where once again he found himself in the company of those he could trust. Fellow Buddhists. More than seven centuries earlier, in the days when the great Mongol warlord Kublai Khan had ruled over China and most of Asia, the Khan had ordained that his empire would follow the Tibetan faith. While the empire had long since been hacked to pieces by a hundred thousand swords, in Mongolia the faith remained. Here Gompo found shelter. And new identity papers. And days later, just across the border near Lake Baykal in Russia, he also found the Trans-Siberian Railway that had borne him many thousands of miles westward, to the Buddhist Temple in St Petersburg.

The temple was an anachronism. It had been built at the time when the authority of the Tsars was falling apart, before the Bolsheviks arrived, a small outpost of Oriental culture in the most Western of Russian cities. Then Stalin had happened. And with him came intolerance. Inquisition. One night his secret police, the NKVD,

148

had burst through the door and dragged all the monks off to their headquarters in Litenyi Prospekt, where they had been tried, convicted, sentenced. That same evening they had been taken down to the soundproof cellars and shot. Not one survived. The granite temple with its tapering tower and vivid red porch had been confiscated by the state and afterwards used for dismembering animals in the name of experimental vivisection. It had taken almost fifty years and the collapse of Communism before the building, now dilapidated and stripped of all its religious artefacts, had been handed back and the presence of incense and prayer was once again felt within its walls.

The temple was both an accident and a victim of history and still displayed many of its scars, but it served Gompo's purpose well. Here he could rest while his friends obtained for him the necessary visa to continue his journey to Britain. The temple in St Petersburg was another place the Chinese would never think of finding him.

But somehow they did.

Gompo, although worldly, was yet highly spiritual, and while he waited for his documents and the chance to travel onward he spent much of his time in prayer. Every day he took himself to the prayer room with its dark wooden walls and heavy atmosphere. It held a tall gilded statue of the Prince Shakyamuni, the historical Buddha, with lotus stems growing from each hand, but on this image there were no precious stones and few inlays. This was a temple that lived on optimism rather than ostentation. Alongside Shakyamuni they had placed an effigy of Je Tsong-khapa, which literally translated meant Lord of Onion Land, the founder

149

of the Gelug school. Then, in another corner, there stood representations of what was called the Tibetan Trinity, the great Buddhas of Wisdom, of Compassion and of Enlightened Energy. Tibetans love their images and before each of these in turn Gompo would prostrate himself. The floor was wooden and polished smooth by the knees and mittened hands of those who had been there before him, prostrating themselves full length while they paid their respects to the Buddhas.

It was a Monday morning, early, while the mists still clung to the rivers of the great city, that Gompo began his devotions. Focusing. Cleansing his thoughts. He fell to his knees, then extended his hands on the floor in front of him until his body lay at full stretch. In the words of his ritual text, he took refuge in the Buddha. And, slowly, he withdrew his body and pulled himself back to his feet. Then he started all over again.

Three times he repeated the series of devotions before each image while the monks engaged in their hypnotic chants and beat rhythmically on their drums and cymbals. It was tiring. As he prayed, Gompo would stay stretched out on the floor, prostrated, while he gathered his thoughts and spiritual strength. So no one thought it unusual when he did not move for a moment, indeed several moments. By the time other worshippers had begun to grow curious at his stillness, the two young men in the gallery had already disappeared. Even before the monks had discovered Gompo was dead, the two were weaving their motorbike through the heavy traffic of Primorsky Prospekt. And by the time the police surgeon discovered the tiny biochemical pellet embedded in Gompo's neck, the two were a thousand miles away on the other side of the Urals, getting drunk on imported whisky with four under-aged and youthfully inventive hookers.

Gompo had evaded his pursuers' attentions for too long. He would not be given the chance to evade them again.

My enemy's enemy is my friend. The Chinese had never cared for their Russian neighbours. Even when both had been Communist, they had grown to be bitter rivals. Race before religion. And when the Russians had finally discarded Marxism, they had in effect stripped away Beijing's last remaining ideological fig leaf, leaving them cruelly exposed. So the Chinese gained more than a little satisfaction when the new Russia began to be comprehensively gutted by the robber barons of organized crime. And when they wanted a favour, some small act of brutality performed on Russian soil, informally and in an untraceable manner, the Chinese never had much trouble in finding willing hands to assist. Often those hands had been trained by the KGB or now-decrepit Soviet military. Feed off the enemy, as Sun Tzu would say. Money rarely changed hands, it was usually explosives or weapons or occasionally opium and, in one case, irradiated cobalt dust with which disgruntled and unpaid officers of the Murmansk Fleet planned an attack on their old headquarters. By comparison, the assassination of a man in St Petersburg had been little more than a training run.

And then there was but one . . .

CHAPTER SIX

Goodfellowe had done with democracy for the day. He'd voted at ten p.m. on a matter of great public sensitivity—at least, that's what the Whips had told him, which is why they had commanded his presence in the Division Lobby, although the details of the measure almost totally eluded him. Something to do with drains? That was it! Measures to renew the crumbling Victorian sewer system beneath London while finding various exotic ways of getting others to pay for it. And about time. In Disraeli's day they'd had to hang perfumed curtains over the windows to block out the foul smell of the river. All the fault of the infamous Thomas Crapper and his devilish invention, the flushing toilet. When such systems had been installed in the households of the rich, who lived in the hills overlooking London, they had washed all the effluent down towards the river. The result was that the working classes huddled along its banks were repeatedly ravaged by lethal outbreaks of typhoid and militant socialism. Whole communities were wiped out as a result. Thomas Crapper had a lot to answer for.

Goodfellowe had given his name to the Clerk who marked it on the voting list and he had re-emerged into the Chamber, which was beginning to empty rapidly as the day's business was all but dispensed. At the door he found Baader.

'Hoped I'd find you here, Tom.'

'Paddy, what a surprise. Didn't think they'd whip in the heavy cavalry for a little light skirmishing over drains.'

'No, I'm paired, Tom. Not voting. I hurried over from the Foreign Office. Needed to see you urgently.'

They sat down in the corner of the Chamber, well away from the few stragglers who remained.

'Your visa case. The man Gompo,' Braader began. He looked agitated. 'You haven't heard?'

'Heard what?'

'He's dead, Tom. Killed in St Petersburg.'

'The balls of Buddha!'

'No details. Of how he died. Whether it was an accident or . . .' He trailed off, seemed ashen with shock. 'I had to see you as soon as I heard, Tom. I feel almost . . . responsible in a way. I am sorry.'

It took Goodfellowe several moments to take in the news. 'Not your fault, Paddy, couldn't be. Don't blame yourself.' He shook his head. 'But what the hell is going on?'

'I asked Consular & Visa to consider the application in principle without telling them of his whereabouts. I did what you asked, kept it in the strictest confidence. It couldn't have leaked from our end.'

'I'm grateful for that.'

'Must have been an accident.'

'He'd only been in St Petersburg a few days. How could they have found out?'

'Must have been an accident,' Baader repeated.

'Do you really believe that?'

'I want to believe that. Look, the Chinese Government doesn't go round knocking off political opponents all over the place.'

'They do in China.'

'But not on the other side of the world. It doesn't

153

make sense.'

'You're right. It doesn't make sense.'

The business of the House had now finished and they were sitting alone in the Chamber, silent, all but lost against the great expanse of green Gilbert Scott leather. Eventually Goodfellowe stirred.

'Thanks for telling me, Paddy.'

'It's rotten luck, Tom. But probably nothing more than a terrible coincidence.'

'Of course,' Goodfellowe replied softly. 'Trouble is, I'm a sceptical bastard. I don't believe in coincidence.'

*   *   *

Even deserts can bloom. And so had Goodfellowe. He'd grown accustomed to—but never accepted—life on his own. Breakfast with no companionship other than a transistor radio. A half-filled pot of tea, for one. Tubs of stale butter lurking at the back of the fridge. The sink he was going to clean, tomorrow. His domestic habits had grown increasingly lethargic.

But since Elizabeth, so much had changed. He now talked with her over breakfast, even though she wasn't there. A little obsessional, perhaps, but lonely people often grow obsessive. He shared smiles with strangers on the street. He could see colours again.

But he still had no money. How the hell was he to finance a love affair when he could barely afford to live? You had to come out from between the sheets at some point and eat, and a Marks & Spencer tandoori dinner for two had considerable social limitations, particularly when your dinner guest was the proprietor of one of the smartest restaurants in Westminster. The Kremlin had come to be an icon to which half of Westminster seemed to gravitate—the half, that is, with expense accounts, where a single meal surrounded by the glittering memorabilia of Marxism could wipe away Goodfellowe's entire food allowance for a week. He was going to have to make what little he had go a long way.

Salvation, at least for their second date, came in the form of a request dropped by hand through his letter box in Gerrard Street asking him to visit the owner of The Himalaya Restaurant, just off Leicester Square, less than five minutes' walk away. The letterhead announced that it was the only Tibetan restaurant in the entire country, but the letter itself didn't explain clearly the purpose of the request. Still, Tibetan food might be fun and if he turned up in the evening there had to be some free hospitality thrown in. He'd take Elizabeth.

The Himalaya, located on the first floor up a narrow set of stairs, was, as with all things Tibetan, simple and unpretentious. It was like being invited into someone's front room, with hand-painted walls—the usual glaring Tibetan colour scheme—covered in old photographs and images of the homeland. And, again like all things Tibetan, in pride of place hung a portrait of the late Dalai Lama, smiling quizzically as though he were just about to burst into laughter. Which, knowing him, he probably was. As Goodfellowe walked through the single small room of the restaurant he could feel the eyes of the portrait following him. Wretched man! The Lama seemed to be pursuing him not simply through the restaurant but through

155

most aspects of his life. Suddenly Goodfellowe chuckled. He'd almost said lives. Buddhist-speak. A mental slip. There couldn't be such things as previous lives and reincarnation, could there? From his place on the wall, the Lama stared indulgently.

Wangyal, the proprietor, a small man with a face as round as the sun and a full set of sparkling teeth, appeared agitated. 'Mr Goodfellowe. Thank you, thank you for coming. This is so important.' But for a while there seemed nothing more important to the proprietor than to ensure that Goodfellowe was taken through the menu in considerable detail. In truth, the pleasures of Tibetan cuisine were simple. Spicy soups. Meat and vegetable *momo* dumplings. Dishes of meat and egg noodle that were related much more closely to China than India. And butter tea, the staple of all Tibetan living. Goodfellowe took the cup in both hands and sipped. Elizabeth copied his example, and immediately spat out the tea.

'Disgusting!' she complained.

'Mine's all right.' He took her cup and tasted. 'Yours is fine, too.'

'Then take it with my best wishes.'

'An acquired taste,' the proprietor explained.

'And you seem to have acquired it,' she said to Goodfellowe.

'I'm enjoying it. It's like . . .' He searched for the comparison, but couldn't find it. Bells within his memory were ringing as though across a great expanse of time. 'I've tasted something like this before. But what, or when . . .' He shrugged. 'Bit like mother's milk, I suppose.'

So they sat and took pleasure in their meal and in each other's company. Her marmalade eyes

156

reflected the low lights and her lips, full and unusually expressive, grew animated as they spoke and smiled for him. Her clothes were immaculate, although he had a mind only for what lay beneath.

The pursuit of women, he reflected, was very similar to the pursuit of politics. Both were indulgent, intrusive, often utterly irrational. Men would squander without restraint until their lives and reputations were left in ruins, then pick themselves up and do it all over again. The mistakes they made were eternal, yet somehow the lessons were never learned. But, oh! The joys of success, they drove a man onwards, never flinching, heedless of the fact that failure would devastate him utterly. Goodfellowe had a lot of experience of both the joys and failures of politics; it was time for a practice run with a woman, he thought. With this woman. And soon she would be in his bed. Idly he speculated about what his dying wish would be—to receive one final standing ovation from a political audience, or to lie one last time with Elizabeth? Hell, even for an Englishman there was no contest. An Italian or a Frenchman would have thought him mad simply for posing the question.

As they lost themselves in each other, Goodfellowe and Elizabeth scarcely noticed the passage of time or that the restaurant was now all but empty. Wangyal, who throughout the meal had kept disappearing into the kitchen, was standing beside their table.

'He is here,' the proprietor announced simply.
'Who?'

Wangyal glanced anxiously as the only other couple still in the restaurant prepared to leave. 'Wait,' he instructed Goodfellowe, until he had bid

157

the other customers farewell, the door was locked behind them and the blinds drawn. He also turned off the lights, it was only candlelight now. And conspiratorial. From behind the decorative curtain that led to the kitchen emerged a gnarled, stooped man, dressed in jeans and a casual shirt too large for him, who raised his withered hands together in traditional Buddhist greeting.

'My name is Kunga Tashi. I have waited a long time to meet you ...'—he stumbled over the name—'Tummo Godfella.'

Up on the wall, the portrait of the Dalai Lama was laughing at him.

'I am happy to meet you, Kunga Tashi,' he responded. Goodfellowe discovered Elizabeth looking at him curiously. To his own surprise he had raised his hands in imitation of the Tibetan's greeting. He wasn't usually so open to suggestion, but he found everything about these people disarmingly easy to copy.

'No, Tummo Godfella. You should not be happy to meet me. For I am on a venture of great danger. Of death. But hopefully, if we prosper, of new life also.'

'If we prosper? If we prosper?' Goodfellowe enquired suspiciously.

'I have much to explain.'

And Kunga had sat down and told him about the circumstances surrounding the death of the Dalai Lama. About his instructions concerning the reincarnation, and the Search Group. 'Three of us set out. One was murdered in India ...'

'And the other in St Petersburg.'

Kunga smiled grimly. 'Do you believe in coincidence?'

158

'No. Not in coincidence.'

'Then the pursuit of eternal peace has become a surprisingly dangerous occupation, my friend,' the monk offered.

'You are the last one?'

'I am the last of the Tibetan Searchers. And if I die, our mission is at an end, our country will be destroyed and our great faith will be wiped from the earth. The end of everything.'

The walls of the darkened restaurant suddenly seemed to draw in on them, and Goodfellowe felt a shiver of concern creep down the nape of his neck.

'I'm sorry about Gompo. Somehow I feel responsible.'

'It was not your fault. Our enemies are all around us, nowhere is safe. Which is why I have a small confession.'

'You've sinned?'

'In a manner. I have entered your country secretly. Illegally. That makes me a fugitive, not only from my enemies, but now also from your own Government. As I said, the search for the child is full of perils.'

Goodfellowe cleared his throat uneasily. 'That's one of my many problems. About the child. I'm not sure I believe in all this talk of reincarnation.'

'But why is it so very difficult?' The old monk smiled. 'Even in your Christian faith there exists the concept of a life after death. We are only discussing the nature of that life.'

'But how can you hope to identify the right child?'

'Because we know His Holiness so well. His characteristics. His mannerisms. And have known him through many lives. We set the child tests to

159

ensure that we have not made a mistake.'

'But surely you might make mistakes.'

'Tummo Godfella, for more than a thousand years your country has followed the principle of hereditary monarchy, based on the belief that the queen on that particular night slept with the king and not some courtier. Are you suggesting that in a thousand years there has never been a ... an opportunity for confusion on that matter? We apply stringent tests in the process of identification. You simply take the word of the mother.'

Goodfellowe could sense Beefeaters rushing up the stairs, ready to drag them off to the Tower for sedition.

'And some might suggest that basing a religion on the notion of a Virgin Birth is scarcely scientific. Although,' Kunga hastened to add, 'we regard your Jesus as one of the great enlightened teachers.'

Trouble was, that was also a problem for Goodfellowe. He was pretty doubtful about the Jesus thing, too, and about concepts such as turning wine into blood and arriving at a heaven filled with fountains and laden vines, but this was hardly the time for a tussle with philosophical principles. 'OK, let's start from the premise that he has been reborn. What makes you think he's somewhere in Britain?'

'Signs, portents. And what His Holiness told us. He said his rebirth would be dedicated to reconciliation, peace on earth, in part between East and West. It makes sense that he should be reborn in the West.'

Goodfellowe wrinkled his nose sceptically. 'What other clues?'

'As he died he turned to face the West. And he

160

had laid out some stones in front of him in the form of a letter *I*. The name for your countrymen in Tibetan is *Inji.*'

The nose puckered once more. These were merely debating points, of little substance. Thin gruel.

'And also this.' Kunga held up his palm with the vivid red scar.

Goodfellowe recognized it immediately. An extraordinarily accurate outline map of England. He could even place Marshwood. And there was a dark purple mark in the precise position of London. 'Remarkable,' he conceded. 'But surely nothing more than . . .'

'Coincidence?'

The monk had a point. 'I was going to say, nothing more than a scar.'

'One might say nothing more than the marks of the cross I have to bear,' Kunga offered provocatively. But what he did not tell Goodfellowe was that, for the first time since the death of the Dalai Lama, the scar had ceased to burn. At the very moment the Eurostar shuttle on which he travelled had emerged from the Channel Tunnel. One minute the hand that held his false passport was on fire. The next minute the pain was gone. It was as though his wound had come home.

Goodfellowe was unimpressed—at least, he wanted to be unimpressed. His experience as a politician led him to be dubious of not only coincidence but also excessive conviction, and he didn't swallow this monk's diet of omens and oracles. Yet he warmed to him, wanted to trust this strange elf-like figure with the pointed ears whose hands told of a lifetime of suffering, whose eyes

161

spoke of little but hope. And he couldn't forget there were two corpses to account for.

'Let's just suppose, for the sake of discussion, that there is something in what you say. What do you want from me?'

'You do not know?' The monk smiled mischievously, like a politician about to announce a tax cut.

'How can I?'

'You are the only Englishman I can trust. Who can help me in the search. I am a stranger in your land, but you will know where to go, what to do. You are a member of your Parliament, a former senior Minister, who knows what questions to ask and where to ask them. You must help me find the child. Without your help the task becomes impossible. The boy will be lost. And with him, Tibet.'

'You want to make me part of your Search Group?'

'You are already part of the Search Group, Tummo Godfella.'

'Goodfellowe,' he emphasized in correction, a little irritated. 'Come off it. You said you were the last one.'

'I said I was the last of the three Tibetan Searchers. But before he died His Holiness told me, and me alone, that there was a fourth member of our group.' The candle between them guttered and spat. 'An English Searcher. You.'

'Me?' Goodfellowe sat incredulous.

'He felt he had a special connection with you.'

'This is ridiculous, I only met the man once.'

'In this life, yes.'

'In any life,' Goodfellowe responded defiantly.

162

'You say he was so very wise and was able to foresee so many things. So how did the other two Searchers wind up so very dead?'

'Some things are meant to be. And was there any other way you might be convinced?'

That took his breath away. It was an accusation so immense and cruel. And yet so accurate. He didn't want to get involved, his diary was far too crowded. Wasn't he already fully occupied with saving mankind, well, at least Marshwood? He couldn't fit in the time needed to debate the meaning of life with these strange people. And yet . . . There was blood on the floor, and whether he liked it or not some of it had spilled onto him.

'What do you want from me?' he repeated, a touch aggressively.

'Help us find the boy, Tummo Godfella. Before the Chinese do. They will kill him. Save the boy and save my country. You are the only one who can.'

'But isn't that your job? You're on the Dalai Lama's wretched committee.'

Kunga ignored the sarcasm. 'I have no idea where to start. I am a stranger in this land and I trust no one. Except for my old friend Wangyal here. And you.'

'Aren't there other Tibetans you can trust?'

'Two have already died. Already we have trusted too much.'

'So how do you expect me to find the boy? Without any name or description, without any team to help? It's like looking for a snowflake on a mountainside.'

The monk smiled mischievously. 'His Holiness said you would be difficult. Would need some considerable convincing.'

'He was right about that bit.'

'But he said you would find a way. And you will help.' It was not put as a question, merely a statement of simple faith.

Exasperating, stubborn, opinionated bloody people, Goodfellowe thought, just like . . . well, just like himself. The unexpected comparison started to make him splutter.

Kunga raised his cup of butter tea. 'A La La Ho,' he offered in toast.

'A La La Ho,' Goodfellowe responded, drinking deeply.

'And you will help.'

'I'll think about it,' was all Goodfellowe could find to say. He had been certain he was going to say no.

The monk started to chuckle as though he was gurgling water and the atmosphere was broken. At which point Goodfellowe returned to reality and remembered Elizabeth. Grief! She'd been sitting through all this, not only silent but completely forgotten. Now she was looking at him curiously, serious-eyed, as though trying to carve from within him what he was truly feeling. About danger, about death. And about her, too. Goodfellowe cursed. He knew the moment had gone. The sexual chemistry had fragmented under the weight of all this death-and-damnation stuff and he knew it wouldn't be put back together that evening. It left him grappling morosely with his thoughts. Would he help? Would he be risking his life? And would he get in at least one more great knee-shaking shag before he died?

Minutes later, as they left The Himalaya, Goodfellowe glanced ruefully up at the smiling face of the Dalai Lama. He could have sworn it winked.

They were walking through Leicester Square when Elizabeth put her arm around his shoulder and brought him to a halt. 'Do you believe in all this?' she asked.

He bit his lip. '*All* of it? Do I believe in *any* of it? Me, the Dalai Lama, Tibet, visas, maps on palms. Corpses everywhere.'

'One hell of a—what's the word? Coincidence?'

He had no response. At least, nothing that made any sense to him. So he said nothing.

'And what did that mean? That toast of yours in the restaurant. A La La Ho?'

'It's a sort of toast in Tibetan. You know, good health,' Goodfellowe muttered, still distracted. Later, he wondered how on earth he had known that.

That night in his lonely bed, biblical images dredged from his childhood kept crossing his dreams. Of three wise men travelling the world in search of an infant king. Of a child born to be a Messiah, a great Saviour. And of Herod sending out orders that the child should be found, and killed. It was almost like the Christmas story. Except that in Goodfellowe's dream, Herod was dressed in a Mao tunic.

*   *   *

It wasn't an earth-shattering election, so far as these things were concerned, nothing more than the opportunity to choose the leader of the party's backbenchers. One of life's little consolation prizes. But it was an election nevertheless, and fought with the usual weapons of any parliamentary terrorist

165

group, namely, alcohol and innuendo. The terrace of the House of Commons was crowded with partisans and those who, like Goodfellowe, were there largely for the drink and the drollery. His mind wasn't truly engaged in the conflict; indeed, since his resignation as a Minister he had found himself growing increasingly aloof from the game. It wasn't a sulk but merely that he preferred to be a player, not a substitute or a spectator. Yet in this contest, at least, and in contrast to most votes taken at Westminster, his voice might count.

He'd spent an engaging half-hour discussing the merits of the leading candidates, for none of whom he had any high regard. 'We can't have Bert,' he had told a group of colleagues, irrespective of the fact that they were drinking his wine.

'Could do worse,' one had countered. 'Elder statesman and all that.'

Goodfellowe examined his colleague, Windell, a young man but already a time-server, known as 'Windy' not simply for obvious reasons but also for his habit of blowing with the prevailing wind and his aptitude for allowing others to sit on and extinguish his opinions. The sort of apparatchik Goodfellowe would gladly have tipped over the terrace wall and into the Thames.

'Precisely,' he agreed. 'An elder statesman. Too bloody old. Going deaf, you know. How's he going to find out what's really going on? Who's going to gossip with him when you have to shout so loud that half the room can hear?'

Wicked, of course, and only partly true. But the party needed new blood, not old duffers, even though this particular duffer was barely ten years older than Goodfellowe. Anyway, since his

166

resignation Bert Travers had barely found two words to exchange with Goodfellowe, until he'd decided to run for this election.

'So it's Duggie?' Windy had enquired.

Goodfellowe rolled his eyes in despair. 'A man of such limited imagination. Always spends the first five minutes before dinner praising the quality of the house wine.'

'So who's it to be, Tom?'

Goodfellowe examined his glass as though the answer might be found in the fragrances of the Napa Valley. 'I'm thinking about Charlie,' he offered, entirely mischievously. The bugger had no chance. 'A bloody little Bonaparte, I know, but young and enthusiastic. New energy. I don't much like him personally and he seems to have no time for anyone over thirty, but heavens, he speaks well. And the press like him.'

Windy began nodding his approval. 'Yes. Good public image.'

'Although apparently in private our little Napoleon prefers to dress up more on the lines of Josephine. But I don't think that matters nowadays, do you, Windy?'

Windell's head had been nodding in a languid fashion as though rolling with the breeze, but the current appeared to have picked up a few knots for his head was now rotating in a stiff and awkward fashion, as though trying to see all round Goodfellowe's question and desperate not to give any clear sign of commitment.

'D'you know, Windy, in a couple of years' time I reckon you could be up for this job,' Goodfellowe had added.

'You serious?'

'As serious as anything I've said.'

'No, Tom, I can't agree,' Windy offered, suddenly decisive. 'I think I'd need at least another four years before I'm ready. But thanks anyway.' And overwhelmed by his own modesty, he took himself off in search of further praise.

The colleagues watched him depart. 'A man destined for the hospitality tent of life, never for its playing field, I fear,' Goodfellowe remarked quietly.

'You're on form this evening, you old bastard.'

In fact, Goodfellowe was feeling sour about his lost night with Elizabeth and disturbed by what the monk had told him. He had little precise idea of what they wanted him to do, still less about how he would achieve it. When at that moment Baader strolled onto the terrace it seemed like—well, to borrow from the monk, almost an omen.

'Paddy,' he waved, 'save me from this nest of vipers. But not before we've liberated one more drink.'

They took their glasses to the river wall and peered into the silt-stained waters. The tide was running.

'Life's a bit like the river, don't you think, Paddy? Sweeping you on. Then shoving you straight back again.'

'Are you preparing to jump or simply trying to make the rest of us feel bloody miserable?'

'You know you said if I needed your help . . . ?'

'Sure.'

'I've got another one.'

'Another what?'

'Another Gompo. Another monk.' He sighed. 'Another bit of madness.'

'Another monk? You want another visa?'

'No. He's in the country already. Illegally, Won't trust the system after what happened to the others.'

'Who can blame him?' Baader mused, before stiffening. 'But he *will* be blamed, if he's an illegal. And you with him if you're protecting him.'

'That's what I want your advice about. I can't tell him to give himself up, not just like that. Not after everything that's gone on.'

'You're talking heartstrings and humanity. But I'm a Minister. I've got to talk about the law.'

'Is there any way we can bring him within the law, Paddy? I dunno ... give him political asylum or something?'

'Can we prove he's being persecuted?'

'Can Gompo prove he's dead?'

Baader turned to face Goodfellowe, his body language designed to emphasize his words. 'You're taking a huge risk getting involved in something like this, Tom.'

'You can't think I'm going to end up like Gompo.'

'If you're knowingly harbouring an illegal immigrant there'll be a small army of select committee members and press editors who'll insist on it and who'll be lining up to do the job.'

'Safer in St Petersburg, you reckon?'

'Almost certainly.'

'Well, I'm not harbouring him. I've simply met him. But I'd like to help him.'

'What's he here for?'

'Meeting up with old colleagues,' he offered vaguely. 'But mostly simply trying to stay alive, I think.'

'Why are you getting yourself mixed up in all

this, Tom? There's no votes in it, and damn all satisfaction. And no national interest, not when you consider how little Tibet matters compared with what we've got in China.'

'Lost causes, I guess. I seem to collect them.'

'Drop it, old son.'

'Can't.' For the first time Goodfellowe realized he'd made the commitment.

'You want to take great care you don't become a lost cause yourself, Tom.'

'At times I think I already am. But enough of me. Will you help the monk?'

Baader shook his head in exasperation. 'I shouldn't. I'm a Minister, for God's sake, I've got codes of conduct shoved up every orifice. And yet ... hell, but I did promise you. Guess I'll have to. I'll make some enquiries with the Home Office about asylum and any other alternatives, just in principle. In the meantime maybe we ought to arrange some form of protection. Name?'

'Kunga Tashi.'

'Where's he hiding?'

Goodfellowe took a deep breath. Then he thought of Gompo.

'Come on, Tom. I can't help him without knowing where he is,' Baader pressed.

Goodfellowe shook his head. 'Not yet. If he comes out into the open now they'll have no choice but to lock him up. You have a chat with the Home Office first. Find out about asylum or some other status. Then we'll see if he wants to play ball. Until then I think he wants to be a bit like Greta Garbo. On his own.'

'You get this wrong and you'll be on your own, too. Sorry for being bloody, old chum, but you must

170

realize that. Nothing I will be able to do to help you.'

Goodfellowe's smile was bitter-sweet. 'On my own? Don't worry, Paddy. I'm used to it.'

*   *   *

Past two in the morning, with most of the city asleep. Nevertheless the telephone conversation was cryptic, with both the man and the woman anxious about eavesdroppers.

'He's here. In Britain. On our doorstep.'

'Who?'

'The monk.'

'So, the storm clouds gather. Right above our heads.'

'What will you do?'

'Find them. Find them quickly. Both of them.'

'The child too?'

'The child in particular.'

'And when you have found them?'

A long silence. Then: 'You have done well. Very well.'

Another silence. Then the question repeated. 'What *will* you do when you have found them?'

'Take care of them. As we always do.'

'In the Chinese fashion?'

'If you like.'

'Like Gompo . . .'

They rang off. The storm was about to burst upon them. Neither slept that night. Betrayal had its price.

CHAPTER SEVEN

Goodfellowe's name had obviously found its way onto a circulation list. The second invitation for a restaurant visit dropped on his mat within as many days. Still, this was Chinatown, with more restaurants than lamp-posts. An invitation didn't imply that he had gained acceptance, only that they had noticed he was passing through.

He had moved into his garret apartment in Gerrard Street a year before, after the mortgage and catastrophic overheads had forced him out of his house in Holland Park, just as they were likely to do in Marshwood. Gerrard Street was noisy, aromatic—he lived above a kitchen that prepared duck and *char siu* pork—and was close to ideal for someone who was clinically depressed and whose internal signposts were encouraging him to run away from life. You couldn't run in Chinatown, it was too small, there was nowhere to go. And the busy clatter of business until three or four every morning meant that the nights were never too empty for a man who couldn't sleep.

Chinatown was also a convenient location for a man who needed to get to Westminster in a hurry on a collapsible bike. He had become a well-known figure around its narrow streets and local traders valued having an influential and highly placed neighbour. Except, of course, he wasn't highly placed. A former Minister who has resigned 'for family reasons' is usually regarded by his colleagues in the same light as a paper cup at a party— something to be used only as a last resort, then quickly discarded—but there was little point in trying to disabuse ambitious Chinese traders. They wouldn't believe him, things didn't work that way in their system; if a former Minister wasn't in prison then he still had his hand in the cookie jar. Anyway, Goodfellowe didn't have the heart to protest his impotence: it still hurt too much.

Neither did the local Chinese believe he had no money. His frugal shopping and eating habits merely confirmed their opinion that he was a man of discretion and a tough negotiator, a useful man to have on their side. So they gave him good deals, greeted him when he came to eat in their restaurants and always gave him double helpings and 'doggy bags'. But he never accepted a free meal—that would establish a debt on his part which he knew they would later call in. There never was such a thing as a free meal in Chinatown.

But at least the invitation from Mr Jiang to attend the opening celebration for his new restaurant would cost him nothing other than a little time, since The Peking Palace was less than fifty yards from Goodfellowe's own front door. He was being asked as a local dignitary in order that Jiang could show off his pulling power, which appeared to be considerable. The place was packed with luminaries. These included the Chief Superintendent from the local constabulary in Agar Street and the Deputy Lord Mayor of Westminster. The local Member of Parliament (City of London and Westminster South) was missing, detained by a minor surgical procedure, but he had sent his wife to offer his apologies in person. It was going to be quite a bun fight. The tables groaned beneath an avalanche of the usual colourful and chaotic

Chinese *dim sum*.

After a year on these streets he was beginning to see through the clutter of Chinese faces, too. He had long ago discovered that the wispy old lady in the ill-fitting silk jacket, Madame Tang, was one of the area's most honoured inhabitants. She owned dozens of buildings in the area, including the building in which Goodfellowe lived, and carried her empire about on a huge bunch of keys that never left her side. She rattled as she walked, which was the only warning that troublesome tenants received before they found themselves in the street and on their way. There were many other pieces in this mosaic of Chinatown that Goodfellowe was only just beginning to put into their appropriate place. Like the group huddled in conversation in the corner. It included not only businessmen with strong mainland connections who were scheming with a trade official from the Embassy, but also two Taiwanese. The enemy. The implacable opponents, or so he had thought. But he had met one of the Taiwanese a few weeks earlier. 'Politics is passion, Mr Goodfellowe. But money is life. You show me politician without money and I will show you politician without prospects.' Didn't he know it. 'You must not misunderstand China,' the Taiwanese had gone on to explain. 'I am Taiwanese. Hate Communists. Fight to death. About politics. But prefer alive. And alive, we must all eat.'

These streets always held an air of inscrutability, an agenda which those unpractised in the art found difficult to read. Like the hand-written posters in the windows offering services and goods that only a Chinese could read. Or the sign above the club

174

door that in carefully painted English letters announced 'Strictly Members Only', while the scribbled characters underneath had suggested 'Everyone Welcome!' Everyone who could read Chinese, that is. These were streets in which asking for a VAT invoice was like announcing you were visiting from Mars. These streets had their own rules and codes of conduct, and laws Goodfellowe had had no part in writing.

Chou was at his elbow. Chou was the owner of a rival restaurant just off Gerrard Street and had always reserved a warm welcome for Goodfellowe, although like many Chinese he remained completely incapable of pronouncing his name. He simply called him 'Minister'. Chou had been conducting a meticulous inspection of Jiang's new establishment and was now ready to pass judgement to anyone who would listen. 'Old equipment in kitchen, Mr Minister. Not good. Cheap.' Chou paused, as though considering his next line, although Goodfellowe knew it had probably been carefully prepared. 'Everything cheap. Perhaps Jiang runs out of money. Jiang a big gambler, you know. Perhaps lose at tables. He also has expensive girlfriend, Mr Minister.' Chou shook his head. 'I don't think Jiang last long.'

Such gossip was, Goodfellowe knew, usually palpable nonsense, but he was growing accustomed to the rumours that ran like a flood tide through the streets of this small community. Against the outside world the Chinese community fought as one family, but once the door was closed their rivalries were never far from the surface. They fought not with weapons—at least very rarely, for these were streets of considerable safety—but with words. They threw everything at each other. Calumny. Denigration. Speculation and outright slander. There were more ways to cut down a rival than with a kitchen knife. A whisper that started in the morning from the back door of a kitchen or across the counter of a betting shop would have grown to a shout by lunchtime, and before evening would be echoing around every corner of the community. And sometimes these rumours were believed. So by the following morning new rumours started by yesterday's victims would be making the rounds. As Sun Tzu would suggest, 'destroy your enemy with his own anger'. And by God how they tried.

Chou was about to launch into another round of vilification when they were distracted by a commotion from the door. At first Goodfellowe couldn't see through the throng, but suddenly people began to step back and make a way. The guest of honour had arrived. To Goodfellowe's delight he saw it was Madame Lin. Jiang preceded her, hopping from foot to foot like some court jester with his Rolex sparkling at his wrist, while she made an almost regal advance through the room, acknowledging greetings on all sides. Then she saw Goodfellowe. Her face lit up.

'Mr Goodfellowe, what a surprise. And a pleasure.'

He held out his hand. 'It has been a few years, Madame Lin.'

'Five. Almost exactly. I remember our last conversation well. And with considerable sadness. But . . .'—she clapped her hands—'tonight is a time of celebration. You must do me the honour of celebrating with me.' She turned to the owner. 'Mr

Jiang, please ensure that my friend is sitting next to me. We have much to catch up with!'

And so they did. Outside the restaurant lion dancers performed traditional rites accompanied by a noisy fusillade of firecrackers, while inside Madame Lin and Goodfellowe sat and talked family, sharing sorrows at the death of her daughter, recovering their spirits with the mischief and mirth brought into her life by her small grandson. The Wheel of Life, crushing, uplifting. Then she had grown softer.

'Mr Goodfellowe, tell me of your wife.'

Somehow it was easy to talk with this wise old woman. It was as though they weren't in the middle of a crowded room but alone, locked away in that deep and private place where Goodfellowe hid his emotions. 'She hears voices,' he said. He shook his head as though he might be hearing them too. 'They tell her that the world is wicked. She trusts no one, least of all me. So she withdraws. Says nothing. Seems to hear and see nothing either.'

'My father was a doctor. I have a little understanding of these things.'

'They call it involutional melancholia. A catch-all term that means the doctors don't really know what they're dealing with. Neither do they truly know how to treat it. So they throw drugs at her. Prozac. And when that doesn't work, they throw different drugs at her. Nothing has worked.'

'Sometimes doctors find it easier to concentrate on their games with drugs than on the patients they are treating.'

'And when they find the new drugs don't work either, they bring in a new team of doctors. And the whole thing starts over again.' He couldn't hide the edge of distress in his voice.

'Our Oriental medicine looks at these problems from a different point of view,' she replied. 'Just as you cannot cure a bad back or a bad liver unless the patient changes his habits, so you cannot treat such terrible depression unless you get the patient to help. Yet she fights you, shuts off all her senses to protect herself. She sits silent, because it is safe for her that way. But as a result she cannot be cured. Drugs on their own often don't help.'

'So how would the Chinese treat her?'

'By trying to open up her senses once more. By stimulation rather than medication. So we might put her in a cold shower, then rub her down with hot towels. We might sing to her, or perhaps shout at her. To encourage her senses to shout back.'

'Better shouting than always sitting in silence.'

'Or we might use something as simple as a herbal pillow, so that some of her senses might be stimulated by the different fragrances, which in turn might stimulate other parts of her body. Slowly. They creep past the patient's resistance without their knowing.'

'My wife spends most of her time in bed or sitting in a chair.'

'Of course. It's easier for everyone that way. No trouble. But also no stimulation. No appreciation of beauty. No happiness. Yet happiness is a risk, Thomas. If we are happy, we risk losing it and suffering hurt. So some choose, like your wife, to do without happiness at all.'

Perhaps he'd been doing that himself, Goodfellowe thought. At least until he'd met Elizabeth.

'I've tried Chinese medicine,' Goodfellowe
178

responded. 'It certainly stimulates the senses, particularly some of the herbal brews. Couldn't fail. The smell is unspeakably foul. Upsets my neighbours for weeks. I simply never thought that something as simple as herbs might work with Elinor's type of problem.'

'Try it.'

'What have I got to lose?'

'And, if it works, you might get your wife back.'

Get his wife back . . . Her words exploded inside his brain. Illuminating places he had been trying to avoid. Forcing him to recognize what previously he had been unable or unwilling to see.

'But I don't want her back.'

He gasped out the words as though kicked by a horse. 'I'm so sorry,' he stammered, trying to recover. 'Please forgive me. I don't know what made me say that.'

But it was true. He didn't want Elinor back. It was past. Even before the accident they had drifted apart, contact maintained only by habit and the children. Not a corrupt relationship, but not much of any sort of relationship. One that had existed only by turning a blind eye. Yet now his eyes were open and it was a relationship he could never willingly pick up again. It left him in a state of shock. He was trembling.

She laid her hand upon his. 'You have no need of apology to me, Thomas. We are all—all of us—torn by divided loyalties. Conflicts inside us. Your conflict is simply more cruel than most.' There was no pity in her eyes—he couldn't have taken pity— merely recognition of the facts. He could deal with facts. And the fact was that he had come to a great turning point.

179

'Madame Lin, you once told me we were very much alike. I think we are. I shall remember this conversation, and your kindness, for the rest of my life.'

'And so shall I.'

As they talked and grew closer, around them the celebrations proceeded with enthusiasm but without, for a considerable period, the presence of the owner Mr Jiang. For Mr Jiang was a man of many roles. A restaurateur. A trader. A man with important contacts. A gambler and womanizer, as Chou had recognized. But he also had a role about which Goodfellowe knew nothing and Chou guessed only little. He was the key figure in one of the local Triad gangs.

While the title of Triad inspired awe, in truth the local London Triads were not like the mighty Hong Kong or Shanghai empires but little more than a loose family of villains. Jiang's ran one of the local gambling dens and a little rent collection alongside. There were also the counterfeit videos and stolen credit card scams, nothing mucky. He'd never bothered with the prostitution and protection rackets because the profit margins on his white-collar villainies were far higher and the penalties, if anyone got caught, much more manageable than those imposed on old-fashioned vice, The courts almost expected the Chinese to be running bootleg videos; the magistrate's son probably had several in his own home. So in the event of a problem a junior member of the Triad would plead guilty, receive a rap across the knuckles and be back on the street, usually within weeks, along with a substantial bonus. Everyone was happy. The police would have their conviction while the Triad member would hold onto his steady job. And no one would get within a million miles of Jiang. He hadn't had a finger laid on him in years. Wiped himself as clean as one of his counterfeit videos. Hell, he was such a pillar of the community that even the Chief Super came to help him open his restaurant.

So when he disappeared from the celebrations, those who noticed assumed he was busy in the kitchens. Instead, he was locked in his tiny back room. With Mo. For nearly forty minutes they huddled together, unnoticed and undisturbed. Up to no good. When eventually they emerged their business had been completed and it was all but time for the Ambassador to depart. Jiang presented her with an extravagant gift and she offered her farewells accompanied by the applause of the crowd—even from the Taiwanese, Goodfellowe noticed. Then she was gone.

Her car was well on the way to her Residence in Hampstead before she spoke to Mo.

'How went your evening, little Mo?'

'It can be done, Ambassador. But there will be a heavy cost.'

'Only blood flows for free. How heavy?'

'Who knows? A lot.'

She sighed, gazed into the darkness. 'Then, little Mo, you had better tell your cousin not to disappear on vacation. There is little time. He's going to be kept busy.'

*   *   *

It was his sense of guilt that drove him to do it.

Like most politicians, he hated his postbag. And like most men with overdrafts he opened it with as much delay as possible. Not all envelopes contained invitations to free dinners. Many envelopes contained misery, some of the most unexpected kind.

One in particular caught his attention. It was addressed to Sam, which was unusual, She didn't normally receive letters at Gerrard Street. Why hadn't it been sent to her at school?

The envelope in question was one of carefully constructed anonymity. Small and obviously inexpensive, brown, with nothing but a hand-written address with an incomplete postcode and a business postmark. No logo or embellishment, no clue as to its origin. A mystery. Goodfellowe didn't like mysteries, but that was no excuse for what he did.

He was worried sick about Sam, even more so since his miserable failure the previous weekend to offer her fatherly advice and comfort. His imagination had spent too much time wandering over all the possibilities of how she was, and what she was. And what she'd been up to. There were so many question marks over his daughter's life, and here was another. He needed to know what was in this envelope, his need driven by his own sense of guilt.

He could scarcely believe what he was doing. In the kitchen. Over the stove. Steaming it open with the kettle, just as he'd seen it done in those black-and-white films of his childhood with Maigret and Fabian of the Yard and clanging police bells on old Wolseley cars. As he watched, the flap of the envelope curled in distaste. And out dropped a cheque. Signed by Sam. And stamped 'Refer To Drawer'.

The cheque was made out to the Unplanned Pregnancy Advice Clinic.

Of course the Clinic and its staff were scrupulous in maintaining the confidentiality of its patients— or, rather, clients. But its finance department was less sensitive, there had been a glitch in the system. Bounced cheques were returned.

His hand trembled, and not simply from the fact that he was scalding his fingers. More confusion and fear. Fear for Sam. Fear for himself. He'd already lost a son and a wife. How much more could he take?

He knew he was not well equipped to deal with this dilemma. His sense of judgement was distorted, his emotions still too bruised from his own life to be able to cope adequately with hers. Which was why he had relied so heavily on Elizabeth's advice. Advice which so far he had embellished to catastrophic effect. Sam hadn't spoken to him in more than a week. The rollercoaster of their relationship had come off the rails once more. And Elizabeth, just when he needed her, was away tasting wines in France. With fellow restaurateurs. With other men. Drinking. Laughing. Letting them fall in love with her. Suddenly he was having trouble breathing.

He knew he must not make the wrong decision, yet he had no clear idea what 'the wrong decision' was. Did that imply there was 'a right decision' in such circumstances? If there was, it'd slipped past him damned quick. But he knew that what above all else would be wrong would be for Sam to face that most transforming decision of her life alone, by herself, It must ultimately be her decision, but she would need support to make the right choice, and

183

still more support if the choice she made was wrong. She needed her father, even though at the moment she didn't want him. He closed his eyes and wept inside.

How long had it been? She must've been pregnant at least nine or ten weeks. He wept a little more. If she remained silent he'd have to confront her, and soon. He would risk losing her, but she risked losing herself if it was left any longer. Time to come off the fence. He would give her three weeks. Three weeks from today, No more. Three weeks. That's all the time they might have left.

*   *   *

The leafy avenue of Prinsengracht was within walking distance of Amsterdam's red-light district but belonged to an altogether different world. Stately, secure, a little sedate even. Lined by banks, bakeries and bourgeois florists, with not a knocking shop in sight. Which made it an excellent cover for the many skulduggeries practised by little Mo's cousin.

He'd come a long way since he'd arrived in this city and earned his first few guilders by running errands for the punters in one of the smoke-filled hash cafés. Now, several years and an amnesty for illegal immigrants later, he occupied a large studio and a workshop overlooking the Prinsengracht from which he ran a lucrative business in Oriental antiques.

The Mo cousins had been born in northern Jiangxi province. In Jingdezhen, to be precise. Which produced ceramics. Not just ordinary ceramics but some of the finest pieces ever known

184

to mankind. Legend insisted there hadn't been a moment in two thousand years when the fires of the kiln had ceased to burn, a sight that had inspired the poet Longfellow to verse: *'Three thousand furnaces that glow/ Incessantly and fill the air/ With smoke uprising, gyre on gyre/ And painted by the lurid glare/ Of jets and flashes of red fire.'* The Mo family had inherited many of the ancient potters' skills and—far more significantly—they had also inherited some of the original potters' moulds. Thanks to such legacies this city of fire still produced artefacts of timeless beauty in the original style. Which was part of the problem, of course, for although these artefacts might support all the aesthetic qualities of the original pieces, they didn't support the same hugely inflated prices.

This was where Mo's cousin came in. His skill was in taking brand new pieces still warm from the kilns and reducing them to antiquity. The moulds were the same, as were the clay and the production methods, but the pieces didn't have the special patinas and markings that came from centuries of being exposed to the elements or, in some cases, being buried underground. So Mo's cousin would scrape the rims, corrupt the glaze, embellish and undermine with time. Dull clay was transformed to the finest blue and white or underglaze red, Ming mark, Yuan mark, all the items most sought after in the galleries of Europe.

He also brought in other ceramics, from factories in Macao and Taiwan, and bronzes from Thailand, all pieces of great skill and beauty, waiting simply for the patina of age to increase their value a hundred-fold. Unglazed funerary pieces were covered with layers of authentic

185

Shandong mud from near the great burial site at Long Xing. He had the mud shipped in by the crate. Stucco pieces were nibbled at by weak solutions of liquid manure, jade aged with acid. The bronzes were a special expertise; he left them soaking in the outflow of the urinals from a local bar, after which they would reappear with the most beautiful lime encrustations that could defy the forensic abilities of all but the most diligent of dealers. Within weeks they looked as if they had been under environmental assault for a thousand years.

There were strict rules, of course, for the export of antiques from China, but in the chaos that had become the People's Republic so much material was slipping through into the hands of unscrupulous foreign dealers that nobody bothered questioning how he kept discovering still more sources of Tang, Ming, Sung or Han. That's what collectors wanted. And that is what the dealers got.

It was a good business—but regrettably not good enough for Mo's cousin. The only form of security a refugee like him recognized was cash, lots of it and placed in some location the authorities couldn't even guess at. Why bother having to rely on the state to guarantee his happiness in old age when, without the state, he could guarantee it himself?

So, ever the entrepreneur, Mo's cousin had begun to branch out. Alongside his artefacts he had taken to packing not only forged certificates of thermo-luminescent date testing that bore the stamp of the Oxford Research Laboratory for Archaeology, but also bags of pure heroin, carefully concealed in the interior cavities of appropriate items. And through Mo's network of Embassy contacts, many of these were smuggled out under cover of the diplomatic bag.

Business was booming, not least because of Mo and the London situation. By moving the genuine antiques around the Embassy, no one became too familiar with any one piece. The only real check was the official inventory—'Banshan Jar. One. 2000—3000 BC. Condition—first.' Which, somewhere around the Embassy, is what they would find. Complete with authentic encrustations. Or so they thought. Meanwhile Mo's cousin would have passed the authentic pieces through a dealer for a truly authentic price. Everyone was happy.

Mo's cousin ripped off the top of the wooden packing case he had just received from London, revealing the most wondrous jade carvings, which until three days ago had adorned the main staircase in Portland Place. Another three crates were already on their way. More were promised. This was Mo's best supply yet and his cousin celebrated. Over the next few weeks there would be little rest for his team of restorers, acid dippers, pissoir plumbers, fudgers and forgers.

From the other side of the canal, and through the branches of a rowan tree that only slightly obscured his view, a young man watched the many comings and goings of Mo's cousin. He sat in the window of a brown-house bar, enjoying the sharp taste of a cube of mature edam and wondering whether he could make his non-alcoholic beer stretch the rest of his watch. As stake-outs went, this wasn't so bad. The weather was warm, the women conspicuously underdressed. And there were results. The pace of activity at the workshop had picked up, there was new business afoot.

Mucky new business, if it involved little Mo's cousin. Which was why, even in liberal Amsterdam, the Drugs Task Force of the city's Serious Crime Squad had begun to take a keen interest in his activities.

They had begun to track every consignment in, and every one out. It had proved a curious mix. Antique porcelain and pottery. Museum pieces some. And pornography. A little marijuana, only enough for personal consumption. Traces of heroin. And lots of mud. A crate of it had arrived just last week and they'd all been convinced they'd find a dozen kilos of powder hidden in the middle, or maybe some uncut diamonds. But that's all it was, mud. And a hell of a mess it had made in the customs shed as they poured out, sieved and threw back every single cupful. Maybe the bastard liked bathing in it.

He was a resourceful fellow, this cousin of Mo, with fingers in all sorts of pies. Too many pies, the policeman concluded. The Chinaman was going to get his fingers burned.

*   *   *

He had suggested a light lunch, but when she opened the door of his Ministerial office in the House of Commons she could see he had more than food on his mind. Why else was he stark naked? Before Mickey had time even to giggle, Baader had scattered half her clothing and was leading her to the leather Chesterfield. There was no hint of romance, this was straightforward pillage and plunder and, right at this moment, Mickey loved it. It was crazy, he hadn't even locked the door and could only rely on any visitor knocking first, but it seemed to be the element of risk that drove him and made him such an energetic lover. She marvelled at the way he was able to adjust his body so that he fitted not only her but also the awkward sofa, and wondered whether they'd ever get to doing it in bed. He'd probably find it boring. Unless, of course, the bed was being wheeled in broad daylight down Whitehall.

Afterwards she lay gazing distractedly at the ceiling. Was it the highest ceiling she'd ever studied, she wondered? She'd seen a few, particularly since she had broken off her engagement the previous year. Occasionally she wondered whether there might have been too many ceilings in her life, but she didn't care to analyse things too much, let alone keep count. She'd enjoyed the variety, that she knew. Yet she'd give them all up, for just one. Preferably in a house rather than an apartment. With roses round the door.

The wall, too, told a story. Covered in cartoons and photographs. Of Baader. Standing beside the Prime Minister. Beside the President. Beside other leaders. Suddenly it all became clear. His frustration. A life spent at the shoulder of greatness, never at the centre of the stage. A man with such strength of mind, always required to follow the opinions of others. He effected a lack of concern, of course, an almost casual approach to power, but looking at these walls she understood how it must gnaw at his entrails and leave him smothered by failure. Now she knew the secret behind his bravado, his recklessness and risk taking, all this marvellously impossible sex. Although he might not admit it, Paddy Baader hated himself.

189

Deep down, within his guts, he regarded himself as a failure, perhaps had always thought he was a failure. In politics. At university. In his marriage. In his relationship with all women. So he wanted to destroy himself. And he'd failed even in that. So far.

She found she couldn't move. All that heat and sweat had stuck her back firmly to the leather. When finally and with some effort she sat up, the movement was accompanied with a ripping sound that left her skin raw and angry. Baader laughed, then began kissing it, soothing the pain. He had nibbled halfway down her backbone when suddenly he stopped.

'Mickey, how much do you know about what Tom's up to with his Tibetans?'

'We don't have many secrets. We share pretty much everything.'

'Hey, should I be getting jealous?'

'Not that, you fool!' she laughed. 'Anyway, the poor mutt's in love. Terribly distracted.'

'You bet he is. Got himself into some very deep water. Two Tibetans dead. A third . . . you know about the third?'

'Kunga Tashi? Yes.'

'Getting involved with an illegal immigrant might be very serious for him. Particularly if the immigrant ends up like the others, dead. I'm worried for Tom. He's out of his depth.'

'Can't you do anything to help?'

'Not officially. Not unless the monk comes forward and asks for protection or asylum. It's crazy for him to be wandering the streets of London if he's in danger. I suppose he is in London?'

190

'Guess so. They met at some Tibetan restaurant. All very cloak and dagger.'

'At least he's not likely to starve.'

She braced her shoulders impatiently and slowly his lips began their work once more. 'I'd like to help.' Nibble. 'If I can.' Nibble, nibble. 'Give him some advice. You know, something friendly . . .'—he guided her hand—'but firm.' She giggled. 'But you know what Tom's like. Bloody stubborn. Independent.'

'Of course.' Her back shivered in enjoyment. 'That's why I love him so.'

'Look, help me, Mickey. To help Tom.' His tone became suddenly more practical. 'Keep me in touch, eh? Before he gets in too deep and discovers he can't climb out?'

She straightened up. 'You're scarcely the man to preach caution with your balls dangling over Her Majesty's carpet and about as defenceless as a duck in a desert. Questions will be raised in the House.'

'Oh, God. They'll crucify me!' He leaped into the air. Naked men always looked ridiculous, she thought, when viewed at any distance greater than about twelve inches. 'Questions!' he continued in alarm. 'It's my bloody turn today. I'm supposed to be at the Despatch Box in ten minutes.' He began a desperate scramble into his clothes. She laughed furiously as his milk white bottom disappeared into carefully pressed trousers. Then he was at the drinks cabinet. A stiff whisky. Neat. Down in one. Back to the dressing. Grabbing for his briefing book.

She was still laughing as he disappeared out of the door.

'I suppose a quickie's out of the question . . . ?'

At first sight, two of the raids looked like normal burglaries. They cleared out the three computer terminals from the Tibet Foundation in Bloomsbury and trashed much of what was left, which didn't amount to a great deal since the Foundation was a relatively small charitable enterprise dedicated to supporting the cultural needs of the Tibetan community. None of the terminals were of any great value. Strangely, however, they also took all the floppy disks, which had no commercial value whatsoever, just jumbles of information ranging from recipes to subscription reminders. Perhaps the raiders were amateurs.

That same night the home of the chairman of the Tibet Association was also broken into. His still more ancient computer was practically candle-powered but nevertheless joined the list of stolen Tibetan property, along with a boxload of paper records. Nothing else was touched, apart from the small shrine in his front room, which was trashed. The burglars, if amateurs, had attitude.

There was nothing amateurish about the following night's raid. Fire investigation officers who later sifted through the debris couldn't be certain it was arson—with all that kitchen equipment around on which to lay the blame there was always likely to be an element of doubt. What was without doubt, however, was that the fire needed only seconds to take hold and within minutes had turned The Himalaya into an inferno. Nothing survived. What the flames didn't consume was obliterated when the huge Victorian roof joists collapsed and fell through two floors.

It was suggested afterwards that only a miracle had enabled Kunga and Wangyal to survive. But the monk knew better.

Kunga had been finding sleep increasingly elusive—a combination of impatience and impotence, perhaps, as he waited for Goodfellowe. So he had sat up late with Wangyal, talking, reminiscing, then they had gone for a walk through the night. Kunga had insisted. He'd suddenly found the small back room of the restaurant oppressive, closing in on him, like a hand pushing him out. He could actually feel the hand between his shoulder blades. Survival had been as simple as that. As simple as faith. But no miracle. They had missed the fire by minutes.

When they returned from their walk there was nothing to be done except stand and watch as everything Wangyal possessed was destroyed. From within the building came a mighty growl, a floor collapsed, and showers of glowing embers were sent angry into the night.

'The breath of dragons,' Kunga muttered grimly.

They both knew this was no accident, and who was to blame.

The flames were at their peak, blazing with the sound and wrath of stampeding buffalo. Wangyal felt as if they were heading straight for him. By the time they had passed there would be nothing left, the landscape of his life would be beaten flat. 'I came out of Tibet with nothing. But I cannot watch this,' he sighed.

'Then it is time. No more delay. We must go.'

'Go? Go where?'

'To Tummo.'

And with a sense of renewed urgency the monk dragged Wangyal away. There was no point in staying, nothing left to stay for. He could inspect the ashes in the morning.

Goodfellowe, woken at almost three a.m., was rumpled and heavy in both eye and limb. He'd been to the gym again and was finding all this exercise exhausting. At times he wondered whether he would have any strength left for Elizabeth. Fit, maybe, but fast asleep. So they had sat over tea— Pu-er tea from Yunan, dark and fierce to restore his wits, letting the steam bathe his eyes—while they outlined what had taken place. The burglaries. The fire. Their utter helplessness.

'At last you bring me good news,' Goodfellowe yawned, waiting for the caffeine to strike.

'I have heard a little about your British sense of humour,' Kunga began, 'but I do not understand it.'

'No humour. There's good news in what you tell me.' He poured more boiling water into the pot. The Pu-er would take several flushings, and so would he. 'But first, I am so sorry about your restaurant, Wangyal.'

Wangyal nodded wearily. 'We have a saying in Buddhism . . .'

'I know. Everything is impermanence. Even so, I'm sad.'

'When you turn things upside down, they look different. When you have lost your country, the loss of a few tables and a kitchen seems somehow trivial.' He managed a half-smile. 'At least, you try to make it so.'

Goodfellowe marvelled at the simple self-control of these Tibetans. None of them would make a politician.

194

'But how is this good news, Tummo?' Kunga interjected impatiently.

'At first sight, it's not. Your enemies clearly know you're in the country. They're also in a hurry, no doubt of that. They want you dead. Like Gompo. To stop you from getting to the boy. To give you no chance of spiriting him away. You should think again about going to the police, Kunga.'

'And while I was enjoying the hospitality of your police, they would be out there searching for the child. If tonight tells us anything, it is that we have no time to waste.'

'Fair point. But—if you turn it upside down— that also gives us two advantages. Your secret's out and your enemies know you're here. So there's no point in hiding *why* you're here. We can start the search for the boy in earnest.'

'*We*, Tummo Godfella?' Behind their sorrow, the monk's eyes had begun to glow.

Goodfellowe's brow wrinkled. This monk was exasperating. 'Don't get any ideas about me; this is purely self-interest. Since I live above a restaurant, let's just say I object very strongly to them being burned down.'

Kunga tried to hide his smile of satisfaction. 'And the second piece of good news? What is that?'

'The Foundation and the Association. You can be sure they are entirely loyal.'

'Why?'

'Because if they weren't it wouldn't have been necessary to burgle them.'

'But how does that help?'

'It means that at last we've got a team.'

*   *   *

195

Kunga had insisted that they be summoned from their beds.

'But it is only just past four in the morning,' Wangyal protested.

'And past midday in Tibet. We have no time to lose. Call them.'

So, while Goodfellowe replenished the pot of tea, two of the most prominent leaders of the local Tibetan community had been hauled from their places of sleep—Phuntsog who headed the Foundation, a surprisingly tall and thin man for a Tibetan with a nose like a traffic cone, and Frasi, who was chairman of the Association, a compact man with worry lines on his forehead like a mountain range. As dawn broke they had crowded around Goodfellowe's small dining table—he had only four chairs and was forced to commandeer the kitchen stool—while Kunga related his story of the reincarnation and the Search. The two newcomers had listened awe-struck.

'This is a particularly great honour. If the child is amongst us,' Frasi had whispered.

'It is also a particularly great danger,' Phuntsog had responded forcefully, agitated by the news of the murder. He'd been in the West perhaps a little too long, and had begun to lose the sense of detachment that characterized his countrymen.

'But why were you both burgled?' Goodfellowe interjected. 'What did they take?'

'Old computers, that's all. Antiquated and practically valueless,' Phuntsog had responded. 'And useless computer disks.'

'And a box of paper records,' Frasi added.

'Of what?'

196

'Of my members.'

Goodfellowe began balancing on the legs of the kitchen stool, rocking back and forth like a monk in prayer. 'So, it wasn't the computers they wanted but the information they contained. The details of your members. I'm afraid it means they can all expect a visit. Every single one of them.'

'Won't take long,' Phuntsog sniffed through that pointed nose. He seemed to sniff a lot.

'Why?'

'We Tibetans are a tiny community in this country. Fewer than a hundred of us scattered around—only two hundred even if you throw in the families.'

'And how many children?' Goodfellowe demanded.

'Boys. Aged two or less,' Kunga added.

'Why two or less?' Goodfellowe asked.

'Simple arithmetic,' the monk replied. 'Even gods have to be conceived! His Holiness died almost four years ago, and there is a short period of transition through which every spirit, even the most enlightened, must travel before being conceived and reborn. So he will be less than three. But probably not much less. Every omen and sign tells us that the incarnation is ready to be discovered, yet a child younger than two is scarcely capable of talking and walking let alone being able to reveal to us that he is the new Dalai Lama.'

'How on earth will he do that?'

Kunga smiled, an expression full of time and mysteries. 'That is not so easy to define. Perhaps a little like recognizing one of your saints? But this is no ordinary child. He will have characteristics that are exceptional, that will have been passed down

197

from his previous incarnation. Perhaps he will have some physical feature, the twist of his smile, something in his eyes. Like recognizing the features of your own family. But most certainly he will show many spiritual signs, these are the most important. Which is why the team of Searchers must be steeped in the traditions, and must have known His Holiness so well. When we believe we have found him, we test the child by getting him to recognize items and articles from his previous life. So this child can be no older than two. And probably no younger.'

Phuntsog piled in once more. 'Which makes it all the easier for the Chinese. There will be so few boys of the right age. Most of us came to Britain in the seventies, when visas were easier. We're middle aged. Past the baby bit.'

'Speak for yourself.'

'I am, yak head.'

'I can think of two with daughters. In Milton Keynes.'

'And there's Samya-ling in Scotland.'

'It's a monastery! You know—monks? Nuns? You expect to find children in a monastery?'

'But there must be some families with young sons.'

'Must there?' It was Phuntsog, distant to the last.

A silence of uncertainty settled across them. Goodfellowe was growing increasingly exasperated at the Tibetans' apparent lack of coherence.

'Look, how long can it take to contact a hundred families? Two days?' he demanded.

'We must move faster than that. Warn anyone with a young child to move them to safety. There is no time to lose,' Kunga insisted, sharing

198

Goodfellowe's concern.

'The Chinese have had the lists for a whole day. They're probably tracking down the Tibetan families already, even as we speak.'

A chill rippled around the table.

'But there's another problem that worries me even more,' Goodfellowe continued.

'Which is?'

'They tried to kill you tonight, Kunga. Yet how on earth did they know where to find you?'

CHAPTER EIGHT

So Duggie had won. Done the only sensible thing and lied about his prospects. Now he was leader of the Government back-benchers, a prince amongst the prawns.

His strategy had been immaculate. His supporters had gone round the House suggesting that Bert, the only other likely contender, was home by a landslide—although in the case of the backbench committee it might be more aptly described as a mudslip. In the Tea Room, in the Smoking Room and corridors, along the benches of the House, the word was heard. 'It's Bert.' Good old solid, dependable Bert. Wisdom of ages, even if he was a little deaf. Would do the job splendidly, everyone agreed.

Trouble was, no one liked the pompous ass. (Not that liking someone particularly mattered in politics. Brutus liked Caesar, even loved him. Always claimed he would be the last man to stab his friend in the back . . .) Many colleagues would have been happy for Bert to have slipped home by a handful of votes and got on with it, but heaven preserve them from having to listen to him in the bar sounding off about his bloody landslide. He would become a bigger pain in the butt than the Chief Whip. A little humility was called for and so—no landslide. And, in the expectation of just that, even many colleagues who were content to see Bert elected had voted for Duggie.

So Duggie had won.

Things were never as they seemed, Goodfellowe reflected, having congratulated and commiserated with the two candidates, neither of whom he'd voted for. He had given a write-in vote for Windy, the only write-in vote of the election, on the grounds that none of it mattered. What was the point of running for office as leader of the backbenches? No power, no patronage, no real role, nothing but pretence. Like a Janet and John video that he used to play for Sam. The characters would sit around pretending to be stuffed dummies, only coming to life when all the grown-ups had turned their backs. For the rest of the time it was all sitting back and waiting. Yes, just like being a backbencher.

Things were never as they seemed.

And that was it. That's what had been nagging at Goodfellowe ever since this nonsense started with the Tibetans. The Tibetans, of course, assumed that their enemy was the Chinese, the hated Han. But Goodfellowe didn't hate the Han. He lived among them, had many friends within their number who had shown him considerable kindnesses. The Chinese Government was a different matter, was ruthless as even their Ambassador Madame Lin had acknowledged, and would crush all things Tibetan without compunction. But Goodfellowe didn't live in Tibet, he lived in Chinatown and loved it. He was the last person to lead a crusade against all things Chinese.

There was also the fact that even if 'the enemy' in this case was the Chinese Government, how could they have known where Kunga was? Only a few Tibetans had known that, plus Goodfellowe himself, and he hadn't told anyone. But someone had. And that someone had to be Tibetan.

His suspicions and frustrations grew when, later the following afternoon, they were once more gathered around his dining table. Three people manning telephones can make rapid progress through a list of names less than a hundred long. As Phuntsog explained, there was only a handful they hadn't so far been able to contact.

'And?' Goodfellowe demanded.

'That's the problem, Mr Goodfellowe. There's not a single boy aged two in the entire Tibetan community. Four girls. A boy aged eight months. Too young. But no one aged two.'

'Impossible,' groaned Kunga, his breath expiring as though it were his last.

'What about those you haven't been able to contact?' Goodfellowe suggested. 'The boy might be a member of one of those families.'

Phuntsog shook his head. 'All those families are known to other Tibetans, who say there is no such child.'

'But . . .' Goodfellowe clenched his fists in exasperation. But what?

'The child doesn't exist,' Phuntsog said.

'He has to,' Kunga insisted. 'He must exist. Too

many people have already died for him not to exist.'

Frasi was agitated. 'All around the country, wherever there is a Tibetan family, it seems there are Chinese. Waiting on the doorstep. Watching. Asking neighbours about the children. Offering money for the right information. Like bounty hunters. Some Tibetan houses have been broken into. Already one attempt has been made to snatch a baby from its mother's arms. There is still much danger.'

'But also some relief,' Goodfellowe offered. 'If they're still searching it means they haven't found the child either.'

'Many Tibetan families are not happy,' Frasi continued. 'They blame us for bringing them this trouble. Many have difficulty believing that the reincarnation of His Holiness could be born in Britain.'

'Frankly, I have trouble believing it, too,' Phuntsog added.

'Phuntsog!' Kunga exclaimed in disbelief.

'So if the child exists, where is he?' Phuntsog demanded in his own defence.

The teamwork these colleagues had managed to mount was visibly fraying at the edges. 'What are we to do, Tummo?' Kunga asked. All their faces were turned in his direction, looking to him for guidance. They were out of their depth. He was none too sure of his footing, either. He very much wished he'd never started with this.

'We must work on the assumption that the child is here in Britain,' he began. 'And that somehow, in ringing around, one of you has missed him. So—we exchange telephone lists. And start all over again.'

'What are you suggesting . . . ?' Frasi exclaimed.

202

'Or suspecting?' Kunga enquired more softly.

'. . . that we have made a mistake? Missed someone out?' Angrily Phuntsog pushed the three telephone lists across the table at Goodfellowe.

'It's possible.'

'But not by accident,' Frasi continued.

'Which is why I suggest you exchange telephone lists and start all over again. To double check.'

'You suspect one of us, Tummo?' Kunga asked grimly.

'Someone betrayed you, Kunga Tashi, almost got you killed. They would also betray the child.'

There was a long and awkward silence as they looked around the table at each other—which one was it?—before Phuntsog turned to the monk. 'Why should we listen to this man, Kunga Tashi?'

'Because he is one of us.'

'He is a foreigner. He lives among the Chinese.'

'Nevertheless . . .'

Slowly, as though moving bars of gold, Goodfellowe pushed the telephone lists back across the table. Without another word and with a prolonged scowl from Phuntsog, the Tibetans left.

$$*\qquad*\qquad*$$

There was only one piece of good news that day but it was the best. She was back. He called as soon as he got her message.

'Damn it, but I've missed you,' he began as soon as he heard her voice.

'That's great.'

'I've missed your body, too.'

'That's also good to know.' She laughed. It merely encouraged him.

203

'I want it. I want you. Right now.'

'Fine, but . . .'

'But what?'

'Who is this?'

Goodfellowe was stunned. His jaw dropped. How many men . . .?

'Oh, Goodfellowe, you're such an idiot,' she interrupted his thoughts. 'It's no fun pulling your leg when you make it so easy.'

He couldn't find the right words, or indeed any words. Her tone softened.

'It's been that tough without me?'

'Tougher.'

'I'm flattered.'

'Sorry to be so dense. A sense of humour bypass. While you've been playing havoc in foreign parts, foreign parts have been playing havoc with me.'

'Eh?'

'A long story. Which I desperately want to bore you with. Tonight. Please. Come over, Elizabeth.'

'To be bored? Sounds irresistible.'

'What if I also said that I want to bonk your brains out?'

'That's better. You're improving.'

'I'm stuck in the House until ten, I'm afraid, but after that . . .'

'Hmmm. You're suggesting I bring my toothbrush.'

'In the morning I'll make you the finest cup of Souchong you've ever tasted.'

'Sorry, I'm strictly a ground-coffee girl.'

'So come over and we can argue about it. In the morning.'

'But I'm dog tired after my trip around France,' she countered.

'And I promise to keep you up all night.'

'In which case . . . That is a promise, is it, Goodfellowe? To keep me up all night? Not just another of your idle threats?'

'I'm a politician. You can trust me.'

'Then there's only one thing to do.'

'Which is?'

'I shall bring my own coffee.'

*   *   *

Sam and Edwina were in a hurry. There was a train to catch. They'd had an enjoyable meal, in the circumstances, sweetcorn and crab meat soup, fried seaweed—Edwina's favourite—and a shared plate of Singapore noodles. Less than a fiver a head at Mah's Kitchen, and the owner didn't mind their stinginess. Sam had eaten there often with her father; Mah was always glad to see her. And both Sam and Edwina, the closest of friends, always felt in need of a little fortifying after their visits to the pregnancy clinic.

They were on half term and staying with Edwina's mother. After their last row, Sam was avoiding her father and anyway he was up to his eyes in parliamentary work. As always. Even worse, he had explained to her that it was most unlikely the Chief Whip would allow him time off to see her Cleopatra. She took it badly. So although the direct route from the restaurant to Charing Cross Station would take them practically straight past his front door in Gerrard Street, they made a small detour to avoid it, just in case they bumped into him. Didn't want to visit, let alone stay. After all, she argued with herself, the studio apartment was so cramped, such a come-down from Holland Park. Only later did she take time to consider her feelings, then thoroughly scold herself. A come-down it might be, but he was the sad, mad mongrel who had to live there.

They were a little late. Mah had delayed them with a free dessert, egg-custard tarts, and they were hurrying now. Sam wouldn't normally have used the quiet alleyway that cut through towards Little Newport Street, not at night-time, but it would save them a few necessary seconds. It seemed clear, apart from the binned rubbish outside the barber's shop, and it was less than fifty yards long.

As soon as they turned into it, Sam realized she had made a mistake.

A leering wolf whistle came first, then two Chinese youths were pushing past them to block the way ahead. Another four followed behind, and increasingly closely. They were all wearing jeans and sneakers, with T-shirts or windcheaters, most of which were emblazoned with Hollywood logos.

'Please let us pass,' Sam said, trying to sound unflustered as the first two youths stood in their path. They simply laughed and spread their arms to cover the way. Sam turned but the others were right behind them.

'No hurry, ladies.'

'We have a train to catch.'

'Trains? There are hundreds of trains.'

The youths were now surrounding them, the sense of menace growing, and backing them into the darkened doorway of the barber's shop. The girls held hands.

'I'll scream!' Sam spat, tossing her head defiantly. The beads amongst her braids gave the

206

sound of a rattlesnake.

'She wants to scream?' the gang leader mocked. 'We'll show her how to scream.' And the youths had whooped and shouted at the top of their voices until the sound echoed down the alleyway. No one paid the slightest bit of notice.

'What do you want?' Sam asked, knowing that she sounded very much less brave. 'We don't have much money.' She opened her bag as if to show them, although in the dark they wouldn't have been able to see.

'Please ... don't hurt us,' Edwina begged. She was trying very hard not to cry.

The youths said nothing, but pressed more closely in upon the girls.

'Take our bags,' Sam said, holding out hers. The offer was ignored.

After the gang's cries and screams, the silence in the alleyway had become terrifying. Sam could barely make out the youths' faces, even though they were close enough for her to smell the leader's deodorant, cheap and sweet. She wanted to vomit. Then he spoke.

'Lovely hair.' The words had a sinister sound. He reached out and began fingering the braids and the beads. Sam pulled back but there was nowhere to go.

'I like your hair,' he insisted, tugging at the tresses.

Sam shook her head.

'I *want* your hair.'

Meaning? Then, in the darkness, she saw something flash. And flash again. It was a Stanley knife, sharp as any razor, its blade exposed. She wanted to scream but discovered that every part of her was frozen.

He waved the blade slowly in front of her face, so that he could watch her eyes following it from side to side. 'It is very sharp,' he whispered, relishing her terror. Then he put the back of the blade to her face, drawing it across her eyebrows like a pencil. She choked, waiting for the blood to trickle into her eyes. But none came.

'Are . . . you going . . . to rape us?' Sam gasped.

'No. I simply like your hair. *Very* much.' And he slit through one of the braids. She gave a strangled cry but dared not move her head, the blade was still circling.

Then another braid came off.

Tears—or perhaps it was blood, she could no longer tell—began burning down her face like tiny streams of lava as once more he hacked, and yet again. Some of the beads fell to the pavement, bouncing around her feet, and one of the youths sniggered. All she could see was dancing of the blade, and the purpose in his eyes.

Again and again the blade hovered in front of her cheeks before the knife cut and carved and hacked its way through her hair, until it was all gone. He held out a fist full of her braids. 'I *like* your hair,' he whispered.

'I like the rest of her, too,' one of the other youths muttered. Then his hand was on her breast, pawing.

And the blade flashed again, slashing across the back of the youth's hand. He screamed in surprise.

'You little banana,' the leader spat, 'that's not what we came for.'

The youth was whimpering and wrapping a handkerchief around his hand to staunch the flow of blood. No one else said a word. The leader waved his fistful of hair once more, a victory trophy, the amputated braids wriggling like serpents between his fingers.

Then they were gone, into the night.

*   *   *

Goodfellowe pushed eagerly on the pedals as he cycled back from the House. He'd bought some candles—the lighting in his apartment was of a strictly utilitarian and non-seductive nature and he had begun to recognize its limitations. There were also two bottles of wine in his basket (something exploratory and Argentine from Sainsbury's), some mineral water and a file of papers Mickey had insisted he take home, but which he had no intention of even opening. Oh, and a box of matches. For the candles. He'd almost forgotten the matches and had to make a special stop at the all-night store on the corner of Trafalgar Square. Candles with no matches. Like a plane without an undercarriage. Not going to get him anywhere.

As always at this time of night Gerrard Street was busy and he weaved his way carefully through the throng, sounding his bell, an incongruous figure in the crowd. People smiled, he smiled back. Such a change, he thought, from that time when there had been no smiles, only dark depression, when he'd had nothing, and no one, except for Sam and the Black Dog. And even Sam had often not been there. He would sit alone, surrounded by memories and debts. In silence. Eventually it had begun to affect his judgement. He had grown isolated, extreme, lost many friends. Only the best had

209

stayed. He'd even lost Elizabeth. She complained that life for him was always a fight, that if he wasn't already embroiled in a confrontation he'd go out looking for one. But life *was* a fight, he'd argued. Kids from his background weren't born to expect reward, only retribution. Oh, but she'd been right, though. You couldn't fight all the time. It wore out not only the body but also the soul; it also wore out those you loved. So nowadays he picked his fights more carefully—at least, he thought he had, until he'd bumped into these troublesome Tibetans. A real rust spot on life's burnished armour, that lot. He was fed up trying to be another Lancelot roving the world in search of injustice and infant gods. Mind you, if there was a Guinevere to help out . . . He couldn't deny that his aspirations on that front usually turned out to be about as collapsible as his bloody bike, but, he promised himself, not tonight. Not tonight!

He stabled his bike in the small cupboard beneath the stairs and hurried up to his second-floor apartment. He had a lot to do—shower, fresh clothes, candles, select some music—and only about ten minutes before Elizabeth was due to arrive. He scrabbled in his pocket for his keys but found he didn't have to bother. The door was already open.

He had been burgled. No vandalism, nothing obvious missing, but his desk had been ransacked and papers were strewn everywhere. Why burgle him? he demanded of the walls. He had so little of value. And what the hell had they expected to find among his papers, nuclear missile codes and lists of Ministerial mistresses? He felt victimized, almost violated, and for a moment teetered on the brink of

210

melancholy. Then he stepped back, angry with himself. No way was he going to let these bastards win, no matter who they were. But first things first. He opened one of the bottles and poured himself an exceptionally large glass.

He was on his knees, tidying the papers, a half-empty bottle by his side, when there was a knock at the door. He turned. It was Elizabeth.

He swore.

'And greetings to you, too, Tom.'

'Sorry. Not quite the candle-lit welcome I'd planned,' he apologized. 'Been bloody burgled.'

'Have you called the police?'

'Doesn't seem a lot of point. I'm not sure anything's missing. And they didn't break in, the lock's not damaged.'

'A professional job, then?'

'Not very professional if they chose me as a target!'

'Unless they knew who you were, that it was you.'

'Of course they did.' Sod it.

That was why he couldn't call the police. He was a target, too, and there would be too many clumsy enquiries—about god-kings, about the Chinese connection, about Kunga. He couldn't tell them about Kunga; it might end up killing him. So he wouldn't tell them anything at all. Oh, but why tonight of all nights, when the only thing he wanted to dwell upon was Elizabeth? He looked across the room, she was all ankle and thigh and—oh, bugger the burglary. It was time to get shot of this Tibetan tangle. He had no time for all this. OK, so the Tibetans were decent, but also chaotic, and Tibet was a million miles away. What did it matter to him? Not as much as Elizabeth. He'd done

211

enough—no, too much! Time to wash his hands. He was about to tell her of his decision and put his life back on course when he was interrupted by a persistent, almost violent ringing of the bell downstairs. It hesitated, but started up again almost immediately. Then, through the night, came a wretched cry of despair.

'Daddy . . . !'

Goodfellowe found himself flying down the stairs three at a time, almost tumbling in his haste. Sam was kneeling on the step, Edwina standing behind her. There were tears on her face, and blood splashed on her blouse. Her clothes were dishevelled, she seemed to have vomited and her hair . . . Her hair was grotesque, like the Medusa, and for a moment he could not move. Then, with all the tenderness he could find, he gathered her in his arms and guided her up the stairs.

Sam stood trembling and speechless in the middle of the room. Edwina sobbed quietly. Goodfellowe was in turmoil. Then Elizabeth was beside him, taking control. 'This is woman's work,' she instructed, ushering him aside and leading the girls in the direction of his small bathroom.

'It's all right, Daddy,' Sam whispered over her shoulder, trying to find a brave smile. 'I haven't been raped, nothing like that.'

He closed his eyes and felt sick inside. 'I'll call the police.'

'No, Daddy! Please, we're all right. No questions.' Not about why they had come to London or where they had been. So for a change both father and daughter found themselves of one mind—no police. But it was with great reluctance and more than a little doubt that he allowed the phone to fall.

It hurt, how it hurt. He was her father. This shouldn't have happened, not to his daughter, not on his doorstep. Somehow he had let her down. Again.

Yet perhaps in all this there was something to hold on to. Sam, in trouble, had come running to him. That made him feel a little better inside. And she appeared to have accepted Elizabeth's presence without qualm or question. That might yet prove to be the brightest blessing of all. Later, after the women had re-emerged and Sam and Edwina were reliving and only modestly reinventing their ordeal for him, Elizabeth busied herself with making coffee, finding tissues, being an unobtrusive comfort.

It was also Elizabeth who voiced the fear that had been lurking in Goodfellowe's mind. 'A burglary and an attack. All in a few hours. You're going to tell me it's coincidence, Tom?'

'Tell me again, Sam, what he said at the end. The leader. As he attacked the one who . . .'

'Who pawed me? He called him a little banana. What did he mean, Daddy?'

'Banana? A Chinese insult. Yellow on the outside, white on the inside. And bent.'

'Then he said, that's not what they had come here for.'

'Oh, Buddha,' he moaned. 'Do you understand what this means?'

'That it wasn't an accident. They knew who I was. That I was your daughter.'

'My fault. All my fault.' Remorse flooded his voice.

'Don't be silly, Daddy.'

'I've been helping save Tibetans. It's caused a lot of trouble. I was going to give it up. I shall have to stop now.'

'Not bloody likely,' retorted Sam.

'What?'

'Give up? Because of this?'

'Of course because of this.'

'You want them to win?'

'No, but I can't have you—'

'Daddy, you think it's the first time I've been felt up in a dark alley?'

The veins in his neck bulged in alarm.

'Although normally I don't take on six guys at once,' she continued. Edwina managed to muster a giggle. Not much of a joke, but in the circumstances any joke was better than tears.

Was this what he paid thousands of precious pounds for every term? he wondered. But there was also pride. She was a fighter.

'Honestly, Daddy, you can't stop just because of this; it's all the more reason to carry on. And somehow it helps to know that it was for a purpose, for you. Much better than having been chosen at random.' She put her arms around him and squeezed, like she used to when she was half her age. 'Look, no harm done.'

He looked down upon his daughter's hacked and savaged hair. 'Can you forgive me?'

'On one condition, perhaps.' She buried her head in his chest.

'What condition?'

She looked up, her eyes sparkling through tears. 'That you pay for my hair extensions.'

She was laughing at him, the laughter running like spring water and washing away their pain.

'The girls have missed their last train, Tom,' Elizabeth reminded him, practical as ever.

'They can stay on the sofa.'

'Then you'd better call Edwina's mother and explain.'

As he helped the girls prepare the sofabed, he kept turning the events in his mind, examining them from all sides. There were no coincidences, only connections. He had no doubt that the burglary and the attack were intended to be a warning to him to stay out of the Dalai Lama matter. They wanted him to know that next time, perhaps, Sam might lose more than her hair. But how did they know about him and what he was up to? He had no public connection at all with Tibet. Yet, as always, the Chinese seemed to be one step ahead, to know everything that was going on.

He telephoned Edwina's mother, explained simply that they had missed the last train, nothing to worry about, that he would make sure Edwina ate something other than chocolate for breakfast—'Thank you, Mr Goodfellowe, preferably fresh grapefruit and a little Earl Grey with lemon; she's so casual about her diet.'—then turned to find the girls already clambering unselfconsciously and exhaustedly into their bed. He, too, felt as though he had been folded a hundred times. And the papers were still scattered everywhere. He swept them up in his arms and threw them into a pile for the morning.

Wearily he finished off the last glass of wine and put away the unlit candles. They would have to do for another day. He looked round for Elizabeth. As he did so the last of his energy drained through the soles of his shoes.

215

She was at the door. Coat on. A mournful smile that seemed to twist her full red lips in sorrow, an expression of both disappointment and determination in her eyes that brooked no argument. She stood only across the room but might have been a million miles away. And growing more distant. Then, without a word, she was gone.

CHAPTER NINE

Goodfellowe was not a man long on patience and neither was he a creature of the morning. By the time he had got the two girls roused, restored and off to their train, he was already grinding his teeth and in need of a little pampering. So he wandered down Gerrard Street to Chou's place for some tea. Like Goodfellowe, Chinatown woke slowly. The mid-hours of the morning were still sleepy, almost gentle. Goodfellowe sat himself down with a newspaper and a pot of tea while he watched Chinatown stir itself and come slowly to life.

Chou's restaurant could best be described as rudimentary, dressed in an assortment of cheap veneers and gaudily coloured lights, and frequented largely by Chinese who used it as something of a social club. Far more business was conducted across the tables by his customers than by Chou himself, but this caused him no great concern. It gave him contacts, enabled him to keep many friends and, in the margins of their friendship, to maintain a sound investment portfolio. And the modest surroundings helped keep the tax man off his back.

Not that everything was harmony. At the rear of

the restaurant, full-scale hostilities had broken out in guttural dialect between Chou's wife and the fishmonger who was trying to get her to accept the day's delivery of fish. Chou was keeping well out of the way; he preferred the quiet life. Which was why any Westerners who came through his door with push chairs were told the place was full up—'No room! No room!' he would gesticulate, shooing them off—while he allowed in any number of Chinese children. They knew how to behave themselves. Unlike Western kids. Or his wife. He lit a cigarette and drew deeply, filling his lungs and getting the kick-start to the day that would see him through until the small hours. He smiled encouragingly at Goodfellowe. Chou was an inveterate chatterer. He always had something to say. Goodfellowe waved him to a seat.

'Trouble?' Goodfellowe enquired, nodding in the direction of the battle.

'My wife say prawns look . . .'—he struggled for the word—'unhappy. It happen every day.'

'Then why not fire the fishmonger?'

'No, no, Mr Minister! He my best friend. Come from same village in Hunan.' Chou smiled broadly through crooked teeth. 'Prawns always very good. Frozen very fresh.'

'So why the row?'

'Just business. My wife want to make sure prawns are also frozen fresh tomorrow.' He shrugged philosophically. 'Marriage is business, too.' Chou had no intention of intervening; the fishmonger would have to earn his money the hard way.

'Everything is business in Chinatown, Mr Chou.' Goodfellowe chuckled.

Chou nodded enthusiastically, and a thought

217

began to rattle around in the back of Goodfellowe's head.

'Tell me, if I had lost something very precious, or even someone, a person, and I wanted help looking for him, could I get any help? Around Chinatown?'

'Sure-sure.'

'How?'

'Chinatown like a big notice board, Mr Minister. You want something. Somebody find it for you. For a price.'

'And if I wanted a lot of help. In a hurry?'

'Sure thing, Mr Minister. Bigger hurry, bigger price. You want something, you let me know. I put word around for you. I good at putting word around.' He beamed. Being a gossip of gargantuan proportions was part of his trade, and he was a master at it.

Goodfellowe studied his cup. 'And what if I wanted something a little unorthodox? No questions asked. If I had made a bad friend, for instance? Wanted him to feel . . . uncomfortable?'

Chou nodded thoughtfully, his head grown heavy, along with the price. 'Then more money. Up front.'

'And if I had made a very bad friend . . . ?'

Chou drew once more on his cigarette, enveloping himself in a cloud of blue haze. At last he reappeared, smiling, with a mouth full of broken and badly stained teeth. 'Very bad friend, very good business.'

'You could help me, Mr Chou?'

Chou's smile suddenly shrivelled. This sounded all too much like a leading question. 'No, not with very bad friend. For that you go elsewhere. Four or five places in Chinatown for such very good business. Clubs. Families. You know?'

'You mean gangs. Triads.'

'Perhaps.' Chou thought he had already said too much but did not wish to give offence. 'But no good for you, Mr Minister. You not Chinese. Sorry.'

'That makes a difference?'

'Don't mix with Chinese bad boys, Mr Minister. Look, Chinaman want to screw Chinese girl, you go ask barber and he give you address in Queensway. Westerner want to screw a Chinese girl and price double. Then she take him to hotel where she says she has a room. But front desk suspicious, she explain. So she get him to wait outside back door while she go round front to open it. You know what? He still waiting at Christmas.' Chou began to laugh, hoping that the tale had diverted Goodfellowe's enquiries. 'Anyway, she probably not Chinese but Filipino. So don't mix with bad boys, Mr Minister. Or bad girls!'

Goodfellowe nodded indulgently. 'I shall accept your advice in everything, Mr Chou. Including the prawns.' Chou looked relieved. 'But if I were Chinese, with bad friends, I could get help in Chinatown?'

'Maybe.'

'A lot of help? An entire army, perhaps?'

The answer dribbled out slowly. 'May-be.'

Oh, no, concluded Goodfellowe, no maybe about it. For sure. And someone had done it. Got themselves an entire private army roaming the country looking for one small boy.

'I hadn't realized there were so many—how can I put it?—possibilities in Chinatown.'

'Two hundred thousand Chinese in Britain. Plenty possibilities, Mr Minister.'

219

Two hundred thousand, thought Goodfellowe. And barely two hundred Tibetans. A thousand to one. He hadn't realized the odds were so immense. Or that it might be so easy to get someone burgled, battered or even burnt out.

You could do anything in Chinatown with money. Buy a woman, a man, a life.

Or a child.

*   *   *

Mickey arrived carrying a pile of mail, behind which were lurking two new shirts. She had a habit of bringing him items of clothing—shirts, sometimes a sweater, and since he'd begun to trim up in the gym even some exotic underwear. She had a cousin in the trade, she told him, which was true, who gave her samples, which was only half the truth. The items were inexpensive, for what they were, but not free. Her treat. And, for the sake of his male pride, her little secret.

Goodfellowe was a challenge. It wasn't that he enjoyed being unkempt, more that he had mislaid the art of looking at himself critically. With a wife in a nursing home and a daughter at private school, the end of most months left him with little to look at other than bank charges. His own needs came so low down his list of priorities that all too often they simply dropped out of sight. So Mickey helped. In little ways. And usually without Goodfellowe knowing. Getting deals on office equipment. Making sure he claimed all his allowable expenses—and, it had to be admitted, occasionally some that might not have been technically allowable. Finding a dry-cleaners that didn't kick the stuffing out of his suits. And, of course, fresh shirts and ties. His life was a mess, but he didn't have to look it. Not all the time, at least. Not until his next bike ride in the rain.

This morning, however, she seemed to have lost the battle. 'You've got that completely bonked-about look. As if you've had no sleep at all,' Mickey offered, studying the tussles in his hair. She took a flier. 'Your date with Elizabeth catch fire?'

Goodfellowe growled like a cornered dog. He'd been trying to call Elizabeth all morning and kept getting the answering machine.

'It's very simple,' he began. 'I've been burgled. I have a pregnant teenage daughter who's been attacked in the street, and a girlfriend who isn't talking to me. I also have a splitting headache, a rude letter from the credit card company and you as my secretary. In ascending order of aggravation. I also have a group of Tibetan friends who are a complete and utter pain in the bicycle seat. Meanwhile I'm also expected to rescue the rainforests by lunchtime. Does that explain it. clearly enough for you?'

'Great. Here's your mail,' she replied, dumping the most enormous pile of papers on his desk. 'And there's a running three-line Whip that should keep you out of mischief until well after midnight.'

'Bugger off.' It was all he could find to say.

'There you go, being all intellectual again.' She smiled sweetly, and kissed him on his forehead. 'And here's a couple of new shirts. Pink. And a cheerful primrose yellow. To brighten up your miserable life and that bloody awful grey suit.'

She dropped them on the desk in front of him. He had the grace to look suitably mortified.

'Oh, hell,' he mumbled, as though her kindness had cheated him of an excellent opportunity to denounce the wickedness of the world. 'You know, at times I get fed up having to say sorry to you. Anyway—sorry.' He struggled to find some way out of the hole he had dug for himself. 'Er, so how was your evening?'

'Me, I had a wonderful night. Dreamt of ceramic tiles and a deposit on my own flat.'

He didn't want to do it but he had no option. He laughed.

'That's better then,' she concluded.

'Oh, if only it were, Mickey. It's just that I haven't got the slightest idea what to do about any of the complications in my life. What did Sun Tzu say? Something about being killed with confusion?'

She retrieved the slim volume from the shelf and placed it on top of his correspondence. He'd grown attached to it and would often spend an idle moment meandering through its pages.

'Anyway, if you've got time this morning for anything important, you might want to join the fun about the Minister for Sport,' she continued. 'Seems she's got herself pregnant, which is wonderful. Historic. Never happened before, a Minister giving birth. Trouble is, her husband had a vasectomy five years ago and we've opened a book about who the randy rogue is. It's neck-and-neck at the moment between the Junior Minister for Agriculture and the goalie at Blackburn Rovers, although she did take a close interest this past season in the English rugby squad and my money's on ... Goodfellowe? Are you joining us today, Goodfellowe?'

He was lost in another world, the volume of Sun

Tzu open on his lap.

'Could it be? Could it be?' he whispered softly.

'Be what?'

'That the Dalai Lama was telling us all along where we should look?'

'How would he know? He's dead.'

'Mickey, this might just—'

The ringing of the telephone cut through his thoughts. Mickey answered it.

'Confusion travels fast, and has arrived,' she answered. 'Your Tibetans are waiting in Central Lobby.'

'Of course they are!' he exclaimed, suddenly full of enthusiasm, and dashed for the door. He was about to disappear when he turned. 'Oh, and the shirts are great. Thanks. I mean it. For everything.'

'Go lose yourself, Goodfellowe.'

Five minutes later they were all gathered in one of the airless basement meeting rooms beside the Great Hall, booked on the telephone that morning when he'd realized they could no longer go on meeting in his compromised apartment. His home had become a target, too. The Palace of Westminster offered security and, amongst the crowds of tourists flocking through, four foreign faces were unlikely to attract attention. But he found the Tibetans downcast, deflated. Their mood grew even darker as he recounted the story of his burglary and the assault on Sam.

'There have been other assaults, too,' Phuntsog added, 'on Tibetans. The Chinese are growing more desperate.'

'Which means they haven't found the child.'

'But neither have we.'

The Tibetans fell to arguing amongst themselves.

223

'We've checked every family twice and three times. Found nothing.'

'There is no boy in the whole of the Tibetan community who is two years old, or anything like it.'

'There is. There must be.'

'A different age, perhaps?'

'Not possible.'

'Another country?'

Kunga gazed at his palm and shook his head.

'I told you. We've got it wrong. He doesn't exist,' Phuntsog muttered.

They were on the edge of despair; defeat would not be far behind.

'Or maybe he's not Tibetan at all.'

Goodfellowe's words hit them like smelling salts. They looked at him as though he were mad.

'Of course he's Tibetan,' Wangyal exclaimed. 'He's the Dalai Lama!'

'Not one of us? You may as well question whether the sky is blue.'

'Or a mountain high'

Only Kunga did not join the attack. 'What is in your mind, Tummo?'

'When I met His Holiness, he said something very curious to me. I've always remembered it, though never understood it. He said the future had a Chinese face. What did he mean?'

The question was met with a row of blank faces.

'Then just a few days before he died he sent me this book,' Goodfellowe continued, waving the volume of Sun Tzu. 'Once more he wrote in it, that the future has a Chinese face. He emphasized the point.' He passed the book around for them all to see.

'A message of failure?' Wangyal asked mournfully.

'Or perhaps a message of hope,' Goodfellowe replied.

'Hope, Tummo?'

'Do you accept that the new Dalai Lama is the future?'

'Of course.'

'And the future has a Chinese face?'

'If His Holiness said so.'

'Then the new Dalai Lama is Chinese.'

'Impossible!'

'Unthinkable.'

'Monstrous!'

'But wait.' It was Kunga, holding back their outrage. 'His Holiness spoke to me of how his rebirth was to be dedicated to peace. Reconciliation through reincarnation, he said. Bringing China and Tibet together. Saving our country. Showing the Chinese they have nothing to fear. What better way might he have chosen than this?'

'No, Kunga!' The other Tibetans were as one.

'But when has the colour of his nose or the slant of his eyes been of such importance? What matters is the spirit inside, not the shape of the body.'

'Can you truly believe this, Kunga?'

He picked up the battered book, one of the last things his master had touched before he died. Kunga examined the inscription, stroked the spine, closed his eyes to make contact, to hear its message. He spoke simply. 'These things are a matter of faith. But I believe you, Tummo Godfella.'

They fell to silence. Most of them didn't want to

225

believe what they were being told. It went against the grain of their history and all the lessons it had taught them. But who were they to argue with a holy man? They had no choice. It was Phuntsog, caustic and sceptical, who eventually spoke.

'So how on earth are we supposed to find one small boy amongst two hundred thousand Chinese?'

'A good point,' Goodfellowe conceded. 'But at least we have one advantage. We'll be the only ones looking.'

But, once again, he was wrong.

*　　　*　　　*

It was barely a day later when Mo found her in her study. Froggie was with her kicking up a racket that echoed from every wall of this vast office, running back and forth between her desk and the door and discovering he could slide on the polished marble floor. He was sliding just as Mo entered the room, which resulted in him banging himself on the door and erupting into tears.

'Mo! If you can't be more careful I shall put a bell round your neck!' Madame Lin rebuked, hugging the child to her.

'My apologies, Ambassador,' Mo managed to mutter through clenched teeth. She'd been in such a foul mood in recent days that he wasn't keen to provoke any unnecessary outburst. The necessary ones would more than suffice.

The flood of tears was stanched with a bribe of chocolate and Froggie was soon back at his game of slide 'n' scream. 'Such a wonderful boy,' she exclaimed. How could she be so blind? Mo thought.

226

She read his mind.

'You think I'm an old fool, don't you, little Mo?'

'Never!'

'You see me as nothing but a ridiculous grandmother.'

'Ambassador, I would rather die—'

'And you probably will.' She paused, her jaw working in agitation. 'With me right alongside you.'

'Ambassador?'

She picked up a diplomatic telegram that lay on the top of her pile of papers and waved it in his direction. 'It seems our mighty masters in Beijing are displeased with us. They demand to know how it is that we keep asking for so much money yet cannot find the boy.'

'And how are we supposed to find the boy when the money we ask for is not sent?' Mo countered angrily.

'They are suspicious of everything nowadays. So much corruption. It seems that everyone in Beijing is lining their own pockets and assumes the rest of us are doing the same.'

'Then I pray we get back to Beijing speedily, Ambassador.'

Disconsolate, she let the telegram fall back to the desk and lit another cigarette. The morning's ashtray was already full, the atmosphere heavy. 'You may get your wish more speedily than you realize. The Ministry of Foreign Affairs is threatening to recall me. In disgrace.'

'That cannot be,' he gasped in astonishment. 'But why, Ambassador?'

'Because we have failed. Because *you* have failed, Mo. You have not found the boy!'

'Ambassador, I have just this moment returned

227

from Jiang. They are searching everywhere but still there is no trace.'

'Remember, Mo, if I get sent back to Beijing, you will be sent back too. And thanks to the revolutionary zeal of our masters there are now even more football stadiums in which you can be shot!'

'We will find him.'

'But when? Time runs out.'

Madame Lin scowled in distraction. Froggie was standing beside her, pulling the leaves off a large spider grass plant. Madame Lin reached out and smacked the back of his hand. He howled. Mo started. He had never seen her chastise the boy before. She was anxious. She meant business.

'It is not an easy task, Ambassador. Many of the Tibetans have hidden their children, even the girls. So I have instructed Jiang that any child who is even suspected of being the right target is to be taken. By whatever means. You understand?'

'I understand, Mo, that you are a ruthless peasant who would do anything to save his own skin, including slaughtering half the children in this country.'

'And you, Madame Ambassador?' he challenged.

For a while she did not answer. When she finally spoke, her tone was more matter-of-fact.

'Your instructions will have to be changed, Mo.'

'But why?'

She exhaled a long plume of tobacco smoke. 'Because you have been looking in the wrong place. The child is not Tibetan. He is Chinese.'

'This must be a joke. And a poor one.'

'I am not in a mood for joking, Mo. Not with the threat of being recalled to Beijing hanging over my head!'

'Chinese? It sounds absurd.'

'No! Open your imagination, Mo. It is a brilliant ploy. The Lama's master stroke. Identifying such a successor will confuse everything. Appealing over our heads to the Chinese people. He is laughing at us from beyond the grave.'

'What will Beijing say?'

'To damnation with Beijing! Curse them!'

'But don't forget them.'

'No. We can never forget them.'

'So what must I do, Ambassador?'

'You need a new approach, Mo. Tell Jiang to look for a Chinese child. Ransack the community. Get everyone looking for him. But ...'—she wagged a finger in warning—'no threats, no intimidation. Offer inducement. Tell them that when the child is discovered, he and his entire family will be taken back to Beijing in luxury. They will be heroes, with riches beyond their dreams. They will never have to worry about being in want again.'

'Will that be true?'

'Who knows? I will try to make it so, but our masters in Beijing are as constant as the wind in autumn. Yet it must be done. Your life and mine depend on it.'

'This will cost far, far more money.'

'Then get your cousin to work all night. Strip the Embassy. Sell the secretaries into slavery for all I care. Just make sure it is done.'

Froggie had grown bored with being ignored and was tugging at his grandmother's dress demanding attention. She lifted him onto her lap and began a counting game on his fingers. But Mo was still unsettled.

'How will we know when we have found the right child, Ambassador? There must be a thousand of the right age out there.'

'According to the Tibetans, this child is not like others. He has the wisdom of ages sitting on his shoulders. It will leave its mark.' She was running her fingers through her grandson's hair. He looked up and chuckled with pleasure.

'But even so,' Mo persisted, 'there may be a dozen or more like that. How can we tell which one the Tibetans will choose?'

'We may not be able to tell.'

'Then what shall we do?'

She kissed the child's forehead. 'In that case, dear Mo, we shall just have to take the lot.'

*   *   *

The child had developed the habit as soon as he was old enough to be released from his high chair. He would sit at the end of the table, in the position of authority, as though in charge. When he had first done so his father had laughed and pushed him aside, but the ensuing riot had convinced everyone that it wasn't worth the hassle. So he sat and banged his spoon, and soon was not simply repeating their mealtime grace but initiating it, even adding new words and thoughts. The new thoughts were usually humorous. At least, his parents found them so, although the boy was clearly too young to understand the true wit of his own words.

Yet he clearly understood laughter. After his breakfast he would stand before their small shrine, with its prayer scarves and photograph of the Dalai Lama and offering bowls, and place a small amount of his own cereal in one of the bowls. Then he would laugh, pointing at the photograph and shaking with mirth as though it were a cartoon show.

A strange lad, his father occasionally thought, with his spontaneous outbursts of laughter and yet with a deep frown that made him appear as though he were struggling with the problems of the whole world. But he and his wife had waited so long for children, so many anxious fruitless years, that this child was always going to be special. For them at least. And the boy possessed an extraordinary ability to surprise. When one of the laundry machines had broken down the father had spent several frustrating hours trying to fix it, until the boy had toddled along, reached around the back and presented him with a small spring. A missing spring, without which the machine wouldn't work. It was almost as though the boy knew.

*   *   *

Elizabeth picked up the phone.

'At last!' Goodfellowe exclaimed. 'Been trying to get hold of you since yesterday morning.'

'Sorry,' she offered, but it lacked any hint of contrition. 'Hadn't realized that availability was part of our deal.'

Goodfellowe's humour died. He was in trouble again. With all his experience he should be accustomed to it, but still it froze him inside. 'Look, I'm so sorry about the other night. But it was scarcely my fault.'

'Tom, you're always sorry and it's scarcely ever your fault. It's simply that your life is so full of demands you don't appear to have much room for me any more.'

'No, not so,' he protested, and was preparing his arguments when Elizabeth interrupted.

'How's Sam?'

'She'll be fine, I think.'

'I felt sure she would be. She's a remarkable young lady.'

'And so are you.'

He heard an extended sigh, like the deflation of hope.

'Tom. We can't keep going on like this.'

'Like what?'

'Like trapeze artists, always threatening to make contact but somehow never quite succeeding.'

'Don't be impatient, Elizabeth. It's just that this Tibet thing is—'

'Is very important. You and Tibet were meant to be. And all I'm doing at the moment is simply getting in the way.'

He groaned in exasperation.

'Don't take it too personally, Tom—'

'What other bloody way is there to take it?' he spat, provoked. She was being so ridiculously unfair.

'Try to understand. We all come to relationships with experience, and my experience has been pretty unconvincing. My ex-husband could never treat me as more than someone who should be standing at the end of a long line of his daily disasters, to be dealt with if ever he found the time. Which he never seemed able to do. He couldn't find the time to make the alimony payments, not even with a

232

court bailiff standing on his doorstep to remind him. Then . . .'—she sighed—'I made the pathetic mistake of sleeping with my divorce lawyer. I should have known. Because he was busy, too. No sooner had he added me to his extensive list of keenly solicited leg-overs than he found all sorts of other distressed women who required his personal attentions.'

'I'm not like that.'

'You're not? But this isn't just about you, it's about me. I'm walking wounded, Tom, and the wounds take time to heal. And that's more than you can give me right now. Time.'

'What are you trying to say?'

'That I don't want to be squeezed into another man's diary and his bed, then just as quickly squeezed out again.'

'I don't want a casual friendship, I want a commitment!' he protested.

'A commitment you can't give yourself,' she responded softly.

'But I want to try.'

'Sure, and you want to save the world, too, or at least Tibet. I don't mean that disparagingly. I wish I could help you, but I can't.'

Desperately—'I'll give it up.'

'No, Tom. Sam was right; you've got to see it through. It's crazy, out of the question, reckless, perhaps even dangerous. It's you all over.'

'But I want to see you,' he insisted stubbornly; 'I need to.'

'After you've saved Tibet, Tom. Come and see me. Then we'll talk. In the meantime we won't have to keep finding excuses.'

He won't have to find excuses, she meant. But by

233

the time he'd focused on that one, the phone had gone dead.

CHAPTER TEN

Jiang couldn't do it, not on his own. A hundred Tibetan families with names and addresses he could cope with, but a couple of hundred thousand Chinese spread all over the place was entirely another matter. He would have to sub-contract and that, he explained to Mo, would cost more money. A lot more money. There was no register, no central list of Chinese in Britain, and a large number of them were illegals anyway so not on anyone's list. They were scattered like leaves in autumn to the four corners of the kingdom.

So Jiang's men went to see the caretakers of the clan clubs. The clubs were the family associations of the Tangs, the Hans, the Chungs and many others, the focal point within the community where immigrants gathered to keep the flame alive. And at the heart of these clan clubs were the caretakers. They might live in the humblest of circumstances, squatting in their club buildings with little more than a bed roll and a toothbrush, but—and this was a central part of their responsibilities—they knew everyone. So Jiang's men explained their purpose and handed over five hundred pounds to each, with a promise that there would be more if the child was found through any of their contacts. It was not made clear how much more would be paid, because whatever figure might be mentioned would inevitably be haggled upwards and Jiang didn't have the time to waste. So he relied on unspecified dreams of greed to motivate his sub-agents.

The next target was the Chinese education associations. There were hundreds of Chinese schools scattered around the country. Many operated only on a Sunday when parents sent their offspring to learn the mother tongue and the culture of the homeland, and they were hugely well attended. The Chinese were ambitious, great achievers, even the school principals. All of the principals were seen individually, and told that there would be not only great honour but much money showered on their school if one of their pupils turned out to be The Special One.

But even above their education, Chinese value their food. So Jiang's men approached the big food distributors, whose delivery vans visited every Chinese restaurant and supermarket in the country. The drivers were each handed fifty pounds as a down-payment to ensure that the message would be spread and a lookout maintained. It was explained that any firm, and any driver, and any food outlet, which could claim a share of the responsibility for finding the child would receive a substantial proportion of the reward fee. By this time Jiang's men had thrown caution to the winds and were openly suggesting ten per cent, knowing that in the event it would be forced up to twenty. But so what? It wasn't their money.

The word was put round, on every street corner where Chinese gathered, in every restaurant, at every gaming table, through every travel agent, accountant's office, school and social club. Find the child. Gain the glory of having claimed the Tibetan god-king for China. Honour your ancestors by being the one responsible for bringing Tibet once and for all beneath the mantle of the motherland. Oh, and by the way, get rich. One hundred thousand pounds rich. Simply for finding a child.

Rumour grows like bindweed when fed by that sort of money. Even with so many Chinese dispersed in such a far-flung manner, it could be only a matter of days before practically all of them had heard. And even if the parents of the child might prove to be nervous or uncertain of the Beijing Government's promises, there would always be a neighbour or friend who carried no such burden of doubt and who could find all sorts of exhilarating ways to use a hundred grand.

But for the Tibetans, even as Jiang's henchmen were called off from spying on their families, there was only despondency. They heard the word echoing around the streets and knew they had no means of competing. They could not find that sort of money. And they were vastly outnumbered.

Even worse, they knew they had been betrayed. By whom, to whom and for what reason they could not know, but no sooner had they agreed on a course of action than the Chinese seemed to know exactly what they were up to. And to be that vital step ahead.

They had known of Kunga's hideaway.

And of Goodfellowe's involvement.

Now they knew of the Chinese connection.

Everything had been betrayed. And betrayal brought despair. Their race was all but lost.

*   *   *

The pace of activity in the workshop studio of Mo's

236

cousin had increased to almost frantic proportions. The lights burned all night, empty cartons of takeaway food created little avalanches outside the door and Mo's cousin looked exhausted. Exhausted, but happy. Even villains can take pride in their work.

But that was his problem. He looked too happy, And too busy. Such a dramatic change in his normal circumstances was bound to excite still further the attentions of those who already doubted his integrity. Or rather, those who knew that he was a drug-dealing little creep but who hadn't yet gathered sufficient evidence to prove it.

So they watched ever more keenly.

There was no proof that the crates being moved around inside the studio actually contained drugs. Some crates had come in by diplomatic courier from London and elsewhere so the Drugs Task Force hadn't been able to touch them. They could have contained anything. But clearly they contained something, and if the contents were drugs then this would be one of the biggest operations ever.

It could prove to be one of the classic coups of any policeman's career. Commendations for sure, and probable promotion. And the little Oriental bastard had to be up to something. So even though there was no direct evidence and there was the worrying diplomatic connection, a combination of suspicion and ambition swayed the day. The drugs squad wanted a result, and so did the Public Prosecutor. The decision was taken. They were going to bust little Mo's cousin.

*   *   *

Things had changed between Mickey and Baader. They had, at last, taken to bed. Yes, conventional sex. He had borrowed the keys to a friend's house in Gayfere Street—'for a diplomatic meeting that required the utmost privacy'. The friend had smiled indulgently, and given instructions about coffee and clean towels.

It was an old beech-panelled ferryman's cottage built two hundred years ago when Horseferry Road had no bridge, and when there was nothing but the sweat of man and beast to guide people across the river. Now this worker's cottage would probably pull nothing short of half a million pounds if it changed hands. Crazy prices. But Downing Street itself had been nothing but a speculative investment, built without proper foundations. Around Westminster not only the inhabitants but even the buildings seemed to get ideas above their station.

Mickey wondered whether the things she was feeling might also be described as ideas above her station. For the first time they had just done it in private, without any danger of being discovered and exposed. It was such a completely different experience, with so much more meaning. Perhaps that was why he had wanted it this way. Not this time the frenzied discarding of clothes and the almost instant gratification, instead there had been a soft, tactile, mutual disrobing, a new sensuousness, taking the time to explore and discover in a way that made all the difference. He had touched not just her body but also, it seemed, a part of her heart. In the normal course of sexual events he was a buccaneer prince, but today he had seemed nothing less than a king.

He lay cat-napping while, seemingly for the first time, she studied him up close. It was folly, of course. Not the screwing around in dangerous places, because that was up to her and him and she didn't give too much of a damn what the world thought about it—although it might take a little awkward explaining to her mother if it ever became public. No, what was folly, she realized, as her eyes travelled across every crease of his face and around those firm, masculine lips, was falling in love with him. He was married, sure, and a quarter of a century older. He'd be dead before she was a grandmother. But she could deal with all that, in her own way, that in itself was not the folly. What was utter foolishness was that this was the wrong man, a man who would never reciprocate or return what she was willing to give. A love doomed to damnation.

Mickey sighed, uncertain for a moment, then nestled closer beneath his arm, smelling him, wanting him. Hell, what use was folly if you couldn't curl up and enjoy it?

*　　　*　　　*

He sat in his apartment beneath the overhead light. It was a harsh, ugly light which he rarely used, but it was the first switch his hand had reached. He didn't give a damn.

The Black Dog was back, and had brought friends. They were sitting all around, in each corner of the room, their eyes red and sharp in the light of the lamp, waiting for him to weaken, just a little more. Then they would pounce. And they sensed it would not be long. He had known this feeling

239

before, of being lost inside himself, particularly in the years after Stevie had died and Elinor had begun to fall ill. He had followed her down that path, pursued by the pack, although not so fast and in the end not quite so far. Not yet. But that was when he had lost his wife, his only son, his career. Now he had also lost his daughter and the woman he loved. Oh, and the Dalai Lama, too. He stank of failure.

The half-empty bottle didn't help, either. What was he drinking? Come to think of it, he neither knew nor cared, and not caring was another signpost down the path. He had to care, or he was lost.

He sat in the harsh shadows surrounded by his problems, struggling to decide which of them he might do something about.

Not Elinor. For her he could do nothing. And so far as Sam was concerned, there was still more than a week to run of his denying-she-was-up-the-duff ordinance. Elizabeth wasn't speaking to him, in spite of the flowers he'd sent. God, she could be tough, even cruel. As for his career, he had all but forgotten what it was like to be a Minister, just as most Ministers—particularly the Prime Minister—had all but forgotten him.

Which left the Dalai Lama.

And alongside every thought he had of the Dalai Lama, Goodfellowe found the overwhelming stench of betrayal. Who was it? Who was betraying them? He swirled the possibilities around in the bottom of his glass then drank deep, but found nothing except dulling uncertainty.

Was it Wangyal? He'd lost his restaurant, everything he owned, but he'd seemed remarkably philosophical about it, even for a Buddhist. So it might be Wangyal.

And what of Kunga himself? He had been the supposed target, but it was Kunga who had suggested they take a walk at the crucial moment. Convenient. Perhaps a little too convenient.

The burglaries had given Phuntsog and Frasi alibis, but were they no more than that, alibis, perhaps intended and even invented to cover the truth?

Yet although the facts might loosely fit, Goodfellowe knew they did not make sense. He had come to know these men, had seen their agonies, even that of the caustic Phuntsog, and trusted every instinct in his body that none of these would ever betray the Dalai Lama. Yet these four, and he, were the only ones who had known. The only ones.

Then the dark mists parted for a moment and he saw something he had never wanted to see that caused him to cry out in pain. He didn't want to see this. He wanted the darkness to come back and envelop him, but there it was, right in front of him. Understanding. Which brought with it agony. And as the pain racked him his body jerked, his muscles flinched in torment. Without even being conscious of what he was doing he launched his glass against the wall where it smashed to pieces, but still it left him in misery. So he picked up the entire bottle and did the same. It left a vivid blood-coloured smear that dribbled down the wall. Like a monk's robes melting in the fire.

To understand is to suffer, said the Buddha. Goodfellowe knew what it meant.

But there was something to be grateful for. The

241

noise had startled the Black Dogs. They had fled in bewilderment.

*   *   *

When Mickey walked into his office he was standing at the mullioned window, gazing out. It wasn't much of an office, small and cluttered, but it did have a window with a view. Again, not much of a view, because there was a balustrade that obstructed the line of sight, but with a little stretching of the neck Goodfellowe could see across the river to the brick towers of Lambeth Palace on the south bank. The view seemed to preoccupy him. The sun had caught the window, casting lurid shadows into the room, making it seem to Mickey a little like a condemned cell with the prisoner struggling for his final glimpse of freedom.

Goodfellowe didn't turn round, simply instructed her in a quiet voice to sit down. She thought he sounded strained, distracted. There followed an extended period of silence when he didn't move and scarcely seemed to breathe.

'You OK, Tom?'

'No,' he replied simply.

'Can I help?'

'Too late for that.'

Another silence. Then he started.

'I've always thought of you as a friend. Someone I could rely on. You helped get me through the worst times of my life. You were there for me when everyone else had disappeared, apart from Sam.' It sounded as though he were writing an epitaph.

'That's what friends do,' she responded,

242

beginning to grow concerned at his morbid tone and the sepulchral atmosphere.

'I shall never forget it.' He was still staring out across the river, but his manner changed, suddenly becoming more businesslike. 'I'm afraid this Tibetan thing has rather got the better of me. Bloody business. I wish I'd never started, I truly mean that. You know at first, when I met the Dalai Lama and was sent his book—you remember . . . ?'

'Of course.'

'I viewed it as something of a game. Nothing too serious. A squabble on the other side of the world that made me giddy simply trying to think about it. Reincarnation? Child gods? What on earth did this have to do with me? But then . . .'—he hesitated, reflecting—'it changed. Men started dying. In foreign countries, to be sure, but men I was supposed to be trying to help. And the killing didn't stop. It was brought right to my doorstep. They tried to burn out Kunga, and didn't seem to mind who else might have been in the building. Then it crossed over my doorstep. They attacked my daughter, invaded my home, endangered my friends. Can you understand why I've begun to take this very personally?'

'For sure . . .'

'But one thing above all else—above the physical dangers and sacrifices—one thing has got to me more than anything.'

'What, Tom?'

'The fact that the Chinese were always one step ahead of us. Not simply guessed what we were doing but knew what we were doing.' He paused. 'Were being told what we were doing.'

'Being told? By whom?'

243

'Ah, but isn't that the question? I've even suspected Kunga himself.'

'Could it be?'

'No.' Goodfellowe shook his head. 'If Kunga wished to betray the child, all he had to do was to find him then hand him over. Like a Judas.'

'Then Wangyal.'

'Not Wangyal. He could have betrayed Kunga at any time yet still he protects him.'

'So it was one of the other two.'

'No, not Frasi, not Phuntsog. You see, they never knew Kunga was in the country, not until after the restaurant had been burned down.' He shrugged. 'Which only leaves *me*. Because who else knew that Kunga was in town? Who else knew that I was helping him? Who else knew that we were looking for a Chinese child? Who else could have betrayed every part of this to our enemy? Nobody!' He turned, a faceless and threatening figure silhouetted against the window. 'Except you.'

Mickey, normally so at home with words and wit, was suddenly stripped of all her powers. She could only stare at this menacing form in front of her as though he were quite mad.

'There was nobody else, Mickey.'

'You can't seriously believe I would betray you,' she stumbled, already in deep shock.

'But you have. I don't know why, but you have. There is no other explanation.'

'Stuff your explanation. What sort of woman do you think I am?'

'I no longer know.'

'You . . . you just go swivel on it, Goodfellowe!' she spat, thrusting her index finger into the air with great ferocity. 'You're out of your mind. Your

244

brains have turned to bollocks.'

He did not respond in kind. His voice was soft, like the lining of a coffin. 'You knew. About Kunga. About me. About the Chinese boy. And you told someone.'

'No!'

'You told someone,' he insisted with rising heat.

'I never would. I never did. I . . .' She suddenly caught herself, grew defensive. 'The only person I've talked to about this is Paddy Baader. But it was you who talked to him first. He knew you were involved because you bloody asked for his help.'

'Correct. But I didn't tell him that the boy was Chinese. Did you?'

Her jaw dropped, trembled. 'I was only . . . He said . . . Look, you talked to him first. He told me he only wanted to help you.'

'Mickey, did you tell him the boy was Chinese?'

Her lips were quivering in uncertainty. 'I might have done. Yes.'

'And about Kunga?'

'No! You told him Kunga was here. Asked him to arrange political asylum. You told him!'

'But I never told him where Kunga was hiding. Where he might be found.'

'And neither did I! How could I? I didn't know where he was staying. All I might have said was that he was above some sodding Tibetan restaurant. I never knew which one, not until it was firebombed.'

'Oh, Mickey. Oh, Mickey. What have you done?'

She was sobbing now, gulping in air, wanting to fight but overcome by confusion. 'What *have* I done?'

'You told him about the restaurant.'

'But not which one.'

245

'There *is* only one. One Tibetan restaurant in the whole of the damned country.'

'Oh, God. Are you telling me that it's been Paddy? All along?'

'Why? Why did you tell him, Mickey?'

She couldn't seem to breathe, couldn't answer. Something inside was imploding.

'Why? What could make you tell him such things? Share such secrets?'

Her lips moved but made no sound. Then her eyes, damp and desperate, fell in shame.

'Oh, hell, Mickey. Is it as simple and pathetic as that?' There was venom in his voice. 'That he's had you on your back?'

Silence.

'If you'd betrayed me for a great fortune, even betrayed me for a minor principle . . . But for nothing better than a bit of over-mortgaged prick. How low can you get?'

'Tom, believe me, I never knew. I've been betrayed too.'

But her words fell on ears that would no longer hear.

'I'm so sorry. Please forgive me, Tom. What can I do?'

She couldn't see his eyes against the sunlight and for that would be forever grateful, but she could sense all the energy and revulsion that he focused on her. And his words she would never forget.

'What can you do? You're a slut. You can get out.'

*   *   *

The editor of *The Times* enjoyed giving parties at

his extensive home in Hampstead and his favourite occasions were those when he was able to erect a marquee in the back garden and cram literally hundreds in. Even people like Goodfellowe. For his own part Goodfellowe hadn't wanted to go, wasn't in the mood, but it was also because of his mood that he feared not going. Sitting alone with his thoughts in the dark he knew would be corrosive. Drinks with *The Times* was in his diary, so drinks with *The Times* it would be.

Because he was not in a sociable mood he was content to linger on the fringes and feed off the conversation of others. There were many dishes from which to choose. Like the columnist pressing the Minister for what really happened in Cabinet— although it was remarkable how little pressure was truly required. Or the brusque businessman and the willowy actress sharing the confidence that life in front of the footlights could be so lonely, and exchanging telephone numbers. And the bishop and the eco-activist, disputing in increasingly lurid terms how green was God. Did bishops really require full-time chauffeurs to round up their flocks? Then there was a parliamentary colleague of Goodfellowe's, a woman he had always regarded as mutton dressed up as crispy duck, who was demanding to know from a literary agent how much a book might be worth that would expose half the amorous liaisons within Westminster of the last ten years, including details of the dinner party for eight members where the young black waiter had worn nothing but a pinafore and a broad smile. Potentially a fortune, he had advised, but in practice very little. The lawyers wouldn't allow it without the corroborating evidence of someone

247

who actually took part. She puckered her lips. But it was me who took part, she purred.

The agent had just added a zero to the figure under discussion when, in the swirling current of the marquee, Goodfellowe found himself standing near to Madame Lin. She had been much in his thoughts. During his struggle over Tibet, Goodfellowe had never had any doubts that the enemy was Chinese. Not all Chinese, many of whom cared little about Tibet and who would have trouble locating it on a map, and not the ordinary Chinese with whom he lived and shared, but official Chinese. That meant the Beijing Government. And that also meant the Government's representatives, amongst whom Madame Lin was the most senior. Nevertheless, as mayhem had followed murder, Goodfellowe had been unable to convince himself that she was directly involved. She was a grandmother, personable, cultured, had been a friend. It couldn't be, for no better reason than he didn't want it to be. But now their eyes met and they both knew the truth. Her eyes were not unfriendly but defensive. Wary. She knew. She was part of it. And Goodfellowe's eyes, hard and deep-set, burned like a night sky under attack from a shower of meteorites.

He was thinking of moving away when she approached. She did not extend her hand.

'I am sorry we should find our meeting like this difficult, Thomas.'

'Me, too, Ambassador.'

'There are many difficulties in leading official lives. We are not always our own masters.'

'I think I can remember those times.'

'I am glad you understand.'

'Understand, perhaps. But I do not excuse, Madame Lin.'

She nodded, considering. 'Do you not accept that there are times and circumstances when it is justified for a Government to take exceptional measures? To require sacrifice from its own people, perhaps even sacrifice of other people? At times of war, or great crisis? Such as you have had in Northern Ireland, for instance?'

'Of course I do.'

'Tibet is our Northern Ireland. Sadly there have been sacrifices on all sides. I regret very much we are on different sides. Politics makes for bad bedfellows.'

'But for me this is not politics, Madame Lin, this is personal. You have violated my own home. And you have attacked my own daughter. That is what I will not excuse because, before I am a politician, above all I am a father.'

'Your daughter was attacked?' Her voice betrayed genuine shock. 'Please believe me, Thomas, I did not know. And I would never have allowed, particularly with your family.' She shook her head in bewilderment. 'We Ministers give orders, we do not always know how they will be implemented. You will remember how such things work, Minister Goodfellowe.'

'I don't remember ever giving orders to hunt down a child.'

'He is not just a child. He is a great symbol. A great force for good or for evil. Depending.'

'On what?'

'On who controls him. The legitimate authorities. Or terrorists. Just like Northern Ireland.'

249

'But he is a child!' His voice was beginning to rise.

'And I am a diplomat,' she responded with equal force. 'As also I was once your friend,' she added more quietly. 'And perhaps later, when this matter of Tibet is settled and behind us . . .'

He shook his head. 'Neither of us will live that long, I fear.'

'Perhaps not. Then maybe in another life.' It was a strangely ambiguous note on which to finish.

'Goodbye, Madame Lin.'

She was about to take her leave when she hesitated. 'Oh, Thomas. I hope you will forgive me, but last week I took the liberty of sending a herbal pillow to your wife. A small gesture. I hope you will be able to accept it in the spirit in which it was sent. The spirit of friendship. It might bring her, and you, some comfort.'

With that she turned and was gone.

*   *   *

Goodfellowe had barely been able to sleep, troubled by vivid dreams of sitting in his own apartment and hearing cries of lust coming from behind the bedroom door. He didn't have a bedroom door, of course, not in a studio apartment, but this was a dream and it appeared all too horrifyingly real. He had run to the door, determined to throw it open. He knew the man inside was Baader, there was no mistaking his cries of triumph. But who was the woman? It had to be Mickey, her cries of fulfilment growing deeper and more abandoned with every beat of Goodfellowe's racing pulse, taunting him until he could stand it no longer. He was grasping for the handle when suddenly the cries changed, as though from a different voice, then changed yet again, casting him into a torment of uncertainty. There was more than one woman. Baader had more than one woman, was screwing them all, in Goodfellowe's bed, and Goodfellowe hated him for it! In a fury of jealousy and disgust he threw open the door. There, stark naked and with smiles of fulfilment, were Baader's conquests. Mickey. And Elizabeth. Oh God, and Sam too. Tied willingly to the bed. He could see her in every detail, every tensed and articulated muscle, every fold of her young skin. And beside her on the bed, Baader was stretched out, laughing at him . . .

He had got to his office in the House unusually early. He found Mickey, equally red-eyed and sleepless, clearing her desk.

'I won't be long,' she said, not looking up from the papers.

He coughed. Such a stupid, nervous gesture, he thought. But he felt stupid and nervous. He coughed again.

'I was too hard on you yesterday, Mickey. After all, you were entirely unwitting. You didn't mean to—'

'To betray you. I think those were the words you used. Betrayal.' With considerable vehemence she threw a pile of papers into the waste bin, still not looking at him.

'Yes, but . . . as you said, I was the first one to raise the matter with Baader. It wasn't entirely your fault.'

'Personally, I don't believe any of it was my fault. What I did I did for you and in what I believed to be your best interests. It's scarcely my fault that politicians can't be trusted.'

He was still standing by the door, and only now took a tentative step forward. 'It could've been worse. No one died.'

'So you're not blaming me for the St Petersburg fiasco? That's very generous of you. Which leaves me carrying the can only for a little casual arson, burglary and assault on your daughter.' She was looking at him now, her eyes brimming with bitterness.

'This has got out of hand.'

'Well, it's certainly out of my hands now. And good bloody riddance.' Another avalanche of old correspondence descended into the waste bin, which shuddered in protest and then toppled, strewing its contents across the floor.

'Look ... Mickey ...' He coughed again, swallowed hard. 'Please stay.'

'Are you serious?'

'We've been working together, been friends, for how long?'

'You've got fingers. You count.'

'Nearly five years. That's a hell of a lot of friendship to walk out on.'

'Forgive me for correcting you, I know it's not a secretary's place to correct a politician, but I'm not walking out. You bloody well threw me out!'

'I'm sorry,' he said. 'Very sorry.'

'Oh, I see. That's supposed to make it all right, is it?'

'I hope saying sorry helps.'

Flames began to lick around her eyes. 'I said sorry yesterday. And I meant it. Remember how you responded? Remember, damn you? You called me a slut.' She kicked the pile of papers, which

252

scattered like a snowstorm about the room. 'Then you threw me out.'

'Look, I was overwrought.'

'Screw being overwrought. You were way, way out of order. Who the hell do you think you are?' The flames had now consumed any restraint she might have retained. 'You call me a slut because I happened to have sex with a politician. Does that make Elizabeth a slut because you managed somehow to find your way into her underwear?'

'Look, this is—'

'Does it make Sam a slut because she gets into the back seat of a BMW? Lets the boys fondle her. Fumble with her? Then FUCK her? That makes her a slut, does it? Does it, Tom?' She was on the point of screaming.

'Please, Mickey, this isn't necessary.' His lips felt as dry and unforgiving as sandpaper. He worried who else might be listening to every word through the open door.

'Then what makes me a slut in your eyes, Tom? Is it because I enjoy sex? Because I like being penetrated? Because if I want it I take it?' Then a look that suggested she wanted to do damage. 'Or is it because you're jealous of other men having me?'

'For pity's sake,'

'Pity doesn't come into it. You showed me no pity yesterday. All you showed me was your typical male double standards, and it makes me want to throw up!'

He advanced a pace towards her, trying to find a placatory note. 'Mickey, calm down. I've already apologized.'

'But you haven't suffered. You men make us

253

women suffer yet you refuse to take any of the blame.'

'I don't follow.'

'How old were you when you got married, Tom?'

'What's that got to do with—'

'Just answer the bloody question.'

She had stopped shouting now; he'd made some progress. He decided he'd better co-operate. After all, this was nothing to what he knew he would be in for later.

'Twenty-eight.'

'Fooled around with a lot of women before that, eh?'

'A few. Sure. Doesn't everyone?'

'And that's all fine and dandy. For a man. You brag about it, how many times you scored, how many notches you had on your bedpost. You get led around by your dicks. But when any girl reaches out to take you up on it, all of a sudden she's a slut. Because she brings you face to face with all your male hang-ups. That you aren't big enough. That you won't last long enough. That she knows someone who's always going to be better than you are. All the things you worry about with Elizabeth.'

His eyebrow twitched.

'So you take it out on us. Because you daren't accept that a girl might have the same approach to sex as you yet with none of your pathetic schoolboy insecurities. That's why you're all control freaks, because we threaten you. And that's why you feel you have to bring us down.'

'I'm not trying to bring you down.' He supposed he had this coming. He had no choice but to take it.

'Then why in your eyes, Tom, am I a slut?'

'Mickey, you are not a slut. I can't apologize

254

enough for what I said. If there is any way I can make it up to you . . .'

'I'm not proud of the mistake I made with Paddy. And I don't mean the sex; that wasn't a mistake. That was fun. But I misjudged him.'

'I did that too.'

'I know it was moronic and always going to end in disaster. But I was blind. Because I made the biggest mistake of all.' There was a huge intake of breath. 'I fell in love with him.'

Women, he'd never understand them. She was an Amazon who had just gone to war and reduced him to incoherence and shame. Now she burst into tears. She was in his arms, sobbing her heart out. 'Oh, God, how I hate blubbing bitches,' she cried.

He could feel her tears, her heat, her passion. He knew she was right. He was jealous of Baader.

'Tom, is there any chance it wasn't Paddy? Not directly? That perhaps he told someone in all innocence—a civil servant, a colleague?'

'He promised he wouldn't. And after St Petersburg? After they tried to burn out Kunga? No, not in innocence. Sorry, love. It was Paddy.'

'I've made such a fool of myself.'

'I want you to stay, Mickey. Please. I can't do all this without you. I need you. We're a team, you and me. I want your help.'

'And I want to help, too.' Her head was buried deep in his chest. 'How can I help, Tom? To make it better. Tell me.'

He shocked himself almost as much as he outraged Mickey with what he said next. He hadn't thought it through, had arrived with only an incoherent and half-formed idea of what needed to be done. Now he expressed it with stunning

255

simplicity.

'You have to go on seeing Paddy.'

She looked up, her eyes full of confusion. 'But I can't. Not now.'

'You must. It's the only way. We've got to find out what the other side is up to. He's our only contact, the only chance we have of keeping up with them. Otherwise we are lost.'

'But you know I can't go on seeing him without sleeping with him.'

He could find nothing to say.

'I can't just go and say to him, sorry about the shag, let's have a cappuccino instead.'

'I know.'

Her next words were formed very deliberately. 'You complete chateau-bottled shit.'

'Think about it, Mickey. It's the only way.'

'Complete. And utter.' She pushed herself away from him.

'He's used you, Mickey. I want you to use him.'

'But I love him. Don't you understand? That doesn't just stop.'

He swallowed, trying to find a more persuasive argument. He couldn't. 'It's our only chance. Otherwise we have nothing.'

'Let me get this clear, Tom. You don't think I'm a slut. Is that correct?'

'Of course.'

'But you want me to have sex with someone, practically to prostitute myself, simply to get information from him. And that won't make me a slut?'

Deep breath. 'No.'

'I see. But I don't believe. So tell me, Tom. Would you ask Elizabeth to do this? Or Sam?'

256

'That's hypothetical . . .'

'Would you even ask yourself to do this?'

'What do you mean?'

'Here's the deal.' Her lips drew back in a smile, but it was not a pleasant expression. This was revenge, and she was going to take it hot. 'I'll go on sleeping with Paddy. Spying on him, Betraying him. On one condition.'

'Name it.'

'That you sleep with a woman I nominate first.'

'What? Why?'

'Because it's the only way to prove you don't think me a slut. For me to do only what you have done.'

'You're joking.'

'I mean every word.'

'But . . . I'm married.' He shook his head like a dog trying to get rid of a tick; He knew that was the most pathetic excuse. Try another. 'I mean, what about Elizabeth?'

'Explain to her what you've just explained to me. That this is no more than a noble sacrifice. Giving up your body for the cause of justice. I'm sure she'll understand.'

Somehow he had his doubts. He looked alarmed. 'Mickey, I'm in enough trouble with her already. I really don't want to do this.'

'Frankly, the way I feel now I don't give a toss. But that's the deal. You want my help. You lead the way.'

'A bit bloody Faustian, isn't it?'

'Oh, no, Goodfellowe. For me, watching you is going to be fun.'

CHAPTER ELEVEN

Another night without sleep. At some point in the far-off future, the time would come when he would simply fall into bed with nothing more to cloud his mind than thoughts of vineyards and mountains of votes, all of which had been cast for him. But he knew that so long as he went to bed thinking of women, he was lost. Like last night. He'd spent the time thinking of what Mickey had said, and knew he had deserved it, even if he was paying not only for his own sins but for those of all mankind—or at least the mankind Mickey had come into contact with, which seemed a fair proportion of the whole. He was filled with horror at being used, of being treated like—well, OK, like he was proposing to treat Mickey, but being sexually submissive went against the grain in a man. Yet in the very same breath he also found the prospect undeniably electrifying. It sent a charge shooting right through him, his body twitched in anticipation. Trouble was, he had this awful feeling this was a process that was way out of his control, that he was strapped helpless to a chair and would suddenly find himself frying. Oh, but what a challenge . . . His senses were intrigued. Half of them said go for it; almost all of them shouted that this was destined for nothing but trouble.

Anyway, it was no more than an outburst of temper. She'd have calmed down by now.

He found her in the small kitchen of the Dragonaria, the basement beneath the House of Commons where the secretaries toiled. She was making tea.

'Feeling OK?' he asked cautiously.

'Never better.'

'Sorry about yesterday. I truly am.'

'Don't be. I thought we came to a perfect understanding.'

'You mean . . .'—he stumbled—'you expect me to go ahead with this?'

She banged the pot of tea down on the counter and turned. He had rarely seen more resolution in anyone's features. 'England expects, dear boy.'

'Seriously? There must be some other way.'

She went back almost light-heartedly to making the tea. 'Her name is Andrina Capp. She's one of the secretaries here in the Dragonaria. Over in the far corner, in front of the blue filing cabinets. The ones that are usually covered in flowers and thank-you cards. Tea? It's fresh!'

She poured a steaming cascade of the liquid into a mug until it frothed and bubbled, waving the spout of the teapot up and down like a . . . Well, he had no illusions as to what he was intended to think.

'But how do I know that she'll . . . you know, agree?'

'But that's where I've been kind to you, Tom. She'll do it for anyone. Even you. But she's not the least bit party political. After hours she goes in for proportional representation. Reckoned to have gone through half the Shadow Cabinet, practically any of them who's under eighty and not a lesbian. Although she's even believed to have had some of the lesbians, too. You'll do!'

'I don't want to embarrass her.'

'You won't embarrass her. She's brazen.'

'Please, Mickey. Think again. We can surely find some other—'

'You're the one who should have thought, Tom. Burnt bridges, and all that.' She pushed the mug of steaming tea in his direction. 'So that's the deal. You do your bit, honey. Then I'll do mine.'

*   *   *

He had expected a harridan. Instead he found a petite young woman of perhaps twenty-five with blonde bobbed hair, freckles and a hugely engaging personality. Well, it would be, wouldn't it?

'Goodness, what a magnificent bunch of flowers,' he offered somewhat ludicrously by way of introduction. She smiled in the sort of manner that suggested goodness had nothing to do with it.

'You're Mr Goodfellowe.'

'Tom. Please call me Tom.'

'As in Dick and Harry!' She laughed. Or did she say Hurry? He could've sworn she said Hurry.

'How long have you worked here?' he enquired, feeling the eyes of the Dragonaria burning like night scopes into his back.

''Bout five months.'

God, a fast little worker. Hadn't taken her long to settle in.

'Your name is Andrina?'

'Andy.'

'I'm sorry we haven't met before. Would you have time for a drink one evening, perhaps a bit of supper? I'd like to know what you think about this place.' He threw his arms around expansively, trying to sound like an opinion pollster out on a

260

canvass.

'Sure.'

'Er, tonight?'

'Be fine.'

And that was it. He'd picked up a date. Out of the blue. He hadn't done that in—well, since about the time Andy had been born—and he'd come to imagine it would be more like storming a medieval castle, all battering rams and boiling oil, defying wave after wave of repulsion before breaking down the final resistance. He'd expected more obstacles than 'Sure' and 'Be fine'. It had rather taken him by surprise and before he had recovered he'd invited her to dinner at The Canasta in Charlotte Street. Four times what his normal noodle-fest would have cost him. Impulsive fool.

But the evening had brought out the sun. Charlotte Street was abuzz with pavement diners and Andy turned out to be a delightful companion who held views and amusing gossip about almost everyone in the House. He listened attentively— after all, he reminded himself, her views were so well informed. Only two things marred the progress of the evening. Over the wild cherry soup he discovered that she was only twenty-two. Then, too late, he remembered that the restaurant was managed by a friend of Elizabeth, one of those he'd met at her dinner party and who, after Goodfellowe's initiation of the debate about adultery, had walked out no longer speaking to his wife. Now he had spotted Goodfellowe. And Andy. Suddenly she was looking extraordinarily adolescent.

'Tom! Unexpected. But a delight. No point in asking how you are, you're clearly in very good spirits.' The restaurateur deliberately allowed his eyes to linger on Andrina a fraction too long. 'And you, young lady, are in very experienced hands.' He allowed the thought to twist and turn for her inspection before shifting his attention to their starter, one of the cheapest items on the menu. 'I hope you'll enjoy the evening. Why not try the lobster, miss? I can recommend it. Know Tom enjoys it. Flown in from Maine today. First class.' And a price to match. A small revenge for what Goodfellowe had served up with the lobster at Elizabeth's dinner party. 'Be happy!' He turned to leave before throwing in his final offering. 'Oh, I'll be seeing our mutual friend later in the week, Tom. I'll be sure to tell her we met up. Bye now.'

It seemed that in a few short words the restaurateur had taken a meat cleaver to both his love life and his wallet. Still, he'd find an explanation for Elizabeth. He doubted whether he would be able to satisfy his bank manager as easily.

It was with a mixture of pain and rising apprehension that he paid the bill and they left the restaurant. Their conversation had been relaxed and flowing, but as the purpose of the exercise began to preoccupy his thoughts he found it increasingly difficult to discover the appropriate opportunity to ask her back to the apartment. It had been too long since he had approached sex simply as a shag rather than as an expression of a relationship. He and Andy didn't have a relationship and weren't going to develop one, and the words for this sort of situation failed him. He had to find the right vocabulary, and quickly, before they got into the taxi.

He was rescued by the fact that there were no

taxis. Bloody no man's land. 'Let's walk,' he suggested. 'Let's walk,' she agreed. So they set off as dusk was falling and London was beginning to glow with pride. Twilight fell across the city and the frenetic pace of day slowed to one of intimacy, a time when hands were held and bonds were built. Not that Goodfellowe had any intention of holding hands with Andrina, but they were able to stroll and laugh—she laughed most readily—lost in the anonymity of the crowd and without being conscious of the passage of time, until they had wandered through the gaiety and tinselled grime of Soho to a point where they were at the fringes of Chinatown.

'Coffee?' he suggested.

'Coffee,' she replied.

He marvelled. As simple as that. At this rate he reckoned he could become a stud. He climbed the stairs two at a time and threw open the door. 'I don't often bring people up here,' he found himself apologizing.

She looked around. 'I can tell.'

Ouch. Still, he couldn't pretend it was designer territory. Utilitarian, second-hand, a little threadbare, so unmistakably Goodfellowe. Anyway, she was up here, that was the main point. He felt relieved that he still had the candles, and guilty when he lit them. They had been meant for someone else. For Elizabeth. Still, needs must. By this point his hormones were beginning to blur the moral niceties. A little music, a bottle of something Chilean—to hell with coffee—and they were sitting on his small sofa, knees brushing.

'You have very beautiful eyes,' he offered. It would have sounded trite, except for the fact that

263

he so obviously meant it. And they were. Almond, green, like a cat's but not cold.

'You're very sweet, Tom. Not at all like most of the rest.'

'How so?'

'You've noticed my eyes. Been looking at them all evening. Not just staring at me below the neck.'

'Doesn't mean I haven't noticed.'

'Of course you have. But you had the decency to start at the right end,'

'Decency scarcely comes into it.' He swallowed half a glass of wine. 'Hell, I'm almost old enough to be your father.'

'You're older than my father, actually.'

He swallowed the other half to dull the pain. 'And that's a turn-off.'

'Why should it be? I haven't been out with anyone as old as you before, Tom, but you've got all your hair. Most of your teeth. The rest of you looks in reasonable shape . . .'—he gave thanks for the hours of agony in the gym—'and I suspect it all works.'

Was she teasing him? he wondered. Was this part of her turn-on technique? Andy had come with Mickey's mileage guarantee, yet she seemed so natural, so new. With a sudden burst of insight he realized Mickey had set him up, but not in the way he had first imagined. This was going to be a deliberate disaster. Mickey and Andy were in it together and would be sniggering over him in the morning, with the rest of the Dragonaria joining in by lunchtime. Humiliation was to be his punishment.

'Although you wouldn't pass my mother's scrutiny.'

264

'Why not?' he demanded—as if he needed to ask.

'Before I came to work in Westminster she gave me very firm advice. If I'm to make it into *Hello!* magazine, I'm to make sure it's with nothing less than a rich hereditary peer.'

So that confirmed it, she was mocking him. He needed a drink, but his glass was empty. 'Another glass of wine?' He made to rise.

'No. No thanks.'

There was a pause as she looked into her glass. He knew she was finding the words to say not on your life, old man, and goodnight. Then she'd have a bloody good laugh in the taxi home. A little part of him was relieved, most of him was furious, although all of him still wanted her.

'No thanks, Tom,' she repeated. 'I don't want to have too much to drink. Not if you're planning to take me to bed.'

He sat speechless. A little awkwardly she reached out for his hand, then stretched and kissed him. It was a tentative, clumsy kiss. She drew back almost immediately, her eyes full of questions. Goodfellowe knew what was going on. Mickey's plan was to take him to the limit. To bring him right up to the very peak of the mountain and show him all the sights. Then push him off the top.

Now Andy was back, this time not so tentative but soft and warm, her tongue wriggling, greedy, hungry for more. She was up for it. He could feel every masculine instinct within him responding, and had no doubt she could feel it too. She used her own body to urge him on. He felt desperately overdressed. He was still wearing his tie.

And he kept it on. Something within him turned,

the bowstring snapped. He drew back. He still wanted her, more than ever. But not like this.

'Sorry, Andy. I can't. I mean . . . I won't.'

There was no disguising her expression of disappointment.

'Forgive me, but I'm not going to feel right about this in the morning.'

'Why not?'

He took a deep breath, not certain of what he would say. 'Hell, I'm not very good at this but . . . There's somebody else. Somebody I think I love. I want to give that a chance. This would only confuse things.'

'She wouldn't know.'

'But I would. And I can't respect you or anyone else by not respecting myself.'

She thought about this for a moment, searching his troubled eyes. 'I said you weren't like all the rest.'

'Sorry. Hope I haven't misled you.'

She leaned forward. 'You haven't. And I'm the one who's sorry. But not angry.' She kissed him again, very gently.

'Please understand, Andy, this is my problem, it's not because of you. I guess you probably noticed I'd like to sleep with you very much.'

She smiled. 'I noticed. And thank you. Perhaps some other time. If things don't work out elsewhere.'

'I suppose you'd like to go.'

'No, not particularly. I don't want our evening to end just here, in embarrassment. You offered me another drink. I'd like to have it now, if you don't mind.'

And so he had opened a new bottle and they had

266

sat and talked and been friends until well after two, when it became apparent to them both that she was far too tired to go home. She slept on the sofa.

'It's been a wonderful evening,' she offered sleepily as she made herself comfortable under the spare sheet. 'Everything turned out perfectly for me.'

'Me too,' he lied.

While Andrina dreamed, he lay awake thinking of Elizabeth. Of her time in the security services. Wondering whether she had ever 'sacrificed herself' in the public interest. Wondering why he couldn't. Wondering whether he could ever tell her, and whether she would understand. And worrying how on earth he was going to explain all this to Mickey.

*   *   *

In the morning he felt the age gap with a vengeance. Andrina rose with the sun, bright and brimming with youthful energy while he felt and looked like the bottom of a laundry basket. After she had bade an embracing farewell, still friends, he decided he had to do something drastic to come to terms with his dehydration. Time for tea. He took himself off to Chou's. The restaurateur appeared glad to see him, scurrying over in a cloud of tobacco smoke that reminded Goodfellowe of Woodbines tainted with diesel oil. At the back of the restaurant the fishmonger and Chou's wife were already locked in combat and taking no prisoners.

'Mr Minister! Mr Minister!' Chou greeted. 'You arrive at difficult time. Yesterday's swordfish was defrost not fresh. My wife want to chop me up and lock me in freezer with it. I am a coward. Hide me, please.'

Goodfellowe waved him into a chair. 'Sun Tzu wrote that he who fights for victory in front of bared blades is not a good general.'

'Sun Tzu very wise man,' Chou acknowledged, gratefully accepting the seat with his back turned squarely against the hostilities.

'So, Mr Chou, how's business?' It was meant as no more than a pleasantry. His mind was elsewhere. On Andrina. On Mickey. On Elizabeth. At times there seemed to be too many women in his life. So how could he feel so lonely?

'Business bad, Mr Minister, but plenty of it. Which is good business, you understand.'

'What bad business?'

'The child. You must have heard of child. Everyone heard of child. Everyone looking. Big money for finding him.'

Goodfellowe felt the veins in his temple beginning to throb.

'Back home in China this boy regarded as great religious leader. But he lost, so Government wish to find him. Put word out on street. Offer big reward.'

'So why is that bad business?' he asked, very slowly.

Chou lowered his voice. 'Because word put out by bad men.'

'Which men? Who is putting the word out on the streets, Mr Chou?'

The Chinaman looked around nervously, as if to check whether anyone was eavesdropping. 'You know, Mr Minister. *Bad* men.'

'You mean criminals? The Triads?'

Chou didn't deny it. Madame Lin cast a long shadow.

'But why is the Chinese Government using such bad men?'

'Big hurry. Everything big hurry. Want child very quick.'

'So who are these bad men? Who is organizing this search, Mr Chou?'

Chou's thin lips were working furiously, as though nibbling rice crackers. This was a *gweilo,* but a senior and very influential *gweilo.* One he wanted to impress. Chou was torn between his instinct for caution and the desire to share a confidence, to show that he, Chou, was important enough to know about such matters. It was a finely balanced judgement, but one that in the end was resolved by nothing more complicated than commercial rivalry. Jiang was growing altogether too haughty, his dining tables too crowded. He had just bought another vanity number plate, and a new Audi coupé to carry it. The time had come to pay for it all. Chou shrugged his shoulders. 'It's Jiang.'

'Jiang's one of the bad guys? The Triad?'

'He should stick to things he knows,' grumbled Chou. 'Like credit cards. His gambling den.'

'He runs a gambling den? An illegal one?'

'In basement below travel agency.' Chou had lost eighteen hundred on the tables almost a fortnight before and he was still sore. 'But nobody gamble there any more,' he lied.

Except that it was not a complete lie. Several of the illicit gambling dens had closed in recent years, clobbered not so much by the law as by growing competition. The legitimate casinos in Leicester Square and Shaftesbury Avenue had come to realize that nobody gambled with the intensity of a Chinese kitchen hand, particularly one who worked seven days a week and slept amongst boxes of lychees and water chestnuts in the storeroom because he had no entry visa. They had nowhere else to take their money. So the legitimate operators had thrown out their prejudices and their normal dress codes and opened their doors to small-stake Chinese waiters in T-shirts and jeans. Everyone could join in. There was one snag, however, which threw a lifeline to establishments like Jiang's. In order to keep their licences the casinos were required to run games of chance whose rules were recognized by the licensing authorities, like roulette and blackjack. But these were not always to Chinese tastes, and the dens that survived were still the only places to get an authentic game of *fau-ten* or *pei-gau* in which you could win—or lose—an entire business overnight, Chinese style.

In Chinese eyes, Jiang ran a valued public service, but Chou would never dream of admitting it. 'Business not good for Jiang,' he spat. 'Soon he disappear, I think. With VAT money.'

It wouldn't be the first time that a business in Chinatown had folded and the proprietor disappeared along with the taxman's share. Chances were the business would then reopen with a new proprietor who would turn out to be a close relative, if only the records were there to establish the family link. Which they never were.

Chou took a deep drag on his cigarette and drank his tea without offering any sign that he had exhaled. Perhaps he simply swallowed it and converted the nicotine directly into bile. The eyes

270

blinked rapidly as he planned a new thrust on the integrity of Jiang. Meanwhile, Goodfellowe considered the options, all of which looked grim. He was up against not only the Chinese Government but an entire private army. Against them he could muster nothing more than a battered monk and three hopelessly confused immigrants. The odds were overwhelming; he stood not a chance. Not unless he got a break, learned something new. He needed his luck to change. He needed Mickey's help, with Baader. Which he'd just blown. He desperately needed time.

He studied his cup, an invigorating brew of 'eyebrow' tea, so called because the leaves were as slender as the fine hair on a lady's brow. In the green liquid he thought he could see Andrina's eyes, smiling at him. And suddenly he found inspiration.

'As you say, it's a bad business, Mr Chou, this search for the child. I shouldn't perhaps tell you this but . . .'

'Yes, Minister?' Chou was suddenly attentive, his face alert, totally round, like a satellite receiving dish.

'The boy they're looking for—you know it's a boy, don't you?'

Chou had only referred to him as a child. The Chinaman nodded furiously. Goodfellowe had established his credentials in the matter.

'I think it's very sad. These bad men say the boy and his family will be taken care of. But do you know what is truly going to happen?'

The satellite dish swivelled aimlessly, as though searching the heavens for the answer.

'I shouldn't say this but . . . Let me put it this

way, Mr Chou. You're a man of much experience. Do you really trust Jiang and his men?'

The dish moved vigorously from side to side.

'They say that when they find him they'll take the boy back to China. They'll do that, of course. But not in luxury. The boy is regarded as a threat. He'll be shipped back, in a crate, his family with him. And they'll never be seen again.'

Now the receiver was locked on target.

'I'm afraid the boy and his family are in great danger.'

A tremor ran through the dish, as if it was struggling to unscramble all this new information.

'And Jiang is spreading wicked lies about the boy's safety simply so he can get his hands on the reward money.'

Suddenly a power surge seemed to flash through Chou's face, which grew unusually agitated. Moral signals about the plight of an unknown boy were difficult for him to decode; dissecting the financial plight of Jiang, on the other hand, was his daily routine. Chou's eyes clouded in anger. 'That man very bad!'

'I hate to think of an honourable Chinese family being misled by Jiang,' Goodfellowe piled in. 'Giving up their son, giving up their safety, simply in order to make Jiang even richer.'

'That is terrible.'

'But there's nothing to be done.'

Goodfellowe was all pained impotence but Chou had begun rubbing his hands as though about to strangle a chicken. Or, given the current circumstances, to gut a fish. For behind him the hostilities had been resolved and the fishmonger was preparing to leave. Chou knew what to do.

272

'Excuse me, Mr Minister. I must talk with my friend.' Chou jumped from his chair and scuttled off after a man who would be visiting dozens of establishments in the course of the day. Chou wanted to ensure he took with him not only fresh fish but also bad news. The bad news about Jiang. And bad news, Goodfellowe knew, travelled so much faster than the good. Almost as fast as the speed of sound. Spreading such news around the Chinese community might not make it any easier for Goodfellowe to find the boy, but it could confuse the opposition and buy a little time.

And that would not be all. There was more disruption Goodfellowe could throw at Jiang, and retribution to be exacted. For the burglary, for Sam. Retribution for the whole sorry mess. Goodfellowe wanted very much to inflict pain.

Of course, retribution heaped upon the bastard Jiang might not help the Search. But that wasn't entirely the point. It would simply make Goodfellowe feel so much better.

*   *   *

When finally he arrived at the House that morning Goodfellowe went directly to his office. He'd been there less than thirty seconds before Mickey appeared. Her expression declared that this was not intended to be a civic welcome.

'Goodfellowe, what have you done?'

'Done?'

'You slept with Andrina.'

A chink of light burst in upon his doubts. Maybe he could save the deal after all. 'So?' he responded defiantly, if somewhat vaguely.

273

'You weren't supposed to do that!'

Goodfellowe took pause for thought. Then, cautiously, he responded: 'Let's start again. The whole point was—'

'The whole point was to wind you up. To humiliate you. Just like you humiliated me. Bring a little balance back into this equation. That's why I chose Andrina. Because I knew you'd get turned down,'

'Hang on, you told me she'd had more MPs for breakfast than the Chief Whip.'

'So I lied. She's been here less than six months. Hasn't slept around. With anybody, so far as I know, let alone a bloody pensioner like you. That's what made her so perfect. You'd try to get your leg across, make a complete arse of yourself and come crawling back with a little contrition.'

'You mean . . . ?'

'Yes, I mean.' She had the good grace to shake her head in a manner that indicated she had lost control of this one. 'It wasn't supposed to happen. You're full of surprises, Goodfellowe.'

He paused. It was a moment for decision. One of those moments for taking risks. 'I've got another surprise for you. We didn't.'

'What?'

'I couldn't go through with it, Mickey. Wasn't right. She slept on my sofa. I guess I was going to lie to you, to pretend. But that wouldn't be right either.'

She offered no response.

'How do you feel about it?' he asked cautiously.

'Angry. A little silly. Mostly relieved.'

'Because it means you won't have to see Paddy Baader?'

'Because if you'd slept with Andy, in trying to shame you I would only have succeeded in shaming myself. Unlike you, Tom, I'm really not into meat markets and sex swaps.' There was an uncharacteristic vulnerability in her eye.

The ensuing silence tormented them both. Eventually he spoke, very softly: 'What will you do?'

'You mean will I go on seeing Paddy?'

'I suppose that's precisely what I mean.'

She bit her lip to hide the tremble. 'The whole thought of it makes me loathe myself. Makes me feel unclean. This isn't something I can simply wash off afterwards, Tom.'

'I know.'

'No you bloody don't! You broke your part of the deal, yet you still expect me to go through with mine, don't you?'

He couldn't answer, or even look her in the eye.

Her body was as tense as steel, she was struggling to be brave but tears were tumbling down her face. 'I have to do it. There's no other choice. We don't have any other way to fight.' Her lips twisted in defiance. 'But this is my choice, Tom. I'll do it because I think it's right. Because *I* think it's right. Not because you ask me to.'

'I wish this had never had to happen. I wish there had been some other way, Mickey. I wish—'

'Yeah. Me, too. I wish lots of things. I wish I didn't hate you.'

'I deserve it.'

'Suddenly we seem to agree on everything.' She tried to compose herself. 'This has been so demeaning.'

He was about to agree but she talked straight

275

through him.

'So demeaning. To think I could ever believe that you managed to screw Andy.'

He swallowed the temptation to protest and offer evidence to the contrary. Then the implication hit him. 'Hang on. How do you know she spent the night with me?'

'Andy told her flatmate where she was going last night. You got a mention in there somewhere. And she didn't make it home.'

'So who is her flatmate?' he asked with rising concern. 'Discreet, I hope.'

'Her flatmate?' Mickey looked at him curiously. Then mischief shone through the drying tears. 'Her flatmate? Why, her flat-mate's the biggest bloody gossip the Dragonaria's ever had.'

Suddenly his sense of humour had vanished. 'Everyone thinks I . . . ?'

'Played the dirty old man? Seduced an innocent twenty-two-year-old? No, not absolutely everyone.' She began to smile. 'But they will by lunchtime.'

He flushed at the thought of what lay ahead the next time he walked through the Dragonaria. He would have to march past Miss Firebrace who perched behind her Olivetti typewriter—yes, she still used correcting fluid, one of the old timers with old values—like a bird of prey. From her eyrie old Eagle Eyes caught everything. She would stare at him, say nothing. But once he was no longer looking she would pounce and pull him and his reputation apart tuft by tuft, like some piece of rabbit.

He was already writhing in embarrassment. Perhaps Mickey had won after all.

'What are you laughing at, woman?' he

276

demanded.

'Nothing much. Only you.' Her humour suggested the wound had begun to heal. Time to get back to business.

'Then why not do something useful for a change?'

'Such as?'

He pondered. 'Well, you could start by fixing me a meeting at Charing Cross police station. With Chief Superintendent Hardin.'

*   *   *

During his thirty years on the force, Chief Superintendent Hardin had grown cautious about approaches from Members of Parliament. They only ever approached him with problems, never the praise he and his colleagues deserved. A towed car, a little difficulty with a breathalyser, an influential constituent who'd been taken for an expensive ride in one of the clip joints, occasionally a daughter who had been found in unexplainable circumstances surrounded by unexplainable substances. At least, unexplainable to a doting father. Somehow the whole world and its troubles seemed to congregate in Hardin's parish, and some still expected him to have the solutions. But it didn't pay to let these matters fester. Better to tell the bloody politicians to get lost at the first opportunity, before they got the wrong idea. Even those like Tom Goodfellowe, whom he knew slightly and rather liked. He agreed to see Goodfellowe the following morning.

They met on the steps to the station in Agar Street. Hardin had come in his chauffeur-driven

Jaguar; Goodfellowe was pulling up on his bike.

'Good morning, Mr Goodfellowe. How are you?'

Hardin extended a hand, forcing Goodfellowe to juggle with his bicycle clips.

'Hungry, Chief Superintendent.'

'If that's your only problem, it's easily solved. Allow me to treat you to breakfast in the canteen.'

It suited Hardin well. Whatever was bothering Goodfellowe could be aired in a public place rather than within the confines of his office, which would help ensure that whatever demand the politician was going to make would be less unreasonable, and any anger he displayed when Hardin turned him down more restrained. It was difficult to shout for justice or burst into tears of remorse through a mouthful of bacon and egg—except that Goodfellowe chose grapefruit and muesli. He'd been squeezing off too many calories on the hill climber to blow it all on subsidized gluttony.

'So, Mr Goodfellowe, how can I be of assistance?' Hardin enquired as they sat down. He rather hoped for a rambling explanation that, while being delivered, would allow him to get on with his breakfast.

Goodfellowe sipped the tea. Indian probably, although stewed to the point that it would have to go through forensics at Aldermaston before anyone could be sure. 'I wanted a private word, Chief Superintendent. A matter of potential personal embarrassment, I'm afraid.'

So, Hardin thought, he's just like all the rest. Why did they always come to his patch to let their trousers down? He eyed his full cooked English with anticipation. 'I'm used to difficult personal circumstances, Mr Goodfellowe. I can assure you

278

of my discretion.'

'But it's precisely your discretion that's at issue.'

The Chief Super's fried egg seemed suddenly to have turned to wax. 'My discretion?'

'With your friend Mr Jiang.'

'The owner of The Peking Palace?'

'And much more. I've learned that he runs not only restaurants but also illicit gambling dens.'

The Chief Super's fork dropped with a loud clatter. 'Gambling dens?'

'The one in Gerrard Street, beneath the travel agents. Didn't you know?'

'No. No. Not at all. In Gerrard Street, you say? To be honest it's always something of a nightmare finding out who owns places like that. Chinese walls, you know.'

'And Chinese whispers. The word is that Jiang has powerful friends who are protecting him. Friends in the police force.'

'Nonsense.'

'I live in Chinatown, Chief Superintendent. Believe me. The word is on the street.'

Hardin was beginning to look as though he'd contracted a dose of salmonella. 'Who are these so-called friends of his in the police force?'

From the folder he had beside him, Goodfellowe extracted a photograph. It was of the party at The Peking Palace. It showed Jiang standing shoulder to shoulder with none other than Chief Superintendent Hardin. Jiang had his hand on the policeman's shoulder.

'Good God, you're not suggesting that I—'

'I am not suggesting anything. I don't believe for a moment that you have an improper relationship with a Triad leader. But these things are—how can

279

I put it?—open to misinterpretation.'

'That's ridiculous. The evening was an exercise in good community relations. No more. You were there, too.'

'But I am a politician. I'm almost expected to have unsavoury friends. Practically compulsory. I'm judged by different standards to the police. Anyway, I'm reporting my suspicions to you. What more could I be expected to do?'

'So what the hell am I expected to do?' It was a question asked of himself, but Goodfellowe was more than happy to oblige.

'If you'll allow me, I think the answer to that is simple. Cover yourself. Make sure no one can accuse you of showing favours to Jiang.'

'How?'

'Give him a hard time. Why not raid his gambling den?'

His breakfast had become a pool of grease, the yolk staring out like the fading eye of a corpse. Hardin pushed it away in disgust. 'Easier said than done. Proving that these places are used as gambling dens is damnably difficult. They play games no one but the Chinese can understand, games we've never even heard of and whose rules we don't understand.'

'Why is that a problem?'

'Because it makes it almost impossible to prove in court that they're doing anything illegal. Or doing anything at all. No witnesses will come forward. No one will co-operate. All we ever find is a large number of Chinese gathered together with money in their pockets and a lot of rice-paper tokens shoved down the john. Get a good lawyer onto that and we end up paying them for wrongful

280

arrest.'

'But you don't need to prove anything, Chief Superintendent. Simply show that you tried. You raid that gambling den, get Jiang to squeal with annoyance and no one will be able to accuse you of impropriety.'

A shower of female laughter swept in from a nearby table. Four WPCs were setting about a youthful and inexperienced special constable. The topic under discussion was the length of his service and they were firing questions at him with such vivid innuendo that his defences had been overrun and he had turned bright crimson. Hardin seemed unable to share the humour. His eyes were fixed, struggling with the alternatives. 'Jiang's a prominent figure. It would play merry hell with community relations.'

'It's precisely because he's a prominent figure that the allegations of favouritism are so easy to believe.'

'Easy to believe?'

'Even easier if it became known that these suspicions had been reported to you by a Member of Parliament and you'd done nothing.'

His tea was cold but he took a deep gulp. 'That wouldn't get out.' Another gulp. 'Would it?'

'Not from me. But these confidences have a terrible habit of escaping, Chief Superintendent. A terrible habit. We live in such cynical times.'

Hardin examined the photograph once more, looking for a means of escape, hoping it would grow sepia edges and fade to nothing. It didn't. The hand on his shoulder seemed to be stretching for his throat. His mouth had gone dry, he found it difficult to swallow. 'I want to thank you, Mr

281

Goodfellowe, for coming straight to me with this information. You may just have saved my life.'

'No problem,' Goodfellowe muttered in reply. 'I'll add you to my list.'

*   *   *

The delivery men were the first to suffer. They made such easy targets. Any of them who were thought to have a connection with Jiang began to find their paths strewn with unexpected obstacles and cancelled orders.

One driver travelled all the way to Milton Keynes only to be told that the storekeeper had obtained his videos from another supplier. When the driver began to remonstrate, the shop door was locked against him. When he continued his noisy protest outside on the pavement he was diverted by a cry from a first-floor window. He looked up, just in time to catch the full force of last night's noodles.

The protests became a true family affair. In Brighton, while heated discussions were being held inside the store, children were at work in the delivery van itself. By the time the driver departed hurriedly, his argument cut short by the appearance of a kitchen cleaver, the van was trailing yards of disembowelled videotape.

The women proved to be most formidable, chasing off delivery men with a mixture of harsh words and assorted kitchen slops, often accompanied by the banging of woks, which sounded like a drum roll before a battle. Yet even the husbands were angry. They were not only businessmen but fathers, too, and everywhere they kept hearing that Jiang had tried to cheat them.

Many of Jiang's supplies were carried under informal contract by food wholesalers who began to find their own businesses affected by the boycott. No videos, no veg. Soon they were joining in the boycott themselves, suggesting that Jiang find himself other donkeys to carry his burdens.

Grit had been thrown into the smooth-running machine of Jiang's empire. It started to cough and splutter. Even bookings at The Peking Palace began to sag, which from one point of view was convenient since his chef had suddenly walked out. Having spent a fractious morning in his back room trying to sort out his mounting problems, Jiang emerged to discover that misery arrived in many different packages. His new Audi coupé had been penned in by cars that had parked so close they were touching his chrome work. There was nowhere to go. What was worse, he'd left the soft top down, and the bags of refuse from his own restaurant that had been piled at the side of the street had somehow spread wings and begun nesting all over the back seat.

His wife wouldn't speak to him. His girlfriend didn't answer the phone. He found he didn't have enough cash in hand to pay the wages. Then his day really began to turn sour.

The raid on Jiang's gambling club was not a model of its kind, but it didn't have to be. All that mattered was that it took place. Twenty years earlier the basement had been a Cypriot poker club, and not much had changed since. It hadn't even had a fresh coat of paint. Strictly economy class. The steps leading down to the basement beneath the travel agent were narrow and worn, so

283

there was no attempt at a concerted rush by the raiders. An orderly queue of members from Clubs & Vice waited their turn to duck beneath the low doorway, which in the event may have assisted with the element of surprise. The gamblers were still at it as they strolled in. Thirteen Chinese women, none younger than fifty, were in the middle of a game of *pei-gau.* And they didn't welcome the interruption. Their bets had been laid, the money slapped down on the table with characteristic relish, and the young male croupier was counting off a pile of buttons, using a bamboo wand to divide them into groups of four. The object of the game was to bet on whether the very last group would contain one, two, three or four buttons and the croupier was almost there, the tension of the game at its peak, when he looked up in mid-count and froze. The women, however, were constructed of sterner stuff. Their voices rose as one in protest, screaming at the manager for his incompetence in allowing this interruption, before turning their attentions to the police. The room was not large, the mass of elderly women presented an effective barrier of bodies to the officers, and by the time they had surmounted the human blockade and reached the gaming table, all signs of the money had disappeared. They were left looking at nothing but a pile of old shirt buttons.

Undeterred, the forces of the law then inspected the rest of the premises. The tiny back room. The kitchen. The single toilet. The store cupboard. There was nothing more. It was a potential death trap, if not from fire then at least from E-coli. It had no licences of any sort, but then this place didn't officially exist, a sort of black hole for bureaucracy into which official circulars disappeared and never returned. The police stayed for more than two hours, trying to interview everyone present, but the women decided that not a single one of them spoke any English and would communicate only by screaming in Cantonese. And the manager was outraged at the suggestion that Jiang had any form of connection with this place. Jiang who? If there were to be any charges, they would be borne by the manager and the manager alone. But there wouldn't be. You can't build a case on a busload of Chinese matrons and a bowlful of buttons.

Yet the point had been made. The word would get round that Jiang's place had a problem. So Jiang himself would have a problem. His cash flow was getting shot to hell from all sides, his sex life had ceased and it was his turn to have the splitting headache. All because of the child. As rewarding as the project had at first seemed, Jiang was rapidly losing his enthusiasm.

*   *   *

Their relationship had changed, and from both sides. Like Mickey, and in spite of his instinctive abhorrence of commitment, Baader too seemed to have developed something more than solely a desire for physical gratification. She was not simply a great body, there was a mind and exceptionally sharp wit in there too. Not, of course, that the relationship could develop, but he began to feel that at least it might be sustained. The future, as they said, was inevitable, but for the moment it could look after itself. A certain tenderness had

285

developed between them, a familiarity based on contentment, and what had been a strictly private passion had begun to leak into a more public arena. He borrowed houses and flats, let slip the occasional indiscretion. Baader was bending his own rules, because they were his rules and he was masculine and arrogant enough to believe they were also his to ignore. Or was it simply that the risks of exposure which so turned over his testosterone needed to be taken to new and more dangerous levels?

In any event, while his wife was away visiting her sister in the New World, he arranged a drinks party at his own home to which he invited the good and the great. He also bent his rules to breaking point and invited Mickey. Asking for trouble, but he did it all the same. The Baader house was a gracious Georgian affair in South kensington but was not vast and any large number of guests inevitably spread through different rooms on two floors before spilling out onto the plant-filled terrace. His parties were popular because he not only gathered together the standard collection of envoys, politicians and press but sprinkled them liberally with entertainers, sports stars, television personalities and the few famous members of the professions who weren't overweaningly pompous. In such a constellation, Mickey's star didn't seem unduly obvious; there was safety in such a crowded universe.

Yet with the change in their relationship Baader had discovered something that was unusual to him and came as a surprise. He had grown jealous. As he circulated through his guests he couldn't help but notice the attention Mickey was paid by men he

286

knew to be of single-minded and lecherous intent, and found himself circulating rather faster than was usual in order to keep her in view. It annoyed him that he should be distracted in this manner. It was out of character. And it meant that for the first time in this relationship he no longer had it entirely under his control.

So when, during one of his orbits through the stars, he discovered he had lost track of her, he found himself uncharacteristically agitated. Where was she? Who was she with?

As it happened, Mickey was not with anyone. Superficially the evening had been a delight, with several invitations to dinner and an outright proposition from an Arab envoy to fly her the following morning to the south of France in his private jet. Even on the best of evenings it was not an offer she would have considered, but this was never going to be the best of evenings. She had not wanted to come, she shouldn't have come, not to the home Baader shared with his wife, but she was driven by circumstance. She had no choice. It might be the only opportunity she found. Baader's presence was tormenting, all around her, even taking the opportunity of the crush to brush up against her in a suggestive fashion. Every moment, every gesture, every piece of domestic furniture reminded her of what she knew she wanted but could never have. This was going to be a tough one to get over, and was likely to become tougher yet.

Under cover of the crush Mickey took the opportunity to escape upstairs and look around the home. The bedrooms with their lived-in and slept-under duvets gave her particular discomfort. She had never slept with him, except for a brief doze of exhaustion one afternoon on his Ministerial sofa, and for all her liberated lifestyle she knew that one day she wanted nothing more than arguments over toothpaste and car keys. And a duvet under which to snuggle, although the mincing Laura Ashley colour scheme would have to go; she would need something much bolder.

She stopped, screamed at herself. This colour scheme and this duvet would never go. It was his. And hers. It could never be Mickey's.

The study was on the first floor. It was a dark room, made still darker by the failing evening light, half-panelled with rich fabric wallpaper and full-length velvet curtains. Beside the fireplace stood a winged armchair upholstered in deep, cracked leather. It was a very masculine room, his room, not dusted as much as the rest of the house, and she wanted to be in it. The desk stood near the windows and lying in clear view on top of the desk was his Ministerial red box. She knew it would be locked, but she checked all the same, not being quite sure why. It wouldn't be the place for his personal secrets; it would contain nothing that his private office hadn't coded and classified and circulated to a dozen other officials. In Whitehall the distribution lists were often longer than the notes themselves.

If he had secrets they would be in the desk. She walked slowly around it, inspecting it from all angles, stroking its time-polished wood, feeling him there, running her finger along the embossed writing surface. Then she tried the drawers. Those contained in the pedestals on either side were open, stuffed with the usual paraphernalia of folders and papers and assorted pens, but the three

288

drawers across the top of the desk were locked. Not resolutely so, for it was a traditional desk and the drawers were loose and rattled when she tugged. It seemed probable that with only a little encouragement the locks might give. She picked up a letter-opener, a stout object with a bone handle. It seemed ideal. She was about to put it to the test when the door opened.

Baader stood silhouetted in the doorway. 'I've been looking for you. What are you doing here in the dark?'

She almost dropped the letter-opener in alarm, but there had been no hint of accusation in his voice.

'I was waiting for you.'

'Waiting for what?'

'What do you think? All evening I've been surrounded by men struggling to get into my underwear when the only man I wanted to try was paying me no attention.'

'I'm hosting a party, or hadn't you noticed?'

The noise from downstairs was clearly audible through the open door.

'Seems to be managing very well without you.'

He advanced into the darkened room. 'It couldn't manage for too long.' The door swung shut behind him.

'Long enough, I think.'

He chuckled softly. 'You really are incredible.'

'You ain't seen nothing yet.' And she began to move everything from the top of the desk, the red box, lamp, telephone. All the papers she simply swept to one side. By the time he reached her side the desk was bare and he had already removed his tie.

'No,' she whispered, 'let me.' And slowly she began to remove every piece of his clothing.

A battle ensued. War was waged, matching his male appetites, every fragment of which wanted to rip his clothes off and devour her, against her feminine wiles. She teased him, aroused his impatience and ardour, turning every button into a detonator that exploded inside him one by one. Carefully she folded every item of clothing, leaving him standing by the desk like a naughty schoolboy, until he stood completely naked. Then it was her turn, his senses stretched to extremes as he tried to make out every inch of her body, but it was dark and the only light came from the street lamps outside.

Then she was lying on the desk top, adjusting her body to its unforgiving outline, and he was upon her. Even for a man with his unusual drive, his enthusiasm was remarkable. All the time he kept demanding to know which of the men in the room downstairs had propositioned her. And she continued to tantalize him, giving him first one name, then another, and on each he vowed vengeance with growing passion until he was no longer able to speak. For him it was nerve-jangling. Explosive. He drove ever deeper inside her, possessing her in a way he vowed no other man ever would. He never wanted to forget this moment. He felt he had total power over her. It was as near perfection as he was ever likely to reach.

When he was finished it took him several minutes to regain his composure. At last he raised himself. 'Come on, they'll be missing us.'

'No,' she whispered, not stirring. 'I need a little

more time to recover. You go on. I'll see you downstairs. In a little while.'

He dressed in silence. Then he kissed her, more tenderly than he had ever done, and departed.

She did not stir for some moments. Silent tears trickled down her cheek. She hated herself. At this moment she particularly hated Goodfellowe. Still she could not bring herself to hate the man who had just left her.

She hated herself all the more when she picked up the keys she had taken from his trouser pocket and began rifling through his private papers.

CHAPTER TWELVE

It wasn't enough that Jiang should have received an unannounced visit that morning from the Environmental Health Officer demanding to inspect the premises. 'Reports of kitchen refuse being left around in unsanitary conditions outside the premises, sir. And a suggestion that perhaps your kitchen equipment may not be up to regulations.' Three hours of scratching around behind cookers, under hotplates, in the back of refrigerators. Endless notes being scribbled. Then all he would say was 'We'll be in touch.' Like some medieval torturer heating the irons.

Jiang had just sat down with a cigarette to calm his nerves before getting back to wrestling with his cash flow when the telephone rang. Customs & Excise. And not just its stationery department but its Investigation Division. The swindle squad. Not a routine VAT enquiry but an implication of

291

irregularity and urgency. Demanding to come round to inspect the books and paperwork.

His fists beat down upon the table in terrible temper. This wasn't just fate or coincidence, not just a casual and uncomfortable fall of the fortune sticks. Someone was trying to screw him, which made life bad enough. And they were succeeding. But what made it far, far worse was that Jiang hadn't the slightest idea who it was.

*   *   *

Goodfellowe had a favoured place within the Palace where, late at night, he would go to be alone with his thoughts. That's where Mickey found him.

The Great Hall at Westminster was the oldest fragment of the Palace, built six hundred years before with an ancient oak roof that had drawn admiration and imitation from all corners of the world. He regarded this as the place of great survival, the niche of the palace that had defied fire and republic and world war and had stood as witness to so much of Man's tribulation, and even a few of his triumphs. Goodfellowe would stand high on the stone steps that led to the Grand Committee Room, staring down upon the scene and trying to be part of it.

'Let's talk of graves, of worms, and epitaphs.'

'You feeling all right, Tom?'

'Shakespeare. *Richard II,*' Goodfellowe explained. 'Richard built this hall, you know. It was his finest achievement. Something to hand on, something that would survive him. Mind you, a ripe plum would have been enough for that.'

'What happened?'

'They dragged him off his throne and killed him.'

'Terrific.'

'When I come up here at night I think I can feel some of it. You know, this is where they sentenced King Charles. They hauled him away, too. Cromwell chopped his head off and promised an end to all miseries—just like an election campaign. But did it change anything? Hell no. Another of history's over-ripe plums. When it came to Cromwell's turn to die, they couldn't wait to bring back a new king and stuck old Ollie's head on a stick for twenty years, just over there.' He waved vaguely into the gloom.

'There must be a moral to this tale.'

'A pox on Parliament! At the end of it all, this place doesn't make a damned bit of difference,' he muttered, disconsolate.

'That's your job, Tom. To make the difference.'

'But can I? Can anyone? Sometimes I think I can hear their voices, all the great men of the past, and they do nothing but scream and contradict and cancel each other out. What does any of it matter?'

'A little heavy for this time of day, isn't it?'

'I wander through my life convincing myself I'm saving the world from stupidity and bureaucracy. Then I realize that, while I'm out there saving the world, I seem to do nothing but hurt those I love. Like Sam. She's appearing in her play tonight. Cleopatra. She'll be beautiful. And I'll be missing, as always. As I'm always missing for Elizabeth. And somehow I've managed to hurt you, too. Never meant to, never intended it, but it happened and it was my fault.'

She was silent for a moment. Up here, when it was quiet and where dusty shadows fell beneath these great oak hammerbeams, she too could feel the atmosphere. Not understand it, not be in touch in the way that he was, but perhaps that nonsense he had of ley lines and energy channels had something in it after all.

'You know, Mickey, they used this hall not only as a place of execution but also for entertainment. Henry VIII used to play tennis here. A little while ago when they were working on the roof they found tennis balls stuck in the rafters. So that's it.'

'What is?'

'This whole place. Nothing but a load of old balls.'

'Truly profound, Goodfellowe,' she offered caustically, recognizing one of his Black Dog days when it felt as if the whole world was pissing against his trouser leg. 'So you get this far and then start wondering whether it's all worth it, eh? Let me tell you it's too bloody late for that. You don't do what you've done to me—we don't do what we've done to each other—simply to wash our hands of it all. Oh no.'

'But what's the point?'

'The point is you try. Why do you think I can forgive your appalling manners and intolerable tempers that would make me disembowel any other man with my fingernails? Because you try. You make mistakes that are many and sometimes grotesque, but you make them for all the right reasons. The right motivations.'

He heard another voice. Hadn't the Dalai Lama said much the same thing to him all those years ago, that it was his motivation that mattered?

'I think Shakespeare said in the same play that all men are but gilded loam or painted clay,'

294

Mickey continued.

He looked at her sharply.

'Don't do that to me, Goodfellowe. Don't go underestimating me again, thinking you're the only one who can quote sodding Shakespeare. I got my English GCSE, you know.'

He hung his head in remorse.

'So you prove my point. You're not like most men. No one could claim you've much gilding. More a gentle creasing. And you're not painted clay like so many of the rest in this place. That's why I understand. And why I can forgive.'

'I keep giving you things to forgive.'

'Don't ever expect me to forget what I've had to do with Paddy. There will always be a part of me that feels unclean. That will hate you for making me try to hate him.'

The light cast mournful shadows on his face, like a gargoyle on the buttresses meant to frighten the children. 'I'm so very sorry,'

'You said it was necessary. Well, it was.'

'You mean . . . ?'

'Oh, yes. I nearly broke my back on his bloody desk. Then I think I found what you need to break him. Damn you, Goodfellowe!'

He couldn't bring himself to smile in the face of her distress. So he shook his trouser leg. The Black Dog ran off.

*   *   *

Mickey's news had instilled a new mood of determination within Goodfellowe, but it didn't appear to be infectious. When he arrived for the council of war at the small Buddhist shrine in

Bloomsbury, late, trousers tucked into his socks, and breathless, he found troubled eyes turned towards him. The enthusiasms of the band of Tibetan warriors had been ground down by contact with reality. They had survived so long on hope and faith, but the facts kept getting in their way. Particularly the fact that they had no means of finding the Chinese child.

'If only we knew where to search,' Kunga muttered, barely able to conceal his frustration.

'It's like trying to catch a swallow on a summer's night,' Phuntsog complained.

'What can we do but wait,' Wangyal asked, 'until they find the child themselves? By which time it will be too late.'

Frasi simply sat dejectedly and shook his head.

A darkness surrounded them, which the glow of butter lamps and the deep brilliance of the temple colours could do nothing to relieve. They faced Goodfellowe. Not all of their expressions were generous.

'We need you more than ever, Tummo,' Kunga declared. 'I believe you are the only one who can help us now.'

'Be bold, it's not as bad as that,' he encouraged. 'After all, they haven't found the child either. And they're spending most of their time fighting each other.' He told them of the rumours he had planted around Chinatown. And Jiang's troubles. And what was still to come. 'Tomorrow the fire department will be calling. They've had reports of blocked exits. And suggestions that internal fire partitions were removed during renovations.' He made no effort to hide his satisfaction. 'Jiang's not the only one who can spit in the soup.'

'The Himalaya passed every inspection without difficulty,' Wangyal commented gloomily, as if in sympathy with his fellow proprietor.

'And how does that help us find the child?' Phuntsog complained. He always seemed to be the one to complain. Their faith needed to be rekindled. They'd spent too long sitting around, waiting.

'It causes confusion in their ranks,' Goodfellowe argued. 'Distracts them. It buys us a little time. And time may buy us better fortune.' Yet he was all too aware that in their view his words amounted to nothing. A big fat zero. He had to give them something more. He was beginning to find the smell of stale incense oppressive. 'If we were in Tibet, what would we do now, Kunga Tashi?' Goodfellowe asked.

'We would look for a sign, an omen. Listen for the voices that are with us all. In the mountains there are voices on the wind and in the meltwaters as they trickle over the rocks. But we are a long way from Tibet. This is a vast and bustling city, where the voices of the mountains are drowned out. This is your place, Tummo. You must listen for the voices.'

'I've been trying.'

'And what do they tell you?'

'That nothing is ever as it seems.'

'We shall make a Buddhist of you yet. His Holiness used to argue that the facts should never be allowed to get in the way of the truth.'

'But facts are the only means I have of getting to the truth.'

'Your facts haven't helped us get to the child,' Phuntsog offered ungraciously.

'Perhaps because we've been dealing with the wrong facts.'

'What wrong facts?'

'I keep asking myself why we are searching for a boy with a Chinese face.'

'Because you told us to!' Phuntsog exploded in irritation.

'You miss my point. The Dalai Lama's instructions clearly said a Chinese face. But why not simply a Chinese?'

'Chinese? Chinese face? What's the difference?'

'Phuntsog, there is wisdom also in silence,' Kunga interjected, his softness lending the rebuke all the more majesty.

'When the moon in Tibet shines on the mountains, it sometimes appears as light as day. Even though it's not day,' Goodfellowe continued.

'So the Chinese face . . . ?'

'Doesn't necessarily make the boy Chinese. At least, perhaps not fully Chinese. I keep thinking that he may only look Chinese.'

'But not be Chinese?'

'Perhaps part-Chinese. And possibly part-Tibetan.'

'The reconciliation,' Kunga whispered. 'Not Tibetan. Not Chinese. But both?'

'Is there any chance? You keep telling me you know everyone in the Tibetan community but, over the years, could it be that someone has gone missing? Lost contact? Perhaps precisely because they got tangled up with a Chinese?'

The suggestion was greeted in awed silence.

Phuntsog in particular seemed agitated, bracing his shoulders as though forcing his way against a gale, his impatience doing battle with his reason.

His long nose twitched violently. Finally he spoke. 'It is possible,' he said bluntly. 'Most Tibetans came to this country in the 1970s. It took us some time to organize . . . It is possible.'

'Someone might have slipped away?'

'Possible.'

'Forgotten?'

'It was a long time ago.'

'We must ask the old folk.'

'It must be done quickly.'

'Tonight.'

'Could it be that simple?'

'The truth is often a straight line.'

'But where? Where could the child be?'

As they inspected their new hopes, Kunga had prostrated himself before the gilded statue of Shakyamuni, where he remained for many moments, his arms outstretched, withered hands pointing towards the Buddha figure. When eventually and with some difficulty he rose, he stared fiercely, almost wildly, at Goodfellowe. 'I believe you are correct. This is the answer. This is why you were sent to us.' He was rubbing his scarred palm. It had begun to burn again, not the whole scar, simply the small part of it that seemed to indicate the position of the capital city, London. 'He is very close. We must hurry.'

And they did, with new fire in their bellies, enthusiasm on their lips, departing quickly into the night to make contact with their community. Even Phuntsog had spirit in his face.

It was as Kunga was leaving that he turned to Goodfellowe and took hold of him. Goodfellowe felt an astonishing heat-filled, almost burning, sensation coming from the old monk's broken hands.

'The Chinese searchers have been distracted, but they are still looking,' Goodfellowe warned. 'The child has a Chinese face. He is still their target. We may not have much time left.'

'I know. But thanks to you we can at least join in their game. Numbers don't always decide. We may yet win.'

Goodfellowe said nothing. In spite of everything, he didn't believe the monk, couldn't share the optimism he himself had generated in the others. He wasn't an optimist. It was simply that he was congenitally stubborn. Elizabeth was right, he liked a fight. He turned to go but still the monk clung to his hand.

'I have one more thing to ask of you, Tummo.'

'Ask away.'

'How can it be that you know what moonlight is like in the Tibetan mountains?'

And, for the first time that evening, Goodfellowe had no answer.

*   *   *

'Chaos! All is chaos! And it is your fault, Mo.'

'There are rumours everywhere, Ambassador. They are not my fault.'

'Yet it is your neck, Mo. Never forget that. We fail and we are dead, both of us. But you first.'

'What am I to do? What can I do?'

'Forget Jiang. Tell everyone, tell them all yourself.'

'Tell them what?'

'That the reward has doubled. And if it is the right child there will be no questions asked about

300

where he came from. Or what condition he's in.'

'Dead or alive?'

'Mo, why do you think it matters? What do you think will happen to him when they get him back to Beijing?'

'I had preferred not to think.'

'So start to think, Mo. About the child. About a football stadium and a bullet in the back of the neck. Think about it hard. Then double the reward, triple it if necessary. Just find that child!'

*　　　*　　　*

A sudden splinter of fear passed through the mother. She had lost him. As soon as they had reached the park he had begun to run, as he always did, as though he had too much to see and not enough time to fit everything into one life. She had lost sight of him. And now he was gone. She cast around in anxiety then she, too, began to run, short distances, first one way then another. Surely he couldn't have gone far? Unless something had happened. Every mother's unspoken nightmare . . .

She was on the point of crying for help when she heard a familiar gurgle of pleasure. She spun round and found him less than five feet away, sitting, almost obscured by a thick bush of lavatera that was alive with butterflies. His hands were raised in front of his face and on each sat a butterfly with blood red wings shot through with streaks of buttercup yellow.

'Gelug, gelug,' he warbled in delight.

And he was right. They were the colours of the Gelugpa, like monks meditating on the mountain top, their robes being blown by the gentle wind. It was one of her earliest childhood memories, before the great storm of exile. Yet somehow, in a manner she didn't fully understand, this two-year-old who had never lived anywhere other than above a dry-cleaners in the heart of Soho seemed to share it.

*   *   *

So it came to pass. They unearthed faded memories of her. A young girl who had arrived in this country in the early years, a Pestalozzi child who had been brought up and educated at that great school for orphans in Surrey.

She had been made an orphan on the march across the mountains. They had encountered the most terrible storm. Her mother had simply frozen, her face a mask of ice that eventually sealed her eyes and blocked the airways, her tears sparkling like jewels of ice in the moonlight. And when it became clear that the food would run out long before they reached safety, that they were all going to starve to death, her father had sat in the snow and refused to move, insisting that it was enough that he should die facing freedom and that his share be given to the child. So she had survived, with two others out of the ten that had set out, and her last view of her father was as a stone Buddha sitting in the distant snow.

There was no lingering bitterness. Such things happened in the mountains. In her new country she had grown and flourished and when as an eighteen-year-old she had fallen in love, it did not matter to her that he was Chinese. Yet it had mattered to some of the elderly members of her community, and to many in his own, so the lovers had followed

302

their own path, honouring their different ancestries but submitting to neither. And when she had failed to become pregnant and the old wives had muttered about punishment and bad *joss* they had moved away, deliberately distancing themselves from the competing cultures that for others could never be fully reconciled.

But she had left a fragment that had stuck in someone's memory. One word. Her married name. Wong.

'It's enough!' cried Goodfellowe in exaltation when they heard.

'There must be thousands of Wongs,' Phuntsog pronounced with characteristic caution.

'But if she was married and she had a child two years ago, one name is enough!'

His enthusiasm had taken him on the charge to the Family Records Centre in the City. Here were gathered census returns, wills, electoral registers—and a record of every birth, marriage and death dating back to 1837. The anatomy of the nation. Along the shelves in this place could be found every sinew and fibre of the populace—and many of its sins and sorrows. Here you might search forever for your grandparents' marriage certificate, and never find it—not because it was lost, but because it had never existed. And the many fathers who clearly existed but who were not recorded, either because they were not known or no longer required on life's long voyage. Every entry told a tale. It was all here, a comprehensive catalogue of life's miracles and muck-ups.

Which is why, when Goodfellowe arrived with perspiration on his brow and renewed hope in his heart, he discovered it had been taken over by

Americans. The package tours were in town and every second inhabitant of the state of New York seemed to have forgathered with the ambition of climbing their family tree. The place was packed, patience on short ration and the air-conditioning all but overwhelmed. It was a battle, standing shoulder to shoulder with the crowd, fighting for every inch of desk space. All around came the clatter of heavy registers being pushed and pulled across metal shelves like horses being hauled through trench mud. But at least Goodfellowe didn't have to fight across a broad front. His target was specific. Wong. A boy. Last two or three years.

His heart sank. As he joined the fray and examined the first volume he discovered there were, if not Phuntsog's thousands, then many hundreds. Wongs were everywhere. It surely had to be the most common name in the country, he thought, gazing down the endless lists. And a heavy proportion of them in London. Which one? A needle in a noodle factory. Yet there was help, the maiden names of the mothers were also listed. The Chous, the Hos, the Lams, the Lees, the Yips and the Yaus. He found another name, too, and felt the nape of his neck begin to bristle in exhilaration . . .

With a mounting sense of urgency he checked the rest of the quarterly registers, he couldn't afford to miss any possibility. But there was only one. Maternal maiden name of Rinchen. Unmistakably Tibetan. Registered in the district of Westminster.

Oh, but where in Westminster? The register didn't say and there would be a listing of Wongs a foot long in the phone book. He was still no closer. He needed a copy of the full birth certificate with

304

its 'usual address' entry. And he couldn't afford to wait days while it was coughed up by the system.

The line in front of the enquiry desk appeared endless. Earnest Americans sought help in establishing their ancestral link to Richard the Lionheart or John Lennon, it didn't seem to matter which. And they all wanted the answer in the next five minutes, because the bus was leaving for the airport in twenty... This was not a time suited to diplomacy. Heedless of the damage he might inflict on transatlantic relations Goodfellowe thrust himself to the front of the queue and pulled shameless rank.

'Help me. Please,' he asked, ignoring the shouts of protest that came from all around. 'I'm a Member of Parliament.'

'Dammit, all the more reason for you to wait,' came a voice from within the queue, a sentiment which drew immediate and general approval. The enquiry clerk, a large lady with a floral frock and sensitive disposition who had taken the job solely to protect her nervous well-being, let forth a plaintive cry for assistance. From within the small Supervisor's office to the rear emerged a middle-aged woman who brought with her no-nonsense eyes and lips of bitter lemons. Goodfellowe explained his purpose.

'You're a Member of Parliament?' the Supervisor sniffed, viewing her uninvited guest sceptically. It seemed improbable. He was perspiring and wild-eyed, and looked as if he'd just come from riding a bike.

'Not for much longer if he goes on pushing his weight around like this,' the voice in the queue opined.

'Please, this is a matter of life and death,' Goodfellowe implored.

'So's mine,' the voice added, waving a certificate.

Goodfellowe produced his House of Commons ID card, which got him away from the firing line and admitted into the glass-walled cubicle that passed as the Supervisor's office, but it took a phone call to the Palace of Westminster switchboard before she was convinced. It was with evident reluctance that she agreed to foreshorten the procedures, her distaste for disorder overcome by the fact that the departmental budgets were due for review again, downwards, and as improbable as he looked this man might have some sway.

'How quickly do you require the certificate?' she asked.

'How quick is quickest?' he replied.

'Well, I'd have to send a fax. Off to our archives. In Southport. On Merseyside,' she added, making it sound like the back side of the Moon. 'They'd have to find the original reference. Then fax us back.' She sucked in her lips.

'Please, how long?'

'About ten minutes.'

Ten minutes that seemed to twist his bladder into savage knots. He hopped. He sat. Fidgeted. Got up. Hopped again. Prayed that the family might still be at the same address, that the Wongs hadn't moved. Well, nobody else had. The housing market was shot to hell. For the first time in three years Goodfellowe praised the Chancellor and all his recessionary works.

And all the while the Supervisor eyed him as though he was about to run off with her pencils. Then the fax machine began to zip and chatter. The

306

certificate. It was coming through. He hunched over the machine, devouring every detail as it emerged.

Place of Birth: St Mary's, Paddington
Father's Name: Martin Wong
Father's Place of Birth: People's Republic of
China
Father's Occupation: Trader
Mother's Name: Wangmo
Mother's Place of Birth: Tibet
Mother's Maiden Surname: Rinchen

It all fitted. So superbly well.

Usual Address . . .

Goodfellowe could scarcely believe it. He wondered for a moment whether someone was playing a sick joke. It couldn't be. This wasn't credible. How in the name of bloody Buddha could they have been searching all that time for a family who lived at that address?

Brewer Street.

In Soho.

Less than three hundred yards from his own doorstep.

The Supervisor resolved in future always to trust her instincts rather than the Palace of Westminster switchboard when, without another word, her uninvited and obviously unbalanced guest fled through the door.

Brewer Street! Goodfellowe screamed to himself. It couldn't be that simple.

And it wasn't.

He felt as though he had a hand on his back, skirting Smithfields, pushing him on through Holborn. Every turn of the pedals sent his heart racing faster, heedless of traffic signals and the other dangers of the road. Much of Covent Garden was a pedestrian precinct; he hurtled through regardless, coat tails flying and bell jangling in alarm as shoppers turned to shout curses after his fleeting form. Disaster almost struck as he tried to negotiate a tight turn while using his mobile phone; a waste bin went tumbling, leaving behind him a turbulent wake of drink cans and fast food wrappers. And it was fortunate that the traffic in Charing Cross Road had been brought to its habitual standstill, backed up all the way from Trafalgar Square, because he gave it no heed as he hurtled out of the side street and charged into the precincts of Chinatown. Pedals flying, wrenching at the handlebars, shouting for passage, he pounded on, his legs like pistons, down Gerrard Street and onto Wardour. At the point where it crossed Shaftesbury Avenue he had no choice but to dismount and push his bike across the intersection, but he was now only fifty yards from the entrance to Brewer Street and the traffic here was quiet. Too quiet. At the corner, in front of the Ann Summers sex shop and 'Peeperama', he tried to jump the kerb, but something on his machine bent or came loose because now there was a distinct wobble to his progress. And as he rounded the corner he could see why the traffic wasn't moving. Blue and white security tape had been stretched across the

308

road. Two police cars with lights flashing were parked across the road, a third was arriving from the other direction. He knew what it meant. He was too late.

It was not inevitable, perhaps, that the Chinese would get there first, but it had been inevitable that they would get there eventually. While Goodfellowe had relied on inspiration and intuition, they had simply broken down doors, first at all the obvious locations then at locations that grew ever more obscure. But anything with a Chinese link qualified, anything that bore a Chinese face, even an inconspicuous dry-cleaners in Brewer Street. It could only have been a matter of time and, after Mo had raised the reward, that time had run out increasingly rapidly. Goodfellowe had lost the race, only by minutes, but in a world of desperate men and women that was more than enough. There were no prizes for also-rans.

His way was barred by a constable. Goodfellowe waved his House of Commons pass once more. 'I know the family,' he insisted, and was allowed through. The door to the apartment was open, the stairs leading up were crowded. The main room was chaos. An upturned table, a weeping woman, a distraught father and more policemen than the room could comfortably hold. A WPC was bringing tea from the kitchen. A small brass *bodhisattva* stared forlornly from the small shrine on the wall.

A detective sergeant recognized him and took him to one side. A child, snatched in broad daylight, he explained. No apparent reason, no immediate explanation, but—his voice dropping—a difficult area this, with its strip joints and assorted low life. Could be a gang matter. Everyone involved was Chinese. Except the woman, apparently, and she was some other form of Oriental. 'Not much for you here, sir. Bit crowded. Appreciate your interest, but best if you leave.'

Which is what he did. There was no point in staying. He had failed. The child was gone.

*　　　*　　　*

Outside in Brewer Street it had begun to snow. The middle of May yet it fell grey and chilling, right across London. An omen. As though the whole world was losing its way.

Alerted by his death-defying call on the mobile phone, they were waiting for him on the other side of the security tape, their senses in the grip of winter.

'The child gone?' Frasi's voice had a sharpness to it, almost a tone of indictment.

'Yes.'

'It is the end of everything,' Kunga whispered.

Wangyal could find no words, the tears streaming down his cheek witness to his utter misery.

'You have failed us,' Phuntsog said, without adornment. He could always be relied upon.

'You are harsh, Phuntsog,' Kunga rebuked.

'Am I? We search in one place, then he tells us search in another. When all the while we should have been looking here.'

'Our enemies have been powerful.'

'And kept most powerfully informed. Often by Minister Goodfellowe.'

'He cannot be blamed. No one is to blame.'

'We have lost our great protector, our homeland,

everything. Yet you tell me no one is to blame? The very soul of Tibet has been destroyed, Kunga Tashi.'

'We have tried . . .'

'You cannot wash your hands so easily . . .'

'It could have been so very different . . .'

As the snow fell they began to argue amongst themselves and to lay blame for failure. Goodfellowe felt no anger with them, not even with Phuntsog's accusations, for their hearts had been ripped out in front of them and pain was inevitable. Yet he felt soiled. He had helped bring them to this point, where friendship was dying along with their hope.

Eventually the melting snow underfoot began to find its way through their soles and to freeze their need for recrimination. They had argued themselves to sullenness. This group of men represented the future of Tibet, and now it was nothing but fragments. The tears in Wangyal's eyes welled ever more openly.

'I apologize, Tummo,' Kunga offered. 'We have abused your kindness.'

'It is I who have abused your trust. You relied on me. I failed. It was my fault as much as anyone's that we didn't get here in time.'

'But without you we would not have got here at all.'

Brewer Street stood drab and silent in the snow. The policemen on duty had sought shelter, the other spectators had fled to the warmth indoors. It was like a Lowry painting, colours faded and mournful, with five round-shouldered men bound together only by defeat.

'What should we do, Tummo?' Kunga at least

311

still looked to him for guidance.

Goodfellowe wrapped his jacket tightly around him and studied the mean skies. 'You go make your mark with the parents, Kunga. They'll need you as much as we need them.'

'And you?'

'I don't know about you gentlemen,' he sniffed, blowing into cupped hands to restore his circulation, 'but I'm dying for a cup of tea. And I think I know just the place.'

CHAPTER THIRTEEN

There had been a crackdown in Tibet. The Chinese were taking no chances. As the search for the child had intensified, their net had been thrown wide and anyone associated with the Dalai clique had been hauled in for questioning. Monks, nuns, former officials, teachers, particularly elderly abbots, anybody who featured on the political files of the Ministry of State Security—and there were thousands—had been questioned, then frequently cudgelled and bludgeoned. And, in almost every case, locked up.

Under Chinese occupation, imprisonment had become Tibet's largest and fastest growing industry. Even though peasants starved, more resources had been thrown at it than agriculture. While Tibetan schools were closed across the land, new gaols appeared like lambs in spring. Yet still there were not enough, for the prisons overflowed. Prisons like the notorious Drapchi, Prison Number One, a few kilometres north of Lhasa. During the days of independence the place had been best known for its holy shrine, but the Chinese had turned it into a site for what they termed an institute of re-education, intended to accommodate up to eight hundred 'scholars'. Now it held nearly two thousand as Tibet was assailed by a deluge of despair. The prison authorities had little idea for what precise reason or for how long these people were being held but, since they were Tibetans, what did it matter? The cells overflowed, every corner was filled, even those that were designed for purposes other than simple incarceration. Like those places reserved for political prisoners in Unit 5, cells that were less than five feet high and in which no one could stand erect. And those cells where the floor was constantly six inches deep in water and filth and where a single night left most inmates crying for feeling back in their limbs.

A cauldron of sorrows.

And as snow fell across Brewer Street, a great shaking of the earth hit Lhasa. Buildings trembled, people ran in terror through the streets, the skies darkened like night as they filled with dust. Many thought it heralded the end of the world. Cracks and fissures appeared everywhere, in roads, through walls and roofs and across the passions of everyone in the capital. Yet this was no ordinary earthquake. Nothing fell down. Not a building nor a single bridge collapsed. It was a portent, of that few had any doubt, a warning of what was to come.

In Drapchi gaol they discovered that the shifting ground had caused a subtle change to the geometry. No cell had burst, no bars had been breached, but instead the locked doors throughout the gaol had stuck firmly in their jambs. They couldn't be opened. And if they were, there was the thought that the whole stinking place might collapse around them.

So what? The Institute of Geological Sciences predicted that there would be more shocks which might finish off the job. These strange superstitious Tibetans might yet be crushed by their own ungrateful gods. So leave them there! Stuck fast behind the doors. It would save their gaolers the trouble of throwing away the keys.

*   *   *

It was a slow and tiring cycle ride all the way up to Hampstead Heath. He'd buckled the front wheel going over the kerb outside the sex shop and it squeaked in protest with every turn. It made steering difficult in the snow, which was beginning to settle both upon the road and upon Goodfellowe himself. Perhaps he should have gone by Tube after all, his destination was just along from Golders Green Station, but he needed the fresh air and the time to think.

He gambled that she would have taken the child to the Residence rather than the Embassy, where there were too many prying eyes. Madame Lin would not be proud of what she had done and would have little wish to parade a captive two-year-old. But the child would need to be secure, on diplomatically protected soil, until he was flown out on a diplomatically protected flight. So it had to be the Residence.

It lay just off the Heath, a sombre red-brick Gothic mansion that stood behind high walls, its entrance protected by heavy metalwork gates and a phalanx of obtrusive security devices. Outside Goodfellowe slithered precariously to a halt, the brakes jammed with slush and all but useless. He was feeling distinctly damp around the collar where the snow had melted and trickled down his face and neck. In normal circumstances he would have considered this a first-class workout. Now it appeared little short of madness.

He rang the intercom. He could feel the presence of the red-eyed security camera watching him, but there was no answer. He rang again. Still nothing. Perhaps the intercom wasn't working. Or perhaps he'd got this all wrong and they weren't here. The place looked almost abandoned. The rhododendron bushes were unkempt, the silver birch bent in sorrow, the driveway was covered in moss and old leaves. A garden hose trailed along the side of the short drive; it didn't appear to have been used or moved for some time. A fruitless journey. Another screw-up, one amongst so many. He stood pressed up against the wrought-iron gate, peering forlornly through its bars.

Then he saw her, looking out through the snow from one of the leaded windows on the first floor. She was staring directly at him. There was a curious cast to her eyes, not the arrogance of victory but something that might almost be mistaken for compassion. He brushed damp hair from his eyes, returning the stare, trying to hate, but failing. How could he hate her? They were too much alike. All he could offer was futile defiance. Then she stepped back out of sight.

A moment later the buzzer rang and the automatic gates swung apart.

The bicycle made an uncertain track through the

snow to the heavy wooden front doors. Standing before them, Goodfellowe made an attempt to shake the snow from his clothes but they were now so wet that the effort met with only modest success. Then the doors opened and he was ushered inside by an elderly Chinese servant who appeared to have a limp and only one tooth. He spoke no English but there was no mistaking the surprise on his face as he examined Goodfellowe and the puddle that was already beginning to form beneath him on the marble floor. With a quick bow of apology the servant disappeared, returning a few seconds later with two warm, dry towels, one for his hair and the other for him to stand on. It was only now he was standing in the dark hallway that Goodfellowe realized how bitterly cold he had become.

'An omen, perhaps?' Madame Lin appeared at the top of the stairs. 'The weather is an omen?'

'Undoubtedly,' Goodfellowe concurred, finishing the running repairs to his hair. 'But the skill is not in recognizing an omen. It is in deciding what it means.'

'And what do you believe such snow means, Thomas?'

'That many cricket matches are about to be abandoned.'

'Perhaps many kingdoms, too.'

'Ah, but which ones? Omens don't tell us such things. That is for you and me to decide.'

'Then I believe the decision is already made.'

He threw the towel in the corner, an aggressive gesture. 'I've come for the child.'

'Of course you have.'

'You admit he's here?' He looked around as

316

though expecting to see some sign.

'I see no point in denying it. Not to you.'

'You can't take him back to China, you know.' He sounded defiant, but didn't feel it.

'But Thomas, he is already in China. This is a diplomatic residence. Legally it is Chinese territory. Foreign soil. You have no power here.'

'I could make it very tough for you. In the media.'

'Thomas, Thomas. I'm glad to see you have not lost your sense of humour. Did you learn nothing from Tienanmen? You would be no more than a fly banging its head against the Great Wall.'

'And I'll ask questions in Parliament.'

She looked down from her position at the top of the stairs, like a schoolmistress lecturing a dullard class. 'So what would you ask the Prime Minister to do? Make an enemy of China? Sacrifice investment worth billions of pounds? Perhaps the thousands of jobs that depend on it?' She shook her head. 'No one could be so rash and foolish.'

'You obviously don't know the Prime Minister.'

She laughed lightly. 'But I do. And perhaps you are right in his case. But even if you could persuade him to become involved, even if you could convince him that the baby Jesus himself was inside the building with Herod sharpening his knives in the kitchen, there is nothing he could do. Not here. Not in China.' Her voiced softened, no triumphalism. 'And there is nothing you can do either, Thomas.'

He considered the point carefully. 'Except perhaps have tea.'

She smiled and waved him up the stairs. 'I have some waiting. Please join me. It's jasmine, I'm afraid; a little gentle for your taste, perhaps. But

317

refreshing after your long journey. I'm sorry that your time has been wasted.'

She led the way into a sitting room full of narrow windows and light that had been made heavy by the snow. A lonely room, he realized, for a lonely woman. She poured tea from a low table while Goodfellowe started upon a tour of inspection, as though he were looking for something special. He found it above the marble fireplace, a pair of fine Tang dynasty earthenware camels partially covered in a three-colour glaze of deep emerald, brown and cream. He took one in each hand, weighing them.

'Magnificent,' he muttered.

'Seventh century. I am delighted you appreciate them.'

He held one up above eye level, examining it from all sides. 'To look at it you'd almost think it was . . . why, genuine.' He released his grip. The camel shattered into fragments in the hearth.

'Thomas! Are you mad . . . ?'

He shuffled the broken pieces around with his toe. 'To be honest I've no idea whether it was genuine or not. I'm no judge of such things. Not many people are, which is why it's so easy to get away with good forgeries. But was that the genuine article? Or is it this one? Or are they both fake?' The second camel fell and smashed with a sound like gunshot.

She had stopped pouring. The smile had gone. 'I've a feeling you have a message for me, Thomas.'

'Tell me, is it that you are simply a common thief, albeit with uncommon access to works of art? Or are you also involved in the drugs?'

His tone was intentionally provocative. The change of atmosphere took her aback.

318

'That is a remarkably insolent observation. Please explain yourself,'

'But isn't it you who'll be required to offer some explanation? About why you've been involved in the wholesale theft and smuggling of antiques from the Embassy. Shipping them off to Amsterdam where they are switched for copies.' He motioned towards the fragments in the fireplace. 'Were those copies, by the way?'

'I have no idea.'

'Scarcely matters. Either way they can be replaced. By copies. From your usual supplier.'

She sipped her tea. There was the slightest tremble across the surface of the hot liquid.

Goodfellowe, too, was trembling inside. Maybe now Mickey would forgive him, and he could forgive himself. She had found the draft letter in Baader's red box, waiting for his signature, which had spelt out all the details. The antiques scam uncovered in Amsterdam. Its use as a cover for drug smuggling. The desire of the Dutch authorities to bring the matter to court, if the British Government would help. Baader's firm advice that they shouldn't, because the offence had taken place on foreign soil, Dutch and Chinese, and the Foreign Office had neither status nor interest in the matter. Baader's recommendation had been trenchant. No action. Not this day. Not any day.

'Were you involved in the drugs, too?'

'What drugs? I know nothing of any drugs!'

'All those antiques and copies that were moved around between the Embassy and the Residence and Amsterdam. Are you saying you didn't know they were used as a cover to smuggle heroin? In the diplomatic bag?'

'No!' Her cup came down sharply into the saucer, threatening both.

Goodfellowe waved a hand at her. 'You know, Madame Lin, I believe you. Of course I believe you. The trouble is, practically no one else will, not with your connections to the Triads and particularly with Jiang.' He was casting around wildly, indulging in pure supposition, but he had to bring her to believe he knew much more than he did. He had to find some means of scaring her. 'I even have a photograph of you and Jiang together. At his restaurant. Remember? You're shaking his hand.'

Her lips had grown taut, all but disappeared. 'I congratulate you, Thomas. A first-class attempt. But you can prove nothing, of course. And your government will not believe you.'

'Oh, but where do you think I got all this from? It was the government that told me!' he exclaimed. 'Or at least Paddy Baader.'

'What?'

'This isn't my detective work.' He was all innocence. 'Why, I've never been to Amsterdam.'

'Baader couldn't have. Wouldn't have!' She was ruffled.

'But he did.'

'No. No. No.' Her own anger took her by storm and swept her along. 'He wouldn't dare—couldn't be so foolish! I'd destroy him before he even got close to me. Cut him down with his own greed.'

'Greed?'

'Unbounded! A man who turns whispers into profits. And now with a little money in his pocket he thinks he can turn on me?' She fought to restore

320

her self-control. 'The pleasure of cutting him down to size will be for me, Thomas, and in my own time. This is not for you. You could never prove a thing.'

'Proof? That Baader knew in advance about your Government's recent order for aero engines? Or that he bought shares to profit from it? In his wife's name, of course.'

Her jaw dropped, her expression a mixture of admiration and anxiety.

'Then there was the new bridge and harbour contract in Shanghai. Uncanny how his wife seemed to spot every single contractor who'd got a piece of the action. She'd got a little list and not one of them was missed.' He wagged his fingers as though conducting a comic opera, mocking her. 'And profited from it enormously. In Switzerland, of course. You might call it pure prescience. I think others will look on it more as a pension plan,'

The desk drawers. It had all been there, in the privacy of Baader's own home. Under lock and key. Until he screwed Mickey.

'So, Thomas, perhaps you will get to Baader first. To you will go the pleasure of making him beg. First a little, then a very great deal. He will, you know. Beg. A man out of his depth. He was all too easy to control. But what will you choose to do? Control him? Or will you destroy him? Could you destroy one of your own?'

He placed his steepled hands to his lips as though offering up a prayer. ' "Destroy one of your own".' He punched out every syllable. 'A fascinating concept. And quite relevant in the circumstances.'

'I don't understand.'

'You will.'

'But you will never destroy me, Thomas, not with
321

your inventions about antiques and drugs and Triads. It is the stuff of novels.' She was regaining her confidence and her will to fight.

'Oh, but I think I might. On the antiques for sure, and there's nothing new about drugs going through the diplomatic pouch. That's all credible enough. And you see, I don't have to prove anything, I simply have to get people to believe it. That would be enough to make your life impossible. And you've gone too far with the Triads. Maybe I can't produce a written contract, but everyone knows, everyone in Chinatown. Whispers everywhere. And they all lead back to the Embassy.'

She was working hard to appear confident once more, but there were bruises around the eyes. She knew she'd been in a fight. 'Even if it were to lead back to the Embassy, it would not lead to me. To little Mo, perhaps.' She began counting off on her fingers. 'The antiques operation—that began before I became Ambassador. Through Mo's cousin in Amsterdam. The drugs I never knew anything about. And the contacts with Jiang have all been through Mo.' She spread her arms wide as though explaining to a larger audience, or a panel of judges. 'Why, I only met Jiang at the opening of his restaurant. As did you. I am a grandmother, I understand nothing of this talk about Triads. So you see, the waters may get choppy, but my junk will float through this little storm, Thomas. I'll survive. But as for poor Mo?' She returned to her tea. 'There are always casualties in war.'

'Sadly I must agree. War has no compassion, makes no distinction between young and old. It will be hard for you to bear.'

322

'What shall I find hard to bear?'

He was still by the fireplace. There were other items on the large mantelpiece. A clock. A jade figurine. A large rosewood framed photograph of her grandson. He picked up the photo and studied it closely. His tone was sharp. 'Down to business. We are not here to talk about you or me. Or Jiang. Or Little Mo. Or even Baader. We are here to talk about the boy.'

'There is nothing to talk about,' she said, almost abstracted.

'Tell that to Chinatown. You see, before I came here I stopped for tea. I drink too much tea, you know. A personal weakness. Coffee makes me so restless.'

He appeared to have lost his thread, or was playing upon her patience. But she was not the patient kind.

'You mentioned Chinatown.'

'Ah, yes. Tea in Chinatown. And everywhere in Chinatown the conversation was of little other than the boy.'

'My countrymen are great gossips.'

'And it has been so for days; thanks to your efforts.'

'But no more. It is finished.'

'It has only just started.'

'You talk in riddles.'

'The riddle has been why, in spite of all that effort and the reward and even the involvement of the Triads, it has taken so long to find the boy. It's been a mystery. Up to this point. But now they understand.'

'What do they understand?'

'That the boy has been deliberately hidden. By

323

his family.'

'Any family would do the same.'

'Agreed! Exactly! Everyone understands that. But what family could be in a position to frustrate such a search for so long? Only a *powerful* family. An *official* family. A family who knew what was going on. A family in a position to disrupt and divert the search.' Goodfellowe brushed an imaginary coating of dust from the photograph. 'In other words, a family like yours. Just like yours.'

The Ambassador offered no more than a thin gasp of surprise.

'As we speak, every tea room, restaurant, barber shop and betting place in Chinatown is running with the rumour that there is only one reason why the child has been so elusive.'

'What is that reason?' Her voice was pale.

'Because the child is your own grandson. And that in order to protect him you are trying to substitute an entirely innocent and unconnected boy in his place.'

'You cannot be serious.'

'Deadly.'

'Oh, Thomas, but I fear you are.' She was still, breathing deep to calm her racing heart. 'No one will believe you.'

'But they already do. What's more natural in Chinese government than a conspiracy and cover-up? Your masters in Beijing all conspire against each other and in their own personal interests. They will think this explanation entirely obvious. Like a cat taking to cream. And thrown in with allegations of corruption throughout the Embassy ...' He held the photograph of her grandson up high, preparing to drop it after the camels.

324

'No!' she pleaded, holding out a trembling hand in protest. It was only a photograph, but she couldn't help herself. In one small, instinctive gesture she had exposed her weakness, the route to her deepest fears, and there was no going back.

'They will kill your boy.' His words landed with physical impact, slapping across her face and making her head jerk. 'Even if they are not certain, they will kill him. Just to be on the safe side. For what is one life amongst so many?' He paused. 'I understand that is the Chinese way.'

'He is my grandson. Thomas, he is all I have.' She had stopped fighting and was now battling with herself to retain some semblance of control.

'It is a difficult world.'

'They will kill me too, but that is not what I fear. It is for the boy. For him I would gladly give my life a thousand times over.'

'I think they will ask you only the once.'

She looked at him through tears. 'You mock me. That is cruel. Unlike you, Thomas.'

'I see no difference between us. We are only arguing about which child your masters would butcher.'

'Would you, Thomas? Would you willingly sacrifice any child?'

He held his silence, replacing the photograph carefully upon the mantelpiece and reflecting upon Sun Tzu. He'd been browsing that morning in bed and had found the advice staring up at him. *'Don't attack until you have discovered your opponent's weakness.'* Damned fine Chinaman, that Sun Tzu.

'There may be one way, if you are willing to consider it.'

'How could I not? You have the advantage of

325

me.'

'One thing above all else is clear. The fate of you, your grandson and the Tibetan child are wrapped up together. All three of you will survive, or you will be sacrificed, together.'

'I fear Beijing will be most insistent.'

'Then tell Beijing that the boy cannot be found. That he will never be found because he doesn't exist. Not here in Britain. Tell them that this has been a Tibetan plot to distract from the search for the real reincarnation. Send them off to look elsewhere.'

'Such as?'

'Does it matter? Try America. That's big. Or Japan. Enough Oriental faces to send any search party spinning. My Tibetan friends will help with the illusion. We'll start a new rumour. Even start a new search. And in the meantime you and your grandson can find a little peace.'

'And the other boy?'

'Him, too. He and your grandson need each other. They can live together in the same world, in the same country, perhaps. They *should* live together, that was the Dalai Lama's message, I think.'

A faint expression of hope began to play around her lips. 'Strangely enough, they both seem to enjoy each other's company.' As though to confirm the point, from somewhere deep within the house there came a loud crash, followed by two whoops of mischief. 'A drum I bought him for his last birthday,' she explained.

'Then spend the rest of the day thinking what you can buy him for his next.'

'You ask me to betray my country?'

'Or betray your grandson. A simple choice.'

'Oh, we are very much alike, you and I, Thomas.' There was resentment now.

'We both believe in our family.'

'And we are both ruthless, you as much as I.'

Ruthless? He didn't like to see it that way, but perhaps she was right. 'So what is it to be?' he pressed. 'The boy? Or Beijing?' He didn't want to allow her time to think, only to feel. And to fear.

Her eyes flooded in anger. 'I am a diplomat. That is my life!'

'But you will die a grandmother.'

Her eyes welled in torment. He had come to understand her all too well, to know the manner in which she could be twisted and tantalized. She was spinning inside. Then something snapped. Her shoulders sagged, her whole body seemed to deflate, to wither in front of his eyes. She could resist no longer. When the words came it seemed as though she had barely enough strength to whisper them. 'You may have the boy . . .'

He closed his eyes, offered a prayer.

The deed was done.

A few moments later, as he prepared to leave, she called after him. 'Tell me, Thomas, how is your wife?'

He stopped, weighing the answer as though it were gold. Or lead. 'She has made something of a recovery. She's starting to respond a little. Thanks to your pillow, I believe.'

'I am glad.'

He was almost at the door when he stopped and turned once more. 'Tell me, Madame Lin, I've always wondered. About your own husband. What happened to him?'

327

She paused before replying, weighing the memories with care. 'It was a long time ago. When I was pregnant. During the purges of the Cultural Revolution. I was a senior party activist and he . . . Well, he was a licentious fool. An opportunist. I had been at a party meeting. Made a ferocious speech denouncing intellectuals and capitalist roaders. Parasites, leeches, who lived off the rest. Oh, but it was a fine speech, Thomas. Everyone said so. Then great pains began with the child. I came back home early, unexpectedly. I found him in bed with another woman. A whore.'

'So?'

'So . . . I was the party cadre. I had the power. I also had the responsibility. Obligations. I had to decide.'

'What did you decide?'

'He was betraying the revolution.' She was pleading too forcefully. 'And he was betraying me.'

'What did you decide?' he repeated softly.

'I had him shot.'

He knew the guilt hadn't left her for a minute of her life.

'Hard times, Thomas.'

'Aren't they all, Madame Lin?'

Ten minutes later Goodfellowe was back out in the snow, trying to figure out how to get a two-year-old boy to ride in the basket of his collapsible bike.

*   *   *

Goodfellowe had been rescued by that rarest of London phenomena, a taxi in a snowstorm. Progress with both boy and bike had proved distinctly hazardous and the appearance of the taxi

328

had gone some way to restoring his belief in miracles. It was with considerable relief that he stowed the bike and clambered in. The boy had already settled himself in the back seat with a confidence that suggested he had been used to being driven around all his life. He smiled, he yawned, he remained remarkably composed considering the ordeal he had just been through, yet he would say not a word. Several times Goodfellowe asked him his name, but got back only a grin in reply. This proved awkward. The taxi driver was beginning to cast glances of concern in the mirror at this strange combination of a seriously dishevelled man and a young boy. Goodfellowe decided that if he persisted in questioning the boy there was more likelihood of the taxi driver heading for the nearest police station than the destination Goodfellowe had asked for, and he didn't think he was up to the challenge of trying to explain to a distracted police sergeant the difference between a politician and a pervert. Miracles didn't stretch that far. So he sat back and decided to concentrate on rearranging his appearance, searching for a handkerchief to wipe away the perspiration and the melted snow that had mingled on his forehead. As he did so, the driver gave a grunt of relief.

'Stopped snowing. 'Bout ruddy time.'

And the boy was gurgling with delight. While Goodfellowe's attention had been distracted the child had been ransacking his jacket pocket, and when his fist reappeared it had found a trophy.

He was clutching the prayer beads.

'Thank you,' the child said to Goodfellowe. His first words. And he meant them, holding

Goodfellowe's gaze for far longer than might be expected from a two-year-old. Then the boy placed the prayer beads around his own neck and burst into laughter.

*   *   *

The second earthquake hit with more devastating effect. Around Lhasa, many of the buildings that before had been shaken and cracked began to fall. People ran in terror through the streets and a huge shroud of dust hung over the capital. Above the dust, the people looked to the Potala Palace, the ancestral winter home of the Dalai Lamas which, according to legend, had risen overnight from the bare rock. Many ordinary Tibetans prostrated themselves in prayer that the Palace might be saved, some writing mantras to Padmasambhava on its walls. When the tremors had ceased and the dust dispersed, a meticulous inspection was mounted of the Palace. They found not a single crack.

And it was astonishing that the only buildings in Lhasa to collapse were new buildings, those made for the forces of occupation, such as government offices and bars. The old buildings, those built by Tibetans, all survived.

Afterwards some explained this away by suggesting that the old Tibetan buildings had better, broader-based footings than the new Chinese structures, that the old mud-brick-and-stone walls moved and breathed while the cheap concrete simply stood stiff and crumbled. There were all sorts of technical reasons to explain the devastation of the Chinese community and the survival of the Tibetan, if one needed an

330

explanation. But most Tibetans didn't. They believed. That was explanation enough.

To the north, in Drapchi, Prison Number One, the tremors hit with particularly appalling effect. Accommodation blocks housing the security staff were flattened like a row of dominoes. The walls of the prison echoed to the cries of those who were trapped and injured—at least, those walls that were left standing. Because, along with the accommodation blocks, most of the outside walls had also crumbled. Chinese troops ran everywhere, abandoning their posts, trying to find loved ones, using their bare hands to dig through the debris and dust.

Neither did the cells escape unscathed. Their walls bent and buckled and bowed. But the jammed cell doors were made of metal, most robustly built, giving the walls that vital extra strength, and not until after the doors had burst open did the walls finally fall. But by that time those within had scrambled out. The prisoners were free. Drapchi was no more.

*   *   *

As Goodfellowe was paying off the taxi and disentangling his bike, the boy was already marching up the stairs to the apartment above the dry-cleaners, one foot stamping firmly after the other, like the sound of a drum being beaten to announce his arrival. Nobody else made that sound and already his mother was at the door in tears of overwhelming joy. As she smothered him with love, the child chuckled merrily. Then his eyes fell on Kunga. The monk had not left the apartment from

331

the moment he'd first arrived and introduced himself. Now he stood in the corner, staring. The child stared back, his head held first to one side, then the other, examining the monk from every angle, his expression a mixture of curiosity and concern. Gradually his features began to glow with a sharp light which spread, and in a moment his whole face was on fire. With a cry of joy he rushed across the room and threw himself into Kunga's outstretched arms. The monk held him high, filled with an elation more profound than anything he had ever felt. And when at last he relinquished his grip and the boy wriggled away, he looked down at his hand in astonishment.

The scar had disappeared. Completely.

There were fewer technical explanations available for the disappearance of the scar than for the distinctive and discriminatory effects of the earthquake in Lhasa, but in this instance, too, Kunga didn't need an explanation. So far as he was concerned he already had one. He had been holding it in his arms.

*   *   *

Baader was sitting in the window seat of the Pugin Room looking out across the river when Goodfellowe found him.

'Tom!' Baader waved heartily to him. 'I'm waiting for the wife to arrive to take her to dinner. Rare treat. Come join me for a drink.'

'Make mine a stiff Scotch. Very stiff. Make yours the same.'

Baader eyed him curiously. 'Fair enough.' The orders were given and Baader's attention was back

332

on his colleague. 'So tell me. How goes it with the search for the child? Any news?'

'The best. As of this afternoon I'm glad to say he's safely tucked away in our hands.'

'But I thought . . .' Too late Baader reined back his surprise.

'You thought others might have him.'

'Others?' he protested, awash with innocence.

'The Chinese.'

'What do I know?' He tried to blow away the fog of confusion he felt gathering around him.

'Far too bloody much.'

'Look, Tom, I'm not sure what you're getting at, but if the matter is settled then I'm delighted. A problem solved. So it's back to business as normal. British interests. Not getting caught up with a bunch of squabbling immigrants who frankly no one understands and nobody wants.' The drinks arrived, Baader raised his glass. 'Confusion to the enemy.'

Goodfellowe drained his whisky in one. Baader looked on in a mixture of awe and anxiety. 'Er, another one?'

'I don't think that would be appropriate.'

'Why?'

'Because suddenly I find I've taken an intense and very personal dislike to you, Paddy.'

'You serious?'

'Bet your last red box on it.'

A pause for reflection. Baader looked around anxiously in search of his wife and his voice sank to the table top. 'You know about Mickey.'

'I do.'

'For God's sake, isn't it a little pathetic for you to try to elect yourself the moral guardian of a twenty-six-year-old?' His tone had grown derisive. 'Or are you simply jealous?'

Goodfellowe paused to consider the point, as though tasting a good malt. 'Perhaps I am a little jealous. How could I not be? Not a particularly noble sentiment, I'll admit.' He shrugged. 'But you're still going to have to resign.'

'Piss off, Tom. I don't know what's got into you but if you think you can blackmail me because I've been screwing around with your secretary, you're wrong. It's not illegal. She's not pregnant. And you are totally out of order.'

There seemed nothing more to say. Baader began fussing with the sleeve of his jacket as though trying to brush away some unpleasant piece of dirt, and avoided Goodfellowe's eye.

'That's a fine jacket, Paddy. Beautifully cut suit. I think you're one of the few Ministers I know who has actually flourished in office. Improved themselves, know what I mean? Puts my rags to shame.'

'A plastic bin liner would put your rags to shame, Goodfellowe, and what the hell are you prattling on about?' Exasperation flooded his voice. He was still casting around nervously for the arrival of his wife.

'Let me be explicit. You are one of the few Ministers I know who has been on the make during his term of office. Even more explicitly, you're the only one I can prove has been on the make.'

Baader slumped in the window seat, his head almost striking the leaded window. Then he started laughing, 'They always said you were unsound, Tom. I thought they were talking about your judgement. Seems they were talking about your mind.'

'When you resign, Paddy—'

'Me resign? Never!'

'When you resign I want you to be clear about why it is you're going. Not because you've slept with my secretary. It's because you have lined your carefully tailored pockets with money. Unethical profits from share deals using inside information.'

Baader glared defiantly at his colleague, his eyes hardened by contempt. 'I deny it.'

'But you've done it.'

'Then prove it.'

'A savings account number F3-stroke-843921 in the Zurich branch of the Société de Banque Suisse—where the last transaction was depositing the profits you made in your wife's name from the Shanghai Harbour contract. Then there were the 48,513 Swiss francs you paid in a few months ago after the aero-engine order was announced. I congratulate you, Paddy. Your wife has proved to be a pretty shrewd investor. Some might say almost inspired. It might be coincidence, of course, her picking all these winners, but I think we've already agreed that most observers prefer conspiracy to coincidence. Ours is such a cynical world.'

As Goodfellowe spoke, Baader's face had become like chalk, as if the bones of his skull were about to burst through the skin. His voice made a sound that might have been strained through catacombs, full of dust and death. 'You cannot have proof.'

'Not the original documents, but excellent photocopies.' It was a lie, of course. All he had was Mickey's scribbled notes, not proof of anything. But it didn't matter. All that mattered was that Baader believed him. Which clearly he did. The shadow of

335

the gibbet had already fallen across his soul.

'And I shall, of course, be sending the papers to the Parliamentary Commissioner and the Committee on Standards and Privileges in due course,' Goodfellowe continued. 'Should make for an entertaining session or two.' He rubbed his finger around the rim of his empty glass, setting up a sound of complaint that grated on the nerves. 'They'll mince you, then fry what's left in public. It's convenient that your name's short enough to fit across one line of the *Sun*. Should make it easy for the headline writers. Trouble is, I feel sorry for your wife. I suspect you've used her, just like you use most women.'

And just like Goodfellowe had used Mickey. His conscience kicked him. He should stop moralizing and get on with it.

'So you see, you'll have to resign. But I'm a reasonable man. I'll give you a choice.'

'What choice? Jump or be pushed?' The voice was choked, the noose already tightening around his neck.

'Better than that. Get your doctor to give you a sick note or something. Exhaustion in the service of the nation, or some such balls. You resign, and I'll keep quiet about the share deals and the Swiss bank accounts. No public disgrace. No ritual humiliation by your colleagues.'

A flush of colour returned to Baader's cheeks. 'But why? Why would you spare me?'

'Not because I like you, Paddy. Fact is, I loathe you. I wouldn't piss in your ear if your brains were on fire. But I prefer to use you rather than destroy you. We're going to move the child somewhere safe, and at the same time lay down a false trail for

336

the Chinese Government. You can help with that. Concoct some diplomatic telegram that the Chinese will be bound to intercept saying that the true incarnation is in Texas or Timbuktu. So long as the boy remains out of harm's way, I have an interest in ensuring you stay on the payroll. I'll tell you what to do. Then I'll tell you when you're going to resign.'

Baader's breathing had grown laboured, his eyes fixed on some distant, fading destiny. 'Suppose I always knew it would come to this. Eventually. But not yet. And not because of a child. I thought a girl, perhaps. Any number of 'em. But never a child.' He blinked and came back to the room. 'I don't seem to have much alternative.'

'None at all, I hope.'

'Was going to resign soon anyway. Coming to the end of my useful life as a Minister. Time for a few directorships, maybe.' Already he was trying to rewrite events, his tone more defiant.

'Just keep your mind anchored to one point, Paddy. The papers I have will destroy you at any time, whether you are a Minister of the Crown or a monkey on a stick. Now or in years to come. You'll never be free from this one.'

'You're a ruthless bastard.'

'Second time today,' Goodfellowe mused. 'It's almost a consensus. Anyway, I see your wife approaching. Time for me to disappear and for you to tell her the good news.'

'The good news?'

Goodfellowe leaned across and tightened Baader's silk tie, a shade too fiercely. 'That you're going to have so much more time to spend with your investments.' He gave the tie a further, totally superfluous twist. 'And you know something, old chum? By the look on Madame Lin's face when I left her, I think you're going to need it.'

POSTSCRIPT

The cold front had passed and left behind a wondrously clear early summer's evening. This was one of the views of London that Goodfellowe never failed to find inspiring, across the river to the City where the dark-suited dome of St Paul's stood like a conductor before a vast orchestra of lights in the financial centre behind. It was an irresistible panorama of bridges and mirrors and ancient spires, cathedrals and temples of commerce, God and Mammon side by side, a marriage of artifice and aspiration that had lasted for a thousand years. Ambition shone through every window. 'Give me your soul!' they shouted. 'Or give me your savings!' Straightforward and so refreshingly sincere. And so unlike that other city on the river, his city, Westminster, where ambition was found loitering in dark Gothic corners like a playground bully.

On the occasions when he grew weary with the game of politics and had lost both his meaning and his motivation, he would come and soak up these awesome sights along the river bank. So much history gathered together in one spot reminded him that like all men he was but a small link in an endless and infinite chain, one that would soon stretch way beyond him. There was so much he wanted to do, so little time to do it. Yet on this spot he knew, too, that it was possible to make a difference. The view in front of him proved it.

Except that it was his usual practice to admire the scene from the vantage point of the walkway of Hungerford Bridge, a location which although often windswept was entirely free of charge. Unlike the restaurant in the Oxo Tower. Ouch. Sam had insisted on a victory celebration, and Mickey deserved one. This was going to hurt, and perhaps the bill would prove to be the smallest of the evening's troubles.

'Come on, Dad, don't be such a sad haddock. Look as if you're enjoying yourself.'

Goodfellowe dragged his thoughts back to the balcony overlooking the busy river and tried to shake the heaviness from his heart. So he'd won, a great victory, but already he'd lost the mood for celebration. Something mattered more. This was the evening he had set aside for his showdown with Sam, because showdown he had reluctantly decided there must be. Her pregnancy could wait no longer.

'To an extraordinary boss,' Mickey raised her glass in salute. 'Even if at times you bear a close resemblance to a horse's arse.' And meant it. But she was talking. It meant she was healing.

'Thanks. I think.'

'And to the women who spur you on,' Sam offered in her turn.

They raised glasses and Goodfellowe cursed. In his distraction he'd not only emptied his glass but also knocked over the bottle. He watched helplessly as eighteen quid's worth of Ninth Island Chardonnay spilled across the metal table top.

'I've never seen you waste even a drop before,' Mickey observed. 'You cracking up, Goodfellowe?'

'Yeah, what's wrong, Goodfellowe?' Sam repeated. 'Why aren't you enjoying yourself? Has it got anything to do with this mysterious personal problem you wanted to talk about? You been arrested or something?'

His face didn't flicker.

'Ah, is this a moment where my Jewish insight tells me I should suddenly become invisible?' Mickey enquired. 'Not that I do invisible very well,' she added, moistening her lips, 'but there's a couple of wicked-looking fellows over by the bar. I could come back in a week or two.'

'No!' insisted Sam, who wanted to party.

'No,' concurred Goodfellowe, more cautiously. This was a family matter, and Mickey was practically part of it. Anyway, he felt that Sam might soon be in need of her support. The waiter finished mopping up and brought another bottle.

'Sam, you know I'm not a moralizer,' he began diffidently.

'You've got precious little to moralize about,' Mickey muttered.

He flinched. 'Precisely. But I've been struggling for weeks to find the right way and the right words for this, and still I know I'm going to make a mess of it.'

'Like my A-levels.'

He took a deep breath, as though about to dive deep underwater. 'Sam, I know. About the pregnancy clinic. About your treatment. I know it's been going on for a long time. Too long, Sam.' His voice carried an edge of relief. At last it was out in the open. 'I know.'

'Oh, Dad, I'm so sorry.'

He closed his eyes. The whole of London had suddenly ceased to move. And through the silence he became aware of a noise. Like a window shattering, the fragments sounding like bells falling chaotically around him. Except it wasn't glass. It was laughter.

341

Sam was laughing at him.

'Oh, Dad, I'm so sorry.' She bit her lip, struggling to control herself, almost embarrassed at her own reaction. 'It's not funny, but . . .'

'You'd better believe it's not funny, young lady.'

He was smouldering, about to ignite. She reached out and grasped his hand.

'I'm not pregnant.'

'Not pregnant?' he copied, testing the notion.

'Never was.' She stifled her giggles, which had been nothing more than a youthful nervous reaction to the intense surprise. 'And I'm sorry you've been worrying needlessly.'

'Needlessly?' He was beginning to sound like a parrot. 'But what about the clinic? The bills?'

'It was Edwina, not me.'

'Edwina?'

'She refused to tell her parents or her doctor and was terrified she'd get thrown out of school. So I helped her. Insisted she got some counselling. I'd come with her to the clinic. Here in London. Even helped her pay for it.'

'One of your cheques bounced, you know. Was sent back to Gerrard Street.'

This seemed to puzzle Sam. 'She was in a terrible state. Wouldn't use her own name, didn't dare use her own address, so . . . I lent her my name. I suppose she must have used your address. The first thing that came to mind. She was very scared. Please don't be too angry.'

'You . . . are . . . not . . . pregnant. You're NOT pregnant.' He wanted to say it slowly, in a number of ways, trying to discover which version would prove most definitive and convincing. 'You mean— you're really not pregnant?'

342

'No. And neither is Edwina now.'

'The clinic?' he enquired, in evident distaste.

'No, nature. After three months. It happens, you know.'

'I am not going to be a grandfather,' he sighed. Goodfellowe poured himself a fresh glass and sipped. Then he swallowed the rest in one draught and shook his head. 'I think I am about to explode—whether in horror or in happiness I haven't the faintest idea. But either you or Edwina owe me thirty-two pounds for your bounced cheque—I paid the bloody thing myself.' He tried to sound ferocious, but failed. 'I got it all wrong again, didn't I? Perhaps I'd better have another drink.'

Sam poured for him. 'Dad, why didn't you ask me earlier?'

'Didn't want to rush you. It was too important for a hasty row. Elizabeth . . .'—he mentioned her name diffidently, concerned for Sam's reaction—'suggested it was right to wait for you to come to me, in your own time.'

'She was right.'

'So I sat and waited.'

'And worried.'

'A father's burden.'

'And opened my mail.'

'Bloody Buddha,' he sighed. He'd never get it right.

'It's OK. Just this once.' She squeezed his hand. 'Love you, Goodfellowe.'

'You can call me Dad.'

She allowed his hand to fall, deciding the time had come to step out from beneath this shower of sentimentality. The Goodfellowes weren't much good at all that, they operated better with a sharpened edge. 'There are plenty of other things I could call you, too. Do you really think I'm the type of girl who would get herself pregnant? What type of person do you think I am? What type of father are you?'

'Relieved. And so should Bryan be.'

'Bryan?'

'Saves me throttling the little bastard.'

'Oh, Dad, you're so . . . palaeolithic.'

He winced.

'Anyway, Bryan was a long time ago.'

'Six weeks is a long time?'

'Seems like it. At least since I met Phil.'

'Phil?'

'Lives in Brighton. He's got a Kawasaki, looks just great in leathers and . . .'

He waved his hands in surrender. 'Do I have to know all this? I'd really rather not.'

'Oh, Dad, you live in such a cocoon. Break out. Enjoy yourself. Look, I'd be happy to help, You know, if ever you need any advice.' She offered her sweetest, most insincere smile. 'About birth control. Safe sex, that sort of thing. Don't be shy.'

And she was laughing at him again, with Mickey joining in, but Sam noticed the shadow of autumn storms that passed across her father's eyes. She had blundered, been frivolous, taken a pace too far. She knew why. 'How is Elizabeth?' she asked. The name fell like a blanket, smothering the laughter.

'Haven't seen her for a while. Been . . . distracted.'

'You should see her,' Sam responded.

'You think that?'

'I was unfair about her,' Sam apologized. 'I had

344

no right. I didn't get it right.'

'Neither did I. Not with Elizabeth. We had a sort of falling-out.'

'Then give us all a break. Buy some flowers and go see the girl,' Mickey agreed. It was beginning to sound unanimous.

'Maybe.' He seemed wounded.

'No maybe about it. If you don't invite her, I will,' Sam insisted.

'You leave me precious little choice.'

'That's the plan.'

'Call her now,' Mickey encouraged.

Dusk had begun to steal the light, leaving the skyline like a string of bonfires in the distance.

'Too late now. First thing in the morning, maybe.' He swallowed another mouthful of Ninth Island's non-vintage. 'Yes, why not? First thing in the morning.'

*   *   *

There was no chance of him sleeping. Too much anticipation.

Shortly after five he climbed on his bike and set off for the flower market at Nine Elms. This was an entirely new experience for him, cycling through streets empty of traffic, breathing in morning air rather than diesel, being able to enjoy what lay ahead rather than worrying about what was looming up behind. It felt so good he thought he might get up at this time every morning. He wasn't making fast progress, the bump over the kerb at Brewer Street had caused more damage than he'd imagined. Not only was the wheel buckled but the frame alignment was off. The central locking was beginning to work loose. But what did that matter, so long as it got him there? He pressed on.

Most of the traffic that was around in London at that time of the morning seemed to have gathered at Nine Elms, laden with a choice of flowers that quite dazzled Goodfellowe. Flowers he didn't even recognize. He chose a ludicrously large bunch of something stemmy and blue that looked as though only moments before they had been growing on the banks of the Amazon. These were placed in a large cardboard box which in turn was tied precariously across the front of the handlebars, causing the geometry of the bike to become seriously compromised. He'd arrived with a wobble and precious little authority, he was an even greater road hazard as he set off on the last leg of his journey. Next time he'd stick to bringing a bottle, he told himself. Next time.

Next time!

The thought added urgency to his efforts, but he wasn't even sweating. The gym was really toning him up. She would be impressed.

It was shortly before seven when, with the rear mudguard complaining like a witch in a wheelbarrow, he turned into her mews. The cobbles made further progress impossible and he dismounted and pushed. Something dropped from the rear brakes. He felt fabulous.

Her house stood halfway down on the right-hand side.

And she was waiting for him, standing at the door in that fabulous silk robe of hers.

She hadn't noticed him yet, the early sun was shining into her eyes.

She seemed so impossibly beautiful. He knew he

346

was very much in love.

He waved, but still she didn't see him and was moving back inside.

Goodfellowe drew nearer, and the warmth seemed to drain from the day. Someone else was with her. A man. Young, with that unquestionable look of being unmarried. Undeniably good-looking. Kissing Elizabeth goodbye. And smiling with that dusted look around his eyes which suggested—to Goodfellowe, at least—that whatever else the rest of the day might have in store, it couldn't be better than what he'd already had.

Elizabeth.

'Morning,' he offered casually in response to Goodfellowe's stare.

And he was gone.

Now Elizabeth had seen him. And the flowers.

'You should have rung, Tom.'

'You said when the Tibet thing was over . . .'

'I said we should talk. You should have rung.'

'Been keeping busy?' There was no mistaking the damage in his voice.

'I suppose you want to know whether he spent the night on my sofa. Or in my bed. Whether he's my cousin or the latest in a long line of lovers.'

'I suppose I do.'

'Well, you have no right to ask.'

'I thought we had an understanding.'

'That we should keep ourselves only unto each other? No, we didn't. We simply agreed to try again. To see whether you were capable of commitment. Because it's your commitment that's always been in question, Tom. Not mine.'

At that moment the flowers tumbled from his handlebars to lie like dead fish across the cobbles.

347

Still, what did it matter? She'd get more flowers this afternoon. He began to lose it. He imagined her home full of them. She'd probably been keeping Nine Elms in business all by herself.

'I'm sorry you're hurt, Tom. You took too much for granted. As you've always taken me for granted.'

He was burning inside, a bonfire of dreams.

He raised his eyes from the cobbles, met hers, those wonderfully warm marmalade eyes that he wanted to look at across a pillow every morning of his life.

'What do you want to do, Tom?'

'I want . . .' It was all he could manage. What did he want? He didn't seem to know any longer.

'Time to make your mind up, Goodfellowe . . .'

The LARGE PRINT HOME LIBRARY

If you have enjoyed this Large Print book and would like to build up your own collection of Large Print books and have them delivered direct to your door, please contact The Large Print Home Library.

The Large Print Home Library offers you a full service:

★ Created to support your local library

★ Delivery direct to your door

★ Easy-to-read type & attractively bound

★ The very best authors

★ Special low prices

For further details either call Customer Services on 01225 443400 or write to us at:

The Large Print Home Library
FREEPOST (BA 1686/1)
Bath BA2 3SZ